W9-CQJ-878

LETTERS OF COMFORT

THE FRIENDSHIP LETTERS, BOOK 2

LETTERS OF COMFORT

WANDA E. BRUNSTETTER

THORNDIKE PRESS
A part of Gale, a Cengage Company

Thorndike Press, a part of Gale, a Cengage Company.

LIBRARY OF CONGRESS CIP DATA ON FILE.
CATALOGUING IN PUBLICATION FOR THIS BOOK
IS AVAILABLE FROM THE LIBRARY OF CONGRESS.

ISBN-13: 979-8-88579-253-0 (hardcover alk. paper)

Published in 2023 by arrangement with Barbour Publishing, Inc.

Printed in Mexico
Printed Number: 1   Print Year: 2024

To my special friend, Doretta.
Thanks for allowing me to use your
lovely name for the main character in
this book, even though you are not
dealing with the same situation as my
fictional character.

I will not leave you comfortless:
I will come to you.

JOHN 14:18

PROLOGUE

Grabill, Indiana

Holding a letter she had just received from her friend Eleanor Lapp, Doretta Schwartz leaned against the fence near her father's barn and read:

Dear Doretta,
   Vic and I received the invitation to your and William's wedding. Just wanted you to know that we plan to be there. It will be an honor for me to be one of your witnesses, and I can't wait for you to meet our sweet little Rosetta.
   Things are going well at our home here in Paradise. Vic is still in therapy, but he hasn't had a drink since his first session, and thankfully, he no longer blames himself for his brother's death.
   I'm keeping busy with things at home and taking care of the baby, of course. I love being a wife and mother, and I'm sure

that you will enjoy being a happy wife and good mother someday too.

I must close now and get this letter in the mail. I'll see you soon and then we can talk in person. These next few weeks will be busy ones as you and your family prepare for the wedding, but try not to work too hard.

With Love & Blessings,

Eleanor

Doretta smiled as she folded her friend's letter and slipped it back in the envelope. She could hardly wait to see Eleanor again and meet her little girl. And even more so, Doretta looked forward to becoming Mrs. William Lengacher, the man she loved and had promised to marry. She felt sure that nothing and no one could ever come between her and William. They were destined to be together as husband and wife.

CHAPTER 1

Doretta stood in front of the bathroom mirror, staring at her reflection. In two days, she would be getting married, and those dark circles beneath her eyes needed to go. Hopefully, sleep would come tonight, and she'd wake up tomorrow morning feeling well rested. Yesterday, after helping prepare the room where the meal would be served following the wedding service as well as decorating the wall behind the bride and groom's table, Doretta had been exhausted and should have slept soundly. But with so many thoughts swirling in her head, she'd only gotten a few hours of sleep.

This evening, William would be coming by, and they would set their busyness aside for a few hours. They would take a ride in his open buggy, and when they returned to the house, they'd eat a late supper with Doretta's family. She looked forward to the ride, especially because William had said he wanted to show her something special — a surprise he'd been waiting to tell her about. Doretta couldn't imagine what it was, but she was ever so curious to find out. The anticipation of his surprise, coupled with the excitement she felt whenever they were together, heightened Doretta's senses and caused her pulse to race a bit more than usual. She picked up one of the essential oil roller balls nestled in a basket on the counter and rubbed some on her inner wrists. Putting her nose close to her skin, she inhaled the pleasant lavender aroma. *Aw, that's better. . . . I feel calmer already.*

Doretta secured both sides of her head covering with a white hairpin and gave her cheeks a little pinch to add some color. She had never worn makeup, not even during her *rumschpringe,* and she wasn't vain about her appearance. Even so, Doretta's face looked kind of pale this afternoon from her lack of sleep, and she didn't want her intended to think she wasn't feeling well.

Doretta had also been awakened last night from a terrible dream. Her heart pounded even now as she reflected on the dream in which William had called off the wedding with no explanation other than saying they weren't meant to be together. The dream didn't make any sense to her because just

10

the other day, William had told Doretta that he couldn't imagine spending the rest of his life with anyone but her.

"Nor I you," she whispered, giving her cheeks one final pinch before moving away from the mirror. It was time to go out on the porch and wait for her beloved to arrive.

Doretta stepped out of the bathroom, nearly colliding with her ten-year-old sister, Karen.

"What took you so long in there?" the young girl asked. "I thought you were never comin' out."

Doretta tweaked the end of her sister's nose. "You're too *ungeduldich.*"

"I'm not impatient, but you're a *schleich.*"

She smiled, shaking her head. "I'm going out with William soon, and I wanted to make sure I looked satisfactory, so I had every right to take my time and be a slow-poke."

Karen shrugged her slim shoulders. "William's a nice enough fellow, but I don't see why you'd wanna be his *fraa.*"

What a silly comment. Doretta's smile widened. "I want to be William's wife because I love him very much and want to spend the rest of my life with him."

Karen wrinkled her freckled nose. "I'm

11

never gettin' married. I'm gonna keep on livin' right here with our *mamm* and *daed* till the day I die."

Doretta didn't bother to tell her little sister that there was a good chance she would outlive their parents. It might have upset the girl to think about the possibility of either one of them passing on. Doretta did not like the idea either, but she wouldn't allow herself to dwell on the topic of death. Mom was fifty-two and Dad had recently turned fifty-four. They were in good health, and barring anything unforeseen, she figured they would both be around for a good many more years. At least she hoped that would be the case, because she would certainly miss them, just as she did her paternal grandparents who had died of cancer only a year apart. Doretta felt thankful that her mother's parents were still alive and lived in the *daadihaus* connected to Uncle Calvin's home over on Hurshtown Road.

A tug on her dress sleeve disrupted Doretta's thoughts. "Aren't you gonna miss Mama, Papa, and our *brieder* after you and William get married and move into that great big house with William's grandpa and grandma? We'll sure miss you."

Doretta couldn't miss the look of sadness

in her sister's blue eyes. "Of course I will miss you. But William and I won't be that far away. His grandparents' house is only a few miles from here, so we'll see you all quite often." She leaned down and gave her sister a hug. "Now go ahead and use the bathroom, and please stop fretting. You're too young to worry so much."

Karen gave Doretta a crooked grin. "I wanna hear where William takes you on your date after you get home."

Doretta couldn't help but smile. While her curious sister didn't think she ever wanted to get married, here she was eager to know about Doretta and William's date. "I'm sure Mama and Papa will want you to head to bed by the time William and I finish our late supper with them, but I'll tell you all about it in the morning. Okay?"

"You promise?"

"*Jah,* of course."

"Okay." Karen entered the bathroom and quickly shut the door.

Hearing the *clippity-clop* of a horse's hooves, Doretta stepped into the hallway, where she slipped on her dark-colored jacket and black outer bonnet. Turning toward the kitchen, where her parents had gone to have a cup of coffee, she cupped her hands around her mouth and hollered,

13

"William's horse and buggy just came into the yard, so I'm leaving now!"

As Mama called back, "Have a nice time," Doretta hurried out the front door.

William's horse, Carmel, so named for its beautiful caramel-colored coat, had been tied to the hitching rail, and William was heading toward her.

Doretta's breath caught in her throat at the sight of his muscular form, blue eyes, and thick, sandy brown hair. She had to hold herself in check to keep from rushing into his strong arms. Oh, how she wished they were married already and she wouldn't have to say goodbye to him when their date ended this evening. But she only had to wait a couple of days until their wedding took place. Then they would never have to part until they grew old and the Lord called one of them home to be with Him. Unable to bear the thought, she shook that notion aside and clasped William's hand as he helped her into the buggy. All she would think about during their date was how fortunate she felt to be engaged to a man who loved her as much as she did him. Doretta looked forward to the days ahead and eventually raising a family with William. Although it would be difficult to give up her teaching position at the Amish school-

14

house, she felt sure that motherhood would be even more rewarding.

I wonder if our children will have my auburn-colored hair or a light shade of brown like William's, Doretta mused as William guided the horse and open buggy out onto the road. *Will we have boys or girls, and how many children will God bless us with?* Doretta had a fondness for children and would miss teaching school. But the direction of her life was taking her down a new path, and Doretta looked forward to seeing what adventures awaited her as Mrs. William Lengacher. Although her job as a school-teacher had been fulfilling, Doretta had no doubts about the joy and satisfaction she would feel being married to William. As each day had drawn them closer to their wedding, she felt even more certain that God had brought her and William together.

"You're sure quiet this evening."

William's comment drove Doretta's musings aside, and she turned to look at him. "Oh, I've just been thinking, is all."

"Were they good thoughts about us and our future?"

She nodded.

"No second thoughts about marrying me?"

Doretta reached over and clasped Wil-

15

liam's arm. "Of course not. I love you with all my heart, and I can't imagine marrying anyone but you. I promise, William, I will never love any man but you."

He let go of the reins with one hand and took hold of her hand. William's gentle touch felt warm and soothing. "And I promise to only love you. My one regret is that my twin brother hasn't found the girl of his dreams yet. Warren is such a kind-hearted man, yet he's never had a steady girlfriend. I'd really like to see him find the right woman and be as happily married as I know we are going to be."

"I'm sure when the correct time presents itself, Warren will find the right woman. Maybe it will be Margaret Wagler. He has gone out with her a few times," she observed. "Maybe their friendship will develop into something more serious."

William's voice lowered a bit. "I'm just sorry it took me so long to propose marriage to you, but I wanted to be sure I could offer you a good life and provide for all of your needs."

"I don't need anything except you," she murmured, snuggling closer to him. "As long as we're together, I'll be happy and content."

He gave her fingers a gentle squeeze.

"Same here. If I live to be an old man with gray hair, or no hair at all, and end up walking bent over with the help of a cane, my love for you will never die."

Doretta smiled. She couldn't imagine the tall, handsome man she would be marrying in a couple of days with gray hair or walking with a cane. But that didn't matter because they would grow old together. When William's hair turned gray, hers probably would too. And even if they both became frail or bent over, they would love and cherish each other until the day one of them died. Even then, Doretta felt certain that the love she felt for William would remain in her heart forever.

"What are you doing out here all by yourself?"

Warren turned his head at the sound of his mother's voice. He'd been in such deep thought, he hadn't heard her open the door and step out onto the porch. "Oh, just taking some time to *iwwergedenkt* a few things," he responded as she took a seat beside him on the wooden bench his grandfather had made a few years ago.

"Mind if I ask what kind of things you needed to think over?"

He gave a noncommittal shrug, hoping

17

she wouldn't press the issue. Warren had always been on the quiet side when it came to expressing his thoughts — especially when his mother started asking too many questions about things he preferred not to talk about.

"Are you feeling *bedauerlich* because your only sibling will be getting married in a couple of days and you're still single without a serious *aldi* yet?" She placed her hand on his arm.

Warren shook his head. "I'm not sad about my brother getting married, and with William and I getting started with our new business, I don't really have time for a steady girlfriend. So that's not even an issue worth talking about right now, Mom. When, and if, God wants me to have a mate, the right woman will come along." *And it won't be one-sided,* he mentally added, *because she'll love me as much as I love her, and she'll look at me the way Doretta looks at William.* Warren crossed his arms in front of his chest and drew in a deep breath. *Does my brother realize how lucky he is to have found a woman who loves him so much? Will I ever find that with Margaret . . . or anyone else?*

"Aren't you going to tell me where we're going?" Doretta gave William a little nudge

18

with her elbow. "The suspense is making me so *naerfich,* I'm tempted to start biting my *fingerneggel.*"

He chuckled. "Aw, now, don't be nervous, and for goodness' sake, do not bite your fingernails. If my mamm was here right now, she'd say that fingernail biting is a nasty habit."

"Jah." Doretta nodded. "My mother would say the same thing."

They traveled in silence for a while, and as the sun began to drop lower in the sky, Doretta felt herself relax. Although the fall air was a bit nippy, there was no wind, and sitting here so close to William, it wasn't possible to feel cold. In fact, heat flushed her face at the nearness of him. Oh, how she loved this man.

"We're almost there." William snapped the reins, and Carmel picked up speed. "Just a little bit farther and I'll show you my surprise."

Doretta looked to the right and then the left. All she could see were some hardy wildflowers dotting the landscape they were passing by. Nothing unusual out here in the country, and they were still several miles from town. Doretta couldn't imagine what would be along this road that had William so excited, but she remained quiet as his horse and buggy moved on. If they were getting close, surely she would see something more than this soon.

The rumble of an approaching vehicle on the other side of the road caused William's horse to whinny and shake her head. Apparently, Carmel either didn't like the noise or the mare had suddenly become skittish of motorized vehicles. Doretta had never seen his horse act like this before, but she felt confident that William would remain in control. The setting sun was obviously in his face, as it was hers, and he put one hand up as if to shield his eyes from the glare. It was at that moment when William lost control of his horse. The crazed animal reared up and took off running down the road at a pace so fast the scenery became nothing but a blur. William shouted at Carmel, but he couldn't slow her down. The next thing Doretta knew, they were in the other lane, heading straight for the headlights of a pickup truck. Doretta screamed and then braced herself for the impact. They were going to crash, and there was nothing she could do about it. There wasn't even time to utter a prayer.

CHAPTER 2

Warren stepped out of his father's barn and slouched against the rustic, wooden building. He remained like that for several minutes, taking in the sights and sounds around him that he hoped, if only for a little while, would take his mind off the deep grief consuming him.

Glancing toward the closest fence surrounding the pasture where the horses grazed, Warren spotted a squirrel running along the top board. A birdfeeder hanging from a wooden post nearby was nearly empty from neglect on the part of Warren's mother. But then, who would expect her to remember to fill the feeders when she needed someone to care for her right now?

Poor Mom. She can barely get out of bed in the mornings, much less resume her normal duties. It will be some time before she or Dad come to grips with the fact that William is gone. Well, I miss him too, Warren thought

21

as he breathed in the odor of decaying leaves that had been swept and piled up under a maple tree in the yard nearly two weeks ago. Most of the lawn furniture hadn't been put away yet, and Warren figured he'd probably be the one to do it, although he certainly wasn't in the mood. It made sense to him that the normal priorities had taken a back seat with his folks and even himself. Most days, it didn't seem that much of a priority for him to even brush his teeth or shave his face. He would look into the mirror at himself and see William looking back at him, which made Warren even sadder.

He'd managed to take care of the animals inside the barn day to day, but other chores seemed not to be as important, like cleaning his room or fixing the loose floor boards outside on the front porch.

Besides grieving the loss of his twin brother, Warren had an important decision to make concerning the health food store he and William had purchased before William's tragic death. There was no way Warren could run it alone, so he would either need to sell the new business or hire one or two people to work there with him. If William and Doretta had gotten married as planned, she would have helped out at the store, at least until their first baby came along. Now, due to the injuries she had incurred, there was no possibility of her helping out at the nutrition center anytime in the near future. Besides, once her body had healed so that she could function again, Doretta would most likely return to teaching, which only made sense. Warren really wanted to keep the building he and William had bought and try to make a go of the health food store they'd been so excited about opening, but he wasn't sure he could do it alone. Warren couldn't help worrying about what would happen in the days ahead.

He massaged the back of his neck and closed his eyes. *Lord, I need Your help with so many things right now. Please give my family the comfort we need today and much needed support in the things we must do.*

A fluttery ruffle as a chicken preened in the small enclosure nearby halted Warren's thoughts. He watched as a collection of fluffy hens crossed the chicken run in jerks and stops, digging holes, pecking for bugs, and preening, the way the first hen he'd seen had done.

His gaze went to what was left of the vegetable patch. Most of the produce had been picked in late October, leaving only root vegetables still in the ground. Wilted stalks and limp, discolored leaves were a reminder that the remnants of the once-healthy-looking garden had been left unattended. Warren remembered William helping to plant the carrots, which were his favorite vegetable. The same day, he'd also bought and planted a couple of yellow pear tomato plants, which were Mom's favorites. *Gardening was a hobby of sorts that my twin brother truly enjoyed doing,* Warren thought.

For now, everything seemed void around the place and less exciting. He could still picture the sparkle in his brother's eyes when he'd spoken about looking forward to being the best husband he could for Doretta. *It seemed like everything was going so well for my brother. Until the day of the accident, that is.*

Warren's shoulders drooped as he heaved a sigh and moved slowly away from the barn. With William gone, nothing seemed right anymore. All he felt like doing was crawling into bed and pulling the covers over his head. But he had work to do and a major decision to make.

I need to pull myself up by the bootstraps and take one day at a time. Mom and Dad are grieving over the loss of William too, and I need to be there for them.

A vision of Doretta popped into Warren's

head, and he stopped walking. Although he hadn't gone to the hospital to see her, since only her close family members had been allowed to visit, he'd prayed for her every day since the accident. He felt sure that by now Doretta had regained consciousness and been told about William's death.

Warren's vision blurred and he shivered not from the cold but rather the sadness he felt for everyone who grieved William's death. He wanted to help Doretta through this ordeal but didn't know if she would allow him to, as the closeness they'd had as children had lessened after Doretta and William became a couple. It wasn't that Warren wouldn't have liked for him and Doretta to have remained close, but he would never have made a move on his brother's girlfriend, nor would he have expected her to reciprocate if he had.

Warren bowed his head and closed his eyes. *Please, Lord, give me the strength and wisdom to make the right decisions about my future, and show me how to help others who have been affected and are hurting because of the tragedy of my brother's death.*

Paradise, Pennsylvania
Eleanor sat in the quiet, dimly lit living room, rocking her precious little girl. Ro-

setta was such a good baby and hardly fussed at all, unless she was hungry or needed her diaper changed. The baby's silky hair rested against her cheek, and the soft fragrance from Rosetta's lavender bath soap was a lovely welcome to Eleanor's senses. She felt blessed, although a little guilty for being so happy when her best friend lay in a hospital bed with multiple injuries. Sweet Doretta should have been married by now, not broken, and soon would be grieving for the man she had lost. What a shock it would be when Doretta's mother, Amanda, told her that William had lost his life in the accident they'd been involved in. With the way those two had been thrown out of the mangled buggy, it was a miracle that Doretta had survived. The driver of the vehicle they'd smashed into had suffered only minor injuries, but William's horse had also been killed.

Eleanor thought about the message she'd listened to last evening when she'd gone to the phone shed. Amanda had called, wanting to let Eleanor know that as soon as Doretta became fully awake, she would tell her daughter about William's death as well as explain the extent of her injuries. Amanda had asked Eleanor to pray that God would give her the right words and for Doretta to find comfort in them.

Eleanor drew in a deep breath and released it slowly. *My poor sweet friend. I can only imagine what a shock all of this will be to her when she learns the truth. Doretta was such a big help to me when Vic and I went through the problems caused by his drinking, and now it is my turn to help her. Oh, how I wish I could be there for her right now. I feel guilty for staying here in our cozy home with my precious baby cradled in my arms, when Doretta is lying in a hospital room in Fort Wayne.*

She stroked Rosetta's soft cheek and studied the infant's dark lashes as her eyelids closed in slumber. Eleanor and Vic had taken the baby to Grabill for William's funeral a week ago, but they hadn't been able to go to the hospital to see Doretta because she'd been heavily sedated and they weren't part of Doretta's family.

Is it too soon to make another trip there? Eleanor wondered. *Would Vic be able to get time off work again so we could go?* Vic's boss had a lot of indoor work going on, and sometimes Vic worked ten-hour days. Before and after work, much of his free time was taken up by chores. And when Vic wasn't working, he had counseling sessions at the clinic in Quarryville, where he'd received help for his addiction to alcohol.

Maybe he wouldn't mind if the baby and I went to Grabill for a few days or so without him, Eleanor concluded. *I really do feel the need to see Doretta and offer my condolences and words of comfort to her in person.*

She leaned forward and kissed her daughter's forehead. *I'll ask your daadi as soon as he gets home.*

Fort Wayne, Indiana
Doretta groaned and squinted against the invading light permeating the room. *But what room am I in?* she wondered. *I'm lying on a bed, but it doesn't feel like my own. There are strange noises and smells I don't recognize. My head and every place on my body hurts, but I don't know why.*

"Oh, thanks be to God — you're fully awake. Can you see and hear me clearly, Doretta?"

"Mama? Is that you?"

"Yes, dear one, I'm right here by your bed."

Doretta blinked a few times as her mother's face, although a bit blurry, came into view. "Wh–where am I? Why do I hurt so much?"

"You're in the hospital. You were in a ter-

28

rible accident on a road not far from our town."

Doretta felt an uncomfortable tightening within her chest. "Are . . . are you sure?"

"Yes, it happened ten days ago."

Ten days ago? "I don't remember . . ." Doretta squeezed her eyes shut, trying to conjure up some memory of the incident her mother spoke about. *What is the last thing I do remember?* Her thoughts seemed frozen as she attempted to search for answers. She tried to sit up, but the stabbing pain in her body made it impossible to move. In addition, an unyielding, cage-like thing held her head in place and kept it from moving to the right or left. What was this strange contraption that held her captive?

"What's wrong with me, Mama? How bad am I hurt, and what is this uncomfortable thing attached to my upper body?"

"In addition to head trauma, some broken ribs, and a broken arm, you sustained a severe neck break and had to be put into a halo brace to keep your neck and spine from moving while you heal." Mama's voice faltered. "Oh, Doretta, my dear daughter, it could have been much worse. You're lucky to be alive."

Doretta's throbbing head felt as though it

had been filled with cobwebs, and she could hardly process what her mother had said. *I was in an accident, of which I have no recollection. There are broken bones, and Mama said I have a head and neck injury. No wonder I hurt so much.*

Doretta had seen a man wearing a halo brace once, but she didn't personally know anyone who had ever been forced to wear one. The one thing she knew for sure was that the metal contraption was very constrictive. She figured she must look quite ugly and couldn't imagine being able to sit or walk with it on. "H–how long will I have to wear the halo?" she asked.

"The doctor said it will be necessary to keep it on for six to twelve weeks. After it's removed, your neck muscles will be weak, and you'll most likely need to wear a soft neck brace for a time."

Doretta tried to take in her mother's words. This all seemed so unreal — like a bad dream. Only this was all too real. Doretta would not wake up and discover that she'd only had a nightmare. *How can I deal with this pain?*

"Your doctors and nurses are skilled, and you have many people praying for you." Mama's voice had a soothing quality about it. "Your injuries will heal, and after a time, you will get used to wearing the halo. Once you're released from the hospital, I will be your primary caregiver at home. It may be hard to sit or stand in one position very long, and you will need my help getting into different positions. Due to your multiple injuries, you will need some physical therapy during your recovery. You'll have to learn how to lift, twist, and bend so that you don't put too much strain on your neck and back — that's very important, Doretta."

Doretta stared at the ceiling, struggling not to cry. There was one more question on her mind that needed to be answered right now. "Where is William?" she asked. "The last thing I remember is waiting for him to pick me up. He said there was a surprise he wanted to show me."

Mama placed her hand on Doretta's arm — the good one in which she felt no pain. "William did pick you up. You were riding in his open buggy when the accident occurred." Mama paused, and Doretta saw tears in her mother's brown eyes. "It breaks my heart to tell you this, but William died in the crash."

A knot formed in Doretta's stomach, and she saw spots before her eyes. "No, it's not true. William can't be dead. We're getting married on the ninth of November."

Mama clasped Doretta's hand and gave her fingers a tender squeeze. "Today is November the sixteenth, and William's funeral was held a week ago."

Doretta still did not remember the accident, and she tried to shake her head, but the constraint of the rigid halo wouldn't allow her to do so. "This can't be, Mama. William cannot be dead." The pitch of her voice rose higher as she spoke the words. "Oh, Mama, what am I gonna do? How can I go on living without him?"

"You'll do it one day at a time, and your daed and I will be there to help you, as will the rest of our family and friends."

Doretta nearly choked on the sob rising in her throat. No one could help her deal with this terrible tragedy. Not even God. He had taken William from her, and nothing would ever be the same.

CHAPTER 3

Paradise

Eleanor had put the last of the baby's things into a travel bag when Vic entered their room. "Your driver's here. Her van just pulled into the yard."

"Okay, I'm ready." She zipped up the suitcase.

He stepped forward and pulled her gently into his arms. "I'm sure gonna miss you and our sweet baby girl. It'll be lonely here without you."

"I'll miss you too, but we'll only be gone a few days — one or two days at my folks, and part of a day to see Doretta, and then we'll be on our way home. Besides, you will be at work most of the time and keeping busy with chores when you're here, so you won't have much time to feel lonely. Not only that, but you'll have Checkers to keep you company."

Vic shook his head. "That dog of mine

33

can sometimes be a pest, and there's no way he can fill the void for me like you and the baby do. Just thinking about you and Rosetta being gone will make me sad." He leaned down, and his lips met hers in a tender kiss. "Promise you won't forget me?"

Eleanor gave his arm a poke. "Course not, silly. It's not possible that I would ever forget you. You are the love of my life, Vic. And now that we have Rosetta, our bond is even tighter."

"I feel the same way about you and our daughter." Vic gave her another kiss and then gestured to Eleanor's luggage. "I'll carry this out to Helen's van and come back inside for the baby." He looked toward the crib where Rosetta lay sleeping. "I want to kiss you both and hold our little girl one last time before you go."

Eleanor smiled. "You're a good husband, and our daughter is *glicklich* to have you as her daddy."

"No, I'm the lucky one." He grinned and grabbed the suitcase handle. "I'll be right back."

After Vic left, Eleanor wrapped Rosetta in a warmer blanket and lifted the little one into her arms. There were no words to express how much joy this precious child had brought into their life. Eleanor hoped and prayed that someday, when Rosetta was old enough to get married, she would find a man who loved her unconditionally, and that God would bless Rosetta and her husband's marriage with children of their own. Eleanor didn't want the years of raising their daughter to go by too quickly, but she did look forward to her and Vic becoming grandparents someday. She would spoil them, of course, but wasn't that the right of a grandparent?

Grabill

Doretta sat rigidly on one end of the couch in her parents' living room, with her broken arm resting on a pillow. She'd been home from the hospital for two days and still could not find a comfortable position, whether sitting or lying down. How could she be comfortable or feel relaxed with her arm in a cumbersome cast and an ugly-looking top-heavy ring around her head, held in place by four titanium pins? Metal posts attached the halo ring to the bulky vest to keep Doretta's head and neck from moving. The vest, which had been made of hard plastic, was lined with a soft fleecy material. It wasn't comfortable — none of it was — not the halo and vest or the cast on her arm. She still suffered with severe

35

headaches, and her ribs ached too.

Wearing the halo and vest had affected Doretta's balance, making it hard to walk. Doretta had been told at the hospital that, if necessary, she could use the aid of a walker. Safety was important in order to prevent falls or even slips. Any obstacles around the house needed to be addressed. Plus, she couldn't sleep comfortably in a bed right now and had been sleeping in a reclining chair at night since she'd come home from the hospital. Going up the stairs to her room would be difficult for her, so Mama had said that whenever Doretta felt ready to sleep in a bed, she had the downstairs guest room prepared for her.

Even eating seemed like a difficult chore, and it was important that Doretta be conscious of chewing her food thoroughly before swallowing so she wouldn't choke. One thing for sure, she wouldn't embarrass herself by going out to a restaurant for any meals. Besides looking strange in her halo-vest apparatus, it would be terrible if she choked on something while eating out. No, she was better off eating all of her meals here at home.

Doretta had been told by her doctor, nurses, and the physical therapist who had worked with her at the hospital that she would eventually get used to the halo and vest, although everyone recovered at a different pace. They had all said that after a while she would learn to function better, which should include being able to sleep in a bed. Doretta doubted their words, and she shuddered at the thought of having to wear the contraption for twelve long weeks, which was how long the doctor had said it would most likely take for her type of neck break to heal.

I could deal with all of this if William were still alive, Doretta told herself. Tears sprang to her eyes. *He was the love of my life, and I miss him so much. My heart feels like it's been broken in two, and although I've been told that my body will heal, I am sure the pain of losing William will always be with me.*

A knock on the front door concluded Doretta's thoughts. *Oh, no . . . I don't want anyone to see me like this. I hope Mama doesn't let anybody except for our family members come into the house while I look so ugly and wounded.* She grimaced. *But then, if it is someone in our family, they would not have bothered to knock.*

Warren stood on the Schwartzes' front porch, holding a plastic bag containing a fresh loaf of pumpkin bread his mother had

37

made and wondering if he'd made a mistake coming over here to see Doretta. She'd only been home from the hospital a few days and might not feel up to company yet. But when he'd said he was heading out to look at the building he and William had bought for their new business, Mom had asked him to drop off the bread. Truth was, Warren had wanted to see Doretta and find out how she was doing, but at the same time he dreaded it. He felt bad about the injuries she'd sustained, and it would be hard to see her and not think about William and how much he missed him.

I still can't believe my brother is gone, Warren thought as he reached out to knock on the door a second time. *But then I'm sure that Doretta feels the same way and must miss him as much as I do.*

When the door finally opened, Doretta's sister, Karen, greeted him. Since it was late afternoon, she'd no doubt returned home from school a short time ago. The auburn-haired, freckle-faced girl looked up at Warren with her head tilted to one side while she blinked rapidly. *"Ach,* Warren, you scared me for a minute 'cause you look so much like your *zwilling bruder."*

Warren understood why Karen would think he looked like his twin brother. She

38

was not the first person to say such a thing and would probably not be the last. For really observant people, however, it should be easy to tell him and William apart. Warren was the one with a small dimple in his left cheek, whereas William's dimple had been in his right cheek.

"I came to see how Doretta's doing and to bring this." Warren handed Karen the loaf of bread. "My mamm made it, and she added chocolate chips instead of raisins when she mixed the batter." He had no idea why he'd told her that. She probably didn't care one way or the other about what his mother had put in the mix. Warren felt strangely uncomfortable all of a sudden — like he was trespassing and shouldn't be here at all.

Karen took the bread from him and smiled. "Wanna come inside? Doretta's in the living room. I'm sure she'd be glad to see you."

"Jah, that'd be nice. I'd like to see how she's doing and offer my get-well wishes."

Karen led the way, and Warren followed her down the hall and into the living room. When he saw Doretta sitting on the couch with her arm in a cast and the strange-looking apparatus attached to her head, his stomach tightened. He struggled to keep his eyes from widening so she wouldn't be aware of how shocked he was. She looked so helpless and sorrowful, it nearly broke his heart. He'd heard that Doretta had been put into a halo and vest due to the break in her neck, but knowing that hadn't prepared him for seeing her like this. Warren wanted to put her at ease when he approached. He smiled, looking into her sad-looking brown eyes, hoping to receive a similar reaction. But then it dawned on him. *What if I remind her too much of my twin brother?*

When Warren found his voice, he took a few steps toward the couch. "Hello, Doretta. How are you doing today?" Warren could have bit his tongue. *How are you doing today? What a stupid question. . . . I can see that she's miserable and hurting by her quivering chin and the grimace on her pale face.*

Her eyes darted to the left, as though unable to make eye contact with him. Was it seeing Warren and being reminded that his twin brother was gone, or could Doretta be embarrassed by her appearance?

He stood with his hands behind his back, waiting for her response to his question.

After several seconds, her gaze came to rest on him. "The pain medicine the doctor prescribed helps some, but it doesn't take care of all the pain I feel."

Warren struggled to find his next words, but before he could say anything, Karen spoke up. He'd almost forgotten she was still there.

"Warren brought some pumpkin bread. Should I take it to the kitchen and cut you a piece, Sister?"

"No, I'm not hungry right now. Maybe I'll have some later."

"Okay." The young girl gave Warren a quick glance, then she darted from the room.

"Mind if I sit down so we can visit awhile?" Warren asked, moving toward the chair opposite the couch.

"I'm kind of tired right now. Maybe some other time."

"Oh, sure . . . I understand. I'll come by again when you're feeling up to company."

He was about to leave the room but decided he ought to say one more thing. "I am sorry for your loss, and I feel bad that you got hurt in the accident that took my brother's life."

Doretta's eyes glistened with tears, and he saw a few of them roll out and dribble down her cheeks. "If one of us had to die, it would have been better if it had been me," she murmured.

"Oh, please don't say that or even think

41

such a way." Warren swallowed against the thickness in his throat from holding back tears of his own. "I don't understand why God chose to take my brother, but I feel certain that you were spared for a reason, Doretta."

"I can't imagine what it would be." The pitch of her voice rose a bit. "Just look at me. I'm no good to anyone right now, and I may never be again."

Warren struggled with the desire to march across the room and take hold of her hand, but he held himself in check. It might not be appreciated. Doretta needed to grieve and work through her feelings of confusion and despair, the same as Warren. And since she'd told him a few minutes ago that she was tired and didn't feel up to talking, he thought it best to say goodbye to her for now. Maybe in a week or so he would come by again and see if Doretta felt up to a longer visit.

The door had no more than shut behind Warren, when Mama stepped into the living room. "Your sister said Warren was here." She glanced around. "I was in the kitchen starting supper when he came and wanted to say hello, but it looks like he's gone now."

"Jah."

42

"It was nice of him to stop by. Sorry he couldn't stay longer. I would have liked to find out how he and his family are doing."

"I'm sure they're all hurting, same as me." Doretta fought against the fresh set of tears that had quickly formed in her eyes. "At least they all got to be there for his funeral so they could say their last goodbyes." She couldn't keep from speaking in a bitter tone. It wasn't fair that William had been killed or that her injuries had been so bad she couldn't even attend his service. Maybe it would have helped if she could have been there to pay her final respects to the deceased rather than finding out about his death when she woke up in the hospital, unable to recall the accident. Doretta had since remembered it, although she couldn't recollect all the details. The only thing she remembered well was seeing William's horse go out of control into the opposite lane where a vehicle was coming. She must have blacked out after the impact and had no memory of anything after that until she woke up in the hospital with Mama looking down at her.

"Mama, I have a favor to ask." Doretta spoke slowly and deliberately.

"What is it?"

"If anyone else comes here to see me,

43

please don't let them in the house."

"Oh, Doretta, why not? Don't you know that people are concerned about you? They want to offer their support and encouragement." Mama paused a few seconds. "Anyway, Karen was the one who went to the door and let Warren in. But I'll talk to her about what you want for the future, until you are ready to welcome visitors."

Doretta brought her hand up to her mouth to stifle the sob rising in her throat. "I don't want anyone else to see me like this. I don't need their pity or support. I just want to be left alone."

"I'm sorry that you weren't ready for Warren to see you in the condition you're in. From now on we will do it your way."

"Thank you, Mama."

She felt relief when her mother gave a nod and left the room. No one, not even Mama, knew the way Doretta felt. Without William, her life would never be the same.

CHAPTER 4

When Eleanor's driver pulled into her parents' front yard, a feeling of nostalgia washed over her like a warm, gentle rain. Although evening shadows encompassed the yard, several solar lights allowed her to see the house and even the rustic old barn. The sight of battery-operated lights in the living-room window felt like a welcoming beacon. She'd grown up here and had made many fond childhood memories in this home as well as inside the barn and all over the yard. One particular memory was of the old wooden swing Dad had made and hung on a large branch of the big maple tree in their backyard. Someday when Rosetta was older, she would play on that swing whenever they came here to visit. Although Eleanor looked forward to pushing her daughter on the swing, she was in no hurry for Rosetta to grow up. She wanted to enjoy her daughter's babyhood for as long as she could.

Eleanor opened the passenger door and stepped out of Helen's vehicle. After reaching inside and removing Rosetta from her secured car seat, she carried the baby up to the porch, while Helen followed with the luggage.

A few seconds later, the door swung open, and Eleanor's father greeted her with a wide smile. "Sure is good to see you, Daughter," he said, enveloping Eleanor and the baby in a hug. "We weren't sure what time you'd be leaving this morning or when you would arrive, but we're glad you're here safe and sound, and your mamm has supper staying warm in the oven for us."

"I picked your daughter and grandbaby up at six this morning," Helen spoke up. "We were making pretty good time till one of my tires went flat. That little problem set us a bit behind because I ended up having to get a new tire. So what could have been a nine- or ten-hour trip, with a few stops for gasoline and some refreshments, ended up being twelve hours instead."

"Well, you're here now, and safe, so that's all that counts." Dad took the suitcase from Helen. "You're welcome to stay and eat with us, and if you need a place to stay . . ."

Helen shook her head. "I appreciate the offer, but while Eleanor and the baby are here with you, I'll be in Fort Wayne visiting my cousin Cheryl. She probably has supper waiting for me too, so I'd better get going." Helen looked at Eleanor. "Give me a call when you know what day and time you're ready to go home and also if you need a ride anywhere while you are here."

"I will. Thank you."

Eleanor had barely followed Dad into the house when her mother showed up. Her cheeks looked quite rosy, probably from the heat in the kitchen, and she hurried to Eleanor and Rosetta to wrap them in an all-encompassing hug. "I'm so glad you made it okay. I was beginning to worry."

"We had a flat tire and had to get a new one, so that added some time to our trip," Eleanor explained.

"Before we all have supper, I'd like to hold this little one for a few minutes." Mom stroked the baby's cheek with two fingers. "I've missed seeing her."

Eleanor was on the verge of reminding her mother that she'd seen her granddaughter just a few weeks ago, when she, Vic, and Rosetta had come for William's funeral. But before she could say anything, Dad spoke first.

47

"While you're cuddling the baby, Lydia, I'll take our daughter's luggage to the guest room." He grinned. "Then it'll be my turn to hold Rosetta."

Mom nodded. "I guess that would be okay. You can enjoy holding her while I'm getting supper on the table."

"And since my hands will be free from holding Rosetta, I can help with anything you need to get our meal on the table." Eleanor smiled. It made her feel good to see her folks' enthusiasm. Like typical grandparents, they were eager to spend time cuddling their grandchild.

The following morning, after breakfast, Eleanor got Rosetta ready so they could go see Doretta. Helen had agreed to pick them up for the ride over to the Schwartz home, which Eleanor appreciated. It would be easier and quicker than borrowing one of her parents' horse and buggies to make the trip. Besides, with the November weather having cooled so much, it would be much warmer inside Helen's van than riding in an open buggy or even a closed-in one, like some Amish in the area had begun using.

"I don't see why you won't leave Rosetta here with me while you go see Doretta," Mom said as Eleanor wrapped the baby in a cozy blanket she had made. "Wouldn't it be easier for you to visit with your friend without the interruption if Rosetta should get fussy?"

"I appreciate the offer, Mom, but it might cheer Doretta up to see the child who we named, in part, after her."

"I get your point, but . . ."

Eleanor felt bad seeing her mother's downcast expression, but she really felt it was best to take Rosetta with her this morning. "We won't be gone more than a few hours, and when we get back, you can spend the rest of the day with your newest grandchild."

Mom reached out to touch Rosetta's little hand and smiled when the baby grasped her fingers. "Okay. I'll get busy and do the laundry while you're gone. It's not a fun chore, but it will make the time go by quickly."

Eleanor gave her mother a hug, picked up Rosetta, and headed for the front door. Although eager to see her good friend, she felt a measure of concern about whether Doretta would be happy to see her or not. Sometimes when a person came home from the hospital with injuries that needed to heal, they were either too tired for company or didn't feel up to visiting due to the amount of pain they felt. So while it was possible Doretta wouldn't feel like visiting with anyone, Eleanor hoped that would not be the case today. If it was, she would keep her visit short so as not to tire her friend out, but at least she could feel good about having been there, and maybe Doretta would appreciate the visit too.

"I'm going out to get the mail. Will you be all right by yourself for a few minutes while I'm gone?"

Doretta's head remained perfectly still, but her eyes flicked upward and she gave a little huff. "I'll be fine, Mama. I won't get off the couch or try to walk on my own unless you're right here in this room. Are you satisfied with that?"

Heat flooded Amanda's cheeks as she struggled not to react to her daughter's question, spoken in such a negative fashion. "Okay, Doretta, I understand." Amanda slipped her jacket on and hurried out the front door.

I understand my daughter's despondency, but does she have to be so annoyed with everything I say and do? Amanda asked herself as she made the trek down the driveway to the mailbox. *I wish there was something I could say or do to make her feel better physically and emotionally. But I guess that will come with time and the Lord's healing touch.*

She stepped up to the mailbox and opened the flap. Inside, she found a card from Doretta's friend, Irma, who lived in Mount Hope, Ohio. Irma had been invited to attend Doretta and William's wedding, but when she'd received the tragic news that William had died and been told that there would be no wedding, Irma had not responded — not even with a card. Amanda had figured her daughter's Ohio friend might come for the funeral, like Eleanor and Vic did, but she had not. Perhaps something had come up that prevented her from coming, but it would have been nice if she'd called or sent a note of explanation and offered her condolences.

Amanda lifted her shoulders with a heavy shrug. *I guess a card now is better late than not at all. I shouldn't be so judgmental.*

She grabbed the rest of the mail and was about to head back inside, when a silver-gray minivan pulled into the yard. Amanda didn't recognize the vehicle. She waited near the porch steps to see who it was and gave a little gasp when Eleanor got out with a baby in her arms. This was certainly a surprise, because Amanda had no idea that

Doretta's Pennsylvania friend would be coming here today. *I wonder why she didn't call and let us know of her plans?*

Amanda remembered what Doretta had said yesterday, about not wanting to see anyone except for family. But surely that wouldn't include Eleanor because she was Doretta's best friend and almost like family. Amanda concluded that it would be good for her daughter to visit with her friend and see the baby, so she gave Eleanor a hug and invited her in. Once she'd taken Eleanor and the baby's outer garments and given Rosetta a kiss, Amanda excused herself to go to the kitchen to fix a pot of tea and told Eleanor that Doretta was in the living room.

Doretta's mouth opened slightly, and her breathing became rapid when Eleanor entered the living room with her baby in arms. *What's going on? I told Mama I didn't want any company unless they were family, and now she obviously invited someone in who is not part of our family.* Tears sprang to her eyes. Although angry at Mama for going back on her word, Doretta couldn't be rude and ask her best friend to leave, so she remained on the couch and gave a small wave.

Eleanor came over and took a seat on the

couch beside Doretta. "Hello, my dear friend. I came to find out how you're doing and let you know that I, along with Vic's family, have been praying for you."

"You didn't have to come all this way to say that in person. You could have sent a card or left a message on our answering machine." Doretta swallowed hard. She could barely get the words out, and it was with great effort that she turned her body so she could look directly at Eleanor. It wasn't the act of turning her body correctly, however, that made it difficult. It was the challenging task of facing her friend and observing the pity she saw in Eleanor's soft brown eyes. Seeing the pretty baby nestled in Eleanor's arms didn't help either. It was a painful reminder for Doretta that she wouldn't be getting married and would never have any children of her own.

"I did send a card, and while you were in the hospital, I called several times to see how you were doing." Eleanor placed a hand on Doretta's uninjured arm. "We also came here for William's funeral, but at the hospital you weren't allowed to have any visitors except for your immediate family due to the seriousness of your condition. So when I got word that you were finally home, I decided to come here in person and tell you how sorry I am for your loss."

Doretta just sat, staring at the baby. She was a beautiful little girl, with a creamy complexion and brown hair, like her mom's. If she hadn't been confined by her stiff halo vest, Doretta might have asked if she could hold the baby. It may have been comforting to feel the warmth and softness of the baby against her chest. *Then again,* Doretta thought, *if I did hold Rosetta, I'd probably feel even worse, because jealousy might take over and I could very well say something improper. Some things are just better left unsaid.*

Several seconds passed, and Doretta tried to think of something to say that would break the silence between them. "So what do you think of this weird-looking contraption I'm stuck wearing? Pretty *hesslich,* isn't it?" She gestured to the vest and then upward to the halo attached to her skull.

"I don't see it as ugly," Eleanor responded. "I see it as a way to help keep you in good posture while your body heals itself, but it does look uncomfortable. How long do you have to wear it?"

"Twelve whole weeks, or maybe longer, depending on how well my neck heals. It's difficult to walk with it without losing my balance, and it is just one more thing to make me feel miserable." Doretta's lips trembled.

"I'm so sorry, Doretta." Eleanor's words were spoken in a soothing tone, but they did nothing to make Doretta feel better. In fact, she felt worse, seeing her friend sitting here, perfectly healthy, and with a sleeping baby nestled in her arms. How could Doretta help but feel envious at a time such as this? It seemed that Eleanor had everything, while Doretta had nothing but an empty, hurting heart.

"It's understandable that you'd be impatient and probably bored, waiting for healing, and I thought about how you might like some reading materials. I brought a couple of books with me to give you." With one hand, Eleanor pulled a bag from her tote bag and unwrapped them. "One's a daily devotional, and the other is a book on God's promises for our lives."

Doretta didn't comment; she just looked away with misty eyes.

"Is there anything I can do for you?" Eleanor asked after she'd placed the books on the nearest end table. "My driver won't be back for another hour, so I'd be happy to . . ."

"Thank you for the books, but there's nothing you can do for me, and I'm too

55

tired to talk anymore. Why don't you go to the kitchen and visit with my mamm until your driver arrives?"

Eleanor's mouth slackened, and she looked at Doretta with her head tilted slightly to one side.

Is she trying to figure me out? Does Eleanor think I'm being rude? Well, maybe I am, but I can't help the way that I feel. I wish she had not come here to see me. I am not good company, and I don't want her pity or help. An uncomfortable lump formed in Doretta's throat, and she had to force herself to swallow around it. *My friend must think I'm a terrible person, but the sad part is, I don't even care what Eleanor or anyone else believes about me.*

Clasping the baby to her chest, Eleanor stood. "I'll go visit with your mother right now and let you rest. But before I go, I'd like to share a verse of scripture with you."

Doretta stared straight ahead.

"The verse I would like to leave you with is John 14:18. It says, *'I will not leave you comfortless: I will come to you.'* " Eleanor took a step closer to Doretta. "When you're feeling down and things seem hopeless, remember to pray and tell God about it, because we have the promise in His Word that He will not leave us comfortless. And my dearest friend, please remember that I will be praying for you."

After Eleanor left the room with her baby, Doretta closed her eyes against the tears pushing at the back of her eyelids. Hearing the Bible verse Eleanor had quoted did nothing to make her feel any better. In fact, it had made Doretta feel worse. As far as she was concerned, if God wanted to offer her comfort, then He shouldn't have taken William away.

"How did things go in there during your visit with my daughter?" Doretta's mother asked as Eleanor sat at the kitchen table, drinking a cup of herbal tea, while Amanda held the baby.

"Not well, I'm afraid. If anything, I think the things I said to Doretta may have made her feel worse. She didn't respond well to me — especially when I quoted a verse of scripture to her."

"She's still hurting physically and is very depressed over losing William."

"That's understandable. Hopefully, as her emotional and physical wounds heal, she will return to her old smiling, positive self."

"I desperately want that for her, but it's going to take some time. William and Doretta were deeply in love, and it will be difficult for her to move on without him." Amanda kissed Rosetta's forehead and changed the subject. "She certainly is a sweet baby."

"Danki." Eleanor smiled. "Vic and I feel very blessed to have her."

"And well you should. Elmer and I felt the same way with each child God gave us, and someday, when we have grandchildren, we'll enjoy His blessings upon us in having them as well."

"Do you think Doretta will fall in love with someone else in the future and get married?"

Amanda shrugged. "It's too soon to know, but I do hope, whatever happens in my daughter's life, she will find joy and sense of purpose, for that is what we all need."

Eleanor bobbed her head. Although she could not make any headway with Doretta today, maybe a few letters from her in the days and weeks ahead would make a difference. When she and Rosetta got home, Eleanor would make it a practice of sending Doretta at least one note of encouragement every week. She would also pray and ask God to give her the words of encouragement that would hopefully break through her friend's pain and take away the depression Doretta felt so deeply within her heart.

Eleanor also prayed that her dear friend would be open to and accept God's comfort in the days ahead.

CHAPTER 5

Warren entered his dad's barn and took a seat on a bale of straw to ponder his current situation and give one of their friendliest cats some attention. The only parts on the cat's fur that weren't black were two tiny patches of white on top of each paw. Besides, this had been his brother's favorite cat, so the male feline probably missed William too and deserved some extra attention. Warren remembered the day William had found the cat in their woodpile. It was apparently a stray that had wandered off someone else's property or may have been abandoned by his mother.

My brother always had a soft heart for animals, Warren thought as he continued to stroke the cat's silky but matted fur. *If William hadn't joined the Amish church, I bet he would have furthered his education and become a veterinarian.* William had even mentioned the idea to Warren once, confidentially of course, because their folks would have been against the idea. Then again, if William had not joined the church, he probably wouldn't have asked Doretta to marry him. She seemed to be grounded in her heritage and faith, which made it doubtful she would ever leave the Amish faith and become part of the modern English world. Warren couldn't blame her for that, because he too was committed to remaining Amish.

A vision of Doretta came to mind, and Warren felt a heavy feeling in his chest. When he'd gone to see Doretta the other day, it had saddened him to view her sitting there with the halo vest and wearing a defeated expression on her usually happy face. William's death had left a hole in too many people's hearts — especially Doretta's, Warren's, Mom's, Dad's, and the grandparents William and Doretta had planned to live with for a time after they got married. In some ways, Warren was glad he didn't have any other siblings who would have also experienced the agonizing grief of losing William.

He squeezed his eyes shut and lowered his head. *If Mom had been capable of having more children, they'd also be here struggling to deal with the loss of their brother.* But in other ways, Warren wished he had a few sisters or brothers whom he would have bonded with. It wasn't that another sibling could replace William — no one could ever do that. But maybe the grieving process would be a little lighter if they had more people in the family to support one another emotionally. He was now an only child, and it had been ever so hard losing his twin brother. Most twins, especially those who were identical or mirror twins like Warren and William, had a special bond with each other, but now that tie was broken. Warren would have to find his own way, and he'd need to brave this new territory. He reminded himself daily that he must lean on the Lord for His strength, while he grieved for William and tried to offer comfort to his parents and grandparents.

Being alone in the quietness of the big barn gave some comfort to Warren at this moment. He could remember his time spent with William while they'd played in this place. What fun they'd had, pretending and laughing at their made-up roles. A smile came to Warren's lips as he thought about all the new kittens born in this barn and how he and William would name each one.

He opened his eyes, fighting back the tears that were collecting on his cheeks. *I would give anything to have my brother back with me now. But that can't happen, so I have to face things the way they are.*

Warren looked up when he heard the barn door open and close with a click.

"What are ya doin' out here with that *raadich katz* on your lap?" His dad's boots shuffled across the floor as he made his way over to the bales of straw.

"Shadow is not a mangy cat." For some reason, Warren felt the need to defend the furry animal. "He's a good mouser and earns his keep around here. Besides, of all the barn cats, this feline was William's favorite, so Shadow is the one I like best now too."

Dad took a seat on the bale of straw beside Warren. "You're right. Your bruder did favor that katz. You also have a point about Shadow being a good *mauskatz.* It just caught me off guard seein' you out here this morning."

"How come?"

"Figured by now you'd be over at your new place of business, setting things up so you can open it up to the public soon. Christmas is just a month away, and I'm sure if the nutrition center was open, many folks would do some of their holiday shopping there."

Warren slid his fingers up and down the

cat's body, causing Shadow to purr louder than he had before. "I haven't decided if I should sell the place or try to make a go of it on my own. Without William's help, it would be really hard."

"You can always hire someone to help out. Maybe your new girlfriend would be interested. I saw her daed the other day, and he mentioned that Margaret is currently unemployed. I'm surprised you didn't know that."

Warren shook his head. "She might have said something, but with everything that's been going on, I probably forgot."

Dad plucked off a piece of straw that had stuck to his trousers and put it between his front teeth. "It would sure be a shame to sell when you haven't even had the chance to see how well the business would do." He shuffled his feet against the pieces of straw scattered on the cement floor. "We need a well-stocked health food store in the area, and I'm sure you'd have plenty of customers in need of good supplements, health care items, organic cleaning products, and the like."

Warren continued to pet Shadow as he mulled over his father's words. Maybe Dad was right: he would never know if he could have a successful business if he didn't try.

"Jah, maybe I will talk to Margaret about coming to work for me."

Paradise

Rosetta had fallen asleep after her last feeding, so Eleanor put the baby in her crib and went to the kitchen to start supper. Vic would be home soon, and it would be nice to have their meal ready.

Eleanor got out the ingredients for the hearty meatloaf she planned to make, and soon the room was filled with a blend of tantalizing aromas as she mixed the ground beef with chopped onions, oatmeal, spices, an egg, and some tomato juice. She had formed it into a loaf and spread a glaze of brown sugar, mustard, vinegar, and Worcestershire sauce over the top, when Vic entered the kitchen.

"You're home early. I didn't expect you for another hour, and supper's not ready yet." Eleanor lifted her face toward him as he approached her for a kiss.

"No problem," he said after the welcoming kiss ended. "We can sit at the table and visit for a few minutes, and then I'll go out and tend to a few chores in the barn. How's that sound?"

She smiled. "It works for me. Rosetta's still taking her afternoon nap, so we shouldn't have any interruptions." She gestured to the meatloaf. "I'll put this in the oven, and then we can have a cup of *tee* and a nice conversation."

Vic wrinkled his nose. "Haven't you got anything stronger than tea?"

"*Kaffi.* Will that be okay?"

"Jah, sure. I'm always up for coffee."

Eleanor remembered the days when Vic's desire for something stronger meant drinking beer or some other alcoholic beverage. Thanks to the treatments he'd received for his alcoholism, Vic had become the kind of husband and father Eleanor had previously known he could be. Although their life was not perfect and they had a few disagreements now and then, they always prayed about their problems and worked things out between them.

After placing the meatloaf into the oven and pouring them both a cup of coffee, Eleanor took a seat beside Vic.

He grinned at her and glanced at the stove. "I'm betting that meatloaf is gonna be real tasty. I sure missed your good cooking those few days you and Rosetta were in Indiana."

She poked his arm playfully. "Is that all you missed me for — just my cooking?"

"Of course not, sweet fraa. I missed your

cold *fiess* touching my warm legs in bed at night."

She lifted her gaze to the ceiling and chuckled. "My feet are not that cold, and I seriously doubt that you missed them."

"Glad I could get a laugh out of you. You've been much too serious since you got back from Grabill."

Eleanor released a heavy sigh. "I've been worried about Doretta. I've written her two letters, but she hasn't replied to either of them."

"With a broken arm, it may be too difficult for her to write."

"That might be the case if she had broken her right arm, but it's the left one in a cast, and since Doretta is right-handed . . ."

"Have you tried calling?"

"Jah, and I've left messages on her parents' answering machine, but I'm sure in her condition, Doretta's not likely to make her way out to the phone shed to call me back."

"What about her brother, Glen? He has a cell phone, right?"

"Well, yes, but I'm not sure if I have his number."

"Bet I do. Glen and I hung out together sometimes when I lived in Grabill, trying to win your hand. I called him a few times, and I think I wrote his number down and stuck it in my wallet. Want me to check?"

"Yes, please. If I can get hold of Glen, maybe he can take his cell phone into the house and let Doretta use it to talk to me."

Vic took his wallet out and began thumbing through the compartments. "Here you go — this is Glen's number." He handed a small piece of paper to Eleanor.

"Danki. I'll go out to the phone shed and call him right now."

Grabill

Doretta had been sitting in the living room, staring at the pieces of wood crackling in the fireplace, when her twenty-two-year-old brother, Glen, entered the room. He stepped up to Doretta and extended his cell phone toward her. "Here you go, Sister. Someone wants to talk to you."

A flush of heat erupted on her cheeks. "Who would be calling me on your phone?" She spoke in a near whisper.

"It's your friend Eleanor."

Her eyebrows rose. "I wonder how she got your number."

"I'm guessing Vic still has it, and she used my cell to reach you." Glen reached out again with the phone. "Go on, take it."

At that moment, all Doretta wanted to do was escape. Her fingers trembled as she

68

took the phone. "Hello."

"Hi, Doretta. I've been wondering how you are doing and figured you wouldn't be going out to the phone shed, so I decided to call Glen and ask him to take his phone in to you."

Doretta couldn't think of any kind of a pleasant response, so she just sat there, gripping the phone in her uninjured hand.

"How are you feeling?" Eleanor questioned.

"The same. Nothing's changed." *I wish things would change for the better, but they haven't. This surprise call from Eleanor just reminds me more of my misery.*

"Are you still taking pain medication?"

"Jah."

"I bet you've had a lot of company since I was there with Rosetta." Eleanor's voice sounded cheerful, which made it even more difficult for Doretta to talk to her.

How can my closest friend think I'd want to be seen wearing this cumbersome apparatus? "No, just my family," Doretta replied.

"Are you getting used to wearing the halo vest?"

"No. Everything about wearing it is miserable. I can't even take a shower or a bath, and when Mama is helping me sponge bathe, she has to be careful not to get the lining inside the vest wet."

"It'll get better soon. You won't be wearing the halo vest forever."

It's easy for others to say such things, but from where I'm sitting, my healing is taking forever. Doretta said nothing to Eleanor. She wanted to end this conversation. *Why can't my family have empathy about me not wanting non-family members dropping in or calling me to chat?*

Eleanor asked her a few more questions, and Doretta's responses were short. Finally, she said, "Sorry, but I can't talk any longer. I'm really tired right now."

"Okay. I'll call again some other time and will definitely write more letters. Take care, my friend, and remember that I am praying for you every day."

I don't want to be pitied for the way I look or because I haven't improved that much.

After Doretta said goodbye, she handed her brother his phone. "If Eleanor calls again while you are here at home and wants to talk to me, please tell her that I'm sleeping."

He quirked a brow. "You want me to lie to your best friend?"

"I — I guess not, since it would be wrong. Just tell her that I'm not up to talking on the phone."

70

"More like you don't want to talk, right?"

"Jah."

"How come?"

"I just don't, that's all. To be honest, I do not appreciate it when someone says a bunch of positive things that are supposed to cheer me up. It makes me feel like I don't have the right to grieve."

"Course you do. We just don't want to see you pull yourself into a *schaal.*"

Doretta gestured to her halo and then the connected vest. "What do you mean? I'm already in a shell. This contraption I'm stuck wearing makes me look and feel like I'm a *schillgrott.*"

Glen's reddish-brown hair swished across his forehead as he gave a vigorous shake of his head. "Come on, Doretta. You don't look anything like a turtle."

"Well, I sure feel like one, and why can't anyone understand that I just want to be left alone? Grandpa and Grandma came by earlier today, and they kept asking how I was and if there was anything they could do for me."

"What's wrong with that?"

"I don't need people over me all the time or trying to cheer me up."

"Okay, I get it. I won't bother you any-more." Gripping his cell phone, Glen took a few steps back from her.

"I didn't mean you, Brother. I just don't want to see or talk to anyone outside of our immediate family, and I thought I'd made that quite clear." Doretta spoke in a low, but firm voice. "Can you understand that?"

He shrugged his shoulders. "I guess so, but if it were me in your situation, I'd want all my friends around — especially my girlfriend, Irene."

Doretta felt a tightness in her jaw and facial muscles, causing more discomfort than she already felt. *If my boyfriend was here right now, I'd be happy to see him. But William is dead, and I feel like a part of me has died too. I wish I really was a turtle and could crawl into my shell and stay there forever.* She pursed her lips. *One thing's for sure . . . I won't have any more phone calls with Eleanor or anyone else who might decide to call Glen's number so they can talk to me.*

CHAPTER 6

Doretta didn't know how she had made it through Thanksgiving, but Christmas would be here in two weeks, and that was even more difficult for her to think about. Mama was in a festive mood, baking cookies and pumpkin bread to freeze until she would take them out to serve on Christmas Eve. She had tried to enlist Doretta's help, saying she could sit at the kitchen table and either stir or measure out the ingredients for the baked goods, using her uninjured hand. Doretta had declined, stating that she didn't feel up to doing it. Her mother had countered, suggesting that Doretta could simply sit and read off the list of ingredients and baking instructions. Doretta said no to that too and returned to the living room to sit on the couch and watch the flames lapping at the logs in the fireplace.

It won't be long before Mama will hang up all the Christmas cards in the living room.

Doretta grimaced. *Glen mentioned snow coming to Grabill. I'm not thrilled about that, either. I have enough trouble getting around with this uncomfortable halo vest. It feels like it's taking forever for me to heal from the accident. I can't afford to fall in the snow or slip on any ice.* Doretta figured she'd have to stay close to home, mostly indoors to be exact. There was no point in risking any of her slow progress by going out in the bad weather.

Her mind trailed back again to the upcoming festivities that would be taking place around her parents' home. She dreaded their family gathering on Christmas Day. In addition to her parents and siblings, her grandparents would be included. She didn't want to see looks of pity or answer anyone's questions about how she was doing. Doretta wished she could stay in the guest room all day by herself, but Mama would never go for that. She would be expected to join the family for Christmas dinner and afterward sit and visit, sing joyous Christmas songs, or play some board games. It would be difficult to do any of those things, especially sing, because she felt no cheer. So how could she be expected to sing any Christmas songs?

Doretta's negative thoughts spiraled

deeper as she repositioned herself on the sofa and tried to ignore the sweet smell of cinnamon and other spices floating into the living room from the kitchen. She could not get comfortable, no matter what her position. The doctor had said she would get used to wearing the halo brace, but she had not. Doretta felt like a caged animal, constricted and unable to do much by herself. With the exception of the help she received from her mother on a daily basis, Doretta preferred to be alone. The truth was she didn't have anything to chat about on Christmas Day — at least nothing anyone would want to hear. Doretta's broken bones might be in the process of healing, but the sorrow she felt over losing William would linger in Doretta's heart for the rest of her life. She was certain no one would want to hear her talk about that. It was depressing to reminisce about how things used to be when William was alive and even worse to think about her life without him.

When the cast on her arm was removed in a few weeks and the halo brace finally came off, Doretta would be able to move around more freely. That should have been something to look forward to, but since she didn't have a job anymore and had been replaced by another school teacher, Doretta had no purpose in life — no reason to get up in the morning — and nothing to look forward to doing each day. She did not want to feel like this or entertain such negative thoughts, but thinking positive thoughts seemed to be an impossible task.

"Doretta, are you listening to me?"

Her mother's question pushed Doretta's thoughts aside. She hadn't even heard her mother come into the living room. "Uh, no, Mama, I didn't hear what you said."

"I asked if the Christmas card you received from Eleanor yesterday included a letter or note."

"Jah, there was a letter inside."

"That's nice. Did she have anything interesting to tell you?"

"No, not really — just said a few things about the baby." Doretta wasn't about to tell her mother that her friend's letter had mostly been focused on trying to cheer her up. *Doesn't Eleanor understand that I have every reason to be depressed? Why does she keep sending me those letters, trying to comfort me?*

"What about the card you got from your friend Irma? Did she write a note inside?"

"Jah, but it was nothing special. Just said she hoped I was feeling better."

"Are you going to send them Christmas cards?"

"No, I won't be doing any cards this year. And maybe not next year or the one after that. I don't know if I'll ever be in the Christmas spirit again."

Mama came over and took a seat beside Doretta. "You will, Daughter. Your injuries will heal, and after a time, the grief you feel over losing William will lessen."

"I don't think so. I loved William so much and will never get over his death. Also, I wish you'd stop trying to make me feel better, because I don't, and you do not understand at all." Tears welled in Doretta's eyes, and she blinked to keep them from spilling over. "Think I heard the timer go off. Shouldn't you go check on the *kichlin*?"

"Yes, of course." Mama rose from the couch. "Would you like to try one of the cookies after they have cooled some?"

"No thanks."

Mama opened her mouth to say something else, but she seemed to change her mind and instead left the room.

Doretta heaved a sigh. She wished she could find some place to hide, but even if she made her way to the guest room, Mama would probably seek her out again and say something cheerful. *I don't want anyone to*

77

try and cheer me up, Doretta shouted internally. *Just let me deal with my grief in the only way I know how.*

Warren entered a room at the back of his new health food store and went down on his knees to open a box of supplements. He'd been officially in business for a week but had been so busy, he hadn't had the time to get everything he'd ordered out on the shelves yet. It was a good thing he had hired Margaret to help, because there was no way he could run the place by himself. Through an ad in the newspaper, some flyers he'd hung around town, and word of mouth, Warren's new business had been bursting at the seams with customers since the first day he'd put the OPEN sign in the front window.

William was right when he told me that Allen County needed this new business. What a shame he isn't here to see how well the opening week has gone. Warren felt sure that his brother would have been as pleased as he was right now with how things were going. Hopefully, people in the area who had already come in to buy supplements and other health-related items would become regular customers and tell others about the new health food store too.

Warren's thoughts went to Doretta. He'd gone by her folks' place to see her again but had been told that she wasn't feeling up to company. It saddened him to think of Doretta sitting in her house with no one to talk to but the family members who lived there. Although Warren still grieved the loss of his twin brother, interacting with people here in the store and keeping busy were two of the things that had been helping him cope. Two other important items for him were time spent in prayer and Bible reading. It helped to read a portion of God's Word every morning or before he went to bed at night. Warren hoped that Doretta might be doing that too.

His contemplations were interrupted when Margaret rushed into the back room with a panicked expression. "Sorry to bother you, Warren, but there is no vitamin C on any of the shelves, and there are several people in the store asking for that supplement. Do you know when we might be getting some in?"

"As a matter of fact, there's some right here." Warren gestured to the box by his knees. "I'll take several bottles out and put them on the proper shelf."

"Do they have a price sticker on them?"

He shook his head. "No, I'll need to do

that too."

"Okay, I'll let the customers know that you'll be bringing some out." She flashed him a dimpled smile and left the room.

Warren rubbed the bridge of his nose. *I wish she wasn't so cute. That pleasing smile and those pretty blue eyes make it hard to keep my mind on work today.*

Warren had begun putting bottles of supplements on the shelves when he overheard Margaret speaking to a customer at the checkout counter.

When the topic of her and Warren dating came up, his ears really perked up. He didn't recognize the other person's voice, so it obviously wasn't Margaret's best friend, Christina, but it had to be someone she knew personally. Surely she wouldn't be talking to a total stranger in such a way — telling them about their personal life.

Warren knelt quietly and was surprised to hear Margaret say that she was fairly sure he would ask her to marry him someday.

Marry her? His head jerked back, and heat radiated from his face. Warren could not believe what he was hearing. He'd never expected Margaret to be so bold.

"I'm sure the only reason Warren hasn't asked me to go steady yet is because he is still dealing with the loss of his brother, which is understandable. He also has a lot on his mind, trying to get things running smoothly here at the nutrition center." Although Margaret spoke a little more quietly this time, her voice was loud enough for Warren to hear every word.

He wiped the perspiration from his head. *What in the world is she thinking?*

"There is a lot to running a business like this," the female-voiced customer said.

Warren was tempted to go up front and see who it was, but he didn't want to embarrass Margaret, who probably thought he was out of earshot. Why else would she be speaking so boldly to a customer about something as private as the two of them dating?

"I'm glad Warren chose me to help him run this store," Margaret continued. "I'm sure once he sees how well we work together here he will want me to be his marriage partner."

Warren's mouth fell open, and he nearly dropped the bottle of multivitamins he'd picked up from the box. *Now where did Margaret get the idea that I would want to marry her? Have I said or done anything to make her think that? We've only been dating a few months, and marriage is the last thing on my mind right now. Surely she ought to realize that.*

With thoughts swirling in his head so quickly it was hard to follow them, he grabbed two more bottles and set them on the shelf. *Did I make a mistake by hiring her to work here with me? Should I have waited awhile, until someone else answered my ad?*

Although Margaret was a striking young woman, with dazzling blue eyes and hair so dark it was nearly black, she was also a bit of a tomboy. Not that Warren saw that as a bad thing, but from what he'd been able to tell, Margaret had little or no interest in cooking or housekeeping. Her favorite pastime involved horses. In fact, according to what Margaret's mother had told Warren's mom, Margaret preferred spending time with her golden-colored mare, Honey, than cooking, sewing, or helping out with indoor chores. She had a special way with horses, and some folks in their area had brought Margaret their horses that had behavioral problems. The amazing thing was that she had usually done a great job fixing them.

Warren had to admit he'd enjoyed the few dates he and Margaret had gone on this fall before William's death. It had been fun to ride alongside his date on the back of his horse when they had gone fishing. Even so, Warren wasn't sure he'd want a tomboy for a wife.

He gave his head a scratch. *Maybe the kind of woman I envision as my wife is not the one God wants for me.*

At the end of the day, Margaret approached Warren outside his office. "Things went well today, don't you think?"

He gave a brief nod. "Jah, we had plenty of business all right."

"A lot of people mentioned that they'd seen your ad in the paper."

"That's good."

"Have you made any special *blaane* for *Grischtdaag*?" Margaret hoped whatever plans he'd made would include her.

"I've made no plans for Christmas, but I guess my mamm will fix dinner and try to make the best of the day. It won't be the same without William, and I sure won't feel much like celebrating the holiday." Warren's lips pressed together in a tight grimace. "Last year at Christmas, my bruder spent part of the day with Doretta. I bet she won't feel like celebrating this year either."

Margaret had heard him talk about Doretta in this concerned way before. Did she need to worry about having any sort of competition with this other girl? *It would be weird if Warren was attracted to her. After all, she's grieving, same as him, but I want to be the one to lift Warren's spirits.* Margaret peered into his gorgeous blue eyes. *He's such a cute guy, and I can't help being drawn to him.* She reached up and pushed a strand of hair away from his eyes when he bent his head forward. "When was the last time your mamm gave you a haircut?" she asked, hoping a new topic might take Warren's thoughts off his grief.

He shrugged. "I can't remember. Maybe the day before William's funeral. I haven't wanted to bother Mom with it. She's still grieving pretty bad."

Oh, the poor guy. He really needs my help. Margaret tilted her head. "I could do it."

"Do what?"

"Cut your hair. I can bring some scissors with me tomorrow and cut your hair in your office or one of the back rooms before we open for business."

Warren gave a quick shake of his head. "No, that's okay. There are other things we need to do when we first get here. I'll see if my mamm feels up to cutting my hair this evening."

"Oh, okay." Margaret couldn't help feeling a bit disappointed. When she and Warren got married someday, she would be the person cutting Warren's hair. Why had he turned down her offer to do it now?

Maybe Warren has no plans to marry me, Margaret thought as she headed to the back room to retrieve her outer garments. *I might have the buggy before the horse. Sure wish I had the nerve to come right out and ask him. But I guess that would be too bold.* She poked her tongue against the inside of her cheek. *I just need to figure out some way to make Warren see that I would make him the perfect wife.*

CHAPTER 7

Paradise

While Eleanor fixed breakfast on Christmas morning, she thought about Doretta, wishing she could talk to her friend right now and find out how she was doing. If she, Vic, and the baby had gone to Indiana for Christmas, she would have been able to see Doretta. This year, however, Mom and Dad had come here to celebrate the holiday. They'd arrived late last night and were still sleeping, so Eleanor had made a stack of pancakes and put them in the oven to stay warm until it was time to eat. She was glad for this quiet time to be alone and think, because once everyone was up, the house would be full of chatter.

Eleanor's thoughts returned to her friend in Grabill. She knew from the messages she'd received from Doretta's mother that Doretta was severely depressed, and nothing seemed to lift her spirits. This was not like the cheerful, optimistic friend Eleanor had known since they were children. After the accident, everything changed, and now Eleanor worried that if something wasn't done to turn things around, nothing with Doretta would ever be the same.

Eleanor remembered back to the time when Vic suffered from depression and guilt when his little brother drowned in their pond. It had taken quite awhile for him to get over it, and for many months prior to him getting help, he'd tried to drown his sorrows with alcohol, which had only made things worse. *Doretta would never start drinking,* she thought. *But if severe depression sets in, it could cause other problems that would be equally bad.* Eleanor's stomach clenched. *It would break my heart if my dear friend sank deeper into depression and gave up on living. I need to keep in touch more regularly, even if it's via her mother, and pray that Doretta's depression lifts and does not go any deeper.*

Grabill

Ignoring the wonderful aromas drifting from the kitchen, Doretta stared out the living-room window at the gloomy-looking Christmas sky. *At least God could have given us some sunshine or even snow.* She squeezed her eyes shut, refusing to look at the darkening clouds a moment longer. Their company would be here soon, and then she'd have to look at their smiling faces and try to force herself to join the conversation.

Tears clouded her vision. *If only there was something to feel joyous about. If William and I had gotten married, we would be together today, celebrating our first Christmas as husband and wife. It's not fair that he was taken from me. Doesn't God care about me anymore?*

"Whatcha doin' there by the window with your eyes closed?"

At the sound of her sister's voice, Doretta opened her eyes. "I was just thinking is all." She could have said that she'd been praying, but it would be a lie. Truth was, she hadn't prayed about much of anything since the accident. What was the point in praying? Doretta had asked herself that question many times since she'd been told that William was dead.

"What were you thinkin' about?" Karen gave Doretta's pleated skirt a little tug.

"It was nothing important." Doretta moved away from the window, made her way over to one of the straight-backed

88

chairs, and carefully lowered herself into it.

Karen came over and stood directly in front of Doretta. *"Hallicher Grischtdaag."*

"Merry Christmas to you too." Doretta could barely get the words out, but she figured it was good practice, because she'd be expected to say "Merry Christmas" to Grandpa and Grandma Schwartz when they arrived, as well as others in the family. It wouldn't be easy, but she couldn't be rude. And maybe if she forced herself to give everyone a Christmas greeting, it might help pull her out of the dark depression she felt — at least for a few hours.

With all the excitement of a ten-year-old girl, Doretta's sister tipped her head to one side and shouted, "Grandpa and Grandma must be here! I hear a horse and buggy pulling into our yard right now."

Doretta was on the verge of telling Karen to keep her voice down, but the child raced out of the room before she could say a single word. "Here we go," Doretta murmured. She stopped talking to herself and let her thoughts take over. *It's time to put on my make-believe happy face now so that no one will be on my case today.* She shifted her position carefully. *Sure hope no one will ask me to sing and yodel today. I'm truly not in the mood for that. I just wish everyone would leave me alone and stop trying to cheer me up. If something unexpected happened and they were thrown into a situation like mine, I doubt that they'd be thinking happy thoughts all the time.*

Warren lay on his bed, staring at the ceiling. Somehow he had made it through their Christmas meal, but a pounding headache had been the excuse he'd needed to take refuge in his room. It had been ever so hard to look at William's empty chair at the table, and he'd been tempted to get up from his own chair and remove it. But that wouldn't have gone over well with his mother; Dad, either, for that matter. They seemed to find comfort in seeing William's chair, where his winter jacket had been draped over the back as though he might return at any moment. Instead of his brother's outer garment offering Warren comfort, seeing it there was like a knife piercing his soul.

Warren and William had always shared a bond that went deeper than the fact that they were siblings. He'd read a magazine article once about identical twins and the closeness they shared. It had stated that some sets of twins were so much alike that when one of them came down with some illness, oddly, the other twin did too, even if they lived miles apart. However, for Warren and William, it went a little further than that. In addition to being identical, they were mirror image twins, which occurred in about twenty-five percent of identical twins. This type of twinship occurred when one twin carried anatomical features, physical characteristics, and sometimes personality traits that were the opposite of their identical sibling.

Their parents had been told, and later Warren and his brother learned, that some studies had been done on mirror twins. Apparently, the researchers believed that mirror twins happened when the fertilized egg split later in development, usually about nine to twelve days after conception. When the split occurred, the genes that determined the left and right sides of the embryo were already active. Each twin took one side, resulting in a mirror image effect. Although the twins were still identical, some of their features appeared opposite of one another.

Warren smiled as he thought back to the day when he and William were children and they'd discovered that even though they both had the same color of brown hair and blue eyes, their dimples were on opposite sides of their faces. William's was on his right cheek and Warren's was on his left. Another opposite trait was that Warren was right-handed, while his brother wrote and ate with his left hand. Some of their personality traits and interests were different too. William was outgoing and made friends easily, while Warren was more on the quiet side. They both enjoyed a rousing game of baseball and could be quite competitive, but William was the better player and sometimes gave his brother a hard time when they'd played on opposite teams. Warren also enjoyed fishing and played the harmonica. William had never shown much interest in learning a musical instrument, although he did enjoy singing and yodeling. He'd often sang and yodeled with Doretta because she was good at it too. In addition to his enjoyment of hunting and hiking, William liked to play board games with Doretta.

Even with William and Warren's differences, many people often got the twin brothers mixed up. That was the fun part — at least William had thought so. Playing tricks on the kids at school had usually been his idea. The one person, other than their parents, who had said she never got them confused was Doretta. Even before she and William had begun dating, she'd made the statement that she always knew the difference between the twins.

Little did she know, Warren thought. *Doretta sometimes believed the person she was talking to was William, but I didn't want to embarrass her, so I just went along with it and never let on.*

Warren put both hands behind his head and groaned as he reflected on Doretta's current situation. *Today must be as difficult for her as it has been for me.* He closed his eyes and said a prayer on her behalf, ending it by asking God to give Doretta a sense of peace and acceptance of the things she could not change.

"Good morning, girl," Margaret said as she entered her horse's stall to give her mare, Honey, some hay. "Should the two of us go for a ride later today?"

Honey's ears perked up, and her honey-colored tail swished back and forth.

"You like that idea, don't you, pretty girl?" Margaret reached for a brush and began grooming Honey's back while the mare ate. She thought about Warren, wishing he could join her on the ride. It would be more enjoyable than if she went out on the trail and rode alone.

Last night, Warren had stopped by the house, but he didn't stay long and hadn't even brought her a Christmas present. He'd also mentioned that he wouldn't see her until they went to work at his store the day after Christmas. Margaret had tried to hide her disappointment, and rather than cause him to feel guilty about it, she'd kept the wallet she had planned to give him for Christmas, deciding it could wait for some other time. She wondered, though, if there was any hope for their relationship to develop further. Maybe if she could be patient and do whatever it took to make him see that she would make a good helpmate, things would change. *Maybe I should take a ride over to his parents' place with some Christmas cookies. That way I could see Warren and try to lift his spirits.* She pulled a piece of straw from Honey's mane. *But if my timing is off and they have company visiting, it would be rather hard to have any alone time with Warren, so maybe riding over there today is not a good idea.*

"What are you doing out here? Shouldn't you be inside getting changed so you look presentable when our company arrives?"

Margaret stopped brushing and turned her head. She was surprised to see her eighteen-year-old sister, Alisa, standing on the other side of the gate to Honey's stall. Margaret had been engrossed in her thoughts and hadn't heard anyone enter the barn.

"I'm brushing my *gaul*." She gestured to her horse. "Honey enjoys the extra attention I give her, and we'll be going for a ride later on, so I want her to look good."

Alisa's pale eyebrows furrowed. "You spend too much time with your mare. Sometimes I think you care more about that horse than you do your good-looking beau."

"That's not true. I spend eight hours, five days a week with my boyfriend while we're working at the health food store."

"But you're both being busy, stocking shelves, unloading boxes, or waiting on customers. That's not the same thing as hanging out just the two of you while spending quality time together doing something for fun the way Marvin and I do when we're not working at our jobs." Alisa looked straight at Margaret. "Warren didn't stay here very long when he stopped by last evening. Maybe he senses you care more about your gaul than you do him."

What an unrealistic remark, and of course it's not true. Margaret clasped the brush she held so tightly that her knuckles turned white. "That's not true, and Warren knows it. The problem is, he's either focused on making his new business succeed or is thinking about how much he misses William."

"You can't blame him for that. Maybe you should try to be more understanding. It hasn't even been two full months since the accident that took William's life. Warren and his parents are still grieving. This is their first Christmas without William, and it has to be a difficult time for all of them."

"You're right, Sister. Maybe he isn't thinking or acting quite like himself yet. Even so, I can't help feeling sad and disappointed when he shuts me out. We haven't gone anywhere together since his brother died." Margaret flexed her fingers as her frustration mounted. "Guess I need some proof that Warren cares about me more than his business."

"He offered you a job at the nutrition center. That should tell you something."

"Jah, that he needed someone to help him run the store, and since I was without a job, he had no problem hiring me." Margaret stroked her horse's silky muzzle. "I'm afraid Warren doesn't see me as his *aldi* anymore." She shrugged. "Maybe he never did, really."

Alisa wagged her finger. "You worry too much. You and Warren haven't been dating that long. Just try to set your worries aside and give him some time to deal with his brother's death and get his store running well. When things get back to a more normal life for Warren, I'm sure he will start coming by here more often and asking you to go out with him again."

Margaret gave a deep, weighted sigh. She wasn't sure her boyfriend would ever stop grieving for his twin brother, but she would try to be patient and remind him occasionally that he needed to take some time to go riding with her or do some other fun things. Maybe once Warren saw how efficient she was at the store, he would realize that he ought to pay her more attention.

Margaret thought of another inherent problem that remained, one that bugged her to no end. *Doretta seems to be taking up space in my boyfriend's head. Warren has mentioned Doretta several times and the concern he feels about her physical and emotional condition.* Margaret pursed her lips. *I feel like Warren is so worried about the woman his brother had planned to marry, that he's pushing me aside. I'll have to think of something so he will get his mind off her and focus more on me instead.*

Doretta sat on one end of the couch with her hands clasped in her lap. It felt good to finally have her cast off and be able to use both hands. What did not feel good was sitting here in the living room with her mother and both grandmothers, forcing herself to take part in their conversation, while Karen sat on the floor near the fireplace, reading one of the books she'd been given for Christmas. The men and boys had gone out to the barn to look at the new horse Dad had bought Mama, so dessert had been put on hold until they returned to the house.

The current discussion among the older women was on the quilted table runner Grandma Schwartz had made for Mama's dining-room table. Since Doretta felt thirsty and her facial muscles ached from forcing a smile, she excused herself to get a drink of water.

Doretta had only been in the kitchen a few minutes when she heard her name mentioned from the living room. Curious to know what the women were saying, she set her glass of water on the table and moved closer to the kitchen door.

"It's a shame Doretta didn't talk much to anyone during dinner. Whenever I looked at her, she smiled, but it didn't seem genuine. Do you think she's putting up a front so we won't keep asking how she's doing?"

Doretta's fingers curled into the palms of her hands. She recognized Grandma

Schwartz's voice, and it irritated her that as soon as she'd left the room, she had become the topic of conversation.

She remained in place, wondering what else would be said. Sure enough, her mother spoke up, and her words were not in Doretta's favor.

"You're right, Kathryn, my *dochder* only pretended to be interested in the conversation at our table today, and her smile was not genuine. She wasn't one bit happy when Karen asked her to sing a little yodeling song, and I knew right away that Doretta would decline. I know my daughter better than anyone else in this family, and I'm also the person who has spent the most time with her since the accident." After a short pause, Mama said, "I am well aware of her melancholy mood, which she doesn't seem to be able to shake."

"There must be something that will cheer Doretta up and help her realize that there are still some good things ahead," Doretta's maternal grandmother spoke up.

Doretta flinched as a wave of heat flushed throughout her body. She couldn't listen to their conversation any longer. She had to go in there and say something.

Breathing in and out several times, Doretta returned to the living room. Positioning herself where she could see all three women, she spoke loudly and in a clear voice. "If you're going to talk about me, why not do it to my face instead of going behind my back? Didn't you think I could hear you from the kitchen?"

Grandma Schwartz's face flamed. "I'm so sorry. I never meant to —"

"I'm going to my room." Doretta turned sharply, nearly losing her balance, and Mama rushed forward and clasped Doretta's arm.

"I'm okay, and I don't need your help; I want to be left alone." Doretta made as hasty an exit as the confinement of her halo brace would allow. Today was the worst Christmas she'd ever endured, and she would be glad when it was over!

CHAPTER 8

"Our driver is here. Are you ready to go?" Mama called from outside the bathroom door.

"Almost. I'll be out in a few minutes." Doretta turned away from the mirror and glanced at the closed door.

"All right, but remember, this is the day you'll hopefully be getting your halo vest removed, so we don't want to be late for your appointment."

Yes, Mama, I'm hoping to get this awkward thing off today, and I'll be glad, but it won't help me get over missing William like I do. Doretta turned toward the mirror and studied her reflection. If her CT scans and X-rays looked good, she would return home today without the ugly-looking, confining apparatus that had held her captive for the past three months. She had been told that removing it would not be a painful procedure, but she could feel some pressure when her health care team loosened the pins. She'd also been informed that once the pins were removed, there might be some fluid oozing out. Soon scabs would form, and once they fell off, Doretta would need to put some lotion or oils on the pin sites to help reduce scarring. *Sure hope it won't be too uncomfortable having those pins removed. I'm glad I won't have to watch them do it.*

She grimaced. *I wish I could cut the hair above my forehead into bangs so my scars wouldn't show. But then I've never seen a woman who is a member of the Amish church with her hair cut like that. People will think I am vain if I even mention the silly idea.*

Tap. Tap. Tap. "Doretta, please come out now. We need to go."

After taking one last look in the mirror, Doretta opened the door and stepped into the hallway. When she returned home later today, hopefully she would look a little more like her old self. *I hope lying low all this time will have paid off. It might help my mood if I'm able to do more things as I continue growing stronger.*

"Business has sure been slow so far today," Warren said after he'd made his way down the main supplement aisle and joined Margaret behind the checkout counter. "Maybe it's the cold weather keeping everyone inside their homes."

"That could be. The temperature is pretty frigid."

Warren observed her cheerful-looking smile that was enough to warm any man's heart. So why hadn't it had that effect on Warren?

"Are you tempted to close the store early today?" Margaret asked.

He shook his head. "Someone might come in at the last minute and need something. I won't put the Closed sign in the window until six o'clock, like usual."

Margaret's smile faded. "Umm . . . I hope you don't mind, but I need to leave the nutrition center a little early this afternoon."

"How come? This is the first time you've mentioned going home before six."

"One of our English neighbors is having a little trouble with one of his horses, so I agreed to see if there's anything I can do to help with the horse's odd behavior."

Warren resisted the urge to roll his eyes. Although Margaret was good with horses and had helped some with performance problems, he didn't understand why working with this particular horse couldn't wait until her day off. *Of course,* he reasoned, *one of those days off is Sunday, so no work that isn't absolutely necessary will be done on our day of worship, not even on our off-Sundays, when we often visit some other church district.* The other day Warren closed the store for business was Monday, which was only three days away, so he saw no reason that Margaret couldn't wait until then to take a look at her neighbor's horse. Or she could go to their place after leaving work this evening.

As if she knew what he was thinking, Margaret touched Warren's arm. "Normally, I wouldn't ask to leave early unless it was important. And since so few people have come in today, I just thought . . ."

"Okay, whatever. Unless we get really busy, I don't mind if you leave early." Warren figured if he didn't allow Margaret to leave early, she would keep pestering him about it until he finally gave in. She was good at getting her own way, and Warren was disgusted with himself for allowing her to keep pushing until she got what she wanted. Warren didn't know why he was so agreeable where Margaret was concerned. Maybe it was because she was so cute and knew how to flirt with him. *Or maybe,* he thought with regret, *I'm just too much of a people-pleaser.*

Margaret's lips parted, and she released a

deep breath. "Danki for being so under-standing. You're the nicest man I've ever known."

Warren shrugged. "I'm just practicing the Golden Rule."

She flashed him another sweet smile. "If you ever need to leave the store early, I'd be willing to return the favor and take charge of things while you're gone."

He gave a brief nod. "Thanks. I may need to take you up on that offer sometime."

Doretta held onto her mother's arm as they walked carefully through the freshly fallen snow in their yard. Even though she had gotten the halo brace off this morning and now wore only a soft neck collar, her balance was still a bit off, not to mention having to deal with the slippery snow beneath her unsteady feet. Although the removable collar supported her neck, Doretta's head felt heavy and kind of wobbly. She reminded herself that the doctor had told her to expect her neck muscles to be weak from being immobilized for so many weeks.

"We're almost there." Mama spoke in a soothing tone as she guided Doretta along. "We'll soon be inside, where it's warm and toasty."

When they entered the house, Doretta felt

a keen sense of disappointment that no one was there to greet her and see that she'd gotten the halo brace off. Of course, she'd known they wouldn't be home at this hour, since Karen and Jeremy were still at school and it was a workday for Dad, Isaac, and Glen.

"Should we go to the kitchen and fix our lunch, or should we start with a cup of tea to warm our insides?" Mama asked after they'd hung up their outer garments.

"I'm not hungry right now, but tea will be fine." Doretta tried to muster some enthusiasm, but Mama probably knew the smile on Doretta's face was not genuine. It had always been hard to pull the wool over her mother's eyes.

"You look *mied.*" Mama gave Doretta's arm a gentle tap. "Why don't you sit at the table while I put water in the teakettle and get the water heating on the stove?"

"You're right, I am tired. Everything about my appointment today was exhausting."

Mama gave an understanding nod. "I knew it would be, with all of the X-rays and then the removal of the halo brace."

Doretta gestured to her forehead. "I am glad no one but our family will see me like this."

"It won't be long and the scabs will fall

off the pin holes, and then . . ."

"There will be scars, and I'll have no way to cover them up."

"Remember that the instructions you were given today stated once the scabs fall off, you should put lotion or oil on the pin sites to help reduce the scarring. Perhaps we could try some vitamin E. Rubbing the oil on my acne scars when I was a young woman took them all away, although it did take a bit of time and patience on my part."

"Guess it's worth a try." Doretta took a seat at the table.

"What kind of tea would you like?"

Doretta shrugged. It felt good to be able to do that motion without the constriction of the halo brace. "Whatever kind you choose is fine with me."

"Apple cinnamon sounds good."

"I'm okay with it too."

As her mother went about getting the tea ready, Doretta read the letter she'd received from Eleanor yesterday and had left on the table last evening when she'd finally read it. Her friend had written that she was concerned about her, and she had shared some passages of scripture, like Psalm 31:24 — "Be of good courage, and he shall strengthen your heart, all ye that hope in the Lord."

That sounds good on paper, Doretta thought, *but it's hard to have hope when your life has been turned upside-down. Eleanor doesn't understand what I'm going through. She's never suffered an injury such as mine, and the man she loves is still alive and there in the house with her and Rosetta.*

"I see you're reading Eleanor's letter," Mama said as she handed Doretta a cup of tea. "You should write back and let her know that you got the halo brace off today."

"I don't have anything positive to say other than it's off, so what's the use in writing about it?" She blew on her hot tea before taking a tentative sip. "Besides, I'm exhausted right now, so I'll be going to my room to rest as soon as I finish this cup of tea."

Mama pursed her lips a few seconds as she stared at Doretta with obvious disapproval. "How can you state that you have nothing positive to say when you're progressing so well in your healing?"

Doretta fought against the hot tears pushing at the back of her eyes. She did not want to end up crying again. She'd done too much of that already. "I'm thankful not to be wearing the halo apparatus any longer, but I still have a ways to go, since my neck is unstable."

"Yes, you do, but not nearly as much as before. The soft collar will offer you additional protection from overusing your neck, and it serves as a transition to normal use. We'll just need to check things daily to make sure it's not rubbing excessively or causing your skin to break down." Mama took a sip of her tea and smiled. "You can return to light duties now and will be able to attend our every-other-week church services again, since you are free of the halo brace."

Doretta swallowed hard. She hadn't been home fifteen minutes and Mama was already mapping out her schedule. *I'm not ready to parade about yet, and I wish my mamm would stop pushing me to do what she's wanting.* Doretta clutched her cup of tea, feeling the warmth on her hands but not appreciating it. *I need to calm down and think about how helpful my mamm has been to me.* Doretta didn't mind helping with some things around the house, but the last thing she wanted to do was attend church, where people could stare and feel sorry for her. And she'd have to listen to the preachers' sermons and various quotes from the Bible that she no longer believed. This Sunday, Doretta would have to come up with a good reason not to go to church with her family, because the thought of going there was overwhelming.

Paradise

After putting the baby down for a nap, Eleanor decided to brave the cold and go out to the phone shed to check for messages.

She put on her outer garments and called Checkers, who'd been sleeping on a throw rug in the kitchen. He sprang into action, let out a few barks, and raced to the front door.

"Hush now or you'll wake Rosetta." Eleanor opened the door, and the dog ran out, brushing against her leg. She stepped out behind him and shut the door. Although there was only a small amount of snow on the ground, the air felt bitterly cold.

Arf! Arf! Checkers raced around in circles. Holding a stick in his mouth that he'd found somewhere in the yard, he stopped in front of Eleanor.

"Not now." She shook her head. "It's cold out here, and I need to get to the phone shed."

He dropped the stick at Eleanor's feet and looked up at her with his head cocked to one side, as though pleading with her to play the expected throw-the-stick game.

"Okay, but just once." She grabbed the

piece of wood and gave it a good fling. As soon as Checkers went after it, Eleanor made her way to the small shack near the end of their driveway. When she stepped inside the cold building, she was surprised to hear the phone ringing. She hurried to pick up the receiver and said, "Hello."

"Eleanor, I — I didn't expect you to pick up. I figured I'd have to leave a voice mail message for you, like I usually do."

Eleanor smiled at the sound of Doretta's mother's voice. "It's good to hear from you, Amanda. How is everything there?"

"It's cold and blustery — typical for the month of February."

"The weather is like that here too." Eleanor took a seat on the folding chair and shifted the receiver to her other ear. "How is Doretta doing? She hasn't responded to any of my letters, and I've been concerned."

"I've tried to get her to write to you, but she's still very depressed and doesn't have the desire to do much of anything other than feel sorry for herself."

"I'm sorry to hear that. I had hoped that by now things might be going better."

"I've wanted that too. Doretta got her halo brace off this morning, and now she only has to wear a neck collar until her neck muscles become stronger. I thought being free of the halo apparatus would perk her up, but when we came home, she had a cup of tea and then went straight to her room. She didn't even come out when I called her for lunch."

Eleanor heard the frustration in Amanda's voice and wished she could give her a hug. "I'll keep writing letters and calling to check on Doretta. I will also continue praying for my dear friend and you as well, Amanda. I'm sure acting as her primary caregiver these last few months has been exhausting for you."

"It has been tiring, but I've never minded caring for my daughter's physical needs. But the sadness Doretta feels, along with her sense of hopelessness, has left me in a quandary, because I don't know what to do to help her bounce back."

"Have you told her doctor about this? Perhaps there's some medicine he can give Doretta for her depression."

"I did mention it to him, but Doretta became upset and said she would not take any medicine that would probably make her feel sleepy or leave her with a drugged-up feeling. As I'm sure you know, my daughter has always preferred a more natural approach to things."

"You mean like organic remedies and such?"

"Jah. She had to take medication for the pain during the early part of her recovery, but as soon as possible, she quit the meds and replaced them with white willow bark pills and Arnica pellets." Amanda was quiet for a moment. "You know, I'm thinking maybe a trip to Warren's new health food store might be in order. I'm sure there must be something there that could help with her depression."

"That's a good idea. It's certainly worth a try. Would you please keep me posted on how things go with that?"

"Of course. But for now, I'd better let you go, because if it's as cold in your phone shed as it is in ours, you're probably shivering like a leaf caught in the wind."

Using her free hand, Eleanor rubbed her arm. "It is pretty chilly out here, even with my jacket on. And I should get back inside and check on Rosetta. She might have awakened from her nap by now."

"All right then. Please give her a kiss from me. I'll call you again in a week or so and let you know how things are going. I appreciate your support for my daughter as well as for me."

"It's my privilege to do so. Doretta was

there for me when Vic and I were going through a rough patch last year. Now it's my turn to help her."

CHAPTER 9

Soon after Margaret left the store to do her horse-whispering thing, Warren got busy placing orders for some items they were either out of or low in stock. He hadn't yet gotten the hang of knowing how much of each supplement to keep on hand, but eventually he hoped to figure it all out so he wouldn't run out of things — especially those items that people asked for most often.

Warren wondered, if his brother had been able to join this partnership as planned, whether William would have had better judgment about what supplements would be more in demand. William had always been more detailed than Warren, so he'd have probably planned better all the way around. But Warren wasn't stupid and had always learned things quickly, so he felt confident that eventually he'd get the hang of things here in the store.

Warren thought about the piece of land his brother had purchased with the idea of building a home on it for him and Doretta. William had planned to show it to her a couple of days before they got married, as a prewedding gift. As far as Warren knew, that hadn't happened, unless William had taken Doretta there before the accident. Doretta would know the answer to that, of course, but Warren wasn't sure he should ask. It might upset her to talk about it. Doretta seemed to come into Warren's thoughts more often as the days went on, and he had become keenly aware that the feelings he'd had for her since they were in school had never gone away.

I wonder how Doretta is doing today. The last time I saw her, she looked miserable wearing that heavy-looking apparatus. I hope she's feeling better and that she'll be able to have the halo brace removed soon.

He glanced at the shelves again. *I need to refocus on ordering the supplements I'm low on or completely out of right now.* But he felt the urge, a tug at his heart, to pray for her, so Warren closed his eyes and bowed his head. *Heavenly Father, please be with Doretta right now and help her to heal both physically and emotionally. Please give comfort and hope to her during this day.*

The bell above the front door jingled, and Warren ended his prayer to find out who had come in. He was pleased to see Doretta's mother near the door. Amanda was the first person to enter the store since Margaret had left.

"Good afternoon. May I help you with something?" Warren shook Amanda's hand.

She blinked rapidly and cleared her throat. "Well . . . I . . . could use a few boxes of herbal tea and some vitamin C to help strengthen my family's immune system against any viruses that might be going around this winter."

"That would be helpful, but I'd also suggest taking zinc and vitamins A and D. I don't have any zinc here today, but it should be coming in the shipment I'm expecting tomorrow morning, so I'd be happy to bring it by your house on my way home tomorrow afternoon."

"That's very kind, but I don't want to trouble you to go out of your way."

He shook his head. "It's no problem. I'd be pleased to do it. It'll give me a chance to see how Doretta is doing too."

"Speaking of my daughter . . . I wonder if you might have a supplement that would help with her depression." Amanda's brows lowered when she frowned. "It's been three months since the accident, and she's still struggling emotionally. It's rare to see her smile these days, and when she does, I can tell it's not real."

"I'm sorry to hear that. Do you think she's still dealing with pain from her injuries?"

"It's not so much physical anymore. Doretta got her halo brace off today, and now she only has to wear a neck collar for a while." Amanda pressed a tissue to her eyes, as though fighting back tears. "She's very depressed and doesn't seem to see the positive in anything. I talked to her doctor about it, and he suggested a prescription for depression, but that didn't go over well with Doretta. Since my daughter is into the more natural way of doing things, I'm hoping she'll be willing to take something found here in your health food store." Amanda glanced around. "That is, if you have anything that you believe might help with her mood."

Warren rubbed his clean-shaven chin as he contemplated her question. Although he and William had learned a lot about nutrition before purchasing the store, he didn't have enough knowledge to offer sound advice for every physical or emotional ailment. After all, owning a retail nutritional store did not qualify him as a medical, naturopathic, or chiropractic doctor.

"I'm not an expert on this, you understand, but I have read that St. John's wort is a popular herbal treatment for depression in Europe. However, that particular herb could have serious interactions with medication, other herbs, or some supplements, so I wouldn't advise taking it without consulting a doctor first."

Amanda pursed her lips. "Can you think of anything else that might have fewer or no side effects at all?"

"Kava root is known for its sedative and anesthetic properties. It's often used as an ingredient in relaxing teas. I read once that some places in the South Pacific, such as Hawaii, have used kava for stress relief, mood elevation, and other calming effects."

"Is it safe to use?"

He nodded. "Studies have shown that it's safe and effective in treating tension and anxiety, which could help ease depression symptoms."

"Do you have any kava here in the store either by itself or in a tea?"

"Not at the moment, but I'm also expecting a shipment of herbal teas tomorrow morning. If there's one with kava in it, I'll include it with the vitamin C I take by your house on my way home tomorrow."

Amanda smiled. "That would be appreciated."

"If I learn of anything else that might help with depression and would be safe to take, I'll bring that too, in case you decide to try more than one remedy for Doretta's sadness."

"Danki, Warren. You're a very kind young man." Amanda glanced around the area where they stood. "This is a nice place. I'm glad you bought the store. It's definitely needed here in our town."

Warren smiled. "I'm glad I did too. I only wish that my brother could have been a part of it, and . . ." His voice trailed off, and he swallowed hard, unable to finish the sentence.

Amanda stepped forward and touched his arm. "I am sorry for you and your family's loss. Opening this business was a good thing, and I'm sure William would be pleased that you went ahead with your plans after his passing."

When he'd gained control of his emotions, Warren managed a smile. "I think so too. Sometimes I visualize my brother looking down from heaven and nodding his approval. Does that sound *lecherich* to you?"

"It's not ridiculous at all. In fact, I've had thoughts like that about my sister, Lisa. We were only two years apart and had a special bond between us until she passed away at the age of ten."

"What did she die from?" he asked.

"We were playing ball, and when it rolled out into the road, Lisa chased after it. A car was coming fast, and the driver didn't see her until it was too late." Amanda placed a hand against her chest. "I felt like I had lost my best friend, and I'll never forget the agony on my mamm's face when she was told that her youngest child was dead."

"I understand. When my folks and I learned that William had not survived, my mamm nearly fainted." Warren leaned against the checkout counter, feeling a sudden need for support. "To tell you the truth, my legs were pretty wobbly that evening, and I think my daed's were too. The horrible accident was something none of us ever expected to happen. We'd all been happily looking forward to William and Doretta's wedding day."

"Jah, we were too. William would have made a fine son-in-law and a good husband to Doretta. When she became conscious enough to understand what I said, explaining to her how William had died was the most difficult thing I've ever had to do." Amanda slowly shook her head. "The poor girl was devastated and still is, for that matter. It's as though my once-cheerful daughter has vanished like vapor. I've never seen her in such a depressed state of mind."

"Although I still miss my bruder something awful, what has helped me the most is keeping my hands and mind busy. Even when I'm not here at the store working, I find things to do to help out at home. Maybe staying busy would help Doretta too."

"That's possible, I suppose, and there are plenty of projects around the house that could be done, so I'm hoping she'll be willing to pitch in when needed."

Warren was on the verge of responding when his mother entered the store. She was bundled up against the cold, from the black covering on her head, all the way down to the boots on her feet. He excused himself to go see what she wanted, and Amanda obliged, saying she would look around the store for a bit before going home.

After she disappeared down one of the vitamin aisles, Warren greeted his mother with a hug. "This is a nice surprise. I didn't think you'd be out and about on this cold day."

"I had a few groceries to buy and thought I'd stop in here and say hello." Her lips formed a smile, but it did not reach her eyes.

Warren gestured to the aisle Amanda had headed down. "Doretta's mother is here shopping. Maybe you'd like to say hello to her."

"I will after I'm done talking to you."

"Is there anything in particular you wanted to tell me?"

"Just wanted to make sure you're going to be home for supper this evening. I know on occasion you have eaten an evening meal at the Waglers' house or gone out to a restaurant."

"No, I'll be coming home right after work. Margaret is working with someone's horse this afternoon, and she'll probably be there for several hours."

Mom's forehead creased. "You mean she's not here right now?"

"No, she left early."

"So you have no help in the store this afternoon?"

He shook his head.

"Well, that was certainly inconsiderate of her. Margaret should be here helping since that's what you hired her to do, not running off in the hope of fixing some horse's problem."

"Business is slow today," Warren countered without commenting on what his mother had said about Margaret. "So I can manage on my own for a few hours until closing time."

"I could stay and help you. Since I used to work at the bulk food store, I know a little something about retailing."

Warren cringed inwardly. The last thing he wanted was his mother hanging around the store the rest of the day, telling him what to do and perhaps trying to change things around. "I will be fine on my own, but thanks for offering. Now, why don't you go ahead and talk to Amanda while I get busy cleaning the front windows?"

She hesitated but finally nodded and walked away. "Please let me know if you change your mind."

"Okay." Warren bit back a sigh of relief when she headed in the direction of the vitamins. He had a hunch that the real reason his mother had stopped by today was to check on him and see if he was okay. Ever since William's accident, Mom had become clingy and overprotective. While she hadn't spoken the words, Warren felt sure that she resented the time he spent here at the store with Margaret. Mom fussed over him constantly, always reminding him to be careful whenever he left the house. Warren loved his mother, and he didn't want to intentionally say or do anything that might hurt her, but he'd felt smothered by her since his brother's death.

Think I'll have a talk with Dad about this, Warren decided. *He might have some suggestions.*

Doretta glanced at the clock on the far kitchen wall. *It's almost three o'clock. I wonder what's taking Mama so long to run her errands.* After her mother left for town, Doretta had wandered about from room to room, thinking about William, and had finally ended up at the kitchen table with a glass of grape juice. Since Mama had left her alone in the house, Doretta had experienced moments when she'd wept and spoken out loud, with only the four walls to hear her deepest cries of despair. She wondered once again what her life would be like today if she had been able to marry William. What kind of experiences might they be having, and was it possible that she may have been expecting a baby by now? It was hard not to ask God why this tragedy had occurred that had separated her and William. There were so many unanswered questions, and she longed to have answers.

Doretta couldn't face the fact that she needed help in shouldering her emotional burdens, and she was too proud and stubborn to admit it to anyone, especially Mama.

She folded her arms and stared straight ahead. *I'm glad she didn't press me too hard about going with her today. I'm not up to seeing anyone, and I don't know what I'm going to do on Sunday when she expects me to go to church with her and the rest of the family.*

"I'll just say that I have a *koppweh,* and it will probably be true, because I've had a lot of headaches since the accident," Doretta muttered. Although she couldn't stay away from church indefinitely, she would postpone it for as long as she could.

She reached up and gingerly touched her forehead. The scabs bothered her not only in their appearance but in the way they felt to the touch. Maybe once they'd all fallen off, she would feel more like being seen in public. Doretta grimaced. *Of course then there will be scars. How much longer will it take before I experience this long-awaited healing?*

She had to admit that without the halo brace, it was easier to move around on her own. Going to bed at night and falling asleep felt pretty much normal, since she could lie flat or change positions. Even though she had made fairly good progress physically over these past weeks, Doretta preferred to move at a slow and cautious pace.

She thought about the small package she had received from Eleanor yesterday. Inside was a cloth satchel along with a note her friend had written: *There are thirty pieces of paper inside this satchel. If you take one out each day and do what's been written on the paper, it might help you feel better. Love, Eleanor.*

Doretta hadn't bothered to open the satchel yesterday, but she had to admit that she was curious about its contents, so she may as well do it now. She pulled the drawstring open and reached inside. The paper she withdrew read: *"Sing a yodeling song."*

Doretta shook her head. *For goodness' sake, Eleanor, don't you realize that I don't feel like singing, much less yodeling?* Doretta was the only person in her family who had learned to yodel, and she'd done it a lot over the years to entertain friends and family members. She'd been happy to discover that William had also liked to yodel, so many times they had enjoyed singing and yodeling, even when it was just the two of them with no one to entertain.

"I'm not about to start yodeling now,"

Doretta muttered. "What would be the point, anyhow? It certainly wouldn't bring William back or make me feel more cheerful."

Doretta felt guilty for not answering any of Eleanor's letters or cards, although she felt sure her friend would understand. She thought the satchel full of papers was a silly idea, but she would take it up to her bedroom and try to remember to open and read one each day. *Well, maybe not every day,* Doretta told herself. *But I will read one whenever I think about it, even though I don't believe it will help me feel one bit better.*

She got up from the table and moved over to the desk on the other side of the room. While rummaging through some of the cards she'd received since returning home from the hospital, she discovered a newspaper under the stack. Her heart clenched when she saw that it was open to the obituary page. And there, circled with a yellow highlighting pen, was William's obituary. She wondered who had done that. *Probably Mama,* she decided.

Doretta did not want to read it, and yet she couldn't seem to help herself. "William G. Lengacher, age 25, of Grabill, Indiana, passed away unexpectedly from injuries sustained in a tragic accident that took place on . . ."

Doretta's vision blurred as she read the date of her beloved William's death. *Oh my . . . Has it really been three months?* Tears rolled down her cheeks as she thought about his funeral, which she hadn't been able to attend. *Would it have brought me closure if I'd been there to say my final goodbyes?* She shook her head. *I doubt it. I probably would have fallen apart.*

Doretta put the newspaper down, unable to read the rest of his obituary. *I hate feeling like this, and crying so often has done nothing to make me feel better. Will I ever get the pain of losing him out of my heart? It doesn't seem possible that I'll ever feel like myself again and be able to function normally. Is there anything that will pull me out of this terrible depression I'm trapped in and can't escape from?*

CHAPTER 10

Doretta stood watching out the kitchen window at a red-bellied woodpecker as it bobbed its head in and out. Even with the window closed, the *rat-a-tat-tat* sound resonated as the determined bird banged away on a tree trunk, no doubt looking for food. *I'm glad that silly woodpecker didn't choose our house to peck a hole in or else someone would need to go outside and shoo the noisy bird away.* She continued staring as it clung to the bark of the tree with its claws.

Too bad Mama is in the shower right now, Doretta thought. *This particular woodpecker is one of her favorite birds.* It seemed strange to Doretta that such a noisy bird would appeal to anyone; but then everyone's likes and dislikes were different. Doretta's favorite bird was the beautiful male red cardinal. *At least the pretty cardinals aren't interested in putting holes into houses and trees. They seem to like eating out of Mama's feeders, though, and the red males have an appealing song to attract their females.*

Doretta's focus on the woodpecker glazed over as her mind flashed back to last summer, when she and William had gone on a picnic.

"This is the perfect place for a *picknick,*" Doretta said as she helped William spread a blanket on the ground near the pond he told her he'd discovered not long ago. It was set deep into the woods on property that didn't appear to belong to anyone, since there were no signs of any buildings or fences.

He grinned at her. "I thought you might like it."

She put the picnic basket in the middle of the blanket and took a seat. William did the same. "This would be a beautiful place to have a home, don't ya think?"

"I suppose," she responded. "But even if the land was for sale, I'm sure it would be expensive — not to mention the price of building a house and adding a barn, as well as a buggy shed and a few other outbuildings."

"Good point. Guess if I was ever to buy any land, it would need to at least have a barn." He gestured to the picnic basket. "Should we pray now so we can eat?"

131

"Absolutely." Doretta closed her eyes and bowed her head. She'd finished her prayer of thanksgiving for the food William's mother had provided, when she heard the distinctive call of a male cardinal responding to its mate. She opened her eyes and spotted the vibrant red of the beautiful bird. A red crest above the cardinal's head made him look even more outstanding. It felt like God had sent the bird at this moment just for her pleasure.

Doretta's breath caught in her throat. "Look over there, William." She pointed to one of the trees in this open-wooded area. "Isn't that cardinal the most beautiful *voggel*?"

William nodded. "Jah. Although the females are pale brown with just an orange tinge, some touches of red can still be found on their wings, crest, and tail."

She smiled. "I'm glad you appreciate birds as much as I do."

"I certainly do." William nuzzled Doretta's neck with the tip of his nose. "But I appreciate you even more, my love."

Doretta parted her lips slightly for the kiss she knew was coming. She felt safe and whole when William was with her.

A knock on the back door pulled Doretta's thoughts back to the present, and she glanced around, hoping someone would answer it. But Mama was obviously still in the shower, and Karen was upstairs in her room. Doretta's father and brothers had eaten an early breakfast and left for their jobs, which meant she had no choice but to see who was at the door.

Doretta hoped she looked presentable, especially with the padded neck collar she sported. The useful device was helpful in keeping her head well supported, but the whitish material was a total dirt magnet and food catcher. Doretta found herself checking her appearance in the mirror after eating to make sure the collar didn't have any food spills or crumbs on it. Before answering the door, Doretta gave the collar a few swipes and grumbled, "It'll be wonderful when my neck muscles become strong again and I don't have to wear this ugly thing anymore."

Doretta stepped into the utility room, and when she opened the door, she was surprised to see Warren on the porch, holding a paper sack. Her heart raced at the sight of him. *He reminds me so much of William, but that single dimple in his left cheek gives him away,* she reminded herself.

"*Guder mariye,*" he said.

"Good morning." Doretta's words, spoken so quietly, sounded strained to her ears.

"It's good to see that you got the halo brace off. How are you feeling now?" Warren asked.

"I'm doing some better." *At least physically,* she mentally added, dropping her gaze to the floor.

"You've been through a lot due to your injuries. I can't imagine how it must have felt to be constrained in that rigid brace. At least you can move around a lot better now with the neck collar you're wearing."

"Jah, but it's still a nuisance." She lifted her gaze, wondering what he thought of the ugly scabs on her forehead. "Are you here for a reason? If it's to see my dad or one of my brothers, they have already left for their jobs."

He shook his head. "An order I had placed a few days ago came into the store later than I expected, and it didn't arrive until yesterday right before I had closed. I was going to drop by here on my way home from work with the items your mamm had asked me to get, but my driver had an appointment and needed to drop me off at home right away." Warren paused to catch his breath before gesturing to the paper sack. "I decided to come by here on my way to work this morning, so here are the things your mamm wanted." He had spoken all of this so quickly, Doretta had a hard time keeping up with, or understanding, what all he'd said.

Ignoring the sack he still held, she kept her gaze on Warren's chest, not his face. "If your store is open today, shouldn't you be there working right now?"

"I'm sure Margaret's at the health food store already. She works for me now, in case you hadn't heard, so I gave her a key."

"I didn't know that. Since I haven't gone anywhere but to and from the doctor's, I don't see or hear much of anything except for what takes place inside this home."

"Oh, well, I just thought . . ." He extended the sack to her. "Guess I could have waited until the nutrition store closed today to drop this off, but since Margaret is no doubt covering for me, I decided to come over now because I wanted you to have them."

"I'm sure that whatever my mother ordered for herself could have waited until later this afternoon."

"They're not for her. The supplements are for you." Warren reached under his hat and scratched his head. "Also, your mamm seemed to appreciate me saving her an extra trip into town to get these supplements, which we are hoping might be helpful for you."

Doretta slipped two fingers under her neck collar and rubbed an itchy spot. "I'm confused. I did not ask her to pick up or order anything for me. In fact, I didn't even know she was going to your store." She looked at him directly and noticed his lips press together in a slight grimace.

"Well, umm . . . your mamm mentioned that you've been quite depressed, and she asked if there were any supplements that might help with that."

Doretta huffed and clenched her hands. *I can't believe Mama would tell Warren — or anyone else — about my depression. This is worse than having people see my scabs.*

Doretta forced herself to look at Warren while she spoke. "You made a mistake coming here this morning. I don't need any supplements, so you can take them right back to your store." She handed him the sack and opened the back door.

"Please let your mother know that I did come by with the supplements. I don't want her to think I went back on my word." Warren shuffled back a few steps and, with a bewildered expression, turned and hurried into the yard.

"Guess I blew that one," Warren muttered as he approached his driver's vehicle. *I should have never told Doretta that her mother said she needed something for depression.* He climbed in and placed the paper bag on the seat beside him. *Doretta will never know now if any of the items I brought with me today would help. I should have been more discreet or tried to explain things better.*

Warren sighed. Today was not starting out on a good note. Soon after he'd gotten up this morning, Mom had asked if she might go to the nutrition center with him, saying that when she'd been there yesterday, she had taken note of several things that could be done to improve the look of certain things in the store. The last thing Warren wanted was for his mother to start rearranging things. He'd told her that he appreciated the offer but was fine with the way things were in the store for now. Before Mom had a chance to say anything more on the subject, Warren had excused himself to go help Dad in the barn.

While feeding the horses, Warren had brought up the topic of Mom to his father. He'd hoped Dad would volunteer to have a little talk with her about giving Warren some space and not hovering so much. Instead, Dad had merely shrugged and said, "Don't let it bother you so much, Son. Your mamm misses William, just as we both do, and she's dealing with it in the only way she knows."

"You mean by smothering me and worrying about every little thing I do?" Warren had responded with irritation. "If Mom had her way, she'd never let me out of her sight."

Dad had then given Warren's back a few pats. "It'll get better, Son. Just give her some time."

Warren clenched his fists into the palms of his hands. He wondered now why he'd even bothered to speak to his father about Mom. *If Dad had been willing to have a talk with her, maybe she wouldn't need so much time. She ought to go out more and do some things with one of her friends or find some projects to do around the house that would keep her hands and mind too busy to worry about me.*

Warren's middle-aged driver, Sam, looked over at him briefly. "You okay, Warren? The way you're biting your lip and clenching your fists makes me think that you might be upset about something."

"Yeah," Warren admitted. "Things haven't gone well so far this morning, and there's no telling how the rest of the day will go either."

"Some days are like that, all right." Sam kept his gaze straight ahead. "Guess all we can do is try to get through the rough days and hope for better tomorrows."

"Uh-huh."

Warren felt a bit better when Sam pulled his vehicle into the store's parking lot and he saw two cars in the parking lot, plus a horse and buggy at the hitching rail, which meant there were customers in the store. That in itself made him hopeful that the rest of the day might go better.

After telling Sam goodbye and reminding him what time he would need a ride home from the store, Warren picked up the paper sack and went inside. He didn't see any customers at the front of the store, but he did hear some people talking down one of the aisles, so he would talk with those customers soon to see if there was anything he could help them with.

"I see you must have brought your *middaagesse* with you today." Margaret pointed to the sack Warren held as he approached the checkout counter where she sat. "I'm surprised you didn't put it in a small cooler so everything would stay fresh until time to eat it."

"No, this isn't my lunch. There are some supplements inside that I'll be putting back on the shelf."

She tipped her head and looked at him

with lips slightly parted. "How come?"

He held up the sack. "Amanda Schwartz had asked me to get them, so I went by their house to deliver the items on the way here. But Doretta said she didn't want them."

"I'm confused. Did Amanda change her mind, or weren't the supplements what she had actually wanted?"

"I never spoke to her. The supplements were for Doretta, and she's the one who did not want them." Warren hurried down the herbal aisle before Margaret could ask any more questions. It wouldn't be right to tell her about Doretta's reaction or discuss the kind of supplements he'd taken to her. Apparently, Doretta didn't want help for her depression — at least not by trying anything Warren had brought from his health food store. He wondered, though, what Amanda would say when Doretta told her that he'd come by and she'd sent him on his way with the items he'd brought.

Doretta sat at the kitchen table, rubbing the bridge of her nose. *How could Mama do this to me? It's embarrassing to think that she would go to the nutrition center and tell Warren that I needed something for my depression. Doesn't she care about my feelings at all?*

Her stomach tightened. *I can only imagine what Warren must think of me. He probably thinks it's strange that he's busy running his business while I sit home every day feeling sorry for myself. And I'm sure Warren doesn't understand why I do not want to take any of those supplements for my depression.*

Doretta didn't fully understand it herself. She'd always preferred using natural remedies instead of prescription drugs whenever possible. *Guess I'm mostly upset about Mama telling Warren I needed something for my depression. Now that he knows, the word will probably get out, and then wherever I go, people will look at me with curiosity and perhaps disapproval instead of understanding that I can't help how I feel.*

It also irked Doretta to know that William's twin brother appeared to be moving on with his life. Didn't Warren miss William as much as she did? He had a girlfriend too, and eventually they'd probably make plans to get married. Doretta's hope for marriage had been snatched away, as easily as a hawk pouncing on some poor unsuspecting little bird.

She drew in a deep breath. *I sure would like to know where William was taking me the night of his death. He'd said it was a surprise, but I never found out where it was.* Doretta rapped her knuckles on the tabletop. *I wonder if Warren knows. If I hadn't been so angry when he stopped by, I could have asked him about it. Why do I always think of things after the fact?* She frowned deeply. *I tend to let my anger out because of frustration before thinking things through.*

Doretta's contemplations came to a halt when her mother entered the room. "That warm shower sure felt good," she said. "Were you able to come up with anything for breakfast while I was gone?"

"No. Warren stopped by, and I lost my appetite for food after that."

Mama's mouth opened, but nothing came out.

"He came here with a sack full of supplements for me, which he said you had ordered to help with my depression." Doretta crossed her arms in front of her chest and looked straight into her mother's eyes. "How could you have gone behind my back and done that, Mama?"

She lowered her gaze a few seconds and lifted her chin. "I-I'm sorry. I only wanted to help. I've been worried about you, and in desperation to help, I reached out to Warren, hoping he might have some suggestions." Mama glanced around the room. "Where are the supplements? I assume he must have

142

left them for you?"

Doretta shook her head. "I refused to take the sack, and he headed on out."

Mama pressed a hand against her chest. "Oh, Daughter, I'm sorry to hear that. I really wish you would at least have been willing to give those supplements a try."

"I don't need them. I'll be fine. What I really need is for people to leave me alone and let me deal with the grief I feel in my own way."

Her mother stepped forward and gave Doretta a hug. "We should never be too proud to accept help from others — especially one's own *familye.*"

"Warren is not my family."

"He would have been your brother-in-law if . . ."

"I don't need that reminder. He's not part of my family, and he never will be!" Doretta got up from the table and pushed in her chair. "I have no desire for breakfast, so if you don't mind, I'm going back to bed." Before her mother could respond, Doretta fled the room.

"What's the matter, Mama? Why are you sitting at the table all alone with your eyes closed?"

Amanda's eyes snapped open, and she

143

turned to face her youngest daughter. "I was praying, Karen."

The young girl's blue eyes darkened, and then she blinked rapidly. "Oops . . . sorry. Didn't mean to interrupt. Figured you'd be gettin' breakfast made by now."

"I fixed your daed and *brieder* something to eat before they left for work," Amanda explained. "Then I went to take a shower, figuring Doretta might start breakfast for the three of us, but that didn't happen."

"How come? I know my sister's up, 'cause I heard her walkin' around awhile ago."

"Jah, Doretta's up, and she was down here while I was in the shower."

Karen tipped her auburn head. "Did she eat already?"

"No, when I came into the kitchen, she said she wasn't hungry and went back to her room." Amanda saw no reason to tell Karen about the delivery Warren had tried to make or Doretta's refusal to accept any help for her depression. This was not a topic the child would understand, and the last thing she wanted was for her impressionable daughter to talk about Doretta's problem with anyone else.

Amanda got up from her chair and moved over to the stove. "Would you like me to fix you some pancakes this morning?"

With an eager expression, Karen bobbed her head.

"All right then. You can help me by setting the table."

"Sure, I can do that."

While Karen began her chore, Amanda got out the ingredients for buttermilk pancakes. Although she wasn't that hungry herself, she figured her appetite might increase once she tasted one of the fluffy flapjacks with real maple syrup. She wished something as simple as a plate full of mouthwatering pancakes could bring a smile to her eldest daughter's face.

There had to be something that could turn things around for Doretta, but at this point, Amanda didn't know what. *Maybe my daughter will hear something from Eleanor again soon, and whatever she says might bring Doretta around. She can't go on like this indefinitely. If Doretta doesn't find some joy in life, she might drown in her sea of depression. I need to pray harder that the right answer will come.*

Chapter 11

Margaret stood in front of the bathroom mirror, pinching her cheeks to give them some color. She'd worked with a problem horse named Harley on Friday afternoon and again after she'd gotten home from work yesterday, clear up until supper. Once they'd eaten and the dishes had been done, Margaret had returned to the barn to spend more time with Harley. She hoped to see if she could get to the root of the situation of him not wanting to be touched and trying to bite.

The English couple who owned this horse had rescued him from an abusive situation, and when they'd brought Harley over for Margaret to work with him, they had explained that he didn't like being handled. That included brushing and any kind of touching. When they rode the horse, however, he acted fine and didn't seem to mind either of them being on his back. The horse had been seen by a local veterinarian and given a clean bill of health, other than that he was skittish and had to be tranquilized in order to do a full examination.

The new owner had also stated that whenever he or his wife tried to brush Harley, the horse would kick the stall door and try to bite them. Margaret was touched when the young woman had looked at her tearfully and said, "My husband and I care a lot about this horse, and we want to be able to go into the stall and groom Harley without him getting mad."

The first thing Margaret had done was to try coaxing Harley instead of going straight up to him, as the husband said they had done. She'd offered him treats and slowly gotten closer as he took them. Margaret never went straight for the animal's face. She aimed for scratching the horse's neck or withers. Margaret had also been doing some exercises to build Harley's trust, such as lunging him on a lunge line. And before switching sides or finishing up each time, she would make him come to her. She did this by lightly pulling on the line to bring the horse closer, then making him follow her. Margaret knew that once she had this down pat, she could try free lunging without using a lunge line.

Margaret felt confident from past experience with other horses that Harley would eventually come to her willingly, allowing her to touch him with no biting on his part. Even though there were moments of frustration, she wouldn't give up until he did what she expected. Margaret had worked with a few other abused horses, and when she was finally able to pet them, she'd given treats as a reward.

By the time Margaret had gone to bed last night, it had been close to midnight, and now she paid the price for her lack of sleep, because she'd barely been able to get out of bed. In addition to her pale cheeks, the dark circles that had formed beneath her eyes made Margaret think she resembled a raccoon.

It'll be embarrassing to go to church looking like this, she thought, *but what choice do I have? Short of death itself, no one in this family stays home from church.* Even on their off-Sundays, Margaret's father, a deacon in their church, made sure that each of his children who still lived at home visited some other church district in the area when they had a Sunday off from their own district.

Sure wish I was allowed to wear a bit of makeup. She pinched her cheeks another time. *At least then I could cover up the dark*

148

circles and make it look like there was some color on my face.

"Breakfast is on the table! It's time to eat," her sister Alisa called through the bathroom door. "Are you coming, Margaret?"

"Jah, I'll be right there." She turned off the battery-operated light above the sink and opened the door. *Guess I'll just have to attend church this morning looking sleep deprived, and if people stare, I'll try to ignore it.*

"You're still in your night clothes," Mama said with a frown when Doretta entered the kitchen wearing her nightgown and robe. "You'll have to eat breakfast quickly if you're going to have time to change into your church clothes."

"I woke up with another koppweh." Doretta massaged her forehead. "I'll just have a piece of toast and some tea before I go back to bed."

Mama looked at Doretta through half-closed eyelids, and Doretta squirmed under her mother's scrutiny.

"I really do have a headache." She continued to rub her forehead. "The ride to church and then sitting for three hours on a hard bench would only make the pain in my head feel worse."

"She's right, Amanda," Doretta's dad spoke up from across the room, where he stood with a cup of coffee. "What our daughter should do right now is take an aspirin and return to her room."

"But Doretta hasn't been in church for a good many months, and she's missing out on hearing God's Word as well as the fellowship of being with other believers."

"I doubt that she'd get much out of it if her head continued to pound," he countered. "Besides, today we are visiting a neighboring church district, and Doretta might not feel as comfortable worshipping with people she doesn't know as she would with those in our own district. Next Sunday might work out better for her."

"The message we hear today could be even better than next week's."

Dad took a few steps closer to Mama. "Jah, but then again . . ."

"Whatever," she mumbled, moving over to the stove. "I'm always in the wrong whenever we have a discussion."

Doretta's fingers curled into the palms of her hands. She felt like a young child being talked about by her parents instead of a twenty-five-year-old woman who had the right to make her own decisions. She was glad, however, that Dad had taken her side

150

on this. Even so, it was hurtful to hear her parents argue — especially when she was the topic of disagreement. Although tempted to give in to her mother's wishes and force herself to go to church, if she relented, she would be miserable — especially with her head now pounding even more.

Doretta wished she could explain to her parents that nothing she heard in a sermon — today or next week — would make her feel better spiritually. The accident that had stolen William had dampened her faith, so hearing any of the ministers preach and quote verses from the Bible would only be a reminder that God didn't care about her or how much she hurt.

"Go ahead back to your room." Mama's tone had softened. "As soon as I get the eggs scrambled for the others, I'll bring you some toast and tea."

"Danki, Mama." As Doretta left the room, she felt a sense of relief from the tension she'd felt in her head, neck, and shoulders. It was nice not having to run a coarse brush through her long hair this morning too. That would have only agitated her throbbing head. And best of all, Doretta didn't have to get changed out of her soft, comfy nightgown.

Doretta's headache lessened a bit as she climbed back into bed. Her soft mattress and the warmth of her covers provided welcome comfort. She was ever so thankful that she wouldn't have to attend church today, where she'd have had to deal with people's curious or sympathetic stares. During the meal after the service, it would be even worse, because Doretta would have been expected to carry on a conversation with the women who sat at her table and no doubt be the subject of many questions. At least for today, she could stay here and try to relax.

Next Sunday would be another matter, however. Like it or not, to keep the peace in this household, Doretta might have to force herself to attend church with her family.

Betty Lengacher looked up from the Amish hymnal she held, and her gaze came to rest on her son, sitting beside one of his childhood friends, Wyatt Steury. On the other side of Warren sat a young, dark-haired man she didn't recognize. *If William were still alive, he'd be right there in that spot, sitting beside his brother.*

Thinking about it and watching Warren sing with gusto as though everything was normal made the nape of Betty's neck stiffen. Things were far from normal, and they never would be the same, at least not for her. For a child to die before their parent just wasn't right. *Why couldn't God have taken me instead?* she silently lamented. *My son had his whole life ahead of him, with a sweet young woman on the brink of becoming his wife.* She squeezed her eyes shut. *It's not fair, Lord, and I don't think my broken heart will ever fully mend. Of course, I'll keep pressing forward, even if I have to pretend that I'm doing all right.*

Betty opened her eyes and continued to watch Warren. From the time they were little, her twin boys had always sat together during church. They'd enjoyed doing a lot of things with each other over the years — fishing, playing games, and joining lots of team sports, such as baseball and volleyball. Although at times her sons had disagreed on things, they'd always worked it out, and neither was left with hurt feelings. There had to be a huge void in Warren's life now that William was gone, but since the day of his brother's funeral, Warren had given no outward display of his grief — at least not in front of her.

Betty clasped her hands tightly together. *Perhaps he's holding back and doesn't want to show the way he truly feels because he's afraid it will upset me. Warren probably thinks if he lets his emotions show or talks about how much he misses William, I will fall apart.* As far as Betty knew, Warren had not talked with his dad about his feelings concerning his brother's death either. If he had, Raymond hadn't said anything to her.

Should she press Raymond on the topic, or would that compound the problem? It would ease Betty's mind if she and her husband could speak about the way Warren seemed to be handling William's death. Venting was one of many ways for healing to occur. It helped to let out bottled-up anger and sorrow that weighed heavy on the heart.

Betty closed her eyes. *Father, please continue to heal my broken family through this tragedy. Only by Your strength can we keep moving forward and see Your healing touch working in all of our lives.*

She opened her eyes and shifted on the bench. Eva Steury, who sat beside her, reached over and placed her hand on top of Betty's. "Are you all right?" she whispered.

Betty's only response was a quick nod. Tears had gathered in her eyes, and the burning thickness in her throat kept her from saying or even mouthing a single word. She and Eva had been friends since they were teenagers. When Eva married Vernon, she'd become Amanda's sister-in-law, because Amanda's husband, Elmer, was Vernon's brother. Betty had been concerned back then that her best friend might become closer to Amanda than she was to her, given that their husbands were siblings. But she'd had nothing to worry about, and her friendship with Eva had remained strong over the years.

The singing ended, and Betty put the copy of the *Ausbund* hymnal aside. It was time to put her focus on the message one of the visiting ministers would preach soon.

"You were awfully quiet on the way home from church," Margaret's mother commented when Margaret came into the house after helping her father put his horse away. Not that he'd needed her help. She'd offered her assistance so she could be around the horses for a while. Unlike people, the horses didn't try to pry into a person's business. And Dad never quizzed when it came to Margaret's private life. Not that he didn't care, because she felt sure that he did. She could only figure that maybe he felt a little uncomfortable discussing such topics with his daughter.

"Aren't you going to respond to my statement?" Mom asked and repeated what she'd just said.

"I wasn't quiet for any particular reason," Margaret replied. "Just doing some thinking was all."

"Bet I can guess who you were thinking about." Her fifteen-year-old sister, Ruby, spoke up from the card table where she sat in the living room, working on a five-hundred-piece puzzle. "Could it be your boyfriend you had on your mind? Huh? Was it, Sister?"

It was hard not to recoil at her sister's question. If Margaret responded harshly, Mom would come down on her. Ruby liked to tease and was acting childishly right now, but Margaret reminded herself that she shouldn't let her sister's teasing bring out the frustration she felt over Warren. She liked him, and he seemed to be occupying more and more of her thoughts. She paused to collect herself, taking in a couple of calming breaths before responding to Ruby's questions.

"What I was thinking about doesn't concern you." Margaret wasn't about to tell her sister or their mother that she'd been thinking about Warren on the way home. They'd want details that she didn't wish to disclose. What transpired between Margaret and her

156

boyfriend was no one's business but her own. But the fact that Warren had gone back on his promise to go horseback riding with her on their day off tomorrow had gotten under her skin.

Margaret took off her coat and hung it on a wall peg. *I can't help feeling hurt because he broke his promise. I was looking forward to spending quality time with him while we rode our horses.* Margaret had spoken to Warren briefly after the noon meal today, and he'd informed her that there was something else he needed to do and wasn't sure how long he would be. So there would be no time for horseback riding tomorrow.

I wonder if Warren's making excuses not to spend time with me, she fretted. *Maybe he made plans to do something with one of his buddies. Or perhaps he wants to stop by the Schwartzes' place to see Doretta again.* She shook her head slowly. *Warren doesn't seem to care about me anymore. If he was a good boyfriend, he'd want to please me and make the time for us to be together.*

Margaret excused herself to go to her room. Since she wouldn't be going horseback riding with Warren tomorrow, she would spend the entire Monday working with Harley. Maybe by the end of the day he would allow her to touch him without getting upset. That would be Margaret's goal, and she wouldn't allow Warren's change of plans to ruin her day. Perhaps by tomorrow evening she could call Harley's owners with some good news.

CHAPTER 12

Doretta shivered against the cold wind pushing her body and feathering briskly through the wild grass growing along the side of the country road where she walked. As she trudged along toward the Amish cemetery, trying to stay warm, the soft collar around her neck not only gave her head the support it still needed, but it protected her neckline from the chill of winter. At least there was no freshly fallen snow to deal with — just a few half-melted piles here and there.

Doretta had told her mother that she was going for a walk, but Mama had no idea of her destination. Doretta felt compelled to visit William's gravesite today, and she hoped seeing his headstone might bring her some kind of closure . . . and perhaps a bit of comfort.

Her heart pounded as she entered the Amish cemetery and made her way slowly among the headstones. A few mounds of slushy snow, mixed with some debris that had gathered on some of the markers, made hunting for William's resting place more difficult. Perhaps coming here had been a bad idea. But Doretta did not want to wait until spring, so she kept walking and pushing away the fragments with her boot on each of the markers she came to. None of the headstones were easy to read, as she bent low, trying to make out the names of the deceased.

"I could be here looking for a while," she muttered. "There are a lot of graves in this Amish cemetery, and I'm already chilled to the bone." Although Doretta wasn't sure where William's gravestone was located, if it took her the rest of the day, she would not leave until she found it.

The wind whistled noisily through the trees outside the fenced enclosure, and Doretta inhaled the crisp winter air, hoping it would help to calm her nerves. It didn't, however. If anything, the cold air took her breath away. She stopped walking for a minute and tried to visualize what William's funeral service must have been like for his family. Doretta also wondered how she would have reacted if she would have been there among the mourners. She could only imagine the pain his beloved parents and twin brother must have felt that dreadful day. After William's funeral service, held at his parents' home, many people would have gotten into their open buggies. Following the horse-drawn buggy hearse, they all would have made their way to this cemetery for William's burial. Doretta shivered at the thought. Her grief would have increased if she had been here in this graveyard, witnessing her beloved's casket being lowered into the ground.

Holding her arms in front of her chest, Doretta closed her eyes and imagined what the scene must have been. Somber expressions and tears on everyone's faces, including her own, as they witnessed the sad occasion. Doretta's grief resonated so harshly that she rocked back and forth unsteadily, feeling as though she might pass out.

That's how it would've gone all right, she told herself. *I would have been inconsolable and shaking so bad that my teeth would have chattered. Someone, probably Dad, would have needed to stand close to me in case I caved in and fell on the cold ground. In some ways, maybe it's a good thing I wasn't here to witness it. In addition to my own grief, I would have felt the agony William's family also dealt with that day. I'm sure his mother must have* sobbed uncontrollably, and no doubt William's father and twin brother would have shed a good many tears.

A horse's whinny brought Doretta's thoughts to a halt, and she opened her eyes, shutting out the painful scene she had envisioned. Looking to her left, Doretta saw a horse and buggy being secured outside the fence, and then William's brother stepped down from his rig. Her mouth went dry. *Oh, why does Warren have to look so much like his twin?*

After Warren entered the cemetery, he headed her way. Doretta held her breath as he drew closer. Seeing him just now made this visit to William's gravesite more unbearable than if she were alone. But Warren had come here for a reason, and there was nothing she could do about it.

"Doretta, what are you doing out here on such a cold, windy day?" Warren's thick brows drew together. "And where's your horse and buggy?"

"I came on foot to visit William's grave." Doretta's chin trembled as her fingers clenched inside her knitted gloves. "But I wasn't sure where to look and haven't been able to locate the place where he was buried."

"Here, let me show you." Warren reached

out his hand, and she clasped it, thankful for the assistance. With the way her legs were wobbling, Doretta feared she might stumble and fall if she tried walking unassisted.

"My brother's body was buried right here," Warren said when they reached a simple granite headstone with William's name and the dates of his birth and death inscribed on it.

Doretta's vision clouded as her eyes filled with a set of fresh tears. Seeing the exact spot where her beloved's body had been placed made it seem so final. Rocking back and forth with her arms crossed against her chest, Doretta moaned. "I — I can't believe he's dead. It's not fair. I — I wish God would have taken me instead of William."

Warren's heart went out to Doretta. He wanted desperately to hold her in his arms and offer comfort. But Warren hesitated because he thought she might take it the wrong way. On the other hand, a hug might do them both some good, because the truth was, being here in the cemetery, in front of his brother's grave, had brought back all the pain of that day when William was buried. This was the first time since then that Warren had visited the cemetery. He'd stayed away because he knew it would be painful. But today, for some strange reason, Warren had felt compelled to come here. He wondered if maybe he'd been led by God to offer comfort to Doretta, despite the fact that he'd had no idea she would be here.

When Doretta began to sob, Warren threw caution to the wind and pulled her into his arms. She didn't resist and clung to him like a fearful child needing comfort in the middle of a dreadful storm.

"I miss him so much," she wailed. "I feel empty inside without William."

"I do too," Warren admitted, barely able to get the words out. He paused a moment to clear his head and form the next sentence. "I don't express my feelings much to anyone, but if I didn't stay busy most of the time, it would be even harder for me to get through each day."

Doretta sniffed deeply as she pulled slowly away from his embrace. The unoccupied space between them left Warren feeling empty. Although Margaret had offered her condolences to him the day of William's funeral, he'd never felt that she truly understood his loss and the pain he'd experienced the way Doretta did now. *How could Margaret understand?* Warren asked himself.

She never had any real connection with my brother, the way Doretta did. The grieving woman William had planned to marry comprehends the pain I feel over losing my twin brother, and I understand her deep sorrow too.

Doretta shivered as she continued to stare at William's headstone. "Your brother was a Christian who loved the Lord." She looked up at Warren. "Do you think he's in heaven right now?"

Warren nodded. "Jah, I do believe that, although there are some in our church who say that we only have the hope of going to heaven." He placed his hand over his heart. "I am convinced, however, that true believers, who have accepted Christ as their Savior and confessed their sins, have the assurance that their soul will go to heaven when they depart this earth."

Doretta's lips parted slightly as she looked upward. "That's what I believe too, and it gives me some measure of comfort knowing William is in a better place."

"That's right," he agreed. "The Bible tells us in Second Corinthians 5:8 that to be absent from the body is to be present with the Lord. Also in Luke 23:43, after one of the thieves being crucified with Jesus acknowledged who Jesus was and asked God's

Son to remember him when He came into His kingdom, Jesus told the dying man: 'Today shalt thou be with me in paradise.' "

Doretta's eyes widened. "You certainly know your scriptures. I've heard those verses before but didn't know where they were found."

"I don't know as much as some people do about the Bible, but I do try to read several verses every day."

Doretta looked down at the ground. Warren wondered if she read the Bible on a regular basis or only listened to those verses included in the sermons being preached during their biweekly church services.

A few more moments passed, and then Doretta said she felt cold and should start walking home.

"Please don't do that. It's too cold," he was quick to say. "I'd be happy to give you a ride in my carriage. Your parents' house is on the way to my folks' place, so it won't be an inconvenience."

Doretta stood quietly for several minutes, rubbing her arms through the sleeves of her woolen jacket, and finally she nodded. "Danki, I appreciate your offer."

She appeared to be a bit wobbly, so Warren steadied her as they left the cemetery and walked to his horse and buggy. He was going to help her in, but she took a seat on the passenger side before he had the chance to offer his assistance.

"I'll hold the reins while you free your horse from the hitching rack," Doretta said.

"Thanks." Warren skirted around to untie his horse. When he stepped up into the buggy, he took Dutch's reins from Doretta. Then Warren handed her a small woolen blanket to cover the lower part of her body. When they were both settled, he guided Dutch out onto the road and kept the horse going at a slow, even pace. There was no point in traveling too fast — especially if Dutch saw something he didn't like and decided to act up, the way he sometimes did.

"I'm glad we both decided to visit William's grave today." Warren glanced over at Doretta. "It was helpful for me to share my feelings about my bruder and discuss the scriptures that make me feel confident that William's in heaven with Jesus right now. I hope it was helpful for you as well."

She stared straight ahead. "Can we not talk about this anymore? It makes me sad to think about William's death, even if he is in heaven." Her voice rose to a higher pitch. "The fact is, your twin brother is never coming back to us, and I will never be his fraa." Her tone lowered again, and Warren barely heard Doretta say, "I'll remain an unmarried woman for the rest of my life."

He thought better of commenting on her last statement. If Doretta decided to close herself off to the idea of falling in love and getting married when the time was right, there was nothing he could do about it. But he hoped for Doretta's sake that, once her grief subsided, she would end up getting married and raising a family. Warren felt sure that William would have wanted that for Doretta. He would not have expected her to spend the rest of her life alone, grieving for him.

Warren heard a whinny, along with the sound of some fast-moving *clip-clops,* and turned his head. An Amish woman wearing men's trousers under her dress galloped down the road on the opposite side. He blinked rapidly. *Is that Margaret riding someone else's horse?*

Harley whinnied as a horse and buggy approached from the other side of the road. When Margaret slowed her neighbor's horse and lifted a hand to wave, her eyes widened and she had to do a double-take. She recognized Warren and his horse right away, but was that Doretta Schwartz on the seat beside him?

Warren must have seen Margaret at the same time because he waved and hollered something she couldn't understand.

What's he doing with Doretta? Margaret wondered as she urged the horse along. *Did he make plans to see Doretta today? Is that why he said he couldn't go horseback riding with me when I asked?*

Margaret clutched the horse's reins so tightly that her fingers on both hands ached. *I wonder where they've been and where they are heading now.* She remembered the excuses that Warren had offered to explain why he couldn't go riding with her today, and none of them included a trip in his open buggy with Doretta. Margaret's heart stung because it wasn't easy to see Warren with Doretta. She should be the woman sitting with him right now.

She was tempted to turn Harley around and follow them, but what excuse could she give? Margaret was sure Warren wouldn't appreciate it, and she couldn't really blame him. The last thing she wanted was to let him know that she felt envious seeing him with Doretta. Warren had been kind of distant lately, and he didn't need a jealous girlfriend questioning his every move. It was hard not to wonder, though, if she may have said or done something to offend Warren. It was obvious that he had chosen who he wanted to spend time with today. Margaret couldn't help her disappointment over seeing the two of them together. She urged Harley onward as she tried to sort out the matter.

I do need to know what Doretta and Warren were doing together, Margaret told herself as Harley trotted down the road. *If there's something going on between those two, I think I have the right to know. When I see Warren at work tomorrow, I'm going to ask.* Margaret pressed her lips tightly together. *I'll just need to be careful how I approach the subject and not let him know how it made me feel when I saw them together.*

CHAPTER 13

Doretta woke up the following morning in a drenching sweat. She'd had a stressful dream about William, and it had seemed so real. She pushed the covers back, sat up, and let her legs dangle over the edge of the bed. Then she closed her eyes and let the scene play over in her mind.

In the dream, Doretta had been riding in William's open buggy, laughing and talking about their future as a married couple. The dream had seemed so real that even now Doretta could almost feel the warmth of William's hand as he'd clasped hers. She'd heard his deep voice telling her that he had a surprise for her. She'd felt excited and eager to know, until a heavy fog enveloped them. The next thing Doretta knew, she stood in the cemetery staring at William's grave, when he suddenly appeared. *But it couldn't be,* Doretta told herself as she opened her eyes. *William was there beside me, looking ever so sad.*

Doretta gave a slow shake of her head. *It wasn't William because his body is in the grave and his soul went to heaven.* She wiped the perspiration from her forehead and got off the bed. *It was Warren standing beside me in the dream, just like he showed up at the cemetery yesterday.*

Doretta moved over to the window and lifted the shade. She'd hoped to find comfort and some kind of closure by going there; however, seeing Warren, who reminded her so much of William, had made it difficult, even though it also had been comforting.

Doretta's gaze came to rest on the little satchel Eleanor had sent her previously, now lying on her dresser. She'd forgotten about taking another piece of paper from it to see what had been written.

She reached for the satchel, opened it, and pulled out a piece of paper. It read: *"Write a poem about happiness."*

A poem? That's lecherich, she thought. *I'm no poet, and I am not about to try writing a poem now. What in the world was Eleanor thinking? Does she really believe that would make me happy?* Doretta tossed the paper aside.

Doretta reached into the satchel again and pulled out another piece of paper. This one read: *"Drink a cup of your favorite herbal tea."* She threw that one in the garbage can by her desk. *If drinking a cup of tea would take away my depression, it would be gone already because I've had plenty of tea, and it's done nothing for me except warm my insides.*

She stared at the satchel, wondering if she should take out any more papers, or would it be better to throw the whole thing out? Doretta figured her friend meant well, but she was equally sure that nothing Eleanor had suggested would do anything to lift the depression she felt.

Doretta picked up the satchel and carried it over to the garbage can. She was on the verge of throwing it in when a knock sounded on her bedroom door. She dropped the satchel on her desk chair and called, "Come in."

Mama stepped inside and walked over to Doretta. "You must have been awfully tired, because you slept later than usual this morning." She gestured to the battery-operated clock on the nightstand by Doretta's bed.

"Jah. Guess I should have set my alarm clock so I could be up in time to help you with breakfast."

"It's all right. It's good for a person to get a little extra sleep sometimes."

Doretta yawned. "I suppose."

"The others have already had their breakfast and are out the door — Karen and Jeremy off to school, and your daed and the older boys heading to their jobs."

"Sorry I wasn't there to help you feed everyone."

Mama shook her head. "It's not a problem. I ate with them, but if you'd like something special, I'd be happy to make that too."

"Please don't bother. I'm not very hungry, so I'll fix myself some tea and a piece of toast."

Mama's forehead wrinkled. "That's not much of a meal to break your overnight fast."

"It'll be enough for me."

Mama opened her mouth as if she might argue the point, but instead she shrugged her shoulders and said, "I'll see you later then. I'm heading down to the cellar to get some wash started." Her mother left the room before Doretta could comment.

She heaved a sigh. *On one hand, Mama seemed fine with me having slept in, but when I said I'd just have tea and toast for breakfast, she appeared to be a bit frustrated with me.*

Well, maybe not frustrated, Doretta corrected herself. *She's overly concerned. Even so, I wish she wouldn't push so hard all the time. I'm a grown woman and need to make my own decisions.*

Her gaze came to rest on the satchel lying on her chair. She didn't want to read more of those silly papers, but on the other hand, Eleanor had cared enough to send them to Doretta, so she would feel guilty if she threw them away without even bothering to see what the rest of them said. She placed the satchel in the bottom desk drawer and closed it. Maybe someday, if she felt like it, she would open the satchel again and read a few more messages.

Doretta moved toward her closet and took out a clean dress. *And besides that, I've made another decision this morning, and I plan to carry through with my plan.*

When Margaret entered the health food store, she found Warren behind the counter, waiting on a middle-aged English woman. Margaret figured he'd either opened the store a few minutes early or she had arrived a bit late.

She grimaced and hurried to the back room to hang up her outer garments and exchange her boots for the pair of shoes she'd brought along in her canvas tote bag. "Oh great, I'm almost half an hour late," Margaret muttered when she noticed the battery-operated clock on Warren's desk. If Warren should mention this or say it was a problem, Margaret would offer to work an extra thirty minutes at the end of the day. Although the store would be closed for customers by then, she could always do some cleaning or organizing on the shelves. Either way, Margaret felt sure that Warren would show some understanding when he heard her excuse for being late this morning.

Warren finished up with his customer as Margaret made her way up to the front counter. "Sorry for being late," she was quick to say. "One of the horses I've been working with gave me a rough time this morning, so I took a little more time with him than I'd planned. And it didn't help when my driver had to make a stop to put gas in her van." She moved closer and put both hands on the counter. "You're not mad, I hope."

"I understand about the driver needing to get gas, but if you hadn't been messing with a horse that isn't even yours, you'd have been on your way here sooner and probably wouldn't have been late." Warren's toes curled inside of his boots. They'd had a discussion similar to this one day last week, and Margaret had promised not to work with anyone's horse in the mornings on workdays because it might cause her to be late.

"I'm not mad, but I am disappointed that you didn't keep true to your word about not working with any horse before coming here to work." Warren spoke quietly so she wouldn't know how irritated he felt right now. Did Margaret really want this job, or was her primary concern helping people's difficult horses?

"I'd be happy to stay an extra thirty minutes past closing time," Margaret offered. "I can do some cleaning or —"

He shook his head. "There's no need for that. Just please try to be on time tomorrow, because if things get real busy during the morning hours, I'll need the extra help."

"I promise to do my best from now on." Margaret fussed with her head covering ties, flipping them behind her head and back to the front, finally letting them rest against her chest. "Umm . . . before I start working today, there's something I'd like to ask you."

He tipped his head. "Oh, what's that?"

"Remember when I waved at you yesterday, while I was out riding and passed your horse and buggy?"

"Jah. With the way you were galloping that gaul, I assumed you must have been in a hurry."

"Not really. I just wanted to see how well the horse would trot, and he didn't disappoint."

"It wasn't your gaul, though, right?"

"No, it was Harley. He's the one I've been working with lately."

"I see."

Margaret looked right at Warren, then she shifted her gaze to the right and back again. "I saw someone else in the carriage with you. Was that Doretta Schwartz?"

"Jah. We met at the *graabblatz,* and since she had gone there on foot, I offered to give her a ride home."

Margaret's lips pressed together in what appeared to be a slight grimace. "Did you go to the cemetery to visit your brother's grave?"

Warren bobbed his head. "That's why Doretta was there too. It was the first she'd seen his gravesite."

"So you just met there by accident? It wasn't planned at all?"

"No, I didn't have any idea she would be there." Warren's facial muscles tightened. He felt as though he were being cross-examined — like Margaret didn't trust him. Surely she didn't believe that he had made plans to meet Doretta at the cemetery. Warren wondered if his girlfriend might feel some jealousy about having seen him with Doretta.

He was about to say something more to Margaret when another customer entered the store. At least he'd thought it was a customer, until the young Amish man walked up to Margaret and said, "I'm having a problem with my gaul, and I'm hoping you can help me with it."

She blinked a couple of times. "What's your horse's situation?"

"From what I can tell, he's foundered, and I'm not sure what to do."

Margaret's brows furrowed. "Well, don't let him lie down. Keep the horse walking, and don't give him any water to drink for twenty-four hours. Also, no food for twelve hours."

"I knew about not letting him lie down, and my younger brother is seeing to that right now while I'm here," the fellow responded.

"Have you called your veterinarian?" Warren asked. "That would have been the first thing I would have done rather than coming all the way here to talk to Margaret about the problem. She's not an animal doctor, you know."

The young man turned to face Warren. "I am aware of that fact, but she has a way with horses and knows a good many things. And for your information, I did call my vet, but he's responding to another call on the other side of town right now. Since I knew Margaret worked here, I figured I'd stop by and see what advice she might have for me."

"Will the veterinarian be coming to your place when he finishes with his other call?" Margaret asked.

"Jah, he said he would."

"That's good. When I get off work today, I'd be happy to drop by and see how things are going."

"Danki, I'd appreciate that." The man offered Margaret a wide smile. "I'll look forward to seeing you later then."

Margaret walked him to the door, and when she returned to the counter where Warren had remained, she said, "Sorry for the interruption. Now what had you been about to say before that young man arrived?"

"Nothing. It wasn't important." Warren gestured toward the back of the store. "We have some boxes in the storage room that need to be unpacked. If you don't mind staying up here, in case any customers come in, I'll go take care of the boxes."

She shook her head. "I don't mind at all."

Warren stepped out from behind the counter, and after Margaret slipped in, he walked briskly to the back of the building, pausing briefly to inhale the spicy aroma of cinnamon tea, found in the aisle where tea and spices were located. *Maybe having my girlfriend work here wasn't such a good idea. She seems to care more about tending to other people's horses than taking care of things in the store.* If Warren could find someone else to fill in, maybe Margaret would be happier if she only had to work at the nutrition center just a couple of days a week. That would certainly give her more time to do what she seemed to enjoy, because from what Warren could tell, helping him in the store was obviously not on top of Margaret's list.

Doretta sat at the kitchen table, drinking a warm cup of mint tea. It was such a gloomy, nearly sunless day, and she longed for spring, when she could spend more time outdoors in the sunshine and watch the birds build their nests. Being cooped up during the cold winter months only added to her anxiety and the gloominess she still felt.

Doretta took a bite of her raisin bread toast. Reflecting on her unexpected meeting with Warren yesterday, she thought about how he had told her that in order to deal with his sadness over losing William, he kept busy so he wouldn't have to dwell on things. Doretta wondered if she should give that a try but wasn't sure there would be enough to do around here to stay busy all the time.

She finished the rest of her tea and set the cup down. *No matter how hard or long I worked each day, it probably wouldn't be enough to keep me from thinking about William and how much I miss him.*

Her shoulders drooped as she rose from the chair and carried her dishes to the sink. *I wish I still had my teaching position. At least that would give me something to look forward to each day — a reason to get out of bed every morning.*

Doretta's thoughts came to a halt when her mother entered through the back door with a stack of mail in her hands. "This one's for you." She handed Doretta an envelope. "Looks like it might be another card or letter from your friend Eleanor." Mama smiled. "I'll let you read it while I go back downstairs and get some jars of tomatoes we canned last summer. They'll be a nice addition to the vegetable soup I'll make for our lunch."

"Don't go to any trouble on my account," Doretta said. "I'd be satisfied with just crackers and peanut butter."

Mama's brows furrowed as she shook her finger at Doretta. "You eat like a finicky bird, and if you don't start putting some of that weight you've lost back on your bones, you'll waste away."

"I eat when I'm hungry, and please don't lecture me, Mama." Doretta was tempted to suggest that her mother should spend more time worrying about the younger children in the family and stop fretting about her, but Mama would see that as being disrespectful. *And I suppose it would be,* Doretta told herself. *So I'd best keep my thoughts to myself.*

Doretta forced a smile. "I'm going to see what Eleanor's letter has to say, and then I'll help you make the soup." *May as well keep myself busy today so I won't have time to think about things,* she mentally added.

"All right then, but if there's something else you need to do . . ."

Doretta shook her head. "I want to help with the soup."

"Okay." Mama turned and left the room.

Doretta tore Eleanor's envelope open and found a card with a beautiful cardinal stamped on the front. Inside the card another rubber stamp had been used that read: "Thinking of you." A folded piece of paper had also been included, with a personal note from Eleanor. Doretta took the piece of paper to the living room, where she could read it privately in case Mama came back up from the basement before Doretta had finished.

My dearest friend, Doretta,

I think of you often and send prayers up on your behalf regularly. I hope you are feeling better by now, and I wish that I would hear something from you. The only updates I've received since your accident have come from your mamm. I really wish we could sit down together in person and have a nice visit or at least talk on the phone sometime.

If you're feeling up to that, please call me and leave a message stating when would be a good time for me to call when I can speak directly to you. If you'd rather not have a phone conversation, would you please write me a letter or even a quick note so I will know how you're doing? You are still my best friend, and I care about you so much.

I hope that you received the little satchel I made, which I filled with thirty different papers. On each one I wrote something different — all things I thought might help to cheer you up a bit. Please remember that I think of you often and have been praying for you regularly.

Love & Blessings,
Eleanor

Tears welled in Doretta's eyes as she folded the note and put it back in the envelope. She missed her friend — and it would be nice to talk — but she didn't relish the idea of sitting out in the cold phone shed to do it.

She thought about the satchel Eleanor had mentioned, which she'd read from for only the second time this morning. *Thirty whole pieces of paper,* Doretta thought with a shake of her head. *What was my friend thinking? Guess at some point I ought to open it up again and see what else she wrote on those little papers.*

I'll write Eleanor a letter instead of calling and leaving a message, she told herself. *It might be good to put my thoughts down on paper, and I can tell Eleanor how strange it was meeting Warren at the cemetery and then dreaming about it. I'll also ask how Eleanor, Vic, and little Rosetta are doing.* Doretta pinched the bridge of her nose. *I'm surprised Eleanor didn't give me an update on her family in the note she wrote.*

Doretta heard her mother moving around in the kitchen, so she set the envelope aside and went to offer her help. As soon as they had the soup made, she would sit down and get started on Eleanor's letter.

Chapter 14

Paradise

Eleanor put Rosetta down for her nap and went to the living room to read the letter she'd received from Doretta in today's mail. She'd been concerned about her dear friend, and it was good to finally hear from her.

Eleanor took a seat on the sofa and opened the envelope. It was a two-page letter, and she felt pleased. Hopefully, her friend felt better and had shared some good news.

With anticipation, she read the letter.

Dear Eleanor,

Since it's too cold to sit in the phone shed for long, I decided it was time to write you a long overdue letter.

I got the halo brace off, and it's a relief to be wearing a soft collar now, which gives my head and neck muscles some support. I can manage without it for a few hours at a time, but if I go too long without wearing it or do too much, I have to put the collar back on.

My scabs have fallen off now, and I've been putting vitamin E on the scars where the screws on the halo were attached to my forehead. Mama seems to think that eventually the scars will fade and hardly be noticeable, but I have my doubts.

Something unsettling happened yesterday. I felt the need to see where William had been buried, so I bundled up against the cold and walked to the cemetery. I'd only been there a short time and was getting frustrated because I couldn't find William's headstone, when suddenly Warren showed up. It took me by surprise, seeing him there, and for a moment, I thought it was William. Warren was kind and showed me where his brother's grave was located. Then we stood there for a while and talked about how much we miss William. It was good to grieve with someone who understood my pain, because Warren felt it too. He not only lost a brother, but because they were twins, they had a special bond. When it got too cold, Warren offered to give me a ride home, which I gratefully accepted because I was chilled to the bone.

Warren mentioned that keeping busy has

been helping him get through the loss of William. He said that when he's working, there isn't time to dwell on the grief he feels. So I've decided to try that too. I am going to start looking for things to do that will keep my hands and mind too busy to dwell on my grief.

Enough about me, though. How is Rosetta doing? I bet she has grown a lot since the last time I saw her. I hope things are still going well with you and Vic. You're lucky to be married to a man you love, and it must be wonderful to have had the opportunity to become a mother. I'll never experience either of those things — not unless I marry someone I don't love, which I can't imagine doing. The fact is no one could ever take dear William's place in my heart.

Mama's calling me for lunch now, so I'd better close. I appreciate your letters and will look forward to hearing from you again.

Love,
Doretta

P.S. I got the little satchel you sent me. I've only opened a few of the papers, but I haven't done anything that you wrote on them yet. Sorry to say, but I don't feel like yodeling, and I've never written a poem. I didn't think tea would help me feel any better either, because I've had plenty of tea and it's never made me feel happy — just warm. I will read some of the other suggestions soon, and maybe I'll find one that I feel like trying instead.

Eleanor's eyes watered as she laid her friend's letter aside. It was good to have finally heard from Doretta, but in spite of her attempt at sounding cheerful, she was obviously deeply hurt and still suffered from depression. It was sad to think that her friend thought no one could ever replace William and that she'd never love again or get married. Eleanor was disappointed that Doretta hadn't been able to yodel or write a poem. *Maybe some of the ideas I wrote on the papers in that satchel won't be helpful,* she thought, *but I do believe that if Doretta tried some of the suggestions, a good many of them might give her a sense of joy.*

Although she wasn't sure how to address Doretta's situation, Eleanor would continue to seek the Lord for guidance.

Heavenly Father, she prayed, *please give me the right words to say when I respond to this letter. I don't believe that trying to keep busy all the time is the answer to my friend's depression. And if it's meant for Doretta to get* married someday, then let it be to the right man — one of Your choosing. Please open Doretta's heart to the fact that someday it may be okay for her to fall in love again.

Grabill

Doretta paused from window washing and wiped away the perspiration that had formed on her forehead. She'd been helping her mother clean house all morning and wished she could go lie down for a while and take a nap. *But if I did that,* she told herself, *I'd end up lying on the bed, thinking too much, and trying to squelch the depression I'm still feeling when I'm not keeping busy.*

She heaved a deep sigh. *All this hard work is exhausting, and I can't be working and keeping my mind off William every single moment of my life.*

One thing Doretta had gained so far by tiring herself out was that she slept like a log through the night, and it didn't take long for her to fall asleep either. That was much better than lying there in bed thinking about William and all that she'd lost, like she had done since hearing about his untimely death.

Doretta moved on to clean a second living-room window. *If I had a job outside the home, I wonder if that would help. Sure wish I was able to teach school again. But they already have a teacher.*

Doretta's thoughts changed direction. She still hadn't had the chance to speak with Warren again to ask if he knew where William had been planning to take her the night of the accident. *Think I'll go out to the phone shed right now and see about hiring a driver to take me to Warren's health food store tomorrow. If Warren isn't too busy, I'll ask my question. If Mama wants to know where I'm going and why, I'll simply say that I want to buy some chamomile tea to help me relax and fall asleep at night. She'll probably be fine with that.*

The following morning, Doretta's driver pulled into the yard and tooted her horn. Doretta, already wearing her outer garments, had been watching out one of the freshly clean living-room windows. "Mama, Mary Beth is here," Doretta called after she'd stepped into the hall to grab an umbrella.

Mama came out of the kitchen and joined Doretta by the door. "I see you're prepared for *regge.*" She gestured to the umbrella Doretta held in one hand. "From the looks of the darkening sky, we may get some rain before the day is over."

Doretta nodded and opened the front door. "Is there anything I can pick up for you at the health food store?"

"We're getting low on vitamin C again, so you could get a few bottles of those if there's enough in stock."

"Okay. Anything else?"

"I think that's all for now." Mama enveloped Doretta in a warm hug. "It's good to see you going out and doing a few things. Over the last several months, you've spent too many hours cooped up in this house."

Doretta told her mother goodbye and stepped out onto the porch. Little did Mama know that every time Doretta left the house, it was done through sheer determination. If Doretta ran into people she knew, she struggled to engage in conversation. *So why am I going into town, where others from our community might be today?* The thought of talking to Warren again didn't bother her too much, but since Margaret worked in the store, Doretta would no doubt see her and feel obligated to speak with her too. Warren's girlfriend was a horse-loving person, and Doretta had little in common with her, which didn't leave much to talk about other than the weather. Although she didn't dislike horses, she had no desire to work with problem horses or even go horseback riding.

Another thing that made it difficult to converse with Margaret was that she'd always come across as being a bit self-centered, and she rarely spoke of anything that didn't involve herself somehow. Although it was none of Doretta's business, she couldn't help wondering why Warren had chosen Margaret as his girlfriend.

Doretta climbed into her driver's van. *Maybe Margaret will be busy waiting on customers when I get there, and I'll have a chance to speak with Warren alone. Then I will get what Mama asked me to pick up and head for home.*

Warren had put the OPEN sign in the window fifteen minutes ago, but so far there was no sign of Margaret. *What will her excuse be for coming in late this time?* he wondered. *And just how tardy will she be?*

Warren was glad there were no customers in the store yet, and he hoped it would not get busy until after Margaret showed up. He tugged at his suspenders and frowned. *If she even shows up at all.* Warren had been having doubts as to why he'd hired her, because she had been late before and wasn't very dependable. He needed someone he could count on — a person who wouldn't let him down.

Warren's flip-phone, which he used for business purposes, rang, and he was quick to answer it. "Hello."

"Hi, Warren, it's Margaret. Sorry I'm late, but someone brought me another horse to work with this morning, and he's pretty worked up. If I don't get him settled down, he's likely to kick the stall door off its hinges."

Warren clamped his teeth together, frustrated and trying to formulate the best response before he spoke and said something he might later regret. "How soon do you think you'll be here?"

"I'll try to make it there by noon," she said. "If I can't, I'll call again and let you know. Hopefully, it won't be too busy at the store today. Sorry for the late notice and inconvenience for you."

"Yeah, it sure is inconvenient," Warren muttered after he'd said goodbye and clicked off the phone. He was more convinced than ever that Margaret cared more about training other people's horses than working here at the store, and that didn't sit well with him at all. As far as Warren was concerned, she may as well quit this job and do what she liked best. This whole thing with her being so undependable was bound to affect their personal relationship too. If Margaret couldn't bother to show up for work on time, how would she hold down any other job?

He thumped the side of his head. *I can't allow myself to get all worked up over this. I need to take one moment at a time and deal with whatever happens today.*

When Doretta entered the nutrition center, she was surprised to see Warren wearing a grim expression while he swept the floor on one side of the room. Nobody else seemed to be around — no customers in sight — not even his hired help. She waited quietly near the checkout counter until he set the broom aside and came over. "Good morning, Doretta. It's nice to see you here. May I help you with something?"

"Jah, I need some vitamin C." She glanced around the room, then back at Warren. "I also came to ask you a question."

"If it's about any of the supplements I have for sale here, I should have an answer for you." He leaned in toward the counter and placed both hands on top of it.

Doretta shook her head. "It's not about supplements. My question is about something else." She looked around the area one more time. "Is there anyone in the store right now?"

He shook his head. "Just you and me."

"Not even Margaret?"

"No. She's late. She called awhile ago and said she had a neighbor's horse to work with this morning."

"Oh, I see." Doretta didn't say anything, but she thought it was strange that Margaret would be late for her job because of a horse.

"So what's your question?" Warren asked.

"It's about William."

Warren tipped his head. "What about my bruder?"

"The night of our accident, William was taking me to someplace special that he said he wanted me to see. However, he never got the chance to show me where or even tell me what it was." Doretta felt an ache in her chest as she struggled to control her swirling emotions. "Do you know where William was taking me that evening?"

His lips pressed together in a slight grimace. "Jah, I do."

"Where was it?"

"It was a piece of property he'd bought. It had no house, just an old barn and some out buildings, but . . ." Warren's voice trailed off, and he rubbed the heel of his palm against his chest.

She waited patiently, hoping he would continue. When his shoulders sagged and his gaze dropped to the floor, Doretta said, "I see. I'm guessing he must have bought the property with the intent of building us a home. Maybe it was the same place where the two of us had a picnic one day. We both liked it a lot, and if it came on the market. . . . But no, that land didn't have any outbuildings at all, so it couldn't be . . ."

Doretta stopped talking, unable to finish her sentence. If she'd been able to see the place William had planned to take her, it would have been a wonderful surprise. She and William had talked about buying a place of their own someday, but they had decided that until such a time as they could afford it, they would be content to live with William's paternal grandparents since the couple had plenty of room in their large, five-bedroom home.

"What's going to happen to the property he bought?" Doretta questioned, once she'd found her voice.

Warren shrugged. "I'm not sure. I heard my folks talking about it a month or so ago, and Dad mentioned possibly having the land auctioned off. To my knowledge, though, nothing has been done with it yet."

"Since it belonged to your twin brother,

have you considered asking them if you could buy it?" she questioned.

"No, not really. I'm not on the brink of marriage, and even if I was, I don't have enough money saved up to buy the property or build a house. I think it's best if the land gets auctioned off. I'm sure Mom and Dad could use the money, and I've also heard them talking about building an addition on their home for Grandma and Grandpa to live in since they are getting up in years and shouldn't be living by themselves in that big house they currently own."

Doretta understood about caring for grandparents and also the need for funds. If the nutrition center did well, maybe it wouldn't be long before Warren had enough saved up to buy some property or get a place of his own. He would eventually need that when he decided to get married. Warren had been dating Margaret for a while now, and Doretta figured they might be getting serious enough to be talking about marriage. Did she dare ask, or would he think she was prying into his personal business? She concluded that it was best not to question Warren about his relationship with Margaret since it was really none of her business.

The bell above the front door jingled, and

Doretta saw three English women enter the store.

Warren reached up and rubbed the back of his neck. "Oh boy. Looks like things might get busy at the checkout counter soon, and I may need to answer some product questions. Would you consider helping me since Margaret isn't here yet?"

"Umm . . . what would you want me to do? I don't know enough about the items you have for sale in this store to answer any questions, so I'm not sure how much help I would be." A trickle of sweat ran from Doretta's forehead and down to her nose. Helping out at the nutrition store was not something she had planned to do when she'd come here today. Besides, Mary Beth was waiting in her vehicle to take Doretta home.

"Could you check people out while I take care of putting some things on the shelves and responding to any questions from customers? I'll pay for your time, of course."

"Well, I . . . um . . ."

"The cash register is battery-operated, and it's easy to operate. Also, everything in the store has been marked with the correct price, so all you would need to do is take people's money, make change if needed, and write down whatever you sell. There's a notebook and pen next to the register for that."

Doretta nodded slowly. "I'll do my best behind the counter, and there's no need to pay me. I'm sure Margaret will be here soon, and then she can take over." She glanced toward the door. "Oh, and I'll need to go outside and let my driver know that my plans have changed and she's free to go on her way. I'll call her or one of our other drivers later, when I'm ready to go home."

Warren gave her arm a quick but gentle pat. "Danki." He headed for the women who had entered the store and asked if he could help them find anything. In the meantime, Doretta hurried out the front door to speak with Mary Beth. She hoped that when Margaret showed up, there would be no misunderstandings. Doretta did not want Warren's girlfriend to think she might be trying to take her job away, because that was the furthest thing from Doretta's mind.

Chapter 15

Amanda glanced at the kitchen clock and frowned. Doretta had been gone over two hours. Surely it couldn't have taken that long for her to get some vitamin C at the nutrition store. If she'd gone by horse and buggy, it would make more sense, but it shouldn't have been this long for her driver to make the trip to and from town.

She tapped her chin a few times and continued to fret. *I wonder if Doretta decided to run a few more errands before or after stopping at Warren's store. Or maybe her driver had a few stops of her own to make along the way.* It was hard for Amanda not to worry about her daughter, especially after they came so close to losing her last fall. Thinking about it brought a feeling of tightness in her throat.

Doretta still grieved for William, and his parents did as well. Betty and Raymond, however, seemed to be coping better with their loss than Amanda's daughter. She wished she could do something to cheer Doretta up and help her resume a more normal life. *Maybe what my daughter needs is a job outside the home. Although it would increase Doretta's workload, at least her mind would be occupied with something other than focusing on her grief.*

Amanda left the kitchen and went to look out the living-room window. No sign of Doretta's driver yet — only a horse and buggy passing by on the road out front. *I wonder if I should check our answering machine. It's possible that if Doretta was someplace where there's a phone, she may have called and left me a message.*

Amanda slipped on a jacket and headed straight for the phone shed. She found only one message, and thankfully, it was from Doretta, saying that she was helping out at the nutrition center and didn't know what time she would be home. The message ended abruptly with no explanation as to what she would be doing at Warren's store.

Amanda's thoughts raced as she searched for answers. As far as she knew, Margaret worked for Warren at the health food store. Could the young woman be sick today or unable to work for some other reason? Or perhaps things had gotten busier than usual at the store, and Warren needed an extra pair of hands. Whatever the case, Amanda figured her daughter would explain, if she was not too exhausted by the time she came home. *I hope she remembers the vitamin C that I had asked her to get before she left this morning,* Amanda thought.

Margaret entered the nutrition store and froze. She was more than a little surprised to see Doretta standing not in front of the checkout counter as a customer but behind the counter, waiting on a woman who was buying several bottles of vitamins. *I can't believe what I'm seeing,* Margaret fumed. *Doretta, of all people, is taking my place behind the counter? How can that be when Warren recently mentioned that she was dealing with depression and staying home most of the time?*

Margaret glanced around, and when she saw no sign of Warren, she hurried to the back of the store, thinking he might be in his office. When she didn't see Warren there, she headed for the storage room and found him unloading a medium-size cardboard box filled with smaller boxes of various kinds of herbal tea. The strong odor from some of the teas caused Margaret to sneeze.

Warren looked up. "Well, I see you finally

made it. I had begun to think you might not show up at all today," he said sharply.

Margaret flinched. She didn't care for his tone or the way he looked at her with a wrinkled forehead and lowered brows. "I told you on the phone that I was going to be late and explained my reason."

"I get it, Margaret. You cared more about trying to settle down someone's horse than coming here to fulfill your duties."

Her face warmed. "So you hired Doretta to take my place? Have I lost my job now, Warren?"

He stood and faced her directly. "You still have a job if you want it, and I did not hire Doretta to work here. Soon after she came in, things got busy, so I asked if she could check people out while I took care of putting some things on the shelves and responding to any questions from customers. Thankfully, Doretta was willing to help out in your absence, which put my mind at ease and gave me a chance to do other things while she waited on customers."

Margaret's tightened muscles relaxed a bit. "Oh, I see. Well, I'm here now, so Doretta is free to go. I assume she came in to buy something?"

"Jah. And to ask me a question."

"About what?"

"It pertained to William." He moved toward the door and quickly changed the subject. "Let's go see how Doretta is doing. If she has no customers and wants to go home, you can take over for her now."

Margaret wondered why Warren chose not to explain the reason Doretta had asked him something about his brother. Maybe he thought it was none of her concern or was worried that she might repeat whatever had been said to someone else. Or perhaps Warren was just eager to get Margaret working behind the checkout counter again. *After all,* she thought, *I know a whole lot more about working here than Doretta does. So I'm sure Warren is glad to have me back for the rest of the day.*

"What if Doretta doesn't want to leave?" Margaret asked, pausing near William's office door. "Will you find something else for her to do in the store?"

"I don't know. It'll be up to Doretta if she wants to stay longer."

Margaret silently removed her jacket, hung it on the back of a chair near his desk, and headed for the front of the store. It didn't sit well with her to see Doretta behind the front counter, but she wouldn't make an issue of it — at least not openly. Inwardly, however, Margaret couldn't help feeling hurt at seeing another woman doing her job. Doretta seemed to be moving in on her territory, and Warren didn't appear to mind.

If I don't figure out what I'm really wanting from this relationship and do something about it soon, I could lose Warren, and Doretta might step in and try to win him over as his new employee, and maybe she could end up being Warren's new girlfriend. I think he's always had a thing for Doretta — even when we were children. Margaret clenched her teeth until her jaw ached. *I cannot let that happen!*

Margaret came up by the counter and forced a smile as she looked at Doretta. *Maybe Warren feels sorry for Doretta and thought he'd be helping with her depression by giving her something important to do. But it's hard not to be upset with him, and I can't help the jealousy brewing inside me.* Another thought flashed into Margaret's head. *If I say anything more about this to Warren, he might fire me and ask Doretta to fill the position permanently. Then I'd really be crushed.*

By three o'clock, several customers were still milling around the store, and two more were at the checkout counter, with Margaret waiting on them. Warren glanced at Doretta and noticed the lines of fatigue on her face. For the last hour, she'd been busy putting prices on some of the newer items that had come in with the last shipment he'd received. From the time Doretta had arrived this morning, when he'd asked for her help, she had kept busy. It would certainly be an asset to have her working here full-time, but he didn't think it would be right to ask.

Warren stepped into his office and took a seat at the desk to contemplate the situation. *Doretta was seriously injured in the accident that took my brother's life, and she's still not fully recovered. It wouldn't be fair of me to ask her to work here full-time. However, working a few days a week might actually be good for Doretta. If she's willing, maybe she could work here on Tuesdays and Thursdays, and since the store is closed Sundays and Mondays, Margaret could work Wednesdays, Fridays, and Saturdays. That would give her three days a week to work with the horses that are brought to her.* Warren bobbed his head. *I'll bring the topic up to both women as soon as the store is empty of customers.*

Keep busy; don't stop, Doretta told herself as she reorganized several bottles of supplements that were out of place. Working here today had been good for Doretta in that it had kept her mind and hands busy. Despite the positive side of it, she was tired and a little bit stressed from the curious stares from some of the customers who didn't know her. Did they think it was strange to see someone wearing a soft collar that stabilized their neck? Or could they have noticed the indented scars on her forehead? Doretta supposed it didn't matter what anyone thought of her appearance, but even so, she couldn't help feeling self-conscious.

Another thing that had bothered her was Margaret's unfriendly attitude. Whenever Doretta glanced her way, Margaret always looked in the opposite direction. And during lunch, when Warren had ordered a pizza for them, all of Margaret's conversation had been directed at Warren. Doretta understood that the two of them had been dating for a while, but why would Margaret take a dislike to her? *I don't understand — is there something about me that Margaret doesn't like, or am I just being over sensitive?*

As Doretta continued down the row of hypoallergenic cleaning products, she thought more about Warren's girlfriend. *Maybe she's worried that I'm after her job, which of course is ridiculous. Although working here would give me something meaningful to do, I would not try to take someone else's position, and I'm certain that Warren would never suggest such a thing.*

She paused to pick up a package of all-natural sponges that had fallen on the floor. *I'm sure I'm overthinking this. Margaret probably has nothing personal against me, and I don't have to worry about Warren asking me to work here on a regular basis. I'm just tired and not thinking rationally. Since there are only a few customers in the store right now, I should probably ask Warren if he would mind if I called my driver and headed back home. I'm certain that he and Margaret can manage on their own until closing time, which is only two hours from now.*

Doretta headed toward the back of the store, where she'd seen Warren go into his office a short time ago. She was almost to the door when he came out of the room heading straight for her. Doretta stepped to the right. Warren went to the left. Now they were blocking each other's way. She shifted to the left. He moved to the right. After moving back and forth awkwardly a few more times, they both stopped and stared at each other. Warren's shoulders shook as he let out a noisy belly laugh. Doretta giggled too — she couldn't help it. This was the first time she'd found something to laugh about since the accident, and it felt good. If the feeling could only last, but she knew it was fleeting. A few seconds of laughter didn't change the fact that William had died, and Doretta carried scars — both inward and outward.

"I was just coming to talk to you," Warren said after he'd quit chuckling.

"Oh, is there something else you need me to do?"

"Not at the moment, but I do need to speak with you and Margaret, if she's not busy waiting on anyone at the moment."

Doretta turned and looked toward the front of the store. "I don't see any customers at the checkout counter right now."

"Good. Let's head up there then." Warren pointed in that direction. "You go first and I'll follow. We don't need any more sidestep-dancing today."

Her cheeks flushed with heat as she nodded while holding back another giggle. "No, we sure don't."

When Doretta approached the front counter, she was surprised to see Margaret holding a cell phone. It wasn't a small flip phone like Warren had in the store. It was one of those larger, fancy-looking cell phones.

Margaret set the phone aside when Warren stepped up to the counter. "When did you get a smartphone?" he asked.

"I've had it a few weeks," she responded. "Makes it easier for people with horse problems to get in touch with me."

Warren's features tightened, and he reached up to rub the back of his neck. "I hope you're not taking calls when you're working here."

She shook her head vigorously. "No, of course not. I just got my phone out to check for text messages."

Spots of color erupted on Warren's cheeks, and he appeared to be quite flustered. "Well, kindly put the phone away. There's something I'd like to talk to you and Doretta about."

Margaret's dark brows rose a bit. "What's that?"

"It's about your work schedules here."

"You mean my schedule, right? Doretta doesn't work here on a regular basis."

Warren looked at Doretta. "How would you like a part-time position at my store?"

Doretta's mind raced at the possibility of such an unexpected thing. "Well, I . . . uh . . ."

"I was thinking you could work two days a week and Margaret could work three."

Before Doretta could form a response, Margaret's eyes widened, and one hand clamped against her hip as she looked right at Warren. "I can't believe this! You're cutting my hours?"

"Only if Doretta is interested in working here the other two days." He turned to look at Doretta. "What do you think?"

Once again, she was about to respond when Margaret cut her off. "If you want Doretta's help too, then why can't we both work here like we've done this afternoon?"

Doretta held back and waited to see how Warren would respond. Truth was the idea of working here part-time did hold some appeal. She wouldn't agree to do it, though, unless Warren's girlfriend was okay with the idea.

Warren placed both hands on the counter and leaned closer to Margaret. "You seem to be spending a lot more time lately working with horses, and you've been late to work a few times because of it. So I figured you might be happy with a couple more free days without having to worry about coming in here. Wouldn't that be better than all three of us working five days a week at the same time? We're not really busy enough to keep more than two people working."

"You're right, I suppose. I would enjoy having more time off to work with horses, and since most people who seek my help offer me a donation, the money I make at home will balance out or maybe even exceed what I'd be earning here in three days."

"Great!" Warren looked expectantly at Doretta again. "What do you think? Would you be up to working a couple days a week for me?"

Biting the inside of her cheek, Doretta's stomach tightened. Part of her wanted to shout, "Yes, yes, I'll do it." Another part said, "I appreciate the offer, but I may not be up to the challenge." She stared across the room at nothing for a few moments before finally giving a hesitant nod. "I'm willing to give it a try, but if it's too much for me, I hope you will understand."

"Of course. Can you start next Tuesday and then work Thursday again? That will leave Wednesday, Friday, and Saturday for Margaret."

Doretta thought back on how she'd left a message this morning for her mother, letting her know that she was going to be detained because she'd be helping out at the health food store. When she'd left home this morning, little had she realized how much her day would change. The type of work she'd be doing was a lot different than school teaching, but it would be a needed distraction and help her get back into the swing of things.

I'm sure Mama will be pleasantly surprised when I tell her that I've gotten a part-time job at the nutrition center and will be working Tuesdays and Thursdays. She cupped a hand against her chin. *I can barely believe it myself.* She looked at Warren and gave another nod while curling her fingers into the palms of her hands. *I hope I've not made a mistake by saying yes. Working here in Warren's store, even two days a week, may be more than I can handle, but I feel compelled to give it a try.*

CHAPTER 16

Paradise

Pushing Rosetta in her stroller with Checkers running alongside, Eleanor headed down the driveway to see if there was any mail. It felt nice to get out of the house if only for a short while. Eleanor appreciated the fresh air, despite the wind against her face. *At least I can't see my breath today, unlike last month, when it was still bitter cold and I didn't even come out for the mail.*

Eleanor was halfway there when she heard the phone ringing from inside the phone shed. "Guess I may as well see who that is." To keep the dog occupied, Eleanor picked up a stick, turned, and tossed it in the direction of the front yard. Predictably, Checkers let out a few barks and took off after it. Eleanor parked the stroller by the shed door and stepped inside. She left the door open so she could keep an eye on Rosetta and grabbed for the telephone. "Hello."

"Guder mariye, Eleanor. I didn't expect you to answer the phone."

Eleanor smiled. She recognized the voice of Doretta's mother right away. "Good morning, Amanda. Rosetta and I were making a trip to the mailbox, and when I heard the phone ring, I stepped inside to answer it."

"How is that sweet little girl of yours?"

"She's doing well but growing too quickly to suit me."

"Jah, they don't stay babies very long. It seems like just yesterday when Karen was an infant, and now here she is almost eleven years old."

"I know what you mean." Eleanor looked out the open doorway and smiled when her precious baby girl stuck her thumb in her mouth. Rosetta didn't care for a pacifier, preferring to suck on her thumb or fingers instead. She also seemed to want juice over her formula, which wasn't a big surprise, since it was sweeter to the taste buds. But due to the sugar content, Eleanor limited the juices and always watered them down. Rosetta had become more attentive to the things around her too, which Eleanor told Amanda about. "When Vic arrives home every evening, he sometimes will announce that he's there, and Rosetta often looks in

217

the direction of her father's voice and squeals."

"Is she a daddy's girl when he's around?" Amanda questioned.

"She can be, but she's a mama's girl when Vic's not at home."

Amanda chuckled. "That's how Karen was too. Doretta, on the other hand, was a mama's girl all the time, and my boys . . . well, they were all pretty much like Karen."

"How are things going with Doretta these days?" Eleanor asked. "I haven't heard from her in a few weeks."

"So you don't know about her part-time job?"

"I don't. Is she filling in for someone at the schoolhouse?"

"No. Doretta is working two days a week at Warren's health food store, and when she's not there, she always finds something to do around here. I'm all for keeping busy, but I can't help but worry because I believe my daughter is wearing herself out." Amanda's voice lowered a bit. "Whenever I express concern about how tired she looks and try to talk to her about better ways to deal with her depression, she becomes defensive. That's why I decided to call you again. Since you're Doretta's best friend, I was hoping you might be able to influence her to stop pushing herself so hard."

I'm not really sure how I can influence her. So far it seems as though writing Doretta is my only option. I just wish my friend would go and seek a professional to help her with her depression. Eleanor cleared her throat and swallowed a few times before responding to Doretta's mother. "I'm willing to write another letter, but I'm not sure Doretta will listen to me. Ever since the accident, I have tried to comfort her, but as far as I can tell, Doretta hasn't listened to anything I've suggested that might help with her depression."

"She doesn't listen to me either," Amanda confided. "I'm beginning to think my daughter will never be back to the way she used to be before the accident."

"She'll get better. We just need to keep encouraging her and never stop praying."

"Praying I can do, but sometimes I think Doretta sees what I mean as encouragement as though I'm treating her like she's still a child. I'm not deliberately trying to tell her what to do, but there are times when out of concern I speak when I probably shouldn't and often say the wrong things."

"I understand." Eleanor looked at Rosetta again. She wondered if when her daughter grew up, she might be faced with the same problem Amanda was dealing with now with

219

Doretta. There had been times when Eleanor hadn't appreciated her mother's advice. Truth be told, when her own daughter became an adult, the two of them might not agree at times. *I need to remember that,* Eleanor told herself, *and try not to make Rosetta feel like a child once she becomes a grown woman.*

Woof! Woof! Woof!

Eleanor frowned when Checkers darted up to Rosetta's stroller and slurped the baby's face a few times. Her daughter's eyes squinted, and she turned her little face away from the dog. "Sorry, Amanda, but I need to hang up now. My poor little girl is getting her face washed by our exuberant *hund.*"

Amanda chuckled. "I'm sure Rosetta doesn't appreciate that. I'll let you go so you can take care of the situation. Danki for listening and agreeing to reach out to Doretta again."

"Of course, and I'll pray for wisdom and the right words to put down on paper before I write the letter."

"And I will be praying that Doretta will be open and accepting of whatever you say to her."

"All right then. I'll keep in touch. Bye for now, Amanda."

"Goodbye, Eleanor, and thanks for being my daughter's friend and caring about her needs."

"It's been a two-way street. Doretta prayed and counseled me when Vic and I were going through deep waters, and now it's my turn to be there for her."

"That's what friendships are for, jah?"

"Most definitely."

"I'd better let you go tend to your daughter now. Bye again, Eleanor."

"Goodbye."

After Eleanor hung up the phone, she left the phone shed and shooed the dog away from Rosetta. Of course, Checkers came right back with his trusty stick, so she took it from him and gave it a toss. Hoping he wouldn't bother her again, Eleanor pushed the stroller on down the driveway. When she opened the mailbox flap and found a letter from Doretta, she couldn't help but smile. *First a phone call from Amanda and now a letter from Doretta. Talk about perfect timing.*

Although she was eager to see what her friend had to say, Eleanor's first obligation was to get her little one back inside. In spite of the sun shining brightly, a March wind had picked up, bringing a chill into the air. Spring may have officially sprung earlier this week, but it certainly did not feel like it.

Even though Eleanor had bundled Rosetta up pretty well before bringing her outside, with the wind blowing even harder now, she didn't want the baby to get cold.

She looked forward to some spring days when the bright sun would warm the rich earth and encourage shoots to grow. Soon there would be flowering bulbs adding lovely colors to the flowerbeds in Eleanor's yard. The days would grow steadily longer, buds and blossoms would form on trees. And it wouldn't be long before butterflies and bees returned to her garden. One of Eleanor's favorite things about spring was the clean, damp smell after a good rain. There was just so much to look forward to, and Eleanor hoped that Doretta would appreciate it as much as she would.

As she set aside her thoughts of spring and pushed the stroller back up the driveway, Vic's dog ran alongside them, barking frantically.

Eleanor looked down at the stick by her feet and frowned. "Not now, Checkers. I am not going to take the time to toss you that stick again. Besides, it's too chilly right now to keep playing your silly chase-the-stick game. I want to get my daughter inside."

Yip! Yip! Yip! Checkers paused between

yips and nipped at the wheels on Rosetta's stroller.

As irritation set in, Eleanor stopped walking and shouted at the dog. "You'd better knock it off, or I'll put you in the dog run, and you can find something in there to nip and yip about for the rest of the day."

As though he understood what she had said, Checkers settled down and headed for the house with his tail between his legs. At the same time, Rosetta let loose a pathetic wail. Eleanor figured she was the one to blame and had brought it on by raising her voice at the dog.

"It's okay, little one." She stopped walking and lifted Rosetta from the stroller. "Mama's not angry at you. I'm just upset with the hund." She patted the baby's back until she quieted. "We'll all feel better once we get inside where it's warm and toasty and there is no wind or yapping dog." If things went the way they normally did when Vic's dog was in the house, he would probably find some place to flop down and take a nap.

Her daughter had been fed and was down for her nap, so Eleanor made a cup of tea and took a seat at the dining-room table to read Doretta's letter, eager to know what she'd said.

■ ■ ■ ■

Dear Eleanor,

I haven't written for a while, and I figured it was time to fill you in on what's been going on in my life. For the last two weeks, I've been working part-time for Warren at the nutrition center. I was glad when he offered me a position, because the new job is keeping me busy, which helps take my mind off things I'd rather not think about.

When I'm not working at his store, I stay occupied at home, helping Mama with chores, and I've also started a few sewing projects of my own. Basically, I have something to do that keeps me occupied almost all the time, and that's helped with my depression.

Eleanor's brows furrowed. After reading this first page of Doretta's letter, she couldn't help but be concerned. *So, Doretta's mother was right. My dear friend is pushing herself hard in order not to feel depressed. In my opinion, she needs to deal with her grief in a better way than working herself into a state of exhaustion. No wonder Amanda is worried about her daughter.*

Eleanor read the second page of Doretta's

224

letter, which was mostly about the kind of things she did at the health food store, but there had been no mention of the satchel Eleanor had sent with the slips of paper inside. Eleanor wondered if Doretta had read the rest of them. And if so, had she done any of the things that had been suggested?

Eleanor got out a notepad and pen to write Doretta a letter. *Think I'll include a scripture verse along with a helpful food-for-thought saying. Maybe something like that will help Doretta realize that working all the time is not the answer to her problem. Getting into God's Word would be much better than pushing herself too hard.*

Grabill

Margaret stood inside her horse's stall, brushing the mare while thinking about Warren and how she missed spending five days a week with him at the nutrition center. It still surprised her that he would hire Doretta to work for him two days a week. *Did he do it because he feels sorry for her, or does he think she needs the money?* Margaret asked herself as she continued to groom Honey. *I hope Warren's not planning to break up with me. He disapproves of my smartphone and doesn't understand my inter-*

est in working with other people's horses. We actually have very little in common. Sometimes I wonder why we began dating at all. She pressed a fist to her lips and heard the boards beneath her feet creak as she stepped to the right to avoid getting flicked by Honey's tail. *Even so, I like being with Warren. He's good-looking, kind, hardworking, and he has an easygoing, pleasant personality. He'd not only make a good husband but a wonderful father as well. The truth is, even though there are times when I think we shouldn't be a couple, I don't want anyone else to have him.*

Margaret reached up and gave her mare a few gentle pats. She was rewarded with a sweet-sounding whinny followed by a welcoming nuzzle against her cheek. *I just wish Warren shared my enthusiasm about horses. I don't think he understands my infatuation with them or the need I feel to help people with their troubled horses. If Warren would spend more time with me, maybe I'd feel a bit better.*

Warren stepped out of his office, where he'd been paying some invoices, and walked to the front of the store to see how Doretta was doing. Somehow with Doretta there, he felt more determined to comfort and support her. Warren longed to give Doretta as much help as she needed, but he had to be careful in how he approached her. He wanted to suggest that she try out certain supplements that might help with her depression, and he wished he felt free to suggest that Doretta attend some social activities with friends. When she would talk candidly to Warren, it seemed evident to him that she needed more time to adjust to the things in her life that she'd had no control over.

"How are things going here?" Warren asked when he joined Doretta at the checkout counter.

"Fine. It was pretty busy awhile ago, but as you can see, there are no customers in the store right now."

"Maybe that's a good thing," he responded. "We both probably need a break, so let's have a cup of that new herbal tea I got in this morning and get off our feet for a bit."

She gave a nod. "Sounds good to me."

They headed over to the display of new teas. "What kind would you like to try?" he asked.

"The maple-ginger sounds good to me." Doretta pointed to the box.

Warren opened the box and took it to his

office. He figured Doretta would follow, but she held back. "You can come in," he called, motioning with his free hand.

"I'd probably better wait out here in case a customer comes in."

"Good point." His cheeks warmed. "I still have plenty of hot water from the big Thermos I brought from home, so I'll pour some into two cups, add the tea bags, and bring them out. We can sit at the small table up front where I have all the self-help books for customers to look at or purchase."

"Okay." She cast him a brief smile and returned to the front of the store.

A short time later, Doretta and Warren were seated at the table with warm cups of the fragrant tea. "This has such a good flavor." She inhaled deeply and took a sip. "It tastes *wunderbaar.*"

"Jah, it's the first time I've ordered this kind, and I thought it would be good to give it a try. That way, when a customer comes in and asks about it, I can tell them how it tastes."

They sat quietly for a while, and then Warren brought up the topic of his and William's birthday, which would be coming up on March 27. "It's hard to believe I'll be celebrating my birthday without my twin brother," he said, dropping his gaze to the floor.

Doretta swallowed the tea in her mouth and nodded. "I'm sure it'll be difficult for your parents too."

"For sure."

"It's still difficult to accept the fact that he's gone. I often find myself thinking of all the good times we had, and then I get choked up."

"Same here."

They reminisced about some things William had done or said, and Doretta took comfort in being able to talk to someone who understood how she felt and knew exactly what she was talking about when she mentioned some things about William.

"Say . . . uh . . . I was thinking . . ." Warren looked at Doretta. "I was wondering if you would like to come to my folks' house for supper on the night of my birthday. I'd really like to have you join us."

She pondered his question a few seconds before responding. "I would like to be included. Danki for inviting me to join you."

"How about if I come by your place and pick you up around five o'clock that evening?"

"Won't you be working at the store that day?"

He shook his head. "The twenty-seventh falls on a Monday, and the store's closed that day."

"Oh, that's right. I forgot." She finished her tea and set the cup down on the table. "If it's not too much trouble, I would appreciate a ride to your home."

"No trouble at all. I'm glad you agreed to join us for supper. Having you there will make it easier for me and my folks to get through the evening and hopefully it will for you too."

Doretta hoped that would be the case. Being with William's family on his and Warren's birthday might be more difficult for both of them than he realized.

CHAPTER 17

Amanda stood watching out the open front door as Warren guided his horse and buggy out of their yard and onto the road. She still couldn't believe Doretta had agreed to go with Warren this evening to celebrate his birthday. She'd shut herself off from any kind of social event for so long, it was a surprise to see her willingness to go. Amanda wondered if being with Warren and his parents as they celebrated his birthday would drag her further into depression. She felt sure there would be reminiscing about William, and probably some tears would be shed. Doretta had made some progress emotionally this past month, and Amanda didn't want to see her daughter take any steps backward.

"What are you doin' with the *daer* open? The young people have gone, and you're letting in the chilly evening air. Would you please shut the door?" Elmer called from the living room, where he'd gone to read the recent issue of the *Plain and Simple* magazine.

She closed the door and stepped into the room where he sat in one of the recliners. "It's not that cold outside this evening, Elmer, and I was enjoying the fresh air."

He placed the magazine in his lap and looked at her over the top of his reading glasses. "You're having trouble letting go, aren't you?"

"Letting go of what?" Amanda gave her apron band a little tug.

"Who, not what. You're *umgerennt* because Doretta is going to the Lengachers' place to celebrate Warren's *gebottsdaag.*"

"I am not upset about her going there for his birthday. I'm just concerned."

"About what?"

"I believe they won't be celebrating as much as mourning the loss of Warren's brother."

"That could be, and it might be just what they all need."

"I don't think so. And I don't believe it's a good idea for Doretta to be there with them for supper. It will only serve to remind her that William is gone, which could deepen her depression rather than lifting her out of it."

"That may be what happens, all right, but it's her choice, don't you think? She's not a little girl anymore, and no matter how much you try, there is no way you can protect Doretta from emotional pain, any more than you could have protected her from the accident that killed her boyfriend and caused injuries to her body." Elmer spoke in a steady, lower-pitched voice as he asked Amanda another pointed question. "Doesn't Doretta have the right to mourn in her own way the loss of the man she'd planned to marry?"

"Well, yes, but I'm also concerned because she is wearing herself out working at the nutrition center and taking on too much responsibility with things around here."

"She probably is, but our daughter has the right to make her own decisions. If you continue to offer your advice all the time or suggest that what she's doing is wrong, it will likely drive a wedge between the two of you, and I don't believe you want that, Amanda."

"No, I don't. I only want what's best for her, and —"

"Mama, is supper ready yet?" Karen called from the hallway. "I'm *hungerich.*"

"I'm hungry too." Elmer set the magazine aside and rose from his chair. "Let's go to the kitchen, and I'll help you put the food on the table. Karen can set dishes and silverware out, and then we'll let our sons know that it's time to eat."

Amanda couldn't help smiling, and she wasn't about to turn down an offer like that. *I think it's nice when my husband helps me out.* Amanda figured that she and Elmer could pick up their conversation later, because Doretta's situation was not a topic to be discussed with their other children at the table.

"*Hallich* gebottsdaag," Doretta said as she and Warren headed down the road in his open buggy."

"Thanks. It really doesn't feel much like my birthday, though."

Warren kept his eyes straight ahead, and Doretta saw his clean-shaven chin quiver a bit. This must have been a difficult day for him from the time he'd gotten out of bed this morning clear up until now. Doretta understood that, because it had been a difficult day for her too. She'd thought that being here with Warren might make her feel even sadder, but the opposite was true. She felt relaxed, and it seemed as though William was with them too — at least the memory of him.

Doretta shifted on the unyielding seat. *Maybe I'm just imagining it because I wish William was with us right now.* She glanced at Warren again. He kept his gaze straight ahead.

"Will Margaret be joining us tonight?" Doretta asked.

He shook his head. "She was supposed to be working with someone's horse today and will probably be at it all evening. Besides, I doubt that she'd have enjoyed hearing the four of us reminisce about my brother."

"Oh, I see." Doretta thought it was a bit odd that Warren's girlfriend wouldn't want to be with him tonight, if for no other reason than to offer Warren the support he would need. But Doretta kept her thoughts to herself because what went on between Warren and Margaret was none of her business.

"Can I help you with something in here?" Betty's husband asked when he entered the kitchen.

She smiled, appreciating his offer. "Danki, Raymond. The meal is almost ready, but if you don't mind setting the dining-room table, it would be appreciated. You can use our good set of dishes and silverware from the hutch there in the dining room."

He tilted his head. "Are you certain you want to use those? I'm sure Warren and Doretta would be fine with our everyday dishes on the table."

"Maybe so, but today is a special occasion as we remember our sons' birthdays."

Raymond swiped a hand across his broad forehead. "Can we make it more of a celebration rather than just a remembrance?"

Betty gave a nod. "You're right. It should be, but if William were here, I would feel more like celebrating."

"Same with me, but the Lord chose to take one of our sons, and the one we have left deserves a nice birthday. Don't ya think?"

"Jah."

"Okay then, let's put smiles on our faces and try to be joyful this evening if for no other reason than for Warren's sake." Raymond turned toward the dining room. "Guess I'd better get to it then."

"Don't forget to put a place setting by the chair where William used to sit," she called after him.

He halted and turned back to face her, with eyebrows squished together. "He's not coming back and will never sit in that chair again, Betty."

"I know. It's just that . . ." She blinked

against invading tears that wanted to spill over. "Okay, just do as you like."

Warren opened the door for Doretta, and when they entered his parents' house, the tantalizing aroma of baked chicken filled his senses. Mom had obviously made his favorite meal. Of course, baked chicken had been William's favorite too. It was a shame he wouldn't be here to enjoy it.

Warren glanced upward. *I need to accept and deal with the fact that my bruder isn't with us anymore, and he will not be coming back.* There were days with the busyness of work when Warren didn't think about William. But other times something would happen or be said that stirred up a memory of his brother, and grief would set in again. Every day was different, and sometimes Warren's emotions were up and down. Because today was their birthday, it had been difficult for Warren to keep his focus on anything — at least until he'd picked Doretta up to bring her here. Being with her was like healing balm to Warren, and he hoped she felt the same way.

Warren took Doretta's jacket and hung it up for her and then took care of his own.

"Something sure smells good," she said, sniffing the air.

"My mamm's a great cook. I'm sure we're both in for a treat."

"Whenever William used to invite me to eat a meal here when we were dating, I always enjoyed whatever your mother prepared."

Warren felt kind of foolish for telling Doretta that his mother was a good cook. For some stupid reason, he'd forgotten that she'd eaten here several times before. *But those times were by William's invitation, not mine,* he thought. *That makes this evening feel a lot different.*

Both of Warren's parents came into the hallway. Doretta was warmly welcomed with a handshake from Warren's father and a hug from his mother.

"We're glad you could join us tonight, Doretta," Dad said sincerely.

"We are also pleased that you've been helping out at Warren's nutrition center," Mom said. "He certainly needs some assistance there, because running a health food store would be too much work for one person to handle on their own."

Doretta's cheeks colored a bit. "He did have Margaret's help before I began working on Tuesdays and Thursdays."

"True," Warren interjected, "but previously, Margaret came in late several times, so I couldn't rely on her help like I'd hoped." He looked over at Doretta. "I'd hire you full-time if I thought you were up to it."

Doretta's brown eyes widened a bit. "I'm sure I could handle it, but Margaret wouldn't be happy about losing her job and a source of income."

"You're not thinking of letting Margaret go, are you, Son?" The question came from Warren's father.

"Not as long as she gets to the store without being late on the days she is scheduled to work. When I discussed this topic with her a few days ago, she said she would make every effort to be there promptly on those days." Warren crossed his arms. "The trouble is Margaret cares more about the horses she tries to help than keeping true to her word."

"Supper is ready. I just need to put the food on the table." Mom placed her hand on his arm. Warren figured she wanted him to change the subject.

"It certainly smells good, and I'd be happy to help," Doretta offered.

"Danki."

"We can all chip in and carry something to the table," Dad said. "Isn't that right, Son?"

Warren nodded. He was pretty sure now that both of his parents wanted to put an end to his conversation about Margaret. He had to admit, this really wasn't a good time to discuss her tardiness or anything else about her, for that matter.

Everyone headed for the kitchen, and each person carried a different dish to the dining-room table. Warren had the privilege of bringing the platter of chicken, and the smell of it made his mouth water. Mom carried the bowl of creamy-looking mashed potatoes. Dad had the chicken gravy, along with steamed broccoli, and Doretta brought in some cut-up veggies and a basket of perfectly browned biscuits. Everything looked and smelled so good, Warren could hardly wait to sit down and eat himself full.

Doretta looked across the table where William used to be seated whenever she had come here for a meal. It seemed so strange sitting here with the Lengacher family without William. She figured it did for them as well.

As they ate their meal, Betty began talking about the day she'd given birth to her twin boys. "I wish you could have seen them, Doretta. They both had a good crop of sandy brown hair, and they each weighed exactly six pounds." Betty stared off into space for several seconds, as though reliving the past. "Raymond and I thought we were the luckiest parents alive because God had given us two healthy sons who looked just alike."

Raymond bobbed his head.

"Little did we know then that twenty-six years later, we would lose one of our twins." Betty teared up and Doretta did too. She could feel this poor woman's pain.

"The Bible tells us that the Lord giveth and the Lord taketh away," Raymond said. "We need to be grateful for the time He gave us with William and focus on the good times we had when he was with us."

Betty dried her eyes with a napkin. "You're right, but they weren't all happy memories, you know. Some were kind of sad — like the day William fell out of the hayloft and broke his arm. He wasn't too happy about it, but we were glad he didn't have any permanent injuries."

"It turned out okay for him, though," Warren interjected. "Because with his arm in a cast, I ended up doing all of his chores."

"Poor William was kind of accident prone," Doretta spoke up. "I remember one school day during noon recess when William had been running and fell down on some gravel. He hurt his *ellboge,* so I got a bandage and some antiseptic from the teacher and doctored him up."

Betty pursed her lips. "Hmm . . . I don't remember hearing anything about William falling on gravel in the schoolyard, but I do recollect Warren coming home from school one day with a hurt elbow. In fact, he still has the scar to prove it." She motioned to Warren. "Roll your sleeve up and show Doretta."

A visible flush swept across Warren's cheeks, and he gave his shirt collar a few tugs. "Aw, Mom . . . really?"

"Jah. If she thought it was William whose elbow she'd tended, then she needs to see some proof that it was actually you it happened to."

Warren rolled up his left sleeve and stuck his elbow out toward Doretta. "My mamm's right; it was me who fell in the schoolyard that day."

Doretta stared in disbelief at his elbow. "Well, for goodness' sakes. I had no idea it was you, Warren. I even called you William. You should have corrected me."

He shrugged his shoulders. "People confused us a lot, and I never wanted to make a big deal of it. So rather than correct folks all the time, I usually said nothing and let 'em think I was my twin. I don't mean it in a bad way or anything, but William was kind of a tease, and sometimes when he did mischievous things, I'd end up taking the blame."

As Warren's father started to speak, a knock sounded on the front door.

Warren pushed his chair aside and stood. "I'll go see who that is."

I hope I did the right thing by coming here this evening, Margaret thought as she waited on the front porch for someone to answer her knock. She'd seen the light from a gas lamp shining through the front windows and reasoned that someone must be at home.

Margaret took a step back when the door opened.

"Margaret! I'm surprised to see you. Wh–what are you doing here?" Warren leaned against the doorframe.

"I came to see you and say, 'Happy birthday.' " She handed Warren a light blue gift bag with silver trim. "I hope you will like what I got you."

"Danki. I . . . uh . . . wasn't expecting you to buy me a gift."

"Warren, who's there?"

Margaret recognized his mother's voice

and waited to see how Warren would respond.

Warren turned his head. "It's Margaret, Mom. She came by to wish me a happy birthday and give me a gift."

"Well, invite her in. She can join us for cake and ice cream."

Warren turned back to look at Margaret, and a bright pink flush had appeared on his face and neck. "I guess you heard that."

"Jah, but if you're busy, don't feel obligated to invite me in."

"No, I'm not busy. We were just finishing up with our supper." He stepped aside and held the door open wide. "Come on in."

After Margaret hung up her jacket, she followed Warren into the dining room, where Warren's parents and Doretta sat around the table. Margaret felt a prickling sensation creep up the back of her neck. *Why was Doretta invited to have supper here and I wasn't? Is she Warren's new girlfriend now? If so, why did he neglect to tell me?*

"Oh, I'm sorry for the interruption. I didn't know you had company." Margaret looked at Warren pointedly. "If I'd known, I wouldn't have stopped by and interrupted your supper."

Warren felt like a mouse caught in a trap

244

with no way out. It was wrong not to include his girlfriend in tonight's birthday gathering, but he didn't think Margaret would be interested in hearing all their remembrances about him and William when they were kids. Besides, he hadn't invited her because he'd figured she would be working until late this evening with that horse she'd told him about.

Are those the real reasons I didn't invite her? Warren asked himself. *Did it have more to do with the fact that Doretta was going to be here, and I wanted her all to myself?* That thought caught Warren off guard, but he concluded it was true. Trouble was, he didn't feel that he could reveal those feelings — especially not to Doretta. If he ever did tell her the way he felt about her, it would have to be later, when the time was right. He would also need some sense that Doretta felt the same way about him. Warren figured that unless he planned to pay more attention to Margaret and treat her like his girlfriend, he should break up with her. The problem was, he didn't want to hurt Margaret's feelings. One thing was for sure: Margaret was here right now, so he pulled out a chair at the table and asked her to sit down. Warren would pray about his situation and think things through before he made any definite decisions.

CHAPTER 18

Sweet-smelling timothy hay assaulted Warren's senses as he paced restlessly in front of his horse's stall, praying for help in sorting out his thoughts so that he could make the right choice regarding Margaret. It had been two weeks since his birthday supper, and he'd still not reached any definite decision about his relationship with her. He appreciated the nice wallet she'd given him and still felt bad that he hadn't invited her to his parents' house for his birthday supper.

Margaret's quiet demeanor and drooping shoulders that evening had let Warren know that she'd clearly been disappointed, and seeing Doretta there probably hadn't helped. Although Margaret hadn't come right out and said so, Warren had an inkling that she suspected his interest in Doretta went deeper than just the mutual grief they felt over losing William. He was quite sure too that his girlfriend had not been happy when he'd asked Doretta to work for him part-time.

It probably wasn't fair to Margaret to cut her hours, he told himself, *but I needed full-time help in the store, and I couldn't count on her to show up on time. Surely, she must have realized that and should have respected my decision. If she'd really wanted to work five days a week, then she should have been more dependable.*

Margaret wasn't a bad person, and Warren had to admit that he used to enjoy spending time with her, but his feelings did not go deep enough to be called love. For that reason alone, he could not ask her to marry him, although Warren felt sure she anticipated an eventual proposal.

With sounds of rustling hay and creaking boards beneath his feet, Warren continued to roam back and forth while rubbing the back of his neck where the muscles were tight and painful. *Under the circumstances, it wouldn't be fair to keep going out with Margaret when I can't offer her a permanent relationship. So that leaves me only one recourse — I need to break up with her as soon as possible.*

He stepped over to where the tack was kept and grabbed a bridle. Then Warren opened the door to his horse's stall and went in. *There's no point in prolonging this, and since today is my day off, I may as well head on over to Margaret's place and talk to her right now.*

Margaret stood in front of her horse's empty stall, blinking against the salty tears rolling down her cheeks and trying not to sneeze from the nose-tickling straw. She still couldn't believe what had happened the evening before.

She'd let Honey and her mother's horse, Biscuit, out for some exercise. They'd both been in playful moods and didn't seem to mind the April showers that had begun shortly before she'd led them from the barn and into the corral. In fact, the rain seemed to invigorate them — especially Honey, who had trotted around the enclosure with her tail up as she snorted and shook her head from side to side. Biscuit wasn't quite as frisky, but she appeared to be enjoying herself as she followed Honey with perky ears but at a more leisurely pace. Margaret had enjoyed watching them and hadn't minded standing outside in the light rain beneath her umbrella.

She leaned against the wooden boards of Honey's stall and closed her eyes, allowing the events of what had transpired next to replay in her mind.

Margaret clutched her pleated skirt and steadied herself against a blast of unexpected wind. A clap of thunder sounded next, followed by a torrential rainfall. She watched in horror as Honey jumped the corral fence and took off down the driveway. The force of the wind blew Margaret's umbrella inside-out, and she tossed it aside. She had to stop her horse before the mare darted into the road.

Cupping both hands around her mouth, Margaret hollered, "Whoa, Honey! Whoa!"

The horse kept running straight for the road. Margaret ran down the driveway with her heart pounding so hard she could hear it in her ears. "Whoa, girl! Whoa! Come back here, right now!"

A horn honked and a minivan came onto the scene. Margaret heard brakes squeal as the vehicle veered to the right. She shouted at her horse again, but it was too late. The next thing Margaret knew, her beautiful honey-colored horse lay unmoving in the road. A few seconds later, a distraught driver stepped out and hurried over to Margaret with a cell phone in her hand. "Is that your horse?"

All Margaret could manage was a nod. She

couldn't speak around the lump lodged in her throat.

"I'm sorry. I didn't see the horse in time, and I couldn't stop. I'll pull my van out of the way and then call 911 for help."

At the sound of the barn door opening, Margaret's eyes snapped open. She wiped her tears with the back of her hand and stood waiting to see who had come in. When Margaret saw Warren walking toward her, she brought a shaky hand to her forehead and choked back more tears. Oh, how she needed his comfort right now.

As Warren approached Margaret and saw her glazed expression and tear-stained face, he knew something was wrong. He moved closer and clasped her arms. "Is there a problem? You look umgerennt."

Her chin trembled as she gave a nod. "I'm very upset. My . . . my gaul is dead."

His eyes widened. "Oh, no! What happened?"

"Last night during the storm, Honey jumped the corral fence and ran out into the road. I yelled for her to stop, but she kept running." Margaret paused long enough to gulp in some air. "Then a van came along, and the driver couldn't stop in

251

time." She lowered her head and sobbed. "My daed had to get the skid loader to haul her out of the road, and early this morning he buried Honey way out in our back field."

"I'm so sorry, Margaret. I know how much you cared for that beautiful horse."

"Jah. She was the best gaul anyone could ever want."

"What about the driver? Was he or she okay, and were there any passengers in the vehicle?"

She shook her head. "No passengers, and the woman driver wasn't hurt. There was some damage to the front of her van, but it was drivable, and she said she had insurance that would cover the cost to fix it. The woman was pretty upset and kept apologizing." Margaret hiccupped on another sob. "You should have seen the way our collie, Ruby, carried on when Honey got hit. She tried to run out in the road, but my mamm held her back. Then this morning, when my daed went out with the skid loader again in order to move the horse to a proper burying place, he discovered that part of her body had been covered with dirt."

Warren's brows squished together. "That's sure strange. I wonder how it happened."

"Dad was puzzled by it too until Ruby showed up and began digging, which caused more dirt to be thrown on the horse's body. Ruby and Honey had always gotten along well, and I think the hund's instinct was to try and bury my poor horse."

"Wow, that's really something."

More tears rolled down Margaret's hot cheeks. "Even if I had the money to buy a new horse right now, there isn't a single one for sale that could ever replace Honey."

Warren's heart went out to Margaret, and automatically he took her into his arms to offer comfort. As he stood there, gently rubbing her back, Warren realized that this was not the time to tell Margaret what he'd come here to say. As upset as she was over losing her horse, he would not say or do anything that would hurt her any further. Breaking up with Margaret would have to wait until a later date, when she had dealt with the pain of losing her special horse.

Doretta sat on the end of her bed, thinking about the message their bishop had preached the day before and the things he'd said about prayer. He'd stated that when a person couldn't form the words to seek counsel with God, they should pray specific verses from the Bible, such as prayers about guidance and direction. One verse Bishop John quoted was Luke 17:5: "And the apostles said unto the Lord, Increase our faith." He stressed the importance of using this verse as a prayer and stated firmly that we should always praise the Lord and never stop praying. Another verse the bishop mentioned was First Thessalonians 5:18: "In every thing give thanks: for this is the will of God in Christ Jesus concerning you."

Doretta wished she could thank God for everything and offer such prayers, but whenever she tried, the words would not come. After the pain of losing William, Doretta wasn't sure she could ever pray and praise God again.

She thought about the last letter she'd received from Eleanor and how her friend had offered more comforting words and scriptures. Tears sprang to Doretta's eyes and dripped onto her cheeks. *Why can't I accept my friend's encouragement and move on with my life so that I can console others the way I used to?* In all of Doretta's twenty-six years, she'd never felt so far from God or been so despondent. Getting out of the house two days a week to work at Warren's health food store had helped some, but even that had not filled the void she still felt deep in her heart and soul.

With a few exceptions, Doretta rarely laughed or smiled anymore, which was the opposite of how she had been before William's death. She'd always been cheerful and positive. Losing the love of her life, however, and trying to deal with her physical injuries had snatched Doretta's joy, like a robber sneaking up on an unsuspecting victim to take their prized possession.

Doretta had thought keeping busy during her waking hours would help, but the only thing it had accomplished was to make her so tired at the end of each day that she slept solidly at night. She did realize, however, that on the days she worked for Warren, she sometimes smiled and even laughed a little. She crossed her arms against her chest. *I wonder why? Are the topics that come up what makes me smile on occasion, or does it have more to do with Warren's easygoing way and the humorous stories he sometimes shares?*

Doretta's contemplations came to a halt when her bedroom door opened and Karen rushed in. "Have ya seen my katz?"

Doretta shook her head. "And it's not likely that your *beschwerlich* cat would be in here."

Karen gave a huff and folded her arms. "Olive's not troublesome. She is a good katz."

"She's a fair mouser, I guess, but she

belongs outside, not in the house."

"Mama said I could bring Olive in for a while so I could brush her hair, but she got away from me, and now I haven't been able to find her anywhere."

"Can't you take care of grooming her on the back porch?"

Karen gave a quick shake of her head. "No, silly. It's raining again, and since the back porch has no cover over it, we'd both get wet."

Doretta got up and looked out the window. What had started out as a cloudy day had turned into another downpour like they'd had last night. "Well, kindly leave my room and go look somewhere else for the beschwerlich katz, because she's definitely not here."

Karen moved closer to Doretta and squinted her eyes. "How come you're always such a grouch?"

Doretta flinched at her sister's hurtful question. It was true, and she knew it, but Doretta couldn't force herself to be happy. *I could be a little kinder, though,* she reminded herself. "I'm sorry, Karen. I shouldn't have snapped at you."

"It's okay." Without another word, Karen turned and left the room.

Doretta touched her forehead, fingering

the scars near her hairline. *If I keep this up, sooner or later my sister might quit talking to me. I really need to work on my attitude, even if I don't feel any joy.*

CHAPTER 19

Margaret opened the jar where she kept the donation money she'd received over the past year from people who had brought their horses to her for training and help with behavioral problems. After she'd counted it, her shoulders slumped. There wasn't nearly enough money to buy a new horse, and she had no idea how long it would take her to get it. "It doesn't help that I only put in three days of work each week for Warren, now that Doretta's working at his store the other two days," she muttered.

"Who are you talking to?" Mom asked when she entered the kitchen with a slip of paper in her hand.

Margaret's face heated. "Myself. I do that sometimes when no one's around."

"I think most people are guilty of that at times." Mom joined Margaret at the table. "You were fretting about the fact that Warren hired Doretta to work at the nutrition center, right?"

"Jah. Now that I have to buy a new horse, I need more money than I'm making." Margaret released a heavy sigh. "And it still irks me that thanks to Warren's impulsive decision, I'm losing out on two days I could have been making money."

"But it's given you more time to work with the horses that have been brought to you for help," Mom reminded.

"True." Margaret sniffed and gestured to the money she had dumped on the table. "Even with all the cash I've received here, it doesn't come close to what I'll need in order to purchase a new gaul."

Mom reached over and clasped Margaret's arm. "You can use Biscuit whenever you need to go somewhere."

Margaret gave a halfhearted shrug. "I appreciate your willingness to let me borrow your horse, but Biscuit is not trained for horseback riding, and she can't do any of the tricks I had taught Honey."

Mom's brows lowered. "For goodness' sakes, Margaret. Most Amish women your age are not roaming around on the back of their horse." She looked straight at her. "And really, how important is it that a horse does tricks? You just need a strong, reliable animal to pull your carriage, and Biscuit is both strong and reliable."

Margaret pressed both hands against her cheeks. "Sorry, Mom. I didn't mean to sound ungrateful, and for now, I will borrow your horse when you don't need her. I also realize that the neat things my horse did are not important to you, but they are to me. Honey and I had a special bond. She was smart, and I enjoyed teaching her new tricks. Even if I did have the money to buy another horse, I doubt that I'd ever find one that would mean as much to me as my mare did."

"I understand. And speaking of horses . . ." Mom handed Margaret the slip of paper she'd brought to the table. "When I was out in the phone shed a bit ago, there was a message for you from someone new to the area about the possibility of you working with one of their horses. If you accept the job, it'll be another opportunity for you to make money."

"Okay, I'll call that number." Margaret was pleased about the potential of doing what she liked best, not to mention the money she would earn. With the note in hand, she got up from the table. "I'm going out to the phone shed right now and return this man's call."

Her mother nodded, and Margaret hurried from the room. In addition to going out for supper with Warren tonight, if this phone call went well, she would have two things to look forward to.

Amanda stood on the front porch, shaking cat hair from one of the braided throw rugs in Karen's bedroom. She had made a mistake allowing her daughter to bring Olive into the house last week, because now the cat was in more than she was out.

Amanda pursed her lips and gave the rug a few more good shakes. *Elmer says I'm too lenient with that girl. I guess maybe he's right, but she's my youngest, and it's doubtful that at this point in my life, I would ever be blessed with more children. I suppose that's the reason I give in to Karen's requests so easily.*

Amanda's thoughts reverted to her sons. Glen and Isaac, both working and with girlfriends, were away from home a lot these days and didn't need her attention as much as they had when they were young boys. Even Jeremy, at age fifteen, kept busy with school and doing things with his friends. So Amanda's focus landed on her daughters more often these days. Karen, being the youngest, still needed a mother's hand, and after Doretta's accident, she too had needed Amanda's care.

Of course, Amanda reasoned, *my eldest daughter has become quite independent here of late. I don't think she appreciates me fussing over her, so why wouldn't I give Karen more of my attention?*

Amanda couldn't help worrying about Doretta, though. She'd been pushing herself too hard for too long, and if Doretta wasn't careful, she might cave in from exhaustion. She could even have a nervous breakdown. If Doretta were still a child, Amanda would be more in control of the situation and would have gotten her daughter some professional help by now. But Doretta was an adult with a free will and could make her own decisions. *Even Eleanor's letters and cards of encouragement, which she sends regularly, haven't had much influence on my daughter,* Amanda thought with regret. *Surely, there must be something or someone that will help Doretta see a light at the end of the dark tunnel.* She bowed her head. *Dear Lord, please let it be so.*

"Since there are no customers in the store right now and I'm not needed at the checkout counter at the moment, is there something else you would like me to do?" Doretta asked Warren.

He stopped sweeping the floor and gestured toward the back of the store. "You can put some of those gluten-free baking flours that were delivered this morning out on the shelves. I haven't had time to get around to it yet mainly because I spent too much time in my office placing more orders." A frown creased his forehead. "When I decided to open this business, I didn't realize how much was involved. Sometimes it's a little overwhelming, and I often find myself wondering if I bit off more than I can chew."

Doretta noticed the lines of worry on his face and wondered what she might say or do to ease his concerns. "Owning a business is a big responsibility, but from what I can tell, you're doing a good job."

"Just doin' my best and taking one day at a time."

"I've heard good things about the store from many of the customers I've waited on," she said. "Several people have said how much this business was needed, and last week one English lady mentioned that she was pleased with how well stocked the store is with a nice variety of health-related products."

Warren smiled. "Thanks for sharing. That kind of feedback is always good to hear. Makes all the work you, me, and Margaret do here worthwhile."

Warren moved closer to where Doretta stood. "Speaking of Margaret . . . did you hear that her horse died during that storm we had last week?"

"No, I didn't. What happened?"

"The mare ran out into the road and got hit by a van. Margaret was pretty upset about it."

"I can imagine."

"She really misses Honey — that horse was quite *schmaert,* and she would do just about anything Margaret wanted." He sighed. "Of course, it wasn't just about Honey being smart. Margaret is a good teacher. Fact is, she has helped a lot of folks here in Allen County that have brought their horses with behavioral problems to her."

Doretta thought about William's horse and how it had spooked the night of their accident. If his horse had been better trained, maybe it wouldn't have crossed the line into oncoming traffic. *If only there was some way that we humans could go back in time and make things right,* she thought. *But God could have prevented Margaret's horse from running out into the road and getting hit. He could have prevented the accident that killed William and left me with scars.* How many times had she rehashed this whole thing only to end up feeling more depressed? *Keep busy,* Doretta reminded herself. *That's the only thing that can help me forget — if only for a little while.*

Doretta moved out from behind the counter. "I'd better get busy putting that flour on the shelf. If I don't do it now, we could end up with more customers, and then I'll need to come back here to wait on them."

"If anyone comes in while you're taking care of the flour, I'll wait on them," Warren said. "And if I need your help with anything, I'll give you a call."

"Okay." Doretta headed to the storage room. Warren was certainly a nice boss to work for. He was also fast becoming a good friend. She appreciated his friendship more than he could possibly know.

Warren finished sweeping the floor and was about to get out the supplies to clean the front window when he heard a thud followed by a gasp. He hurried to the area where Doretta had gone to set the bags of flour out and was so shocked by the sight before him that he couldn't utter a word. Doretta stood with a dusting of flour on her head, the front of her dress, and even on her shoes. The nearly empty bag lay on the floor by her feet. With her eyes wide and mouth slightly open, she turned to look at him with a bewildered expression.

"What happened?" he asked. "Are you hurt?"

"No, I'm fine. I lost my grip on that bag of almond flour, and now it's ruined, and I am a mess." Her foot slipped when she took a few steps forward, and instinctively, he reached out to steady her. With both arms around Doretta's waist, Warren was so close, he could feel her breath. When he pulled slowly away, it became obvious that some of the flour on her dress had stuck to his shirt and trousers. Warren looked at Doretta's face and noticed a smile beginning to form. Then she giggled, and he broke out in laughter. "What a pair we make." He kept one arm around her slender waist. "We look like a couple of young bakers who don't know our way around the kitchen yet."

Doretta brushed some of the flour off her dress. "I'm so sorry, Warren. I've created a big mess on your clean floor, and now it'll be my job to do some sweeping."

He shook his head. "That's okay. I'll take care of it while you get cleaned up. We'd have some explaining to do if we looked like this and a customer came in."

Doretta nodded. "I can only imagine what

they would think."

"This stuff is slippery. Let me walk you to the bathroom door." He offered his arm to her and was pleased when she accepted it.

As they made their way in that direction and he leaned a bit closer, an unexpected thought popped into Warren's head. *I wonder what Doretta would do if I kissed her right now. Now get that crazy notion out of your head,* he told himself. *Doretta's still in love with William, and I have a date with Margaret tonight. I should not even be having such thoughts. I just got caught up in the moment, that's all. By this evening, when I'm eating at a restaurant with Margaret, I'll have forgotten all about this unexpected moment when I was tempted to kiss the woman my brother had planned to marry.*

"Aren't you *hungerich,* Sister?" Jeremy nudged Doretta's arm. "You took a hunk of *hinkel* and put it on your plate, but ya haven't even taken one bite of that chicken."

"Your *bruder* is right," Papa put in from his seat at the end of the kitchen table. "Are you feeling *grank,* Doretta?"

She shook her head. "I'm not sick, and I'm sure that Mama's fried chicken tastes great. I was just thinking about something, that's all."

"Like what?" Isaac asked.

Doretta took a sip of water and set her glass down. "It was nothing important — not worth sharing at all."

"But your ears are turning pink, so I bet you were thinking about something, or maybe someone, and you're too embarrassed to tell us."

Doretta's jaw clenched. *Why won't Isaac let the subject drop?* She picked up a drumstick and ate a bite. "There, are you all happy now?"

Mama's forehead creased as she gave Doretta a stern look, but she made no comment. Doretta was glad, because she didn't want this conversation to go any further. There was no way she would tell her family about the incident that had occurred at the nutrition center when she'd dropped the bag of flour today. Someone, probably one of her brothers, would most likely call her *butterfingers* or say that they wished they could have seen her with flour all over her face and clothes.

Doretta tried to focus on the boiled potatoes she'd also put on her plate, but an image of Warren and his look of concern came to mind. Doretta had trouble holding back a smile as she thought about the way they'd both ended up laughing. She'd appreciated the fact that Warren had seen the humor in the situation and showed no irritation over losing an entire bag of flour.

Doretta's heartbeat quickened as she reflected on the way she had felt when he'd put his arms around her this afternoon. It had been unexpected, and Doretta's breath had caught in her throat. For one fleeting moment, as Warren leaned in close, she'd thought he might be about to kiss her.

But that wouldn't make any sense, she told herself. *Warren and Margaret are dating, and they'll probably end up getting married. Besides, I'm sure he has no interest in me other than being a friend, and I'm sure he thinks that's how I feel about him too — just a good friend.* Doretta's mind raced at the notion of him becoming more than a friend. If she were being completely honest with herself, she'd have to admit that she enjoyed Warren's company a lot. Was it because he looked so much like William, or could it be for other reasons she hadn't been willing to admit?

"There you go again, Sister . . . staring at your food and not eating."

Doretta looked to her right, where Karen sat. Was everyone watching her this evening? Why did they care so much about what she was thinking or how much she ate? It was rude. *How would they like it if I pointed a finger at one of their plates and asked why they weren't eating?*

To steer the conversation in another direction, Doretta looked over at her mother and posed a question. "I was wondering if you'll be having another sisters' day soon."

"Maybe in a month or so; I'm not sure. Why do you ask?" Mama tilted her head to one side.

"Oh, just curious is all. I know how much you enjoy spending time with your sisters, and since you haven't gotten together in a while, I figured it might be soon."

"Yes, I do enjoy spending time with Anita and Joanna, but we all have busy lives, and sometimes it's hard to plan a day when we're all free at the same time."

"How come we never have a sisters' day?" Karen blinked her long lashes as she looked over at Doretta.

"That's a good idea, Doretta," Papa said. "When Karen gets out of school next month for summer break, you two should make plans to do something fun together."

"That's sounds nice." Doretta gave her sister's shoulder a tender squeeze. "Why don't we both think about what we'd like to do, and then we'll make plans for one of my days off toward the end of May."

"Oh boy! I can hardly wait." Karen's freckled face fairly glowed as she spoke in a bubbly tone.

Doretta forced a smile. *Well, that worked nicely. I not only changed the subject, but now I have to put on my thinking cap and come up with something for us to do. At least it will take my mind off Warren and wondering if I'm beginning to have feelings for him that go beyond friendship. If I do, then I'll have to nip it in the bud, because William's only been gone five months, and I shouldn't even be thinking about a relationship with anyone else at this time. Besides, Warren has already been spoken for; plus I cannot break my promise to William.*

CHAPTER 20

The days flew by, and soon it was the end of the school term. Jeremy had graduated from the eighth grade and already found a job learning a new trade in their local buggy shop. Since today was a Friday, and Doretta didn't have to work at the health food store, she'd promised Karen that they would do something fun together. Although she had a mild headache and didn't feel like going anywhere, she had promised her sister and wouldn't go back on her word. But it had begun raining this morning and hadn't let up by noon. That put a damper on Doretta's original plans to take Karen to the park for a picnic lunch. Even going for a ride in their open buggy with umbrellas over their heads would not be fun on a dismal day like this.

"So where are we gonna go, and what can we do with all this rain comin' down?" Karen tugged on Doretta's skirt as they both stood looking out the living-room window.

Mama stepped up beside them. "I have an idea. Why don't you see if one of our drivers is free to take you into town?"

Karen looked up at her and frowned. "What are we supposed to do there?"

"You could have lunch someplace and visit the library to check out a *buch.*"

Karen wrinkled her nose. "I already have plenty of books to read here at home, so why would I need another one?"

Their mother's suggestions weren't going well, so Doretta decided to give Karen some options. "How about we begin our sisters' day by having lunch at the Woodhouse Restaurant? When we finish eating, we can either stop in at the Dollar General or visit Miller's Country Store. I'm sure we could find something to buy at either one of those stores."

"Can we stop at both places?"

"Sure."

Karen's lips formed a nice smile. "Okay, let's go."

Doretta tweaked Karen's nose. "Let me go out to the phone shed and call one of our drivers. If I can find one who is available, we'll leave as soon as they get here to pick us up."

"Okay! I'd better get my umbrella, though,

so we don't get too wet going out to the driver's van." Karen skipped out of the room.

Mama winked at Doretta. "That went well."

"Jah. Now I just have to hope that one of our drivers is available."

"Did you bring anything for lunch today?" Warren asked when he joined Margaret at the checkout counter.

She shook her head. "I got up early to work with another horse that was brought to me last night, and after I ate a quick breakfast, there wasn't time to fix myself a sandwich to bring to work." She patted her stomach. "I'll be okay until suppertime, though."

"You should eat something to keep up your strength," Warren said. "We've been really busy all morning, and with the weekend coming, a lot of people are out shopping today, so we might be even busier later this afternoon." He shifted his weight and leaned against the front of the counter. "Why don't I run down the street to the Woodhouse Restaurant? I'll bring us both back something and we can take turns eating in my office. That way, someone will

always be up front here to wait on customers."

"Didn't you bring a lunch from home
either?"

"Jah, I did, but the tuna fish sandwich my
mamm made for me doesn't really appeal.
I'm sure there's something on the menu at
the restaurant that would be more appetiz-
ing."

"Okay, sounds good. I'll pay you back for
whatever you bring me."

"Do you know what you want?"

"No, not really. Why don't you surprise
me?"

"Are you sure? Whatever I choose might
be something you don't really care for."

"If it appeals to you, I'm sure it will to
me. We've been dating long enough that you
should know my likes and dislikes by now."

"Yeah, okay." Warren wasn't about to tell
Margaret that he hadn't paid much attention to what she chose for her meals whenever they'd gone out for lunch or supper.
He'd seen what she ordered at the time, but
it didn't seem important enough for him to
remember. Warren did know that when
Margaret had eaten supper at his house,
she'd always complimented his mother on
her good cooking.

He grabbed his hat and umbrella and headed for the door. "Be back soon."

Warren entered the Woodhouse Restaurant and placed his to-go orders. While waiting for the sandwiches to be made, he stood off to one side. Glancing at the section where people had been seated, he was surprised to see Doretta sitting at a table with her sister. It was good to see her out and about, which meant her depression must be lifting some.

With only a slight hesitation, Warren made his way over to their table. "Sorry to interrupt your lunch, but when I came in here to place a takeout order and saw you over here, I wanted to come say hello." Warren shuffled his feet and cleared his throat a few times. He felt nervous all of a sudden and could barely make eye contact with Doretta.

"Doretta and I are havin' a sisters' day," Karen spoke up. "We're goin' over to the Country Store after we get done eating. Our mamm gave me some money, so I hope there's somethin' in the store that I'll wanna buy."

"I bet there will be. They have lots of interesting things there in addition to the tasty pies, doughnuts, and such that they sell." Warren looked at Doretta. "Sounds like you planned a nice sisters' day."

She smiled and gave a slow nod. "We had wanted to go to the park for a picnic, but this rain we're having today put a damper on that."

"Yeah, that makes sense." Warren turned his head when he heard his name being called. "Guess I'd better go. My order's ready."

"It was nice seeing you. I hope the rest of your day goes well."

"Thanks. I'll see you next Tuesday if not before."

"What about Sunday? Won't you be at the church service?"

"It's our off-Sunday, and I'll be going to my uncle's church district with my folks."

Her cheeks took on a rosy hue. "Oh, that's right. My family will probably visit another district too."

When Warren's name was called again, he said goodbye and hurried off. He wished he could have sat down at the table and eaten his lunch with Doretta and Karen. But Margaret was waiting for him at the store, and more customers would be coming in.

Warren still hadn't broken up with Margaret, but seeing Doretta here today made him wish once again that she was his girlfriend instead of Margaret. If he knew Doretta felt the same way about him, he would break up with Margaret this very day.

With his order in hand, Warren gave a frustrated shake of his head and headed out the door. *Of course, that's not likely to happen. Even if by some chance Doretta does have any feelings for me, she's not likely to admit it. I'd have to be the one to make the first move, but I won't do that until after Margaret and I are no longer a couple.*

After Warren left the restaurant, Karen looked over at Doretta and said, "Warren sure looks like William. It's kinda weird, don't ya think?"

"William and Warren were identical twins, so it makes sense that they would look alike," Doretta responded.

"I know, but it was always hard for me to tell 'em apart."

Doretta nodded. "When we were *kinner,* I didn't always know which twin was which, but by the time William and I started going steady, I always knew the difference."

"How could you tell?"

"Sometimes it was by something William said or did, but the dimple in his right cheek, which I never paid much attention to when we were children, also let me know when I was in the company of the man I'd fallen in love with." Doretta stared wistfully out the window. *If William and I had gotten married as planned, I wonder what I would be doing right now. I probably would not be sitting here at this restaurant answering questions from my curious sister. By now, William and I may have been living in the house he'd wanted to build for us, and I would no doubt be there, baking, cleaning, or planning what to make for our supper this evening.* Doretta struggled not to give in to the tears pushing against the back of her eyes. *William and I would have been married for over six months, and there might even have been a baby on the way. Now I'll probably never marry or become a mother.*

Karen nudged Doretta's arm. "Sister, did ya hear what I said?"

"Huh? No, sorry. Guess I didn't. Could you please repeat it?"

"I said I'm done eating now, and I wish you'd hurry up and finish your soup so we can head over to the Country Store. Oh, and don't forget that we're gonna make a stop at the Dollar General too."

Doretta fought the urge to roll her eyes. Her sister was certainly the impatient one today. Of course, she couldn't really blame Karen for wanting to check those stores out. It seemed like years ago when Doretta felt more carefree and would have been enthused about going there too. But now she only wanted to please her sister, which she guessed was okay too. At least it would give them both something to do on this otherwise dreary day.

Margaret glanced at the clock on the far wall. Warren had been gone longer than she expected, but maybe they'd been busy at the restaurant, and it had taken awhile to get his order.

She drummed her fingers on the counter. *It was nice sharing my horse-training work with Warren even though he appeared to be a little preoccupied by something else. I wonder what was on his mind.* She looked toward the entrance. Margaret was bored with no customers in the store, so if he didn't get here soon, she'd need to find something to do.

Before work this morning, she had picked out one of her nicer dresses and had even worn a newer pair of shoes. But it was to no avail since Warren hadn't even noticed her attire. If he had, he hadn't commented on the way she looked when she'd arrived at the store. *I feel like I'm fading away right in his presence, and our relationship seems to have stalled. What if he decides to break up with me in the near future?* She shrugged her shoulders. *Maybe it wouldn't be that big of a deal, since things do seem kind of off between us these days. Then again, it would mean I wouldn't have a boyfriend, and that wouldn't sit too well with me. Besides, people might wonder why we broke up, and I'd have to come up with a good reason.*

Margaret stepped out from behind the counter and was about to head for the back room when Warren entered the building with a plastic bag.

"Sorry I took so long," he said, placing the sack on the countertop. "I got us both ham and cheese sandwiches, but I forgot about beverages. So I hope you're okay with just water from the cooler I fill with ice and keep in my office."

"Water is fine for me," she said, moving back to the wooden stool she'd been sitting on earlier. "Why don't you go to your office and eat first?" Before Warren could respond, Margaret quickly added, "Or, since there are no customers in the store right now, maybe we could both sit out here and eat our sandwiches rather than taking turns."

"I guess that'd be all right. I'll go get another stool and some bottles of water."

"Okay." She seated herself and waited for his return.

■ ■ ■ ■

After their prayer and while they ate their lunch, Margaret began telling Warren about one of the horses she was working with. "The mare's name is Dixie, and she's a real sweet one, but she's afraid of stepping in water — even small puddles. I've been spending a lot of time trying to get her to trust me, and once I've gained Dixie's full trust, it will be easier to teach her that she doesn't have to fear every mud puddle she encounters on a rainy day."

"That makes sense." Warren picked up his water bottle and took a drink.

"Jah, but I'd rather work with a horse like her than the other one who was brought to me last night. He has a nasty habit of bucking his owner off whenever he tries to ride him."

Warren stared at the front door, hoping a customer would come in so this conversation would end and they could get back to the business of working.

"You know, I've lined up several new clients just by word of mouth, and the other day . . .

Warren tried to stay focused on what Margaret was telling him, but his mind kept wandering as his thoughts went to Doretta. At one point, while Margaret continued to drone on, he had patted his face with some water in an attempt to refresh himself and stay attentive. It didn't seem fair that he couldn't have what he wanted and felt trapped in a relationship he didn't want to be in and wasn't sure how to get out of. *And even if I do break up with Margaret, there's no guarantee that Doretta and I will ever be together as a couple. It's probably just wishful thinking.*

"You're home early today," Amanda commented when her husband came through the back door. "I figured you wouldn't be here until closer to suppertime."

He gestured to the kitchen clock. "I'm only half an hour early."

"Oh, guess I didn't realize what time it actually was. The girls still aren't back from town, so I figured I had plenty of time to get some letter writing done." Amanda grimaced. "To be honest, I haven't even started our evening meal."

"No problem. We can eat whenever you get it done." Elmer took a glass from the cupboard and filled it with water. "What took our daughters to town on this rainy spring day?"

"Karen wanted to have a sisters' day, so Doretta agreed to take her to town for lunch and some shopping."

"That sounds like *schpass.* That's probably why they aren't back yet. They're having too much fun." He wiggled his brows.

"My guess is that our youngest daughter is enjoying herself, but I'm not sure about Doretta."

"What makes you think that?"

Amanda pulled her favorite cookbook out and placed it on the kitchen counter. "She didn't act too thrilled about going anywhere today, and I think she only agreed to have a sisters' day just to please Karen." She released a heavy sigh. "I'm still worried about Doretta. Although she appears to be less depressed, I've seen the sorrow in her eyes at times, and sometimes I feel that she's merely putting on an act for our benefit."

Elmer put his arm around her waist. "You need to quit fretting. Our daughter has to work through the grief she feels in her own way and time, and we've talked about this before. You and I both know there is nothing we can do to hasten it."

"I know, but . . ."

He halted her words with a tender kiss. "Be there to listen when Doretta wants to talk, and remember to keep praying."

Amanda managed a smile and a nod. Her husband's advice was good, but as a mother who loved her children very much, it was hard not to be concerned when they were hurting. *If Doretta would just show some signs of her faith in God returning, I'd feel much better about things. Guess that's the one thing I need to pray the most about, and I also need to give my own anxieties to the Lord.*

CHAPTER 21

Spring blossomed into a warm, humid summer, and as the days played out, Doretta's feelings for Warren grew stronger. While she would have liked to have been happy about this change, she felt guilty instead. It wasn't right to have strong feelings for him when he was dating someone else. Worse yet, Doretta felt as if she was betraying William. When they'd confessed their love for one another more than a year ago, she had told him that he was the only man she would ever love. William had echoed that sentiment.

I have definitely gone back on my word to William, Doretta told herself as she removed a pair of her father's trousers from the clothesline. *Fortunately, Warren has no idea how I feel about him, so at least I don't have to worry about the embarrassment or guilt I would feel if I told him the truth.*

Thinking about her feelings for William's

brother was enough to make Doretta depressed again, and she couldn't allow that to happen. *Keep busy,* she told herself. *If I look for things to do, I won't have to think about all of this.* Pulling off one of Papa's work shirts, her thoughts continued. *If I would have perished in the accident instead of William, would he have eventually married someone else, or would he have kept his promise to love only me?*

Doretta reached for another shirt and gave it a shake before placing it in the wicker basket by her feet. *I am sure he would have grieved for me just as I have for him.* She let her arms go limp. *Maybe I'm overthinking my situation. I've had time to grieve for William, and at some point I should move on with my life, but what about the promise I made to him?*

Doretta took the rest of the clothes off the line, placed them in the basket, and headed for the house. She had only made it halfway there, when Karen's cat, Olive, skittered across her path, chasing after one of the other barn cats. Doretta lost her balance, couldn't regain it, and went down, along with everything in the basket. Clearly unmindful of what she had done, Olive made a dash for the barn.

Doretta groaned as she sat up and surveyed the damage. Her father and brother's trousers looked okay, but most of the towels were soiled. "Always trouble somewhere," she muttered. "Now I have another load of laundry to do. Well, at least that crazy katz has been spending more time outside lately instead of in the house, where she's always underfoot and causing trouble. I just wish Olive wasn't so full of mischief. It's really difficult to like her."

"A strange thing happened when I woke up this morning," Margaret told Warren as they worked together putting several new items out on the shelves.

He tipped his head. "What was it?"

"When I went out to feed the horses, before entering the barn, I discovered a mare I'd never seen before in our corral, and a note was attached to the gate." Her forehead wrinkled. "So apparently the horse was dropped off sometime during the night."

"Seriously?"

"Jah, isn't that strange?"

"Very. What'd the note say?"

"Only that the horse has a lot of problems and the person writing the note said they couldn't take care of the mare anymore. The horse's owner also stated that the mare needed a good home and that they wanted the new owner to be me." Margaret placed one hand on her hip. "I don't believe it's anyone I know personally, because I would have recognized the horse. The mare's owner must be someone who has heard about me, though, and my ability to work with problem horses."

Warren bobbed his head. "That's an unusual occurrence all right. What are you going to do about it?"

"I — I'm not sure, but the horse seems nice and calm, so I may want to keep her, unless the real owner changes their mind and comes to claim her."

"Doesn't sound like they want the horse or they wouldn't have left her in your corral with a note. It also seems strange that they wouldn't state their name or give you specific information about the mare's problems." His brows lowered. "Maybe the horse was stolen and someone wants to make it look like you took her."

Margaret sucked in her bottom lip. "I — I can't imagine why anyone would do that, but I do plan to try and find the owner."

"How are you going to go about that?"

"I could hang some flyers or run an ad in the local newspaper."

"Guess it's worth a try." Warren paused to

put several bars of organic soap on the shelf closest to him.

"In the meantime, I'll take good care of Cocoa and try to help with whatever problems she has."

"You've named her already?"

"I didn't have to. Whoever wrote the note said Cocoa is the horse's name. I'm guessing they chose that name because the mare is the same color as cocoa."

"I see."

Margaret set a few jars of all-natural body lotion on the shelf near her, then she turned to look at Warren again. "Would you be free to come by my house after we get off work so you can see the horse?"

"I could have, but I agreed to go to the bishop's house for supper with my mamm and daed this evening, and if I went by your house, I'd probably get home too late to change and head out with my folks."

"Oh, I see." Margaret couldn't keep the disappointment she felt out of her tone. As unfortunate as it was, she felt certain that Warren wasn't really interested in meeting the horse and had used the supper invitation as an excuse to get out of going to her house. If Warren thought it was more important to have his evening meal at the bishop's house, then so be it. Margaret would go home after work and spend some time by herself getting acquainted with her potential new horse before helping her mother prepare supper. Then, when the meal was over, Margaret would go back outside and stay with Cocoa until bedtime.

When Margaret arrived home late that afternoon, she rushed to the barn without even going to the house to change her clothes. She had put Cocoa in Honey's old stall before leaving for work and needed to find out how the horse was doing.

Upon entering the stall, Margaret discovered the mare chomping on what was left of an apple. She smiled. "Someone must have given you a treat recently, didn't they, girl? I bet it was my thoughtful mamm."

Cocoa dropped the piece of apple and nickered. Then she moseyed on over, wrapped her warm neck around Margaret's shoulders, and nuzzled her ear.

Margaret's heart nearly melted like butter on a hot summer day. This horse seemed so loving. She couldn't imagine why anyone would have given her away or what problems Cocoa might have. Margaret hadn't felt so much love coming from a horse since Honey died. "Maybe you need me as much as I need you," she murmured, gently rubbing Cocoa's silky neck. "Any problems you might have, I'm sure I can take care of, and I won't give up working with you until I do."

Cocoa gave a low whinny as if in agreement, and at that moment, Margaret decided that she wanted — no needed — to keep this beautiful cocoa-colored horse as her own. Maybe God had graciously given the mare to her as a replacement for the gentle, sweet horse she had loved and lost.

"Would you like a glass of milk and a few cookies?" Warren's mother asked after they'd returned from Bishop John's place, where they'd had supper.

Warren shook his head. "No thanks, Mom. I'm still too full from all that food John's wife fed us. But maybe Dad will want something to snack on after he puts his horse and buggy away."

"I doubt it, and you're right — it was a filling meal." Mom pulled out a chair at the kitchen table. "You were kind of quiet all evening. Is there something troubling you, Son?"

"Jah, to be honest, there is."

"Want to talk about it?"

He lifted his shoulders in a brief shrug.

"It might help you feel better to share

whatever is bothering you."

"Maybe so." Warren took a seat opposite hers. "I'm stressed out over my relationship with Margaret."

"Have you two had a disagreement?"

"Not really. We just don't have much in common. All she seems to want to talk about is her horse training. I try to be interested, but I have other things on my mind, and it seems like Margaret couldn't care less about anything other than what's going on in her own life."

Mom tipped her head. "What kind of things are on your mind?"

"My business, for one thing. I take my job seriously and am dedicated to providing my customers with the newest and best products beneficial to their health."

"Since Margaret works at the nutrition center with you, I would think she'd feel the same way."

"She does okay at work and always keeps busy, but during our slack times or lunch breaks, all she talks about is all the problems the horses that have been brought to her have and how she plans to fix them. And she's always after me to go horseback riding with her. Guess in Margaret's mind, a really fun date is going riding." Warren rapped his knuckles against the tabletop. "I realize that horses are important to our mode of transportation, but I'm not obsessed with them the way Margaret is. I think if she ever starts making enough money through donations from the people who bring their problem horses to her, she'll quit working for me."

"Has she actually said that?"

"Not in so many words, but she's hinted at it a few times."

"What would you do if Margaret quit her job at your store?"

"If Doretta was interested and felt up to the task, I'd hire her to work five days a week. She's a good worker and seems interested in the business."

Mom sat quietly for several seconds. "You always speak highly of Doretta. Do you have feelings for her that go beyond friendship?"

Warren's eyes widened, and he nearly fell out of his chair. Had he said something to his mother previously that would reveal the way he felt for Doretta, or was Mom's intuition at work? *Should I be honest, try to skirt around the question by changing the subject, or would it be better if I said this was something I didn't want to talk about and headed up to my room for bed?*

Mom reached across the table and placed her hand on his. "You don't have to answer if you're not comfortable talking about it."

Warren drew in a deep breath and decided to go for it. Maybe his mother could offer some good advice. "The truth is, Mom, I'm in love with Doretta, and I have been for a long time — even before she and William began dating."

She nodded. "I've suspected as much — especially since your bruder died."

"I feel guilty about it, though."

"You've done nothing wrong, so why would you feel guilty?"

"William loved Doretta, and if he hadn't passed away, she would have become his wife, and she'd now be my sister-in-law."

"True, but he's not with us now."

"I know, but . . ."

"Have you told Doretta how you feel about her?"

"No."

"Are you going to?"

"I — I don't know, but if I decided to tell her, I'd need to break up with Margaret first."

"That makes sense. Have you prayed about the matter?"

"Jah, but nothing has come clear to me yet." He drew in a few quick breaths. "I know it might seem odd, but I feel as though I need William's approval, and that's sure not gonna happen."

"You're right, so trust the Lord. He is the only one who can give you peace in your heart. And my advice is to keep praying and asking God to guide and direct you concerning Margaret as well as Doretta."

"Okay, I'll do that. Danki for listening, Mom. Oh, and can I ask a favor?"

"Certainly."

"Please don't tell anyone, not even Dad, what I've shared with you this evening. I would feel terrible if Margaret or Doretta got wind of any of the things I've said."

"Don't worry, Warren. I will keep it all to myself and join you in prayer about the direction God wants you to take."

Warren felt a little better hearing that. He would keep praying, but he still had some doubts about how God would reveal to him what he should or should not do.

CHAPTER 22

Doretta and William stood in front of the bishop, answering his questions that would unite them in marriage. She smiled and looked into her husband's mesmerizing blue eyes. He smiled back, but his dimple was in the wrong place.

Doretta's brows furrowed as she continued to stare at him. What's going on here? *she asked herself.* Something is wrong. This can't be William; he's dead. Did I agree to marry his twin brother instead?

The scene changed suddenly, and Doretta saw herself standing in front of William's gravestone with tears rolling down her cheeks. In the next minute, she was enveloped in Warren's arms. "Who do I love?" *she sobbed.* "Is it William or Warren? They played tricks on me when we were children. Are they trying to fool me now too?"

Doretta's eyes snapped open, and she sat

up with a start. Staring into the darkness of her bedroom, she released a heavy sigh that transformed into a deep moan. It was only a dream, but oh, it had seemed so real. She could still see William's face. Or had it been Warren smiling at her on their wedding day?

What did that dream mean? Doretta asked herself. *William is gone, and I'll never be his wife, but am I supposed to be with Warren?* She shook her head. *No, that can never be. He's with Margaret, and I made a commitment to William.*

Doretta's hands shook as she pushed the covers aside and rose from the bed. She needed something to calm her nerves and hopefully relax her enough so that she could get back to sleep. She lifted the shade covering her window and saw a sliver of a moon. It made her remember that the other day she'd pulled the satchel from Eleanor out of her desk and read a few more suggestions her friend had written on the papers inside. One read: *Look up at the moon and thank God for all He created.* Doretta knew deep in her heart that God was the creator of all things. Even so, the faith she'd put in Him before William's death had not returned. *Will I ever feel close to God again?* she asked herself. *What would it take to bring me back spiritually to the way I used to be?*

Doretta had read three more pieces of paper that day. One had said: *"Soak your feet in warm water."* The second one read: *"Put some lavender oil in a roller ball and roll it on your feet at night."* The third one said: *"Get up early to see the sunrise."* None of those things had helped Doretta feel any better, not even watching the sun come up. Eleanor may have meant well by taking the time to write on each piece of paper inside the satchel, but it had been for naught. Doretta did not feel one bit closer to God, and she wasn't sure that she ever would again.

She let the shade fall shut and turned away from the window. After fumbling around for the flashlight on the nightstand by her bed, she slipped her robe on, left the bedroom, and made her way carefully and quietly down the stairs.

As she approached the kitchen, Doretta heard a terrible racket. *What in the world could be happening in our kitchen right now?* As the clattering sound continued, she held the flashlight in front of her until the gas lantern hanging above the table came into view. When Doretta reached up and turned it on, she was surprised to see Karen's cat with her head stuck in a tin can.

"For goodness' sake, Olive, what do you think you're doing, and why are you in the house again?" Doretta bent down and grabbed hold of the squirming cat. "Hold still now, and let me get this can off your head."

Amanda rolled over in bed, tempted to wake her husband and ask if he'd heard the strange, clattering noise that had wakened her. She sat up and cupped a hand over her right ear to listen. The sound continued, and if she wasn't mistaken, it seemed to be coming from the kitchen. Amanda made a hasty decision not to disturb Elmer, so she reached for the flashlight by her side of the bed and turned it on, careful to keep the beam of light away from her sleeping husband's face.

When she felt sure that she hadn't wakened him, Amanda got up, grabbed her robe from the end of the bed, and slipped quietly out of the room. She stopped outside the bedroom and drew in several deep breaths, feeling leery of venturing down the hall on her own, not knowing what was going on in the kitchen or who she might find there. Amanda had second thoughts about her decision not to wake Elmer, and she almost returned to the bedroom. *I'll just walk quietly and take a peek,* she told herself. *If there's a stranger in the house, I will run right back to the bedroom and alert my husband.*

Amanda figured her fears were unfounded. Most likely, one of the children had gotten out of bed and was rummaging through the cupboard or refrigerator for something to eat or drink. That would seem strange at this time of night, and she wondered why they would be making so much noise. Surely whoever it was would have some consideration for other members of the family who were in bed sleeping.

Continuing cautiously down the hall, Amanda saw a light coming from the kitchen. *If it's one of my kinner, I really have to wonder which one of them could be up at this late hour.* As the clattering noise grew louder, and she heard Doretta's voice, Amanda rushed into the room. "What is going on here?"

With Karen's cat in her arms, Doretta turned to face Amanda and grimaced. "I came downstairs after waking up from an unsettling dream and found Olive with her head stuck in a can. It wasn't easy to get it off because she wouldn't hold still and kept trying to scratch me with her sharp claws." She pointed to the cat, who continued to squirm. "But I finally won out and didn't let Olive get the best of me."

Amanda rolled her eyes. "I've lost track of how many times I have told your sister to put that cat outside before going to bed. I bet Karen had Olive in her room, and the troublesome feline snuck down to the kitchen in search of some food she didn't need."

"That's probably what happened all right, and she must have found an empty can that never got put in the garbage." Doretta moved toward the backdoor. "I'm going to put this little stinker outside, and then I'll fix myself a cup of chamomile tea to help settle my nerves. Between the stressful dream I had and having to deal with a squirming, uncooperative cat, my insides feel all shaky."

"I understand because I felt pretty nervous for a little while too. I'll heat the teakettle and join you for tea."

While Doretta took care of the cat, Amanda heated the water and got out the teabags. Soon the two were seated at the table with cups full of warm, calming herbal tea.

"What kind of dream did you have that caused you to feel the need to get out of bed and fix some tea?" Amanda questioned.

Doretta blew on her chamomile tea and

took a sip before responding to the question. "It was about William and Warren."

"Oh?"

"It began with William and me standing before Bishop John to become husband and wife, and then I realized I was marrying Warren, not William." Doretta's mouth trembled. "As the dream continued, I stood at William's gravesite, and Warren was there, holding me in his arms. I felt comforted and safe, Mama. And the truth is, I feel that way whenever I'm around Warren." She paused and drank some tea. "He makes me laugh when I'm sad, and when there are no customers in the store, Warren and I usually take some time to sit and visit awhile. I can share my feelings about William with Warren, and it's a comfort to know that he understands."

"Do you love him?" Amanda asked, seeing her daughter's wistful expression.

"You mean William?"

"No, I was referring to Warren."

Doretta lowered her gaze to the table. "It doesn't matter how I feel about him. I can never be Warren's aldi."

"Are you certain of that?"

"Jah, Mama. You know that he's with Margaret, and they will no doubt end up getting married."

303

"But she hasn't joined the church yet."

"No, but he has, and when he proposes, I'm sure she will prepare for joining."

"If he proposes, don't you mean?"

"I'm sure he will, Mama."

Amanda drank some tea and set her cup down. "That remains to be seen."

They sat quietly for a while as they finished their tea.

"If you love Warren," Amanda said, "I think you should let him know."

Doretta shook her head. "I can't do that. I'm sure he doesn't feel anything more for me than friendship. And even if he did, it wouldn't change the promise I made to William that he would be the only man I'd ever love."

"But he's not here anymore, and I don't believe —"

"I can't talk about this anymore. I need to go back to bed and try to get back to sleep. Morning will be here before we know it." Doretta pushed away from the table and went to place her empty cup in the sink. "Good night, Mama. I hope you'll be able to fall asleep again too, and I'm sorry you were awakened by that terrible racket made by Olive, the ornery katz."

"It's all right. I'm a mother, and it wasn't the first time my sleep has been interrupted." Amanda chuckled softly. "I'm sure it won't be the last either."

Doretta paused by the kitchen door. "Mama, I do have a favor to ask."

"What is it, dear one?"

"Please don't tell anyone about my confused feelings for Warren, okay? I would be so embarrassed if the word got out and Warren heard about it." Doretta's neck bent slightly forward. "If Warren knew how I really felt about him, I'd have to quit my job."

"I won't tell anyone," Amanda said. "But I do think at some point you should tell him."

"I can't, and I've already told you the reasons." Doretta whirled around and rushed out of the room.

Amanda remained at the table listening to the sound of Doretta's feet going up the stairs. *My daughter needs to let go of William,* Amanda concluded. *The promise she made to him when he was alive is no longer binding. Why can't she see that and move on with her life?*

With her head bowed and eyes closed, Amanda prayed silently: *Heavenly Father, please give my daughter a sense of peace about things while You guide and direct her steps. If it's meant for Doretta and Warren to be together, then please let them both know.*

Paradise

Eleanor opened the shade at the kitchen window and looked outside to witness a beautiful sunrise lighting up the sky with dramatic-looking hues of red, orange, and pink. Eleanor had discovered some information about sunrises and sunsets in a book she'd gotten from the library when she was a teenager. She'd learned that at both sunrise and sunset, when the path of light through the atmosphere was longer, the shorter-wavelength blues and greens in the sky were almost completely invisible, leaving the longer-wavelength oranges and reds that so often dominate the morning and evening sky. Eleanor didn't really care about the scientific reason for sunrises or sunsets, though. She simply enjoyed their breathtaking beauty and made it a point to watch them as often as possible.

Eleanor smiled. *I'll never forget the vivid, gorgeous sunsets Vic and I saw during our trip to Sarasota before Rosetta was born. Watching the sun go down over the Gulf of Mexico was the highlight of every day we spent on our vacation. And there were the lovely sunrises too. Oh, such beauty to behold!*

Maybe when Rosetta is a little older, we can visit Florida again. I'm sure our little girl would have a great time playing in the sand, looking for shells, and splashing around in the water with her daddy and me.

Remaining at the window, Eleanor breathed in and out slowly as she continued to watch the sunrise until the mixture of colors disappeared. It was hard to believe they were in the middle of summer already, but the weeds in her garden, along with the bounty of produce coming up from the fertile dirt, was proof. Eleanor did most of her gardening and outdoor chores during the early morning hours, when the weather was cooler and not so humid. While she took care of her outside chores, she enjoyed putting Rosetta in her stroller so the baby could watch her and benefit from the fresh air before the day heated up.

Vic had left for work earlier than usual today, and Rosetta was still asleep, so this gave Eleanor a little time to herself to watch the sunrise, do her devotions, and spend some time in prayer. Doretta was always high on the list of people Eleanor prayed for, and today her dear friend came to mind. She hadn't heard from Doretta for several weeks again, and it concerned her. Had she been too busy to call or write, or was there something else keeping her from corresponding? Eleanor hoped her friend had begun reading the Bible again and that Doretta's faith in God had been restored. But without hearing from her, she couldn't know.

With her Bible in hand, Eleanor took a seat at the table and prayed for Doretta. Then she read First Peter 5:7 out loud: " 'Casting all your care upon him; for he careth for you.' " Eleanor felt thankful for the reminder that she didn't need to feel anxious and that God cared for her as well as Doretta. She would continue to write her friend letters, and if it be God's will, maybe she, Vic, and Rosetta could make a trip to Grabill later this summer. It would be wonderful to see her parents and siblings again and reconnect with Doretta. Seeing her friend in person would give her the best read on how she was doing. She'd have to speak with Vic about this idea soon.

Grabill

Margaret's saddle creaked softly beneath her as Cocoa moved at a gentle, even pace along the trail. She took in the sights of overgrown sections where the trail almost disappeared and noted the wildflowers and berries along the way. She enjoyed listening to birds chirping and the horse's shoes clopping as they moved along the dirt path. Perspiration dampened her skin, but Margaret didn't mind. She felt one with her beautiful horse, and it pleased her to know that Cocoa must have been ridden before, for she had taken to it so easily.

It was an ongoing mystery as to who had given her such a beautiful animal. *If I knew who had left Cocoa here, I could at least thank them.* Margaret clicked her tongue to quicken Cocoa's pace, since Dutch was right behind them. *Well, maybe it doesn't matter who gave Cocoa away. They obviously wanted me to have her, so I'm going to stop thinking about it and be thankful.* It had been almost two months since Margaret found the easygoing mare in the corral, and she was glad that no one had answered any of her ads and reclaimed the horse.

She glanced over at Warren, wearing his helmet and looking straight ahead as he rode on the back of his gelding, Dutch. How nice it was that her boyfriend had finally agreed to spend part of his day off to ride with her along this country trail on such a warm, cloudless day. They hadn't done much together lately, and she'd felt neglected. Warren clearly didn't care as much for horses as Margaret did, but at least he had put himself out by coming with her today, and she appreciated it. In fact, she took this as a sign that he must care deeply for her. Margaret wondered how long it would be before Warren proposed marriage to her. As soon as he did, she would prepare for joining the Amish church, and they would set a date and begin planning their wedding.

"Remember that note I told you about — the one that was left the morning I discovered Cocoa in our corral?" Margaret looked at Warren again.

"Jah."

"The owner said that the horse had problems, but so far I've found none." Margaret laughed. "She does have a habit of pulling her food out of the rack and onto the floor before eating it, but I don't see that as a problem. To be honest, I think it's kind of cute."

"I'm glad the gaul is workin' out for you. I know how bad you felt when Honey died."

"I still miss her, but not as much anymore. Cocoa has definitely become my horse, and I'm glad her owner never came back to claim her."

"It was probably someone who couldn't take care of the animal," he responded. "Maybe they didn't have enough money or had become physically unable to tend the horse any longer."

"That could be. Either way, I believe that Cocoa being left in my care was meant to be. My daed even said it was quite likely an answer to prayer."

"Whose prayer — yours or your father's?"

"Both. Dad knew how upset I was when Honey died, so I'm sure he was praying for me."

She patted the mare's neck and was rewarded with a gentle whinny. As they rode through a sunny spot along the trail and entered a shaded area, the cooler temperatures were a welcome reprieve.

Margaret looked straight ahead to make sure they were still on the path, then she glanced back at Warren and smiled. "If there's one thing I've learned while working with horses, it's that no two are alike. Like people, they all have different personalities and abilities. I have also come to realize that horse training is not just teaching the animals to do certain things or unlearn a bad behavior. It's about the trainer understanding the horse and coaxing him or her toward a specific goal. Trust and building a relationship come slowly. Oh, and I've never believed in using fear as a technique for training," she added. "Horses need to feel safe and cared for. Every gesture we make to our horses means something to them. They can sense our emotions too."

"I'm sure that must be true." Warren nodded, shifting in his saddle as he wiped some sweat from his brow.

They continued down the trail in silence. A doe jumped unexpectedly out of the woods right in front of them. Margaret managed to keep control of Cocoa, but Warren wasn't so lucky. Dutch reared up, and seconds after the deer darted into the bushes on the opposite side of the trail, Margaret watched in horror as Warren slipped out of his saddle and landed on the ground with a sickening thud. Dutch stood nearby, looking confused and maybe a bit guilty, with the reins lopsided and hanging down from his neck. Margaret quickly dismounted, grabbed both horses' reins, and secured them to a nearby tree limb. Her heart pounding, she raced over to Warren and dropped to her knees beside him. "Are you okay? Are you hurt?"

Warren gave no response, but at least she saw from the rise and fall of his chest that he was breathing. Margaret knew that when a person fell from a horse, almost any part of their body could be injured. Breaks or a strain to arms, wrists, and collarbones were common when riders tried to break their fall by putting their arms out. She was also aware that riders could be badly injured when a horse stepped on or fell upon them. The horse could also end up getting hurt if it fell.

Margaret drew in a deep breath in an effort not to panic, but she knew Warren needed help and right away. Thankfully, she had brought her cell phone with her today and was quick to call for help. She hoped and prayed that whatever injuries her boyfriend had incurred, they were not serious.

CHAPTER 23

Fort Wayne

Warren's mother took a seat beside her husband in one of the hospital waiting rooms. A small table covered with glossy magazines was next to them, but Betty didn't care about those. She was eager to hear how their son was doing and hoped his injuries were not serious.

Betty shuddered and stared toward the doors where Warren was receiving emergency care. The thought of losing another son was unbearable, but she had to keep the faith. Surely Warren would be okay. He had to be. She couldn't endure it if he died too.

Her throat felt dry, and she kept shifting against the seat cushions behind her back, trying to find a comfortable position. Her handbag lay in her lap, and Betty began fiddling with the strap. Sitting here so helpless waiting for some word on Warren's condition was fast becoming unbearable. Why didn't someone come and give them some news? Low whispers, throat clearing, coughing, and the rustle of clothing from other people who sat nearby were enough to make her want to scream. Betty held herself in check, though. She couldn't have a meltdown in public. What would people think?

"Stop fidgeting and try to relax." Raymond pried Betty's fingers loose from her purse strap and held tightly to her hand. "I'm sure we'll hear something about Warren's condition soon."

"I hope so. Waiting and wondering how our son is doing is ever so hard." She looked over at Margaret, who sat in a chair on the other side of her, picking at a cuticle on a thumbnail. "Danki for letting us know right away what happened on your and Warren's trail ride."

Margaret's gaze met hers. "Of course. I knew you'd want to meet me here, and I'm glad you were able to get a driver so quickly. I was relieved when Virgil and Patrick came to get Dutch and Cocoa and called a driver for me. I wanted to ride in the ambulance with Warren but couldn't leave the horses until my brothers showed up."

"We understand, and at least you got here before we did, although it's unfortunate that you don't know anything more about Warren's condition than we do at this point," Raymond said.

Betty drew in her lower lip and blurted, "Warren doesn't enjoy horseback riding that much, you know. He should have said no when you asked him to go with you today."

Margaret teared up. "You're right. Warren could have said no, but he didn't, so I just assumed —"

A man wearing a stethoscope around his neck entered the room, called Betty and Raymond's names, and introduced himself as Dr. Woods. They both stood and hurriedly joined him.

"Is our son going to be all right? Is he seriously hurt?" Betty's questions came out in a rush.

"His injuries are not life-threatening," the doctor responded, "but he will be laid up for a while. We've done several tests, including X-rays, a CT scan, and an MRI. Warren's left ankle is broken, and his tailbone's badly bruised. He also has a slight concussion. If your son hadn't been wearing a helmet while riding his horse, it could have been much worse."

Betty drew in a deep breath and expelled it quickly. "Thank the good Lord!"

"Jah, He is always good." Raymond patted his wife's shoulder and then looked back at the doctor. "How long will our son need to stay in the hospital, and how will his injuries be treated?"

"We'll keep him here a few days, but when he goes home, he'll have to rest and keep weight off his foot. We'll get the swelling down with ice and elevation, and then he will be fitted with an inflatable boot to keep the bone in place. Warren will also be given a pair of crutches so he won't be tempted to put his full weight on the injured ankle. If crutches aren't to his liking and cause too much pain under his armpits, another option for getting around would be a steerable mobility knee scooter. That would allow Warren to be more independent despite his injury."

"Where would we get such a thing?" Betty questioned.

"They're available at most medical supply stores, and most of them aren't too expensive."

"How long will it take for our son's ankle to heal?" Raymond asked.

"Normally, it'll take anywhere from six to twelve weeks. During that time, your son will need to come in for regular X-rays to check the bone."

"That makes sense," Raymond said.

Betty's eyes widened. "Oh dear, Warren probably won't be able to work at the nutrition center for some time." She looked over at Raymond. "I could take over for him there, but Warren will need my care at home, so I can't be in two places at once."

"Don't worry; we'll figure something out." Raymond patted her arm again.

Margaret joined them. "I can go back to working five days a week, and maybe Doretta can work full-time with me too."

Raymond nodded. "We can discuss it with Warren when he feels up to talking."

"Speaking of which . . ." Betty looked back at the doctor. "Can we see our son now?"

"Of course. Once he is situated in a room, I'll have one of the nurses come and get you."

"Thank you." Betty heaved a sigh of relief. Warren was hurt, but he would be okay. He just needed to rest and take it easy, and above all, he should stay off the back of his horse from now on and quit giving in to Margaret's requests. She was not the right woman for him. Betty felt sure of it.

Grabill

"Are you doing okay, Son? Do you need anything right now?"

Warren sat up from where he'd been lying on the couch and groaned. "Jah, I need to get off this couch and return to work."

Mom shook her head. "You can't do that yet, Son. Why, your accident was only a week ago, and you've been home from the hospital for just four days. So please try to be patient. Besides, Margaret and Doretta are working in the store and taking care of things there, so you have nothing to concern yourself about."

"I suppose you're right, and I do appreciate them taking over in my absence while I'm laid up." He winced a bit while shifting on the couch. "Guess I'm just feeling restless and impatient right now."

"I understand that. If I were laid up, I'd be impatient too." She handed him a glass of water and a pill. "It's time for your pain meds now."

"No thanks. I don't need them."

"Are you sure? There's no reason for you to suffer needlessly."

"I'm okay, Mom, but I'll let you know if I should need a pill." Warren paused and took a drink. "Thanks for the cold *wasser,* though, because I'm hot and thirsty."

"You're welcome, Son. I'll leave you alone now, but I will be back when it's time for lunch." She gave his shoulder a gentle tap and hurried from the room.

Warren drank the rest of his water, leaned over to set it on the coffee table, and then laid his head back against the pillow. He'd never been one to lie around, and the thought of having his mother doting over him made being home all day seem even worse. He'd known she would try to mother him, because ever since William's death, Mom had been a worrywart. But whenever she hovered, it got on his nerves.

Warren closed his eyes and allowed himself to relive the accident that had put him in this frustrating predicament. After Dutch caught sight of that deer and reared up, Warren had felt himself helplessly slipping out of his saddle. He'd seen the horse's shoulder and realized he was looking up at the animal's mane. That's when he knew there was no way of catching his balance. No matter how much he wished it wasn't true, he knew he was going down. As Warren had been falling, he'd closed his eyes, and that was the last thing he remembered until he'd woken up in the hospital in excruciating pain.

Even now, his bruised tailbone throbbed liked crazy, along with his ankle. He also felt as though his neck had suffered whiplash, although he'd never mentioned it while at the hospital. With all the tests they'd put him through, if it had been a serious neck injury like Doretta's, they would certainly have discovered it. In addition to the major injuries, Warren had plenty of bruises from his rough landing. He'd been self-doctoring by taking *Arnica* pellets, as well as rubbing *Arnica* gel on his injuries, but it would be awhile before the black-and-blue color faded. Warren felt sure that he needed a stronger dose of *Arnica* — the 10m potency, which unfortunately he hadn't kept in stock at the nutrition center. Warren had asked Margaret to order the more potent dose, but as far as he knew, it hadn't been delivered to the store yet. If the homeopathic remedy had arrived, surely Margaret would have brought it by the house for him.

All Warren could do was try to be patient and wait for the remedy to arrive. Then he had to hope and pray that it would help reduce the swelling, bruising, and pain. Warren did not want to continue taking the prescription drug he'd been given at the hospital. He preferred using natural remedies unless there was no other choice. Also, Warren was determined to make the crutches work, because he didn't want to spend extra money for a knee scooter, which would probably have its own set of issues.

■ ■ ■ ■

Doretta made her way to the back room to open a box of supplements that had come in that morning. They'd been quite busy today, and Margaret had been up front handling customers' purchases most of the time while Doretta answered their questions and did some restocking. It seemed strange to be working without Warren. She missed being able to ask him questions, and even more so, she missed the times that she and Warren had spent talking about William and so many other things. Doretta had been deeply concerned when she'd heard about his accident, but she was relieved when she'd learned that Warren's injuries were not life-threatening.

She wondered how Margaret could keep her mind focused on her work with her boyfriend at home, no doubt in pain and needing care. Doretta thought about how yesterday, when they were between customers, Margaret had admitted that it had been her idea for the two of them to go horseback riding the day of Warren's accident. The strange thing was, when Margaret told Doretta this, she didn't seem to show much remorse. She had said it as though she was simply relaying information.

It would be hard for me not to be concerned about Warren, but I should not be judging Margaret because I don't know how she truly feels. Besides, Warren is not my boyfriend. I am glad that he is going to be all right, though, Doretta told herself as she reached into the cardboard box and removed four bottles of magnesium citrate. She couldn't imagine how Warren's parents would have dealt with losing another son.

If Warren had died, it would have affected me deeply as well, Doretta admitted as she opened a box of homeopathic supplements. Several bottles were marked *Arnica* 10m, which were the ones Warren had requested for his own use while recovering from the injuries he'd sustained when he'd tumbled off his horse. Doretta figured Margaret would take them to him on her way home from work, so she took the bottles up front to the checkout counter and waited until an Amish woman paid for her purchases and left the store.

"These just arrived." She handed the bottles to Margaret. "They are the homeopathic remedies Warren had told you that he wanted for his own use, so I figured you'd want to take them to him at the end of our workday."

Margaret pursed her lips. "I would deliver them, but I've recently begun working with another new horse, so I need to get home as soon as I can. Would you be able to take the remedies to Warren?"

"Jah, I could, and since his parents' house is on my way, I'll ask my driver to stop there before taking me home."

"Danki, I appreciate that so much. With me being here all week now, it cuts into my time for working with the horses, and two horses with issues are in our barn right now."

"No problem. I don't mind at all. In fact, it'll give me a chance to see how Warren is doing."

"Okay, good. You might grab an extra tube of *Arnica* gel to take him too. That stuff goes quickly when you're using it on multiple places."

"I will." Doretta took the remedies and placed them in the tote bag she'd put in Warren's office when she'd arrived that morning. *I can't help thinking that Margaret and Warren's relationship seems a little off. Margaret seems to be more worried about a new horse she's training than she is about her boyfriend and his well-being.*

Doretta would be glad when the CLOSED

sign could be put in the window and she could be on her way to see Warren.

When Mom stepped into the room and announced that Doretta was there, Warren pulled himself to a sitting position, eager to see her, as always. "How'd things go at the store today?" he asked.

"Real well. We had lots of customers and kept busy the entire day." She moved across the room and handed a paper sack to Warren. "Your *Arnica* 10m came in today, so I brought that by, along with a new tube of *Arnica* gel. I figured you would want to get those as soon as possible."

"Jah, I sure do." Warren glanced at the spot where his mother had been standing and was relieved to see that she'd left the room. "I had told Margaret to watch for the order and get them to me as soon as it arrived." He leaned slightly forward. "Did she ask you to bring me these remedies instead of her?"

Doretta nodded. "She's working with a new horse and wanted to get home right after work to proceed with her training. Actually, Margaret said she has two horses in their barn that she's working with right now."

That's not much of a surprise. Warren's face

tightened as he squelched a frown. *This is just one more proof that Margaret cares more about spending time with troubled horses than she does doing helpful things for me. I need to find the courage and the right time to break things off with her because our relationship isn't going anywhere, and I'm sure she knows it as well as I do.*

"Would you like to sit down and visit awhile?" Warren's mother asked, coming back into the room, holding a tray with two glasses of iced tea. "I've brought you both something cold to drink." She placed the tray on the coffee table and took a step back.

"I appreciate the offer," Doretta said in a pleasant tone, "but my driver is waiting outside in her vehicle, and I don't want to keep her any longer." She looked at Warren. "Before I go, though, I'd like to know how you're doing."

"I'm still having some discomfort in my ankle and tailbone, but it's nothing I can't handle." He opened the bag and looked inside. "I'm sure these homeopathic remedies will be a big help to me, though. Danki for bringing them by."

"I'm happy I could help." She hesitated a moment, then added, "I'm sure it must be hard for you to be laid up here, having to deal with pain when you'd probably rather be at your store."

"You've got that right," he said with a nod. "I don't like lying around when I should be tending to my business."

"My son is too impatient," Mom put in. "He's never been one to sit around idly, and I think he has the silly notion that the nutrition center will fall apart without him."

Warren bit back a retort. He certainly wasn't going to say anything disrespectful to his mother — especially in front of Doretta. Truth was, Mom was at least partially right. Even though Warren felt sure that the store was in good hands, he couldn't help but worry about how things were going in his absence. After all, the business was his livelihood, and he wanted people who shopped there to say good things about it.

Just as soon as I'm up and around and able to use my crutches with ease, I am going back to work. I may have to sit around with my leg propped up most of the day, but at least I'll be able to see for myself how things are really going.

CHAPTER 24

A week later, Warren hobbled down the hall with the aid of his uncomfortable crutches and sniffed deeply of the delicious aroma coming from the kitchen. When he entered the room, he discovered his mother sitting at the table. "What are you making for lunch?" he asked.

"I have some chicken noodle soup heating on the stove for us, and there's a loaf of gluten-free bread warming in the oven to have with it." Mom's voice sounded strained, and her somber expression made Warren wonder if she might be unhappy or stressed about something. A cardboard box sat in front of her with the flaps open.

"What are you up to there?" he asked. "What's in that box?"

She looked up to him with tears in her eyes. "I put this off long enough. I've been going through the last of your brother's things."

When Warren saw the look of discomfort on his mother's face, he had to fight his own tears of regret. Although looking at William's things would be painful, he felt compelled to see what was inside the box. Maybe going through the last of William's effects would help bring more closure for both him and his mother. He couldn't help being curious about what the square container held inside.

"Can I help you with that?" he offered.

"Jah, that would be nice." She gestured for him to take the seat next to hers.

Warren sat down and reached into the box. The first thing he pulled out was a pair of black suspenders.

"If you need a spare, you're welcome to take them," Mom said.

"No, that's okay. I still have several good ones of my own."

Mom retrieved a harmonica and held it for several seconds. "I miss hearing your brother play the mouth harp."

Warren squinted. "Mom, it's me who used to play that instrument. I haven't touched it, though, since William died, and I have no idea how one of my harmonicas got put in there with William's things."

"I found it on the floor in his closet," Mom said. "Maybe he'd decided to try playing it and borrowed it from your room."

"If he was borrowing it, wouldn't he have asked me first?"

She shrugged her shoulders. "Maybe he was afraid you would say no."

Warren gave a huff. "Now why would I do that? William and I shared a lot of things with each other, and I certainly would not have refused to let him borrow the mouth harp."

"Maybe he wanted to try playing it on his own, and his plan was to surprise you with it."

"Jah, that could be, I suppose." Warren saw no point in continuing this discussion, so he stuck his hand in the box again. This time he pulled out a dark brown leather journal. He'd seen William write in it several times after Doretta had given it to him as a birthday present soon after they'd begun dating. Warren, however, had never read anything his brother had written in the journal. *But I'd like to read it now,* he thought. *It might make me feel closer to him somehow. And who knows — William may have even mentioned my mouth harp and why he'd taken it from my room.* Warren scratched his head. *It's strange, though, that I never even missed it. Of course, that could be because I have several harmonicas in different keys.*

"That looks like the journal Doretta gave your brother." Mom pointed at the book. "I found it in William's desk and placed it in the box, but haven't looked inside of it yet."

"I'm interested in what William has written in the journal, but reading the contents will be bittersweet."

She nodded. "At this point, it won't matter if you look inside to see what he'd written about, unless, of course, there's a personal matter about him and Doretta." She cleared her throat.

Warren didn't comment, but Mom might be right — there could be some personal things about his aldi inside William's journal. He gave the leather cover a couple of thumps with his knuckle. *It could be a little weird to read my brother's thoughts about the same girl we both care for. But I still miss William, and I believe this journal might make me feel a little closer to him.*

"My tailbone is beginning to hurt from sitting on this wooden chair too long," Warren told his mother. "Think I'll go back to the living room and sit on the couch awhile."

"Okay," Mom said quietly without looking at him. She continued to focus on the harmonica she held. "I'll close up the box until we are ready to look through more of it sometime later."

"Okay." Warren got up and, with the journal tucked under one arm, made his way back to the living room. He still didn't understand what his harmonica had been doing in William's closet. *Surely my brother couldn't have been jealous because I played and he didn't. That would be lecherich,* he thought. *William sang well and yodeled way better than I ever could. Shouldn't he have been satisfied with that?*

After seating himself and propping his foot on a pillow he'd put on the coffee table earlier, Warren placed the journal in his lap and opened the first page. Seeing William's handwriting put a lump in Warren's throat. *I hope what I read will give me some peace and not cause me to feel worse about my brother's passing.*

Yesterday was a great day, Warren silently read. *Mom invited my aldi to join us for Warren's and my birthday supper. Doretta and I haven't been dating very long, so I wasn't expecting her to give me a gift, but I was pleased when I opened her present and found this journal. I plan to use it for writing about special events that occur. I will also include my thoughts, hopes, and plans for the future, as well as some other personal things.*

Warren's chest ached as he reflected on

332

his twin's written words. *All those wonderful plans William made had vanished like a vapor the day his life ended. I wonder what my brother would have done differently if he'd known what the future held for him and Doretta.*

Warren closed the book when he heard Mom's voice calling him for lunch. He would read more from William's journal at another time. Right now, he'd better head for the kitchen and have some lunch so he would be ready for his driver to pick him up. Warren figured Mom wouldn't be happy when she discovered where he was headed, but he had to find out for himself how well things were going at his store.

Paradise

Eleanor took a seat on the front porch bench to enjoy the warmth of the sun and read a letter she'd received from Doretta today. Rosetta wasn't awake from her afternoon nap yet, so this was a good time to read the mail that had been delivered this morning. Eleanor would have done it sooner, but she'd been busy washing clothes, and then she had spent some time weeding in the garden while the baby watched from her stroller.

Checkers lay sleeping on the porch, close

to Eleanor's feet. No doubt, he was enjoying this sunny, blue-sky day too. Vic's dog had become a faithful companion to Eleanor during the day, but as soon as Vic returned home from work, the dog stayed close to him, which was fine by her. Eleanor would not have liked Checkers being underfoot while she cooked their evening meal, set the table, or cleaned up after supper. And once that was all done, she had enough to do getting Rosetta bathed and ready for bed.

Eleanor released a heavy sigh and swatted a pesky mosquito that had landed on her arm. She enjoyed seeing pretty fireflies at night, but mosquitoes were aggravating, and their bites could be incredibly itchy. So many other things about summer she liked, however — lush green plants with bright flowers, fruit clusters in the branches of their apple and cherry trees, and backyard barbecues and campfires. Eleanor's mouth watered, thinking about the tasty hot dogs and burgers Vic enjoyed barbecuing on their grill. Even when he overcooked them on occasion, she still enjoyed the taste.

Eleanor hadn't let go of her desire to make a trip to Indiana sometime this summer, but she did not want to go without Vic, even though he'd said she could hire a driver and go with Rosetta. His workload had increased, and the boss had informed all of his crew that, except for an emergency, no one could take any time off until things slowed down. Eleanor figured that may not happen until sometime this fall. Or it might mean they couldn't plan a trip until winter, which wouldn't be nearly as much fun, due to colder weather and probably snow.

Even so, she told herself, *I'm thankful and feeling blessed that Vic has a good-paying job that normally provides steady work throughout most of the year.* Some people weren't so fortunate, and they struggled to buy food and pay their bills. A new family had moved into their church district a few weeks ago, and Robert, the husband, still hadn't found a job. To make matters worse, his wife, Selma, had recently learned that she was pregnant with twins, and they already had five children under the age of ten. Fortunately, their church district had helped out, and so did several others who weren't Amish and lived in the area. What a blessing it was to be part of a community with people who cared about others.

Refocusing, Eleanor opened Doretta's letter and took out the piece of notepaper, eager to see what her friend had to say. Her eyes widened as she read about Warren's accident and the extent of his injuries. Eleanor was equally surprised to learn that Doretta and Margaret were both working full-time together at the nutrition center in Warren's absence. She hoped that arrangement was going okay. From what Doretta had said in a previous letter, Margaret wasn't the easiest person to work with, which was the reason Doretta had stated that she was glad she and Margaret worked separate days. Now, things were different, and Doretta would need to get along with Margaret if for no other reason than for Warren's sake.

Eleanor felt pleased that her friend seemed to be doing better emotionally, but she was still concerned about Doretta's spiritual welfare. Had she begun reading the Bible again? Was Doretta praying regularly and drawing closer to the Lord? Eleanor hoped her friend wasn't pushing herself even harder than she had been by finding more to do at work or home. Doretta needed to take some time to rest and allow God to heal her emotional pain.

Grabill

For the past two hours, Doretta had been working at the store by herself. She'd managed so far without Margaret's help but couldn't help fretting about how things would go if more than one customer showed up at a time. In addition to that, this summer day had brought hot and muggy weather. Even with the battery-operated fans she had placed in various locations inside the nutrition center, the building hadn't cooled down. She hoped it would not be a deterrent to anyone who came here to shop today.

Doretta took a paper towel from the roll they kept under the front counter and wiped the perspiration off her forehead. After throwing the wet paper away, she reached up and touched the scars on her forehead. They were still there but not nearly as noticeable as they'd been before she had begun gently massaging them with vitamin E oil. Maybe with continued use, the scars would fade completely away.

The bell on the front door jingled, and Doretta was surprised to see Warren enter with the aid of crutches. He hadn't told her he'd be coming by, but she was ever so glad to see him.

"How's it been going here today?" Warren asked as he approached the counter.

"Except for the excess heat in here, I guess things are going okay. There hasn't been as many customers as usual, but that could be due to the warmer weather."

"Jah, it's a hot one today. I hear the whir of the fans, so I'm guessing they're all set out?"

"I took care of that as soon as I got here this morning." She leaned forward, resting her elbows on the checkout counter. "I never expected to see you here today. It must be difficult for you to get around with those crutches and being unable to walk like you did before the accident."

"You've got that right. They haven't been easy to get used to, but I'm managing."

"That's good."

"Anyway, I had an appointment in town and wanted to stop here to see if everything is going okay." Warren glanced around. "Where's Margaret? Is she in one of the back rooms?"

Doretta shook her head. "Margaret left a few hours ago."

"Where'd she go?"

"Her home, I presume."

"How come?"

"She said she needed to meet someone who was having a difficult time with their horse."

"You've gotta be kidding!" A vein on the side of Warren's forehead protruded. "She had no right to take off like that and leave you here in the store alone. This really upsets me." His voice rose with each word he spoke.

"It's all right, Warren. I've been managing okay on my own so far this afternoon."

His jaw clenched visibly. "Glad to hear it, but even so, I have every right to be upset. Margaret knows better than to leave you alone while she runs off to look at some problem horse. If I'd known she would be so unreliable, I would have never hired her in the first place, let alone while I'm not here to oversee things." He moved behind the counter to stand beside Doretta. "Well, that settles it — I'll be staying here at the store with you till closing time today."

"There's no need for you to do that, Warren," Doretta argued. "You're still not fully recuperated, and I don't think —"

"I'm staying, and that's all there is to it. I can sit here behind the counter and check people out while you take care of other things."

"If you're sure . . ."

"I am, so please don't look so worried. You know, I'm really not that bad off . . . especially compared to one of the fellows in our church who works at a cabinet shop and recently lost two fingers on his left hand." Warren grimaced. "It would be really difficult for me to work having lost any of my fingers. But if something like that happened to me, I'd do the best I could under the circumstances, because I'm not a person who gives up easily."

Doretta didn't argue. After all, Warren owned this business, not her. "Okay, if you're sure you feel up to it, then you can take my place here, and I'll help out in whatever way you like."

"My ankle's not fully healed yet, but in other ways I'm doing better. I'm sure the higher potency of the *Arnica* I'm taking is the reason my pain has lessened and the bruises are almost gone."

"I'm happy to hear it," she said. "That makes me a firm believer in using homeo- pathic remedies."

He smiled. "Some folks are skeptical about homeopathy, herbal preparations, and different kinds of supplements. Unless they have tried them and seen what good can happen, they aren't believers in holistic medicine."

"Since working here, I've certainly learned a lot about certain supplements that I never knew before. I'm finding it all to be very educational and enlightening."

"I'm glad. It helps if a person who works in a health food store knows more than the customers so they can offer advice and answer questions when needed."

"I've done my best and will continue to do so as long as I'm working here." She got down from the wooden stool and offered it to him.

"Your job is secure for as long as you want." Warren leaned his crutches against the wall behind them and positioned himself on the stool, being careful to keep his foot with the broken ankle off the floor. "But Margaret's walking on thin ice, and I'll be having a talk with her soon." He brought his leg up to rest it on a shelf behind the counter. "Ah, that feels better."

She tilted her head. "Would you like the cushion from your office chair to sit on? It might be more comfortable."

"Actually, that would be a nice idea." He smiled.

Doretta was happy to help him out. From the moment he'd shown up this afternoon, her tension had faded. Doretta felt bad, though, that she'd been the one to tell Warren about Margaret leaving early. She was certain that he wouldn't fire Margaret because of this. After all, she was his girl-friend, and if he let Margaret go, it might affect their personal relationship.

I wish I could say something to smooth

things over, Doretta thought as she walked toward the back of the store to get his chair cushion and a rag to do some dusting. *But it's really none of my business how Warren chooses to handle this situation with her. What happens between him and Margaret is not my concern — although it could be if she gets mad at me for telling Warren why she left early today.* Doretta pulled her bottom lip in with her teeth. *But what else could I do? I wasn't about to lie to him by making up some excuse.*

After Doretta brought Warren the cushion, he placed it on the stool and seated himself again. He thanked her for the idea, and at that point, Warren seemed to be in a better mood.

Doretta brought Warren a bottle of water, and then she got the dust rag and began cleaning off the tops of some vitamin bottles that had a light coating of dust. *If I were Warren's aldi, I'd sure try harder to please him and would make every effort to keep true to my word. Apparently, Margaret doesn't re-alize how fortunate she is to have Warren as her boyfriend. If he and I were dating, I'd never deliberately do anything that would cause him to mistrust me.*

She shook her head. *My relationship with William wasn't perfect, but we were always honest with each other. I trusted him, and I am sure that he believed in me as well.*

A pang of regret shot through her. *Will I ever stop missing what we had together? Is it wrong to wish that I could ever have a relationship like that again?*

CHAPTER 25

"I hope you don't mind, but I need you to make another stop before taking me home," Warren said after climbing into his driver's rig.

"Not a problem," Sam replied as he pulled his van out of the nutrition center's parking lot. "Where do you want to go?"

"Margaret Wagler's place. I'll give you the address if you don't know where she lives."

"I know exactly where it is. I've driven for her dad several times." Sam reached up and readjusted his rearview mirror. "Margaret's that horse whisperer, right?"

"Yeah. Only she doesn't refer to herself as such. Just says she has a good understanding of horses and enjoys working with them and trying to fix their problems."

"I'm guessing there's a demand for that kind of thing, and she probably gets paid well for it." Sam glanced over at Warren. "Does Margaret have any other job besides fixing unruly horses?"

"She works for me at the health food store." *But not for long.* Warren didn't voice his thoughts to the driver. Besides the fact that it was none of Sam's concern, this man, although a good driver, could end up repeating whatever Warren said — especially since he sometimes drove for Margaret's dad. Warren couldn't take that chance.

"How ya doin' today?" Sam asked, taking their conversation in a new direction. "Since you're out and about, I figure you must not be hurting too bad."

"I am dealing with less pain now — at least most of the time, but I won't be getting my inflatable boot off for several more weeks, so I'm still a bit hampered with what I can do physically."

"That's understandable. I remember once, when I was a kid, I fell from the treehouse my dad built for me and my brothers. I ended up busting my right arm." Sam put on his blinker and made a right-hand turn. "Since I am right-handed, I had to do everything with my left hand, and it was no easy task. I think my brothers were both glad it was me wearing a cast and not them." He gave a light chuckle. "Of course, since I was a bit hampered, they ended up doing most of my chores."

"I bet they weren't too happy about that. For me, though, it's been about not being able to walk or move easily without pain, and using my crutches to get around has put a lot of strain on my shoulders, back, and even my wrists. It's also challenging to perform certain tasks that require the use of my hands while I'm trying to manage with the crutches. Fortunately, I haven't needed to worry about chores at home because my dad has been taking care of them — even feeding and watering my horse."

Sam gave the steering wheel a tap. "Until a person breaks a bone or suffers some kind of other injury, I think we all tend to take our healthy bodies for granted."

"You're right about that. It was certainly true for me till I fell off my spooky horse."

"Do you like to ride horseback?"

"Not particularly, but Margaret does, so I've gone along with it a few times to please her. I've never enjoyed it as much as she does, though, and after breaking my ankle, I came to the conclusion that my horseback riding days are over. I'll be content to stick to hitching my horse to the open buggy or calling for a ride in a motorized vehicle like yours."

"Can't blame you for that. If I were Amish, I'd be the same way."

The rest of the way they rode silently, and when Sam pulled into the Waglers' place, Warren turned to him and said, "It shouldn't take me long to say what I have to say here, so I hope you won't mind waiting for me."

"Not a problem. Till you come back, I'll read a chapter or two from one of my Western novels that I keep in the van for times when the person who hired me asks me to wait while they run their errands and keep their appointments."

"Okay, thanks." Warren opened the door and stepped down, using his crutches for support. Even with the medical boot on his foot, it was hard to navigate with the aid of the crutches when he walked too far. He figured Margaret would most likely be in the barn or corral, so that's where he headed.

Margaret passed the chicken coop where the hens were cackling and carrying on. She was about to lead Cocoa into the barn when she spotted Warren heading her way with the use of his crutches. She smiled when he approached. "Well, this is a nice surprise. You must be feeling better if you're up and about today."

His eyes narrowed, and she couldn't miss

the visible tension in his neck and shoulders. "I went by my store to see how things were going and found Doretta working there by herself. Can you imagine my surprise when she said you had left early to go look at some problem horse?"

A warm flush of heat crept across Margaret's cheeks. She cleared her throat a couple of times and averted her eyes from Warren's steady gaze. "Jah, I . . . uh . . ."

"I can't believe you would do that to her, Margaret. What if things had gotten super busy? How did you think Doretta was supposed to handle it on her own without your help?"

She clutched her horse's lead rope and swallowed hard. "Doretta said she could manage, and I figured —"

"Oh did she now? Did you leave her with any other choice?"

Margaret's throat felt thick as she forced herself to look up at him. "I'm sorry, Warren, but the person who called me about their horse sounded desperate and said they needed my help right away."

With a brisk shake of his head, Warren groaned. "It's always the horses, isn't it, Margaret? If they're really more important to you than helping out at my store, I think it would be best if you quit."

She looked up at him and blinked, unbelieving. Surely he didn't mean it. "But . . . but what am I supposed to do for an income if I don't work at the nutrition center? As you know, I'm expected to help out financially while I live with my parents."

"I'm well aware, but I would think by now that you'd be making enough money training the horses that are brought to you with problems their owners haven't been able to fix."

"I do have some cash saved up from the donations I've received, but it's not the same as earning a weekly paycheck. I can't count on having a horse to fix every week, and even if I could, there would be no guarantee that the donation I'd get would be equal to what you pay me each week."

"Don't ya think you should have considered that before you started coming into work late and leaving early some days?" Warren spoke in a stern tone of voice, without wavering, as he drilled her eyes with his stare. Margaret felt sure he would not back down.

"You're right, Warren," she said, fanning her face with one hand as she continued to hold Cocoa steady with her other hand. "I was wrong for putting the horses before my job. If you'll let me keep working in your store, I promise to do better from now on."

Warren continued to look at her for several seconds, then he gave a slow shake of his head. "Beginning tomorrow, I'll be going back to work, and with Doretta's help only. And in case you're concerned, which I doubt, I'm sure that the two of us will manage just fine."

"So you're actually saying that you don't need me anymore?" Margaret struggled to hold back the hot tears threatening to spill over. She'd never been this angry at Warren. Didn't he have any understanding of her situation at all?

"Two people working there is all that's required at this time," he replied, leaning on his crutches as he bent a bit closer to her. "Let's face it, Margaret, you've never been happy helping at my store. I think you only agreed to work there because you needed a job. If you feel that you need another job besides training horses, then you oughta look for something you would enjoy enough to be on time."

"Okay, it really hurts, but I understand you're not going to back down." Margaret stepped forward and placed a hand on Warren's shoulder. "Even though I won't be an employee at the nutrition center, I will still be your aldi, though, right?"

Warren's lips pressed together in a slight grimace. "I don't feel good about saying this, Margaret, but we really have very little in common. You like working with horses and going riding. I don't. My emphasis right now is on my health food store, and you seem to have little or no interest in it."

The tears Margaret had been holding back dripped down her hot cheeks. Warren was right, but she had hoped that he might come to enjoy horses as much as she did if he spent more time around them. Apparently, that was not going to happen because it seemed all Warren cared about was running his business. Then another thought popped into Margaret's head. "Are you in love with Doretta? Is that the real reason you want to break up with me?"

The cords along Warren's neck stood out and sweat beaded on his forehead as he leaned away from her. "What kind of a question is that? Doretta and I are just friends, and I'm sure that's how she feels too."

Margaret stroked Cocoa's neck, needing to be comforted right now. She was rewarded with a gentle nuzzle from the mare. "I didn't ask if she was in love with you, Warren. My question was whether you love her."

His forehead wrinkled. "This is not a topic for discussion right now. I came here to tell you that I don't think you should be working at the nutrition center anymore."

"I get that, but you also suggested that we should break up."

"Jah, but it's because of our differences — nothing else." Warren glanced toward the driveway. "My driver's waiting, so I need to be on my way." He started to walk away but turned back around. "I'm sorry, Margaret. I didn't mean to hurt you, but I need employees who show up for work on time and don't take off in the middle of the day for no good reason."

Margaret swallowed hard. Warren was right; she had let him down. But that didn't make it any easier to accept the idea that she now had no full-time job or steady boyfriend.

Warren's ankle, which had felt a little better earlier today, began to throb as he got back into Sam's vehicle. Although he had hoped he would feel a sense of relief after talking to Margaret, Warren felt like a heel instead. He had hurt her feelings, and he wished there had been a better way of breaking up with her. But he'd let his frustrations get the best of him and ended up blurting it out. *I wonder if there is ever a good way to break up with someone. I have tried to make Margaret happy by bending to her ways, but it seems to me that I've been the one doing all the bending. Everything should not be about her. Apparently, she doesn't believe that the things I'm interested in matter at all.*

Sam looked over at Warren and nudged his arm. "Does that frown you're wearing mean things didn't go well with your girl-friend?"

Thanks for noticing. Guess I should be better at not letting my feelings show. "No, they didn't go well, and Margaret is not my girlfriend or my employee anymore."

"Oh, I see. Hopefully, things didn't end on a bad note."

"I'm afraid they did. Margaret does not understand my disinterest in her work with horses, and she doesn't realize how impor-tant my health food store is to me. The truth is, we're not compatible." Warren didn't know why he had told all of this to his driver. It wasn't like he and Sam were best friends or anything. Besides, Sam might repeat the things Warren had just blurted out. Even so, he'd felt the need to talk about this to someone willing to listen.

"It's better to find out now rather than later," Sam said. "If you ended up marrying the girl and then realized you weren't on the same page with things, you'd have an even bigger problem."

"True, and divorce would not be an option for either of us." Warren decided it would be best to end this topic before he said anything more that could be repeated. He asked Sam not to say anything to anyone and then turned his head toward the side window, barely taking note of the passing scenery as they headed down the road again.

What was I thinking? I haven't even asked Doretta if she would be willing to work five days a week at the store with me. I could ask Sam to make one more stop for me at her house, but my ankle hurts pretty bad, and I need to get home so I can rest and put my foot up for a while. Besides, Sam is probably more than ready to get to his home too. Guess I'll have to wait till tomorrow when I show up at the health food store to ask Doretta if she would be okay working with me now instead of Margaret.

Warren rubbed a spot on his forehead where a headache had started. *Sure hope she says yes, because I can't run the store without help. I won't say anything about me and Margaret breaking up, though, and I certainly will not mention that I'm in love with her. I can only imagine how shocked she would be if I boldly stated that fact — especially if she doesn't feel the same way about me.*

Warren's thoughts went to his brother's journal and the entry he'd read last night. William had written about how much he loved Doretta and that he wanted to ask her to marry him. He'd said he was waiting for the right time, and it couldn't happen until he felt that he could provide a good living for her. He'd also mentioned the health food store he wanted to open and how he and Warren hoped to become partners.

Warren winced and stared down at his hands, now clenched in his lap. At this moment, he was unable to see where his future might go, and it saddened him to know that it no longer included his twin brother.

CHAPTER 26

A round of knocking against her bedroom door brought Margaret awake. She groaned and pulled the covers over her head.

"Are you up, Margaret?" Mom called through the closed door.

"No, I'm still in bed."

When Margaret heard the swish of the door opening, she pushed the covers aside and sat up just as her mother stepped inside. "You'd better get up right now or you'll be late for work. The others in our family have left for their jobs already."

"I won't be going to the nutrition center today." Margaret stretched her arms over her head and released a noisy yawn.

"Why not?" her mother asked, moving closer to the bed. "Are you feeling grank this morning?"

"No, I'm not sick. The fact is, I don't have a job anymore."

Mom's forehead wrinkled as she narrowed

her eyes and tilted her head to one side. "How come?"

Margaret explained about the visit she'd had from Warren and ended by saying she didn't think it was fair that she had no job to go to now.

"I can't believe what you're telling me. Why didn't you say something about it sooner? You sat there at the supper table with us last night and didn't say one word about losing your position at the health food store."

"I was too upset to talk about it."

"What reason did Warren give for letting you go?" Mom asked.

"He said that I'm unreliable."

"Have you made some mistakes while working there or not been courteous enough to the customers?"

Margaret shook her head. "It's nothing like that. Warren is upset with me because I've gotten to work a little late a few times, and yesterday I left early. But Doretta was still there, so it's not like the store was unattended."

"She was there by herself?"

Margaret nodded.

Mom looked at Margaret with her lips pursed tightly together. A few seconds passed, and then she asked, "Did you have a good reason for arriving late on the other days or leaving early yesterday?"

"Jah. At least I thought so."

"What were those reasons?"

"I had a horse to look at for the first time — not to mention the other horse that's here in our barn needing my time."

Mom's eyes narrowed as she tapped her foot in rapid succession. "For goodness' sake, Daughter, what on earth were you thinking?"

Margaret merely shrugged in response.

"Did you tell Warren that you were sorry and plead with him to let you keep your job?"

"I didn't beg, but I did promise to do better." Margaret frowned. "Warren didn't change his mind, though, and he ended up breaking up with me."

Mom's mouth dropped open. "Really? Why would he do that? I thought you two might be getting serious by now, and maybe —"

"Warren said we have nothing in common, and he even accused me of caring more about horses than I do him."

"He might be right about that, Margaret. Your new gaul, as well as the ones you work with that have behavior problems, are what you talk about most of the time."

Margaret knew her mother was right, so she didn't try to argue the point.

Mom pointed a finger at her. "I would like to feel sorry for you, but you've brought this on yourself. Now, I want you to get out of bed, wash up, and put on a clean dress. After you've had some breakfast and done whatever needs to be done with the horses, you'd better call one of our drivers and head into town."

"I'm not going to Warren's store and plead with him to give me my job back. I've already told you that he was firm about his decision to fire me."

"I'm not asking you to do that. What you need to do, however, is go around town to some of the shops there and see if anyone is hiring, because you do need to find a steady job now."

"I'm earning some money from the donations I receive by working with people's horses."

"True, but it's not a steady income that you can count on. And until you get married and move out on your own, you're expected to help out with our finances here, just like your sisters and brothers all do."

"I know, Mom, and I will. But as far as getting married, that's probably never going to happen." Tears welled in Margaret's eyes.

"I had convinced myself that Warren loved me, and I thought it wouldn't be long before I would receive a marriage proposal. But you can see where that notion got me. Guess it was just a silly dream. It's not likely that I'll ever find a man who loves horses as much as I do, so I'll probably end up a spinster who will never marry and have a family of her own."

Mom shook her head. "Don't be so pessimistic. I'm sure the right man is out there for you somewhere. You should be praying about it instead of fretting."

Margaret didn't argue. What was the point? She threw her legs over the side of the bed and stood. *Clearly, Mom doesn't understand the way I feel about anything. Since I won't be getting a marriage proposal from Warren, I see no reason I should bother joining the church.*

"I can't believe you're going to the nutrition store to work today. I was surprised when you told me you'd gone there for a while yesterday." Betty looked at her son from across the breakfast table and frowned. "I'm sure Margaret and Doretta can manage without you, just like they've been doing since your accident."

"I'll be fine," Warren said after finishing

his glass of orange juice. "And I need to go because Margaret won't be there. It'll just be me and Doretta from now on."

"What?" Betty's head jerked back. "What happened? Did Margaret quit?"

"No, I let her go."

"When was this?"

"Yesterday, I asked Sam to drive me over to the Waglers' place before he brought me home."

Betty looked over at her husband. "Did you know about this, Raymond?"

He shook his head.

She looked back at Warren. "What would possess you to do such a thing? Margaret's been working at the store since you first opened it, and you need her there."

"No, I don't. She's not reliable." Warren's knuckles whitened as he clasped the empty glass in his hand. "As I have mentioned before, Margaret has shown up at work late on several occasions. Then yesterday, she left early, leaving Doretta alone to manage things on her own in the store." He set the glass down. "I'd call that unreliable, wouldn't you?"

"Well, jah, it does prove that she's not reliable." This bit of news did not sit well with Betty.

"You were right in letting Margaret go,

Son," Raymond chimed in. "I would never put up with it if any of the employees who work on my construction sites weren't dependable."

Warren wiped his face on a napkin. "So now you understand why I need to get back to working at the store. Sure can't leave Doretta there by herself to manage everything."

"Is she up to the task?" Betty asked.

"Of course. She's been working there five days a week since my accident, and when I was there yesterday, I never heard a word of complaint from Doretta. In fact, after watching her in action, I'd have to say that Doretta is very efficient, and she is also showing a strong interest in learning everything she can about the supplements I sell as well as promoting good nutrition when she speaks to the customers."

Betty picked up her piece of toast and nibbled on it before responding. "That's good, but there might be days when she's not free to work, and it would help if you had someone to fill in for her." She placed the rest of her toast on the plate and looked at Warren. "Don't you agree?"

He shrugged. "I suppose I could look for someone to fill in if needed, but it won't be Margaret."

"I could do it." Betty smiled. "I'm trustworthy and dependable."

"Danki, Mom. I'll keep that in mind."

"I could take your place in the store too. That way you can stay home and rest your ankle."

He gave a firm shake of his head. "My place is in the store, and if I need to rest my ankle, I'll take a break and go to my office for a while."

"Okay, but do keep my offer in mind."

"I will, Mom."

Betty spread some strawberry jam on the rest of her toast and took a bite. It was difficult not to worry about Warren, but she didn't want to be pushy and end up upsetting her son. Betty had offered her help and would be there if and when he needed her, and she would make every effort to leave all things in God's hands.

Eager to be ready on time for her driver to pick her up, Doretta rushed into the bathroom to brush her teeth. She picked up her toothbrush and turned on the faucet to dampen the brush before squeezing some toothpaste on it. She had barely gotten the brush wet, when Karen's cat darted in through the partially open door and leaped up onto the counter. After a quick swish of her paw, Olive took a drink from the faucet.

Doretta rolled her eyes. "Crazy cat. Why are you always up to mischief?" She turned off the water and began brushing her teeth, but the persistent cat did not leave. Olive gave a few pathetic meows and sat staring at the sink bowl. When Doretta finished brushing and turned on the water again to rinse her mouth, the cat made another swipe at the running water and drank again.

Doretta opened the bathroom door fully and stuck her head out. "Karen, would you please come get your cat?"

Her sister showed up a few minutes later with another cat in her arms. This one was all white, and from the size of it, Doretta figured it wasn't more than a few weeks old. "Why do you have to be such a cat lover?" she asked.

"Cause they're nice and soft," came the smiling response. "And I like to hear 'em purr."

"Well, the kitten you're holding should be in the barn with its mother. And this one should not be in the bathroom drinking running water from the faucet — especially when I'm trying to brush my teeth." She pointed at Olive.

"I don't care if she does it when I turn the water on at the sink."

"Well I do, so please take her out."

Karen picked Olive up by the scruff of her neck and carried her out of the room.

Doretta gave her head a shake and rolled her eyes one more time. *I wonder sometimes if my sister and I are really related. We're nothing alike — especially when it comes to the way we feel about cats. If I ever have a house of my own, no cats will be allowed inside.*

When Doretta arrived at the health food store with a basket of muffins in hand, she was surprised to see Warren sitting behind the checkout counter. Would he be working all day or just half the day, like he'd done yesterday when he came by unexpectedly?

"Guder mariye," he said, offering her a pleasant smile.

"Good morning. Will you be working here today?"

"Jah, most definitely." He gestured to the basket she held. "What have ya got in there?"

Doretta walked up to the counter and set the container down. "I brought a little treat to share with Margaret, but I didn't realize you would be here again today." She pulled aside the piece of cloth that she had used to cover the muffins. "There are six muffins in here, so we each can have two. Oh, and I had one for breakfast, so I know for a fact that they are nice and moist."

"That was thoughtful of you. I'll eat one soon because I'm hungry due to the fact that I didn't take the time for breakfast this morning."

"How come?"

"My driver needed to leave earlier than planned, so I had a glass of orange juice before heading out."

"Guess it's a good thing I brought enough muffins then." She cast him a quick smile. "Will you be here all day, working with me and Margaret?"

"Not Margaret. Just you. She won't be working for me anymore."

Doretta touched her parted lips with her index finger. "That's a surprise. What reason did she give for quitting?"

"She didn't. I let her go," Warren responded.

Doretta's eyes widened. "Seriously?"

"Jah."

Doretta was on the verge of asking him why, when Warren spoke again. "Margaret is not a dependable employee. When I stopped by her place yesterday, I made it clear that I won't be needing her to work here anymore. So if you feel up to the task,

I'd like you to continue working full-time for me, and of course, I'll be here every day to help."

Before she'd had the time to think it through, Doretta nodded and said, "Okay, I'm willing to do it." What else could she do? If Warren thought he was up to working at the store again, that was his decision, not hers. She was a bit concerned, though, because even for the short time Warren had worked yesterday, she'd seen the lines of fatigue on his face, coupled with what she recognized so well as struggling with pain. She hoped for Warren's sake that he wouldn't try to do too much and would take it easy today. Doretta knew from experience how terrible he would feel if he overdid it and ended up feeling exhausted and dealing with more pain. So she would do all she could to take the burden off him and suggest that he go to his office and rest if he needed to.

Doretta felt sorry for Margaret, having lost her job. But Warren was right — his girl-friend wasn't reliable when it came to working at the store.

Warren reached for a muffin from the basket and took a bite. "Yum! This is really good, Doretta."

"Danki. I'm glad you like it."

He finished the rest of his treat and grabbed a roll of paper towels from the shelf under the counter. After tearing off a piece and wiping his mouth and hands, he said, "There's something else you need to know before you hear about it through the gossip mill."

Warren's statement jolted Doretta out of her contemplations. "What is it?" she asked.

"Margaret and I are no longer a couple."

Warren said it so matter-of-factly that it caused Doretta to take a step back. "She broke up with you?"

"No, I'm the one who ended things."

"Was it because of something she said after you fired her?"

He shook his head. "It's something I've felt the need to do for quite a while, but I couldn't form the words until yesterday. The truth is . . ." He paused. "Well, the fact remains that Margaret and I have very little, if anything, in common. I'm not sure why we ever started dating."

"She is a pretty girl."

"True, but beauty is only skin deep. It gets old after a while when one person has to compensate in order to make a relationship work." Warren thumbed his right ear. "I suppose what drew me to her in the first place was that Margaret was so upbeat about things. Her excitement about the horses she works with always showed on her face, and the bubbly tone of voice she used when talking about them made me believe she would be happy and interested in the things I enjoy too. For some foolish reason, I thought Margaret would be enthused about me and my new business, but she obviously didn't care much, or she wouldn't have found excuses not to be here helping out."

Doretta wasn't sure how to respond, so she merely said, "I'm sorry things didn't work out between you." *I have to say, though, I kind of thought that relationship seemed a little off.* She leaned against the counter, thinking about how, when Warren needed *Arnica* to be brought to him, Margaret had wanted to go home and tend to a horse after work instead of taking the homeopathic remedy to him. Doretta had been surprised when Margaret asked her to run the supplements to Warren. She was tempted to tell Warren what she thought about Margaret but decided her opinion on this was best kept to herself, because it really was none her business.

"I figured I would feel some sadness after breaking up with her, but to tell you the truth, I felt relieved. Margaret is definitely not the woman God wants for me, and I'm glad I realized that before it was too late."

Doretta debated about whether she should comment on Warren's last statement or not, but she was saved by the bell on the front door as it rang to announce that a customer had come into the store.

CHAPTER 27

The summer months had come and gone, evaporating like steam drifting up from a teakettle. When Doretta looked at the kitchen calendar on the wall, she could hardly believe that today was officially the first day of fall. Things had been going well at the nutrition center, with more and more people from the area shopping there. Warren had run a few ads in the local newspaper advertising a couple of sales, but most of his business had come from folks telling others about the store.

The warm weather they'd had all summer had cooled to a nice even temperature, for which she felt grateful. Soon leaves would begin falling from trees, landing in gutters, and forming drifts in the yard. The green grass would turn yellow or brown, and root vegetables from the garden patch would be pulled up and cleaned. Some jams and jellies had already been made, but Doretta knew there would be more canning, pick-ling, and jelly-making to come. They would be drinking freshly squeezed cider and eating apple butter on buttered toast. Her stomach growled at the thought of it. Doretta liked this time of the year when fresh potatoes, carrots, beans, and beets from the garden would be cooked and served for meals along with canned or pickled vegetables. Autumn also meant baking, with lots of good smells, and she looked forward to eating apple and pumpkin pies. Doretta's appetite had increased, and while she still suffered from mild depression, she had begun to feel more like herself.

Perhaps that's because of the friendship I've established with Warren, Doretta reasoned. *Spending time with him makes me feel relaxed and happier than I've been in a long time.*

Doretta thought about Margaret and how she'd found another job soon after Warren had let her go. She now worked part-time at a harness shop and continued to train people's horses during her off-hours. Doretta couldn't understand why her ex-coworker hadn't tried harder to be there for Warren after the accident or why the young woman had been so undependable when it came to her job at his store.

I guess some people can be so self-

absorbed with their own lives that they aren't aware of other people's needs or desires. Even so, with Margaret's father being a deacon in our church, one would think that he would have taught his daughter a little something about putting other's needs before her own and being more responsible.

Doretta tapped her knuckles on the kitchen table where she sat. *Guess Margaret's daed is not really responsible for how she acts as an adult. She's a grown woman and should take responsibility for her actions. Like all other Amish children I know, Margaret has been taught to do the right things and treat others with respect, so she should be putting that into practice.*

Doretta's lips pressed together. *It's too bad Margaret didn't take more interest in Warren's store. If she had, she and Warren would probably still be a couple — maybe even planning their wedding by now. But then,* Doretta reasoned, *maybe they weren't meant to be together. Perhaps Margaret will find someone more suited to her, and Warren will too. They both deserve to be happy.*

Doretta enjoyed helping Warren in the health food store, and each workday she looked forward to the time that she and Warren would spend conversing with each other when there were no customers in the store. She reflected on the day he had come to work without his inflatable boot or crutches and smiled when she pictured the joy she'd seen on his face to be able to walk normally again and without any pain.

As the days of summer had drifted by, Doretta felt herself drawing closer to Warren in ways she had never expected. Even though his personality was different from his brother's, Warren was easy to get along with, and she'd discovered that they had many things in common, such as a love for going for long walks, an interest in sharing things they'd read in books, and a desire to see that his health food store ran efficiently. Warren also shared his brother's good looks, but of course that came from being identical twins. Doretta thought about Warren often, even when they weren't together. She'd allowed herself to fantasize about what it would be like if she were married to him. That thought always made her feel guilty, though, because she felt sure that if William knew, he would disapprove. The promise she had made to William that she would never love anyone but him was always at the back of her mind.

Doretta reflected on how kind and thoughtful Warren was, and she was reminded of an incident from their childhood.

After school let out on the day the twins graduated from the eighth grade, Warren had told her that he knew God had a plan for her life. "And everyone else's," William had interjected. Then he'd clasped her hand and said, "Someday, sweet Doretta, you're gonna be my wife."

Tears welled in Doretta's eyes, and she blinked to keep them from spilling over. What good did it do to dwell on the past? It couldn't be changed, and she must learn to live in the present.

"Why are you sitting here in the kitchen staring at the calendar as though you're in a daze?"

The sudden question pushed Doretta's thoughts aside, and she turned in her chair to look at her mother, who had just entered the room. "Oh, umm . . . I was thinking how quickly summer went by, and now here it is autumn already." Doretta had been thinking about the change in seasons when she'd first looked at the calendar, but she wasn't about to share with her mother the rest of the thoughts that had gone through her head. It would not only be embarrassing, but more questions from Mama would probably follow.

"It has always wondered me, the way the summer months speed by very quickly, and wintertime seems to drag on and on," Mama said. "Guess maybe it's because we keep so busy with gardening and the never-ending yard work that needs to be done during the summer months, when the weather is warm and humid."

"That's true. Most of my summer days were spent helping at Warren's store, though, so except for my day off on Mondays, I didn't get to help you here as much as I would have liked."

"It's all right. I didn't expect you to stay home from work and help out," Mama said. "Karen assisted me many times by pulling weeds in the garden. In fact, she helped with a lot of things in the yard and here in the house, all the way up until she started school again toward the end of August. And when they weren't busy working at their jobs, your brothers were helpful and took turns mowing the lawn." She took a seat beside Doretta and smiled. "I'm pleased that you have a job you seem to enjoy. I had thought you might quit working for Warren and go back to teaching, but I guess you're happy right where you are."

"Jah, I really like my job, and I've learned so much working there among all the supplements and other health-related products Warren has available."

Mama reached over and patted Doretta's arm. "I know you have, and our whole family has benefitted from the knowledge you've gained. We also appreciate the employee discount Warren has offered you as a benefit of working there."

"It has been nice," Doretta agreed. She pushed her chair away from the table. "Guess we'd better get busy and start the canning we had planned to do today. If we're not careful, it'll soon be time to begin lunch preparations."

"You're so right." Mama bobbed her head. "The canning jars are washed and sitting on the counter, ready to go. We now need to wash the green beans we picked earlier and fill the jars. Soon after that, we'll fill the pressure cooker and set it on the stove. Then we'll just have to hope that all the lids seal properly and no jars get broken."

Doretta cringed at the thought of losing even one jar after they'd worked so hard to pick and prepare the food, but it was the risk they'd have to take, just as they always did each canning season.

"Easy, girl. Settle down now."

Margaret's horse whinnied and kept tossing her head from side to side. Margaret stopped brushing Cocoa, and as soon as she began massaging the horse's neck, the mare settled right down. "You're spoiled, ya know that? You just want my attention all the time, and you think you're something special."

The horse responded with a nicker, and Margaret laughed. It was nice to have Mondays off, like she'd had while working at the health food store. And since her job at the harness shop was only part-time, she was happy to have most Saturdays off as well. This gave Margaret two full days, plus evenings, to work with the horses that had been brought to her lately for help.

Margaret thought about Warren and wondered how he and Doretta were doing handling things at his store with just the two of them working there. *He was right about us not having much in common.* Margaret began brushing Cocoa again. *I suppose it was best that we did go our separate ways, but it still hurt my feelings when Warren broke up with me. I'm not holding my breath, but maybe someone who loves horses as much as I do will come along and ask me to go out with him. If not, then I'll have to accept it and move on with my life without love or marriage.*

Paradise

Eleanor stood in front of the open kitchen

window and drew in several deep breaths, trying to quell her nausea. She had hoped with this baby that she wouldn't have to deal with being sick to her stomach throughout the pregnancy, but it appeared that she might. Toward the end of April, she and Vic had learned that she was expecting. They had shared the good news with Vic's family while eating a meal at his parents' home one evening in early May. Everyone in Vic's family was delighted with the news, as were Eleanor's family members. But she hadn't heard anything back from Doretta yet, and that seemed strange, since she'd sent her a letter in June sharing the exciting news. *Maybe she never got my letter. It may have gotten lost in the mail.*

Eleanor placed both hands against her ever-growing stomach and breathed deeply a few more times, thankful when the nausea subsided. *Maybe Vic's boss would be okay with Vic taking a few days off so we could make a trip to Indiana. Since I haven't heard from Doretta in a while, it would be wonderful to share our good news with her in person. Perhaps this evening, when Vic gets home from work, I'll bring that topic up and see what he has to say. I'm sure he would enjoy getting away for a while as much as I would. For that matter, Rosetta would have a fun time on the*

*trip too, since she would be the center of at-
tention at my folks' house and most likely at
Doretta's home too.*

Checkers let loose a couple of loud barks,
pulling Eleanor out of her musings. She
turned from the window and saw the dog
pawing at the backdoor. "Okay, okay, calm
down, you impatient little dog. I'm coming
to let you out right now."

Grabill

Even though today was his day off, Warren
had gotten up at the crack of dawn. Mom
had a few chores she'd asked him to do,
and he'd wanted to get them done early so
he could spend the rest of the day doing
some things for himself. One of them
involved reading some more in his brother's
journal, so he grabbed the book from the
desk where he kept it and headed for his
room, where he wouldn't be disturbed.
Mom had gone outside to pick any vegetables from her garden that might be ready,
making it unlikely that she would have
disrupted his reading if he'd gone to the living room. But Warren preferred the privacy
of his bedroom, where he could be alone
and shut the door.

After entering the room, he propped two
fluffy pillows against the headboard and

reclined on the bed with the journal. Warren had read quite a few more entries during the summer months, and he'd gained further insight into his brother's thoughts and deepest feelings. In one of the entries, William had mentioned the harmonica he'd borrowed without Warren's knowledge or approval.

It was water under the bridge now, but Warren found his brother's reason for taking the harmonica quite interesting. William had stated that since Doretta had mentioned how much she enjoyed hearing Warren play the mouth harp, jealousy had taken over. So William decided it was time for him to learn how to play the instrument. The only thing was, Warren had never heard his brother play, nor had William made any mention to Warren about having borrowed the harmonica. He figured his twin must have either given up on the idea and forgotten to put the instrument back in Warren's room or William had been so occupied with other things that he'd forgotten all about the idea.

In some ways reading William's journal had offered Warren comfort, but in other ways it made him feel sad because he really missed his twin brother and wished he was still here. Even though William was gone, it gave Warren a sense of peace, knowing that his twin had been a believer in the Lord.

As he read a bit more of what was written in the journal, Warren pictured his brother doing some of the things he mentioned. His throat constricted when he read how much William had looked forward to going over to see Doretta that evening. Warren smiled as he recalled times when his brother was getting ready to go on a date with Doretta. William would be in front of the bathroom mirror for longer than necessary, fussing with his shirt, making sure it was tucked in, and then rubbing his hand over his smiling face, indicating that he'd given himself a nice, close shave.

Warren also reflected on the fun he and William had when they'd gone on a few double dates. Warren swallowed hard. *Oh, how I miss the good times William and I used to enjoy.*

Today, Warren felt compelled to breeze through most of the entries and read his brother's last comments, written two days before William's death.

With an ache in his heart, Warren read the words slowly and in silence.

I can hardly believe that in just a few days, I'll be getting married to the sweetest woman I've ever known. Doretta is everything I could ever want in a wife, and I feel blessed that she's chosen me to be her husband. I feel sad for Warren, though, because I've known for a long time that he loves Doretta too. Clear back when we were kinner, my brother had a fondness for her, which I'm sure is why he hung around us so much. She chose me, though, so I never let on that I knew about my brother's feelings for her.

I have to admit, however, that for a time, I was worried that Doretta would like Warren better than me because they seemed to have more in common. He played the mouth harp, and she liked to sing and yodel, and they had such a good time when he played and she yodeled. That's why I let her think it was me whenever Warren did any thoughtful things for her when we were children and even into our teen years. Truth be told, whenever I saw them together, I felt jealous. It was selfish of me, but I never told her how Warren felt, because I loved Doretta so much and didn't want to lose her.

I've done some growing since then and realize now that if she hadn't picked me and had chosen Warren instead, he would have taken good care of her and been the kind of husband she deserves. If that had happened, it would have hurt, but I would have given them my blessing. I do hope that someday my twin brother will find a woman he loves as much as I cherish what I have with Doretta. Warren is a good man, and he deserves to be happy. I would wish him the best, even if he ended up with Doretta.

Warren closed the journal, set it aside, and lay completely still as he let his brother's words sink in. His thoughts swirled so quickly, it was hard to keep up with them. *William knew I loved Doretta, but he never said anything about it to me. I'm sure he didn't tell Doretta either. And yet he wrote that if she had picked me and not him, he knew I would take good care of her and be the kind of husband she deserves. He also said that even if I had ended up with Doretta, he would have wished me the best.*

To Warren, this news was like receiving his brother's blessing, which he appreciated more than words could say. A knot formed in Warren's stomach, and he placed both hands there as if to squelch it. *What am I supposed to do with this information? Should I reveal my true feelings for Doretta and let her know what my brother said in his journal? Or do I simply tell Doretta that I love her and see how she responds, without her knowing about William's last journal entry?*

A vision of Doretta's lovely, petite face popped into Warren's head. Whenever she smiled, it was as though her pretty brown eyes lit up, and seeing her when she'd looked at him like that always made Warren smile too.

He sat up straight and reached up to massage the back of his neck. *If I tell Doretta what's on my mind, I'll be taking a chance that she might reject me, but I can't hold in my feelings for her any longer. When I am with Doretta tomorrow, before we close the store for the day, I'll declare my love for her and see how she responds.*

CHAPTER 28

After Warren stepped out the front door Tuesday morning to wait for his driver, he pulled in a few deep breaths to help steady his nerves. The cooling air on his cheeks was crisp but slightly damp with a hint of possible rain. A breeze came up that caused goose bumps to erupt on Warren's neck, and he pulled the collar of his jacket tighter. Drying leaves clattered across the driveway, and geese honked overhead as they followed their migration path. Fall was definitely here.

Warren's heart pounded as he thought about seeing Doretta and, for the first time, revealing his deepest feelings for her. Of course he would need to wait until the end of the day, when no customers were in the store, which would be difficult. If Warren had his way, he'd blurt it all out as soon as Doretta showed up at the store. Staring up at the drifting clouds, his mind contem-

386

plated the situation. *Should I say to her, "I would like to talk with you about something?" No, that's not good enough. I don't need to ease into the topic. I should just get right to the point. I'll start by saying, "Your friendship has meant a lot to me, but now my feelings have grown deeper." At least that sounds better.*

Warren bit down on his lower lip. Letting Doretta know that he loved her would be much harder than he'd imagined. *I really hope that I'll say the right thing to this special woman I've fallen in love with.* Warren knew, however, that even if he chose the right words to say to Doretta, she might react negatively. And was all this worrying about the situation gaining him anything?

Warren took in a long, deep breath and eased it out. He did this a few more times, trying to relax and collect his thoughts. He tried focusing on the scenery around him, hoping it would have a calming effect. Warren saw crops being harvested across the way, and he watched several horses in a neighboring field quietly grazing in the morning light. Soon it would be time to rake and bag leaves, and of course he would find the time to help with that. Dad was busy with his own chores, and Mom couldn't handle all the yard work herself, so Warren would set aside some time in the evenings to help with the fall cleanup.

A familiar, rhythmic *clip-clop* of a horse pulling its owner's buggy came down the road, interrupting Warren's contemplations, and when he saw that it was one of their neighbors heading to work, Warren lifted his hand to wave a friendly greeting. The Amish man waved in return and continued on his way down the road.

Lately, Warren's normally optimistic thoughts were full of tension and anxiety. What would it be like to go out with Doretta? Where would be a nice place to take her for their first date? What would they talk about? Would she enjoy herself as much as Warren knew he would, spending time with her? His mind was all over the place this morning, and all this thinking had only increased his concerns.

Warren leaned against the porch railing and tried to lessen the tension in his muscles and calm his thoughts. *What if Doretta has no feelings for me that go beyond friendship? What if I've misread the way she has looked at me on several occasions — with a yearning expression and glowing cheeks?* So many times Warren had wanted to declare his love for Doretta, but concern about being disloyal to his brother had always stopped him from saying the words on his heart. Warren had also been fearful of Doretta's reaction, because she might not return his feelings. His stomach clenched at the possibility. *If I open my heart to her and she responds negatively, I'll be devastated. I can't imagine spending the rest of my life without her, but that's the risk I will have to take.*

The rumble of a vehicle pulling into the yard ended Warren's contemplations. His driver was here, and soon they would arrive at the nutrition center, where his focus needed to be on work.

I'll try to stay as busy as possible today, Warren told himself as he settled up front in the passenger seat of Sam's van. *That should help keep my focus on work and not on the words I plan to say to Doretta at the end of this workday.*

"When you leave the harness shop today, would you mind stopping by the nutrition center and picking up a few things for me?" Margaret's mother pointed to a list she'd placed on the table. "We are nearly out of those supplements, and I'd prefer to get them now, before the bottles are empty."

Margaret gripped her empty breakfast plate as she carried it to the sink. The last thing she wanted to do was go to Warren's store and see him there with Doretta. It would be yet another reminder that she no longer had a job there and that Warren had broken up with her. "Can't you do it, Mom? If I ask my driver to take me there, she'd be going out of her way."

"You know I can't leave the house today," Mom stated firmly. "My sisters will be coming over to help me finish cleaning the house in readiness for hosting church here this Sunday."

"Oh, that's right. I forgot."

Holding her own plate and silverware, Mom joined Margaret at the sink. "I don't see how you could have forgotten, since you helped me do some cleaning yesterday."

"I didn't forget about us having church here. I just didn't remember that your sisters would be coming today to help out."

Mom's pale brows lowered. "You've been quite forgetful lately. Is there something troubling you, Margaret?"

She shrugged. "I have a lot on my mind, that's all."

"Anything you'd like to talk with me about?"

"No — at least not right now. I need to get to the harness shop and be on time. Wouldn't want to get fired from that job too." Margaret couldn't keep the sarcastic tone out of her voice. She picked up the list Mom had placed on the table and put it in the tote bag she took to work. Then she gave her mother a goodbye hug and hurried out the door to wait for her driver.

As Margaret stood on the porch, a gust of chilly wind swept in, causing her to shiver. She reached up to tuck some fly-away hair back under her head covering and frowned. *Sure wish I didn't have to stop at the nutrition center today. It's gonna be hard to see Doretta working with Warren. She took my job, and I wouldn't be surprised if she ends up taking my ex-boyfriend too. I bet anything that the real reason Warren broke up with me is because he's in love with Doretta. He'd never admit it, but I've seen the way he looks at her with longing in his eyes.*

Going over some invoices that needed to be paid, Warren glanced at the clock in his office. In a few minutes, it would be time to put the CLOSED sign in the front window. He unbuttoned the top button on his shirt and reached around to rub the back of his neck. His muscles felt tight, so he closed his eyes and took a few calming breaths. Although eager to tell Doretta what was on his heart, Warren's mind was filled with nagging doubts. *What if she doesn't love me?*

What if Doretta is offended when I express my love for her? How could we continue to work here together once the truth is out if she doesn't feel anything for me but friendship? I could never ask Doretta to quit her job here, even if there is no chance of us being together as a couple. But it would be so hard to spend time here with her every working day, knowing there's no chance for us to be a couple.

Warren tapped his knuckles against the desktop. *Stop being so negative,* he told himself. *I need to be thinking positive thoughts right now, not jumping to conclusions or trying to analyze things. I need to wait and see what happens after I've spoken to her.*

Through his partially open office door, Warren heard a voice he recognized. *Oh boy, this isn't good. Margaret is here. I wonder what she wants. She'd better not have come to ask for her job back, because that's never going to happen.*

He pushed the chair away from his desk and headed down one of the vitamin aisles in the direction of the checkout counter. But he'd only made it partway when he nearly collided with Doretta, who had been coming from the opposite direction. Looking up at him with wide eyes while holding a piece of paper in one hand, she gave a small gasp. "Oh, sorry," she murmured. "I was so busy looking for the items on this list that I didn't see you coming down the aisle." Her ears turned pink, and she quickly averted her gaze.

"It's okay. No harm done." He looked at the paper she held. "Is that something for me?"

"No, it's a list Margaret brought in. She said her mother had asked her to come here to pick up a few things, and she wants me to get them for her." Doretta looked up at Warren.

"Oh, I see. Would you like me to take care of getting those things?"

"No, that's okay. I don't mind doing it, unless you'd rather."

"You go ahead. I'll head up front and talk to Margaret."

"Okay." Doretta hesitated a moment, then proceeded down the aisle with the list.

Warren approached Margaret, standing with her arms folded at the checkout counter, and he quickly walked behind the counter and perched on the stool. "How have you been, Margaret?"

"I'm okay." She gave him a brief smile. "How 'bout you? I've heard that your business is thriving these days."

"Jah, it's doing quite well. Better than I'd even hoped, in fact." He leaned forward, placing both hands on the counter. "You know the layout of this store, so I'm wondering why you asked Doretta to get the items on your list rather than getting them yourself."

Her face blanched. "Well . . . I just figured since she's been working here full-time for a while now, she ought to know where everything is and could get the items I need quickly. For all I know, you may have moved some of the things around since I worked here, and I didn't want to waste time searching for them." She glanced toward the front door. "Also, my driver is waiting for me, so I don't have time to waste while hunting for things."

"I haven't moved much around, although I have several new products available for my customers now and had to find suitable places for those. So you're probably right — it may have taken you awhile to find all the items on your list."

An uncomfortable silence settled between them as they waited for Doretta to return with the products Margaret's mother wanted. For Warren, it was hard to know what to say and keep things positive. Warren and Margaret lived in the same community and were part of the same church district, so there was no way they could avoid seeing each other. It wouldn't feel so uncomfortable if they'd never been anything more than casual friends. Because they'd been a dating couple for a good many months, however, it was difficult for Warren to know how to carry on a sincere conversation with Margaret right now. He felt relieved when an English couple entered the store and said they needed help finding a few things. Although Warren would soon be closing the store for the day, he would willingly keep it open as long as there were customers needing assistance.

Warren told Margaret that Doretta should be back soon and would ring up her purchases, and then he excused himself and went down the first aisle with the man and woman to help with whatever they needed. He hoped that by the time Margaret and the English people paid for their purchases and he'd put the CLOSED sign in the window, he would have the courage to tell Doretta what was on his mind.

When the last customer left, Doretta went to the back room to get her tote bag, lunch cooler, and jacket. Her driver would be here soon, and she wanted to be ready when Mary Beth came to pick her up.

She stepped out of the room and was

surprised to see Warren standing outside his office door as though he'd been waiting for her. "I'd like to talk to you for a few minutes before we both head for home." Warren's words seemed rushed, and Doretta noticed he seemed uncomfortable.

"Did I do something wrong?" she asked.

"No, it's nothing like that. There's something I need to tell you, and if I don't say it now, I'll probably lose my nerve." Beads of sweat erupted on Warren's forehead.

Curious to know why he suddenly seemed so nervous, she asked, "What is it?"

He cleared his throat a couple of times, and she watched his Adam's apple bob up and down. "William's been gone for nearly a year now, and during that time I believe you and I have drawn closer as friends."

She nodded, wondering where he was going with this.

"Your friendship has meant a great deal to me, and sharing our thoughts and feelings about my brother has helped to comfort me in my grief." He paused and took in a breath. "I hope you have been comforted as well."

"I have." Doretta smiled. "My friend Eleanor has sent me many letters of comfort, which helped too. Also, spending time with you and talking about our grief has helped more than you can imagine."

Warren took a step forward and placed one hand on Doretta's shoulder. "I'm hoping we can be more than friends, Doretta, because the truth is I'm in love with you and have been for a long time."

Doretta couldn't believe what she had just heard. Every fiber of her being went numb. "No." She shook her head vigorously. "You can't love me, Warren, and I can't love you."

Thankful to hear the toot of her driver's horn, Doretta ran all the way to the front of the store without looking back. She fumbled with the doorknob a few seconds, then flung open the door and dashed outside. Unmindful of the cold rain that had begun falling, she climbed into her driver's van and collapsed against the front seat. She would have to quit her job at the nutrition store. With Warren having declared his love for her so boldly and unexpectedly, there was no way she could continue to work for him.

Chapter 29

Warren stood silently as though frozen in time. *Doretta doesn't love me, and she never even gave me a chance to explain about finding my brother's journal. Maybe if she knew what William had said, her reaction would have been different and she wouldn't have run out the door like that.* He gripped his head with both hands. *Maybe I should have told Doretta about William's journal entry first, before I declared my love for her.* Warren swallowed hard, trying to push down the lump that had lodged in his throat. *But if she doesn't love me, my brother's written words may not have made any difference at all.*

He looked upward, then closed his eyes. *Dear Lord, please tell me what I ought to do. Should I go after Doretta and try to explain, or would it be better to wait until tomorrow when she shows up for work to try and talk to her about William's journal? I'll need to apologize for upsetting her too.*

Warren opened his eyes, took a seat on the stool behind the counter, and breathed in and out a couple of times. *When Sam gets here to pick me up, I could ask him to stop by Doretta's before taking me home. But I don't know how long I'd be there, and Sam might not have the time to wait.* Warren's breathing came faster and deeper. *I need to wait until tomorrow, when Doretta and I have both calmed down. I'm sure things will go better if I talk to her then and clarify things.*

After Doretta said goodbye to her driver, she made a dash for the house, nearly tripping over Karen's cat, lying stretched out on the porch. "Stupid katz," she mumbled. "You're always underfoot." Normally, Karen would have been here and might have taken the cat inside, but Doretta remembered how, during breakfast this morning, her sister had talked excitedly about going over to her friend Michelle's house after school. Karen would be staying for supper to celebrate Michelle's birthday, and most likely she wouldn't be home until close to her bedtime.

Doretta pushed open the front door and stepped inside, making sure the door closed tightly so Olive didn't get the chance to follow her in. The last thing she needed right now was having to deal with her little sister's irritating cat.

Doretta still shook inwardly as she removed her jacket and hung it up. She couldn't get rid of the image of how Warren had looked at her when he'd blurted out that he was in love with her. She was almost to the stairs, on a desperate quest to get to her bedroom as quickly as possible, when her mother called from the kitchen, "Doretta, is that you?"

"Jah, Mama. I'm going up to my room."

"Well, please come back down as soon as you've changed so we can sit and chat over a cup of hot tea and a few peanut butter cookies I made earlier today."

Doretta cringed. *Not now, Mama. How am I going to get out of talking to her at this moment? What excuse can I use for staying in my room?* It wasn't right to tell a lie, but Doretta needed to be alone.

"I'm really tired," she called, speaking the truth. "So I'm going to lie down for a while."

"Okay. We'll talk later then."

Doretta grasped the wooden handrail and wearily trudged up the creaky stairs. *If I doze off and fall into a deep enough sleep, maybe I won't wake up until tomorrow morning. Of course, my problem will still be there, and as much as I dread it, I'll have to deal with the situation.*

Suddenly, an idea popped into Doretta's head — one that might solve all of her problems if she went with it. *Maybe it would be best if I made my decision right now instead of lying on the bed thinking about it and replaying the scene with Warren announcing that he's in love with me.*

Doretta turned around and came back down the stairs. "I'm going outside to the phone shed to make a call," she hollered through the kitchen doorway.

With a questioning look in her eyes, Mama stuck her head around the corner and peered at Doretta. "I thought you were tired and had gone upstairs to your room to rest."

"I was heading that way but changed my mind because I have an important phone call to make."

"Oh?" Mama's whole body came into view then, and her eyes squinted as she stared at Doretta. "Mind if I ask who you're going there to call?"

"When I come back inside, I'll tell you about it." Doretta put her jacket back on and hurried out the front door before her mother could respond.

■ ■ ■ ■

Amanda put the teakettle on the stove and waited for Doretta to return. *My daughter is acting a bit strange this afternoon. One minute she's too tired to have tea and cookies with me, and the next minute she's racing out the door to make a phone call. I wonder what could be so important.* Since the accident, Doretta had gone through some emotional changes but had seemed to be doing a bit better of late. Amanda hoped whatever was going on with Doretta today had not been a setback. *I hope she's not still struggling with letting go of the past and moving on.*

When the kettle whistled, Amanda poured hot water into two cups, added tea bags, and placed them on the table. No doubt Doretta would only be leaving a message for someone, so it shouldn't take her long.

Amanda picked up a recent issue of *The Budget* and read a post from her favorite scribe's column. She smiled when she learned about a surprise party that was thrown on behalf of the scribe's sixty-fifth birthday, but the surprise ended up being on the scribe's family, because he never showed up at his home that night. Instead, the widowed man had, without their knowledge, packed up his gear and gone on a camping trip without bothering to tell anyone he was leaving or where he planned to go. The biggest surprise, however, was when he showed up the next day with a cooler full of fish he'd caught the day before.

Amanda turned the page and smiled after reading a post by a scribe from upstate New York who had written about a woodpecker he'd seen turned upside-down in the snow. Believing the poor thing must be dead, the *Budget* writer had lifted the bird out by its tail feathers. When the fowl came up with a squawk of protest, the scribe quickly realized that the woodpecker was very much alive. After resting for a bit, the bird flew off as though nothing out of the ordinary had occurred.

Amanda paused from her reading to remove the tea bags and place the cups on matching saucers.

She glanced at the clock. *I really have to wonder what is keeping Doretta. Surely she couldn't be talking to anyone who is Amish, because it's not likely that an Amish person would be in their phone shed at the same time she'd made the call. Of course,* Amanda reasoned, *Doretta might not have gone out to the shed to call an Amish person. It could be one of our English drivers, who would be more apt to answer their phone.*

Amanda picked up her cup and took a sip of tea. It wasn't hot, but still warm enough to enjoy. As she continued to read more of *The Budget,* she ended up finishing her tea. By the time Doretta came in, Amanda figured she would need to start over with hot water for her cup.

Doretta entered the house feeling a little better than when she'd arrived home. After talking to Eleanor for the last ten minutes and hearing about her pregnancy for the first time, she was eager to tell her mother about the call.

She hung up her jacket and entered the kitchen, where she found Mama sitting at the table with the Amish newspaper spread out in front of her.

Mama looked up and smiled. "Oh good, you're back. I'll pour you a cup of hot tea." She appeared to be about ready to push her chair back, but Doretta stopped her.

"It's all right, Mama, I don't need any tea right now. I really need to talk."

"Okay. What do you wish to talk to me about?"

"I just spoke with Eleanor on the phone. Vic happened to be near their shed when the phone rang, so when he picked it up and found out it was me, he went inside and got Eleanor so we could chat."

"Oh, that was nice. Is everything going well with Vic, Eleanor, and sweet little Rosetta?"

Doretta nodded. "But not so well with me."

Mama tilted her head to one side. "What's wrong?"

Doretta quickly told her mother what Warren had admitted at the end of their workday and ended her story with a heavy sigh. "With all that being said, there's no way I can go back to the nutrition store tomorrow and face him." She moistened her lips with the tip of her tongue. "And now I have a favor to ask of you."

"What kind of favor?"

"Would you please call the Lengachers' number and leave a message for Warren? I would appreciate it if you explained that I have decided that it's necessary to resign from my job."

Mama's eyes widened, and her mouth dropped partially open. "You can't be serious, Doretta."

"I am very serious. After what Warren said to me, there is no way I can face him again let alone work with him in his store."

"I don't see why not. You can simply tell

Warren that you can't begin a romantic relationship with him because —"

Doretta held up her hand. "One obvious problem is that the man I have fallen in love with looks just like William. And I'm not 100 percent sure that the love I think I feel for him may be more about his physical resemblance to William." She paused. "If I had acknowledged what I've come to feel for Warren, he would have expected us to become a couple, and that's another problem, because it can never happen."

"How come? If he loves you and you love him, then what's the problem?"

"The problem is that I promised William I would only love him, and even though he's no longer with us, I cannot go back on my word. Warren should realize that and accept it, because William told me once that his brother knew about the promise we'd made to each other." Doretta sniffed deeply. "I — I wish Warren had never said that he's in love with me. Why couldn't he have been satisfied for us to go on as good friends?"

"Well, I just think —"

"It doesn't matter what anyone thinks. I need to get away, and Eleanor has invited me to come stay at her and Vic's house for as long as I need to. I found out today that she's in a family way again, and the baby is due in December. Poor Eleanor has not been feeling the best, so I'm sure she will appreciate the extra help I can offer her right now."

Mama blinked. "She's expecting a baby, is that far along, and hasn't told you before now? That seems odd, don't you think?"

"Eleanor said she had sent me a letter back in June and was surprised I hadn't responded to it. Of course that's because I never got the letter." Doretta pressed a fist against her mouth and puffed out her cheeks. "Can you believe that, Mama? I bet it got lost in the mail or ended up in someone else's mailbox."

"That may be true. Strange things have been known to happen with the mail service."

"So now that I know she's expecting a baby, I'm really eager to go, and it's a good excuse for me to resign from my job at the health food store."

"But Doretta, dear, running away from a problem never solved anything. I really think you should stay here and work things out with Warren."

"There's nothing to work out. He broke up with Margaret awhile back, and I'm sure I was the reason for his decision. He only thinks he's in love with me, and once I'm gone, Warren is bound to think back to what his brother had told him about the promise we'd made and realize that he and I cannot be together." Doretta placed her hand on Mama's arm. "I've made my decision, and after I hung up from talking with Eleanor, I called one of our drivers and she agreed to take me to Pennsylvania. We'll leave here early tomorrow morning."

"I'm not in favor of this idea, and I'm sure your father won't be either when he gets home from work and finds out what you are planning to do."

"I'll make sure that Papa understands my reasons for going to Pennsylvania. I just don't want to discuss it with my brothers or sister in the room. I do not need their input. Besides, Karen's too young to offer her opinion on this, one way or the other."

"That's true." Mama's lips pressed together in a slight grimace, but after a few seconds passed, she slowly nodded. "All right, Doretta, I'll make the call and leave a message for Warren since I assume you're afraid the sound of your tearful voice might let Warren know how much you really do care about him. But I still think you're making a terrible mistake."

Doretta shook her head. "I'd be making a bigger mistake if I stayed." She pushed her chair away from the table and stood. "Don't worry about fixing me a cup of tea. I'm going upstairs to pack. Since winter is coming soon, I'll need to take plenty of warm clothes, and I may need two suitcases."

Mama's eyes appeared to grow larger, and her voice cracked when she spoke. "You're planning to be gone that long?"

"Jah. I'll stay at least till Eleanor's baby is born, and then I'll see how it goes from there. If I should decide to stay longer, I'll have to look for a job."

Mama's eyes filled with tears, and she quickly wiped them away. "Are you saying that you may never move back to Indiana?"

"Possibly. I'll have to wait and see how it goes."

"But Doretta, Paradise will be unfamiliar, and you won't know anyone there except for Eleanor and Vic. Will you be content living that far away from your family?"

"It would be an adjustment, and I'd miss you all terribly." Doretta didn't tell her mother that if things worked out for her in Lancaster County, she planned to remain there permanently. It was the only way she could think of to get all thoughts of Warren out of her head.

CHAPTER 30

Doretta stood in the hallway, tearfully saying goodbye to her mother and father. She had told her siblings goodbye last night since she would be leaving before any of them were out of bed.

"Please let us know when you get there," Papa said after he'd given Doretta a hug. "We'll be visiting the phone shed often to check messages and will let your grandparents and other family members know once we get word that you have arrived safely."

"And we'll all be praying for safe travels." Mama swiped the tears from her cheeks. "We shall miss you every day, and it sure won't be the same here without you."

"I'll miss you too, and I promise to stay in touch through letters and phone calls." Doretta opened the front door. "I'm going to wait on the porch for Mary Beth. She should be here any minute, and I don't want her to honk the horn and wake the rest of the family."

"I'll wait with you while your daed goes out to the barn and begins his chores," Mama said.

"Not until I carry out our daughter's luggage, though." Papa grabbed both suitcases, stepped out the door, and placed them on the porch.

Doretta slung her purse over her shoulder and picked up a satchel filled with some personal items she would need on the trip.

Mama came out the door behind them with a small cooler bag, which she handed to Doretta. "There are some snacks and bottled water in here for the trip in case you get hungry along the way between stops your driver will be making for meals."

"Danki, Mom, that was *gedankevoll.*"

Papa grinned. "Your mamm does a lot of thoughtful things for her family. And others too," he added.

Mama blushed. "Now don't you go trying to make me look good in our daughter's eyes. I am no saint, you know. I simply enjoy doing what any *gut mudder* would do for her family and friends."

"You are a very good mother," Doretta said, swallowing against the lump lodged in her throat. "And even though it isn't said as often as it should be, we all appreciate the way you look out for our needs." Doretta caught sight of Mary Beth pulling in, and she gave her parents one final hug. "It's time for me to go, but I'll be in touch soon."

Doretta's father reached for her two pieces of luggage. "I'll carry these out to the van for you."

"Danki, Papa." Struggling to hold her tears at bay, Doretta hurried out to the van ahead of him.

"Would you mind checking for phone messages before you help your daed in the barn?" Warren's mother asked him as their day started.

"No problem," he replied. "If there's anything important, I'll come back to the house and let you know before I head for the barn."

Mom turned from the kitchen counter where she'd been mixing pancake batter and smiled. "Danki, Warren."

"You're welcome." He grabbed his straw hat from a wall peg, slipped into a jacket, and went out the back door. Warren hadn't said anything to either of his parents about how things had gone yesterday afternoon when he'd told Doretta that he loved her. He wanted to wait until he saw Doretta at the store this morning and got her reaction after he told her the rest of what he'd wanted to say the previous day. If she reacted positively, he would definitely tell his folks. If Doretta gave a negative reaction, he may as well not say anything to Mom and Dad.

Warren hurried around the side of the house and made his way down the driveway to the phone shed. When he entered the small building, the message light on the answering machine was blinking.

Warren took a seat on the stool and hit the message button. There was only one message, from Amanda Schwartz. He reached under the brim of his hat and scratched his head. "That's strange. I wonder what she wants. It's probably a message for Mom."

He picked up a pen in readiness to write down Amanda's message, but the pen slipped from his fingers when he heard: "This message is for Warren. I am calling to let you know that Doretta won't be going to work today." There was a brief pause. "And I'm sorry to say that she has decided to quit working for you."

Warren sat several seconds in stunned silence, rubbing his forehead. *Doretta doesn't love me. What I told her yesterday only made things worse. I doubt that it would have mattered if she knew about William's journal entry. I've lost the only girl I have ever loved, and now I wish I'd kept quiet about my feelings for her.*

Warren remained in the phone shed for several minutes, trying to bring his swirling emotions under control before going back to the house. Not only was his heart broken, but he also had to find someone else to work with him at the nutrition center, and quickly, because he couldn't manage the place by himself for long.

With an ache in his heart and a feeling of heaviness, Warren ambled back to the house. As much as he hated to do it, he would have to ask his mother if she would help out at the store until he could either hire someone else or convince Doretta to come back. He hoped it would be the latter.

Paradise

Eleanor had busied herself all morning, getting everything ready for her dear friend's arrival. She had been wanting to spend some quality time with Doretta for quite a while and would soon be getting that chance. It was too bad their visit couldn't be under better circumstances, though. After talking to Doretta last night on the phone and listening to everything her friend said, Eleanor realized how shocked Doretta must have been to learn that Warren was in love with her. Hearing this hadn't totally surprised Eleanor, however. She remembered how, when they were children attending school and even into their teen years, Warren would often do kind things for Doretta. Eleanor had thought sometimes that he paid her friend more attention than William did. Of course, Doretta had been smitten by Warren's brother, so she probably hadn't noticed that Warren cared deeply for her.

But why is Doretta so upset about it now? Eleanor wondered as she walked into the guest room to make sure it was ready for her friend's arrival. *I would think Doretta would be pleased that Warren thinks so much of her. Guess I'll know more when she gets here and we've had a chance to talk about it.*

After looking things over one last time, Eleanor perceived that it seemed to be in order, so she left the room and headed down the hall to check on Rosetta. If she was awake, she would no doubt be ready to eat.

I bet Doretta will enjoy spending time with Rosetta, Eleanor thought when she entered her daughter's bedroom and found her sitting up in the crib, wide-eyed and with a big grin on her sweet face.

"We'll be having company soon, and I know you will love Doretta as much as she'll love you." Eleanor lifted the child into her arms and smiled when the little girl giggled. It was hard to believe that Rosetta was a year old already and had begun walking a week ago, which meant getting into things within her reach. Having Doretta here would mean an extra pair of hands and feet watching and taking care of Rosetta. It would also give Eleanor a chance to rest during the day whenever she became sick to her stomach or felt exceptionally tired. Of course, those weren't the main reasons Eleanor looked forward to her friend's visit. She was eager to spend time chatting and hoped she would be given an opportunity to comfort Doretta, as she had done through the letters she'd sent to her since William's death. From Doretta's responses via letters and phone calls, Eleanor had become aware that her friend's depression had subsided, but she wasn't sure where Doretta stood spiritually.

Perhaps she is doing better in that area too and just hasn't said so. But if not, I'll pray that the Lord will use me in leading Doretta to a close relationship with God like she once had.

■ ■ ■ ■

Doretta fidgeted on the seat beside her driver. It was nearly two o'clock, and according to Mary Beth's GPS, they were almost to their destination. She looked forward to seeing Eleanor again and getting acquainted with her friend's little girl. Although Doretta had seen Rosetta before, the child had been a baby. Since then, she'd become a toddler, which no doubt kept life quite interesting at the Lapps' home these days.

"Are you certain that you don't want me to stick around Lancaster County for a few days in case you change your mind about staying until your friend's baby is born?" Mary Beth's question broke into Doretta's thoughts.

"There's no need for that," Doretta replied. "I won't change my mind. If and when I'm ready to return to Grabill, I'll let you know."

"Okay." Mary Beth turned right and drove her van up the driveway until a white house came into view. "This must be it." She looked over at Doretta and then pointed. "I see your friend's last name on a welcome sign above the front door."

417

"Yes, I see it too." Excitement welled in Doretta's soul, although it was mixed with a bit of trepidation. What if things didn't work out staying here? She might wear out her welcome after a week or even a few days.

Stop thinking negative thoughts, Doretta chided herself. *I'm sure once Eleanor and I are together again, it will be like old times, and we'll simply enjoy each other's company.*

Once Mary Beth had shut off the van's engine, she came around and helped Doretta get her suitcases taken up to the porch. Doretta reached out to knock, but her fingers hadn't even connected with the wood when the door opened and Eleanor stepped out. "Oh, it's so wonderful to see you! You made good time. How was your trip?" Eleanor spoke in a bubbly voice, and Doretta couldn't miss the look of excitement on her friend's face.

"Our trip went well, and it's great seeing you again too."

Doretta and Eleanor hugged, and then Doretta introduced her driver, whom Eleanor had not met before because Mary Beth was fairly new to the Grabill area.

"It's nice to meet you." Eleanor shook the middle-aged woman's hand, but Mary Beth stated that she was a hugger and pulled Eleanor into a hug. "I've heard so much about you. In fact, Doretta kept me entertained on the trip here with stories about when the two of you were girls growing up in Grabill."

Eleanor rolled her eyes. "I can just imagine what kind of stories she had to tell."

Mary Beth chuckled. "She told some good ones, all right." She stepped forward with one of Doretta's suitcases. "Let's get your things inside, and then I'll be on my way."

"There's no need for you to hurry off," Eleanor was quick to say. "Wouldn't you like to sit down for a cup of coffee or a glass of cold water? The three of us can visit while my daughter entertains us with the toys she has spread out in the living room."

Mary Beth set Doretta's suitcase down in the entryway. "I appreciate the offer, but as we came into Paradise, I saw a few stores I'd like to investigate, and I'd better do that now, before they close up for the day. After that, I'll be checking into a bed-and-breakfast here in Paradise for the night, and then I plan to head back to Grabill tomorrow morning."

"Thank you for everything," Doretta said, handing Mary Beth the money she owed for the ride. "I hope everything goes well on your trip home."

"Thanks." Mary Beth gave Doretta a hug

and turned to face Eleanor again. "It was so nice meeting you. Perhaps we'll meet again when Doretta is ready to return to Indiana."

"It was nice meeting you too," Eleanor said. She looked over at Doretta and smiled. "I hope that trip back to Grabill won't be anytime soon. I've really been looking forward to our time together, and I don't want it to end too quickly."

Doretta gave a nod. "Same here."

After Mary Beth left, Doretta went to the living room to see Rosetta, and after she sat on the floor watching the child play with her toys for several minutes, she stood and said to Eleanor, "I'd better go outside to your phone shed and call my mamm. I'm sure she's been checking for messages off and on this afternoon, waiting to hear that my driver and I got here okay."

"Of course." Eleanor smiled. "While you're gone, I'll set out some cookies and something to drink. Would you like a glass of *wasser* or some *kaffi*?"

"A cup of coffee would be good. The last few hours of our trip I had trouble staying awake, but I made myself remain alert so I could keep talking to Mary Beth in case she felt sleepy."

"That was good thinking. After you return to the house and we've had our refreshments, I'll show you to your room so you can unpack and get settled in."

"Sounds good." Doretta went out the front door and had no trouble finding the phone shed, which was near the end of the Lapps' driveway.

Doretta felt a weird but relaxed sensation as she approached the shed. Just being here and putting distance between herself and Warren made her feel like the burden she'd felt since her last conversation with him had been lifted a bit.

Grabill

"How did I do today?" Warren's mother asked when he put the CLOSED sign in the store window. "Was I helpful enough?"

"You did just fine, Mom," he responded. "I didn't expect you to know where everything was on your first day working here, but you were able to locate most items on your own when I was busy with something else."

She smiled. "I'm glad I can be of assistance to you, Son. It would be difficult for you to manage this store on your own, and I want you to know that I'm willing to help out here for as long as you need me."

"I appreciate that." Warren couldn't believe he had asked his mother to fill in for

Doretta today, because he remembered how he'd turned her down when she'd volunteered to work here before he'd hired Margaret. Although he'd never spoken the words to his mother, Warren had been sure that his mother would have taken over and tried to tell him how to run the store.

He leaned against the front counter while slowly shaking his head. "I still can't believe Doretta's mother called to let me know that Doretta was quitting her job here. She must be pretty upset with me, Mom."

"Just give her some time." Warren's mother patted his arm. "I believe when Doretta has a chance to think about things, she'll realize that she needs a job and will most likely come back and ask you to hire her again."

Warren's hands went limp at his sides. "I'm not so sure about that. Amanda made it pretty clear in her message that Doretta has no desire to work here again. I think I've ruined things between us for good."

"Have you considered going over to her parents' house and trying to explain things to Doretta? Don't you think she has the right to know what your brother wrote in his journal?"

He shrugged. "I thought she should know, until she ran out of here and then notified me, via her mother, that she wouldn't be working here again. She obviously doesn't have the same feelings for me as I do for her, so there's not much point in telling her what William wrote."

"You won't know that for certain unless you try."

Warren tipped his head. "I suppose it's worth a try. Maybe I'll drop by and talk to Doretta after work tomorrow."

"Why put off till tomorrow what you can do today?"

He sighed. "Guess you're right. After our driver drops us off at home, I'll hitch up my horse and head over to her house. But if Doretta is unwilling to talk to me, there's not much else I can do."

CHAPTER 31

Warren whispered a prayer while still in his open buggy, then got down and secured his horse to the hitching rail. When a heady gust of wind came up, blowing wind-tossed leaves across the yard, Warren grabbed hold of his straw hat with both hands and headed for Doretta's house as quickly as he could.

Despite the chilly blast of air sliding beneath his jacket collar, Warren's hands felt sweaty. He heard the tinkling music of wind chimes and knocked on the front door. Several seconds passed before the door swung open. Doretta's sister looked up at him with a curious expression.

"Hey, Karen." Warren smiled at the young girl, hoping she might offer him a warm greeting, but she stood there stony-faced. "Is Doretta at home?" he asked.

"Nope."

"Do you know what time she'll be back?"

The girl gave a brief shrug with her palms

turned up.

He shuffled his feet against the wooden porch floor, wishing for a better response from Doretta's sister. "I really need to talk to her. It's important."

"Mama's here but not Doretta. Wanna talk to her instead?"

He hesitated a moment, then nodded. Surely Doretta's mother would know what time her eldest daughter planned to be home.

Karen opened the door wider. "Mama's in the living room workin' on a giant puzzle. I was helpin' her till you knocked on the door." After closing the door against the howling wind, she led the way and Warren followed.

He approached the card table, where Amanda sat studying the puzzle that appeared to be half done. "Guder *owed*," he said after clearing his throat.

"Good evening," she responded, diverting her attention from the puzzle and looking directly at him.

"I'm sorry to bother you," Warren said. "I came to see Doretta, but Karen said she's not here."

Amanda nodded, her gaze swinging back to the puzzle.

Is she not going to talk to me? Warren

wondered as he waited nervously, overheating in his jacket. He reached under his hat and scratched his head. *I just want to get to the bottom of what is going on with Doretta.* "Do you know when she'll be home?"

Amanda pushed away from the table and stood with one arm clasping the other at the elbow. "Not exactly. It could be some time before we see Doretta again." Her voice sounded strained, as though she might be hiding something.

I can't believe my ears. It could be some time before we see Doretta again? What does that mean? Warren's mind raced like a runaway horse as he searched for answers. Something wasn't right here. He felt it in his gut. Was Amanda trying to keep him from talking to Doretta? Did she know about the things he'd said to her daughter yesterday? Could Doretta be hiding out in her room, unwilling to speak to him? *No, that can't be it, or Amanda would be lying to my face, and I don't think she would do that.* "Do you mind me asking where she went?" he questioned.

Amanda shifted her position, clutching her apron in front of her as if it were a shield.

"I really need to talk to her."

"Ya can't," Karen spoke up. "My big

426

sister's in Paradise. She went there this morning."

Warren quirked an eyebrow. "Huh?"

"Paradise, Pennsylvania. Doretta went there to visit her friend Eleanor," Amanda stated. "And I don't know when she'll be back. She might stay there several months." She looked at Karen and asked her to go set the table for supper. This topic was obviously something Amanda did not want to talk about in front of her young daughter.

Karen nodded and scampered off toward the kitchen.

I hope she doesn't get upset with more questions. Warren rubbed his sweaty palms down the sides of his pant legs. "Did Doretta go there to get away from me, or was it for some other reason?"

Amanda's hand fluttered to the neckline of her dark green dress. "She was very upset by the things you said to her yesterday. That's why she asked me to call you and say that she was quitting her job at the nutrition center."

"I got that, but I never expected she'd run off to Pennsylvania and not even tell her own mother when she would be back."

Amanda looked at him with a blank expression, which only increased Warren's frustrations. *Can't Doretta's mother see how desperate I am?* "I need to talk to Doretta," he said. "There was more I had planned to tell her."

Amanda gave a firm shake of her head. "That's not a good idea, Warren. My daughter has never fully recovered from your brother's death, and she needs this time away, which is probably something she should have done sooner. Hopefully, this will give her a chance to think things through and come to grips with whatever feelings she is still dealing with. Doretta has come a long way from the depressed state she was in for so many months after William died, but her recovery has not been complete." She changed her position and reached out to touch Warren's arm. "My advice is to give her more time. If it's meant for you and Doretta to be together, she must come to that realization on her own without any pressure from you or anyone else."

Warren's hands went limp. "Okay then. Danki for your time." With a feeling of emptiness throughout his body, Warren turned and shuffled out the door. He felt as powerless over his future as he did over controlling the wind. *Even if I had been able to tell Doretta about William's journal, she may have still rejected me,* Warren told himself as

428

he made his way toward the horse and buggy. *Amanda's right — if it's meant for us to be together, then Doretta will need to realize that on her own. Guess all I can do is pray for her and try to keep my focus on running my business. If and when Doretta returns to Grabill, and I feel the time is right, maybe then I'll tell her about the things my brother wrote.*

"Isn't our *nachtesse* ready yet?" Betty's husband asked when he entered the kitchen and saw her peeling potatoes.

"Sorry, Raymond, but I didn't want to get supper ready too soon since Warren's not home yet." She gestured to the refrigerator. "If you're feeling hungerich, why don't you snack on some *kaes*? There's also a box of crackers in there." Betty pointed in the direction of the pantry.

He wrinkled his nose. "I don't want any cheese or crackers. What I'd like is some mashed potatoes to go with that roast you have baking in the oven that smells so good."

"I'll put the potatoes on to boil as soon as Warren shows up."

Raymond got out a glass and poured himself some milk. "I don't see why we have to wait for Warren. There's no telling how long he will be gone, and you can always keep a supper dish warming for him in the oven." He took a drink, then turned to face her. "And you know what else, Betty?"

She shook her head.

"It's not good for you to keep kowtowing to our son all the time. He's a grown man, for goodness' sake, and he can certainly fend for himself."

Betty put the peeler down and crossed both arms over her chest with a huff. "I do not kowtow to Warren."

"Jah, you do." Raymond slurped some milk from his top lip. "You cook, clean, make his bed, do his laundry, and now you're working with Warren in his store."

Her face warmed. "That's not fair. Warren needs help at his nutrition center, and when he asked me to fill in until he could find someone else, I could hardly say no." She pointed a finger at Raymond. "And in case you've forgotten, let me remind you that I cooked, cleaned, made the bed, and did William's laundry too, and you never said anything about that."

Raymond lowered himself into a seat at the table. "That's true, but if he had lived, you wouldn't have been doing all that very long because he would have been married to Doretta by now."

430

Tears welled in Betty's eyes. "I don't need the reminder. And what do you want me to do? Should I tell Warren that he'll have to do everything that he needs done all by himself, when he has a busy store to run? I'm his mudder, and I'm more than happy to help him by doing those chores as well as working with him in the nutrition center."

Raymond left the table and pulled Betty into his arms. "I'm sorry for upsetting you. Guess I'm just being selfish, wanting to have supper ready when I get home from work." He gently patted her back. "You were right in wanting to help out at his store, and if you want to do all those other things for Warren here at home, then I won't bring the topic up again."

"Danki." She sniffed and stepped out of his embrace. "I'll go ahead and put the potatoes on, and then we'll eat as soon as they're done."

He shook his head. "No, that's okay. I can wait to eat till Warren gets here."

"All right, if you're sure you don't mind."

"I'm fine with it." Raymond drank the rest of his milk and had just brought his glass to the sink when Warren walked in with wind-blown hair and holding his straw hat with both hands.

"I'm glad you're back. How did things go

with Doretta?" Betty asked after he'd hung up his hat and jacket.

"I never spoke with her. She's gone."

Betty's brows furrowed. "What do you mean, Son? Where has Doretta gone?"

"I was told that this morning she took off for Pennsylvania to stay with her friend Eleanor. Her mamm said she didn't know when Doretta might come back." Warren slumped against the counter near the sink. "I've lost her, Mom. I don't think she will ever return to Grabill."

Betty gave her son a tender hug. "I'm so sorry, Son. But don't lose heart. Doretta might have a change of heart and return to Grabill to make things right with you. If not, then maybe it's not meant for you to be with her. She may not be the woman God has chosen for you."

He heaved a sigh. "I'd rather not talk about this anymore. I'm going to the bathroom to wash up, and then I'll come in and join you and Dad for supper."

Betty watched Warren leave the room with slumped shoulders and head down. Oh, how she wished there was something she could do to put a smile on her son's face and a spring in his step again. But unless she could come up with something that would help, there was nothing to do right now except pray, and that she would definitely do.

Paradise

Doretta looked around her friend's kitchen table and couldn't help feeling a bit envious. Vic sat at one end, Eleanor occupied the seat across from Doretta, and Rosetta sat in a wooden high chair to the right of her mother. They were a family, and a few months from now, another child would be added. Doretta would never know the joy of getting married and having children — all because of a promise she had made. At the time, it had felt right to pledge her love to William for forever. But she hadn't considered how it would be if one of them died. When he'd promised to love only her, William probably hadn't thought about that either.

Doretta picked up her glass of water and took a drink. *Now I'm in love with William's brother, and I can't do anything about it. What a pickle I'm in — and all because of a promise.*

"You're awfully quiet, and you haven't eaten much. Aren't you hungry, Doretta?"

Vic's question pushed Doretta's thoughts to the back of her mind. "I'm tired from the long trip, and I guess maybe it robbed me of my appetite."

"That's understandable. So when we finish eating, I'll take care of the dishes, and you'll be free to go right to bed." Eleanor's words were spoken in a soothing tone. "I'm sure a good night's sleep is what you need, my friend."

Doretta shook her head. "I wouldn't feel right about leaving you stuck with the kitchen cleanup. I want to help, and I can wait till that's all done before going to sleep."

"It's all right," Eleanor said. "Vic usually helps me do the supper dishes."

Doretta glanced over at him, and she felt a bit better when he smiled and gave a nod.

"Okay then, I'll finish the food on my plate and get ready for bed." Doretta looked back at Eleanor. "Tomorrow, I'll feel rested and ready to help with anything you need to have done. I'm sure between the two of us, we can get a lot accomplished."

Eleanor reached over and wiped her daughter's face, messy with food. "And you'll have the chance to get better acquainted with your little namesake."

Doretta forced a smile despite the lump that had crept into her throat. Oh, how she wished for a child of her own. A vision of Warren came to mind. *I wish I was free to acknowledge the love I have for him that will remain hidden in my heart until the day I die.*

CHAPTER 32

It had been a week since Doretta's arrival in Paradise, and every day she had kept busy helping Eleanor with household chores, shopping, and caring for Rosetta. It was good to keep busy. It kept her from thinking too much about Warren and the strong feelings she had developed for him.

It isn't fair, Doretta told herself as she removed some fresh-smelling towels from the clothesline in Eleanor's yard and placed them in the wicker basket near her feet. *I wish I'd never made the promise to William that I would always love him and no other man.* She swallowed hard as tears clogged her throat and threatened to spill over. *Even more than that, I wish I could banish all thoughts of Warren from my head.*

She was about to add a few more towels to the basket, when Vic's dog, Checkers, bounded up to her with a stick in his mouth. He dropped it next to the basket and looked up at Doretta with his head cocked to one side.

"You want me to throw that stick, don't you, boy?"

Woof! Woof! Woof!

She chuckled in spite of the tears she'd been fighting only moments ago and bent down to pick up the well-used piece of wood. "Okay, Checkers . . . now fetch!" Doretta gave a hefty toss and watched as Checkers raced across the yard in pursuit of his goal. It felt good to have a little fun like this with the dog. It definitely helped her feel more relaxed — at least until a distant memory surfaced.

"Throw me the *balle!*" William shouted. "Hurry now, before my bruder makes a home run."

Doretta stood off to the side, along with some of the other girls in her class who had stayed on the playground after school to watch the eighth-grade boys play a rousing game of baseball. William and Warren played on opposing teams, and there was no doubt about the competition going on between the brothers as well as all the other players.

William was better at baseball, but Warren always did his best. Besides, there were other things he was good at, so Doretta didn't think it mattered who won or lost the game. But the boys had other ideas, and the game continued with lots of cheering from the sidelines, along with dirty, sweaty boys hollering at one another and playing for all they were worth.

Doretta felt bad when Warren fell trying to slide into home plate, but she was glad he wasn't seriously hurt.

When the game was over and Warren's team had lost, Doretta watched as he and some of the other boys walked away with slumped shoulders and heads down. She was on the verge of going over to tell him that it didn't matter who won or lost the game, when William came up to her, grinning from ear to ear. "Pretty good game, jah?" He leaned close to her ear. "Did ya count how many home runs I made here today?"

"No, not really," she admitted. "I was busy watching all the action, though."

"Jah, there was plenty of that, and I'm sure glad my team won." William's grin widened.

"Is Warren okay? He fell pretty hard when he was hurrying to get on base."

William shrugged. "Aw, he's fine. The only thing that got hurt was my brother's pride. He'll get over it, though. He always bounces back whenever things don't go his way."

Woof! Woof!

Doretta's thoughts returned to the present when Vic's dog announced his presence again. The stick Doretta had thrown for Checkers a few minutes ago lay at her feet again.

"Okay, I'll toss you the stick once more, but then I need to finish getting this laundry off the line." Doretta grabbed the stick. Checkers posed in readiness until she'd sent the piece of wood flying, and then he was off and running, his ears streaming back in the breeze.

That dog is a determined one. Doretta pulled two more towels from the line. *Just like William, who always wanted to win at whatever he did. I wonder if what William said to me that day outside the schoolhouse about Warren was true. Does he always bounce back when things don't go his way?*

Eleanor stood at the living-room window watching Doretta alternate between taking clothes off the line and playing fetch with Vic's dog. Her friend was bundled up against the cold, but at least the sun was out, and the towels they'd laundered earlier today had no doubt had enough time to dry.

In the week Doretta had been here, she'd been so helpful — always asking what needed to be done and then jumping right in to complete the task. Eleanor appreciated the extra pair of hands, but she'd hoped they would have more time for sitting and talking. Eleanor knew from the times she had gone to Al-Anon meetings how important it was to get in touch with one's feelings and learn how to reach out to others for help. Although her friend was not dealing with an alcoholic, the way Eleanor had with Vic some time ago, Doretta had been doing some better emotionally. But now, with the situation involving Warren, it had become obvious to Eleanor that Doretta had not fully come to grips with her feelings about the accident that had taken William's life and left her with a broken neck and other injuries. To compound things, now Eleanor's dear friend struggled with the love she felt for William's brother, which she thought there was nothing she could do about. And it was all because of a spontaneous promise she had made to the man she'd planned to marry.

Eleanor thought about the devotional book she'd been reading before going to bed at night. The book focused on the topics of strengthening one's faith and learning to know God's will when making important decisions. *I think I'll place that devotional on the coffee table in the living room,* Eleanor decided. *Maybe Doretta will see it there, become curious, and read some of the chapters and scripture verses on faith and discernment. They have certainly helped me when difficult decisions needed to be made.*

Eleanor heard the timer in the kitchen go off and went to check on the peanut butter cookies baking in the oven. After opening the oven door and testing the cookies to be sure they were done, she grabbed a potholder and removed the tray to place on a cooling rack. She sniffed deeply, and instead of feeling nauseous as she sometimes did when a particular food odor permeated the kitchen, she enjoyed the delicious aroma of peanut butter that whetted her appetite. As soon as Doretta came in with the laundry basket, they would sit down at the kitchen table and enjoy a few cookies.

Doretta gathered up the basket and returned to the house. Once inside, the alluring smell of freshly baked peanut butter cookies caused her mouth to water. It reminded Doretta of a day, not long ago, when her mom had invited her to have peanut butter cookies, hot tea, and sit down for a chat. Doretta sighed. *I'd still be at home right now if Warren hadn't proclaimed his love for me. But I'm at Eleanor's place now, and I want to be helpful, focusing on all the things that need to be done while I am here.*

Doretta's next job would be folding and putting away the towels. After that, she would offer to take care of Rosetta in case Eleanor felt like taking a nap. Even though Doretta had never been pregnant, she remembered how tired her mother had been during her pregnancy with Karen. Poor Mama had often fallen asleep on the couch around the time she would have been starting supper. Fortunately, Doretta had been there to take over, and since she had learned to cook at an early age, she'd managed to fix a decent meal without her mother's help.

Doretta took the full basket to the dining room and set it on one of the chairs. She would fold the towels and stack them on the table, then take them to the linen closet in the hall.

She had done about half the towels when Eleanor entered the room. "I have some peanut butter kichlin and hot cider ready." She grinned. "I was going to fix tea but changed my mind, so why don't you leave the towels for now and come to the kitchen to have a snack with me?"

"That sounds good, but I really should finish these first." Doretta gestured to the towels left in the basket.

"There's no hurry. They can wait awhile."

Eleanor clasped Doretta's arm. "Come now, we don't want the cider to get cold."

"Okay, if you insist." Doretta followed her friend to the kitchen.

Soon, they were both seated at the table enjoying the delicious cookies Eleanor had baked and some tangy warm cider.

"This must be homemade." Doretta licked her lips. "It tastes so crisp and tart — just the way I like hot cider."

Eleanor nodded. "Vic's daed has a cider press, and we provided the apples from one of our trees. It was fun to watch the cider-making process, and Vic's whole family was there for the event. Even Rosetta had a good time." Eleanor laughed. "Of course, that was mostly because everyone wanted to hold her. Rosetta received plenty of attention that day, as she was passed from person to person."

Doretta smiled. "Speaking of Rosetta — where is that darling little girl?"

"She's still napping, but it probably won't be long until she wakes up."

"That's good, then I'll take my turn watching her while you get some rest."

"I'm not tired."

"But you've been baking all morning. Didn't that tire you out?"

Eleanor shook her head. "Not really, and

443

I don't need to rest. Maybe later this afternoon I'll feel like it though."

"Well, if you do, I'll keep an eye on Rosetta." Doretta bit into a cookie. "Yummy . . . this is sure tasty. It was worth the trip to Pennsylvania just to sample some of your kichlin."

Eleanor chuckled. "Danki for the compliment, but I'm no better at baking than you are, my friend."

"I do all right in the kitchen, I suppose. When I was engaged to marry William, I looked forward to eventually having a home of our own, where I could do all kinds of cooking and baking." Doretta released a deep sigh. "Did I ever tell you where William was taking me the night of the accident that took his life?"

"No, I don't believe so." Eleanor thumped the side of her head. "Unless my pregnant brain has forgotten what you may have said."

Doretta drank some more cider and set her mug down. "I didn't even know where we were heading that evening. William said it was a surprise."

"But you found out later?"

"Jah. Warren told me. He said his brother told him that he'd bought a piece of property where he intended to have a house built for us, so we wouldn't have lived with his grandparents very long." Doretta's vision blurred. "It saddens me to think that we never got the chance to have a home of our own."

"Do you know where the property is located? Have you gone there to see it?"

"No, and I don't want to. It would be sad to see the place where William had wanted us to live. Besides, I think William's parents must have sold it by now."

Eleanor reached over and clasped Doretta's hand. "I'm sorry, Doretta. I know how disappointed you must be — not about the house but about not being able to marry the man you loved so dearly."

"Love," Doretta corrected. "I still love William, and I always will."

Rosetta's shrill cry ended their conversation. "I'd better go tend to my daughter. We can continue our conversation when I get back, if you like."

Doretta nodded, but she hoped when Eleanor returned to the kitchen, they could discuss something else. Talking about William made her think about Warren, and that topic was off limits.

Grabill

Amanda entered the health food store to

get a few things she needed and spotted Warren's mother sitting behind the checkout counter.

"Good afternoon." Betty smiled and stood. "May I help you with something?"

"I just need a few items, but I'm sure I can find them." Amanda glanced around, feeling a bit uncomfortable all of a sudden. It seemed odd to come here and not see Doretta working and Betty now in her place. "Is Warren working today?"

"Jah," Betty responded, "but he had an errand to run, so I'm here minding the store by myself for a while."

"Do you enjoy working here?"

"I can think of a few things I'd rather be doing, but my son needs me, so I will keep helping out until he finds someone else who is more qualified."

Amanda wondered if she should mention Doretta, but before she could make up her mind, Betty spoke first with a question.

"Do you have any idea when your daughter will return from her trip to Pennsylvania?"

"No, I do not. Doretta's only been gone a week, and she hasn't said yet how long she plans to stay there."

"Warren blames himself for her leaving." Betty's words were spoken kindly, and she looked at Amanda with sympathy in her eyes. "I'm sure you must miss Doretta very much."

"I do, and if she decides to remain in Paradise permanently, it'll be hard to accept." Amanda rubbed her arms briskly through the woolen material of her jacket. "I wish Warren had never said that he loved her."

"But he does, and he wanted her to know it." Betty came around and put one arm around Amanda's shoulder. "We both love our children, and we want the best for them, right?"

"Of course." She looked at Warren's mother and blinked against invading tears. "I tried to talk Doretta out of leaving, but she said she had to get away. I had promised her that I wouldn't tell anyone this, but I see no reason to keep it a secret from you — although I'd rather that you tell no one else, including Warren."

"Tell him what?"

"The fact is my daughter loves your son too."

Betty became quiet. "I wasn't supposed to tell anyone about Warren's feelings for Doretta," she finally said, "but since he told her himself, I don't feel bound by that promise any longer."

"Well then, there ought to be some way we can get those two together. But it probably won't happen because Doretta feels guilty for loving Warren."

Betty touched the base of her neck and began to massage it slowly. "Why? Because she also loved William?"

Amanda nodded. "You may not know this, but Doretta promised William to love no other man but him. Doretta feels that she is bound by that promise, so she can't give her heart to Warren. Does that make any sense to you?"

"Yes and no."

"What do you mean?"

"It makes sense that two young people in love would promise to love no other. What does not make sense is that Doretta doesn't realize that since her beloved is gone, she is no longer bound by that promise."

"You're right, Betty, but unless Doretta comes to that conclusion on her own, there is no hope of her and Warren ever having a future together."

"We can pray for your daughter, and I'm sure that Warren is praying for her too."

"Certainly, but I don't think it would be good for any of us to put pressure on Doretta. That could cause her to pull further away. Loving Warren and letting her promise to William go has to be her decision, and I will not try to sway her. I have decided to leave it all in God's hands."

Betty nodded. "All right, Amanda. And I will make every effort to do that too."

CHAPTER 33

"How are you feeling this afternoon?" Doretta asked when she entered the living room and found Eleanor lying on the couch with her eyes open. "Did you do too much this morning?"

"I don't think so, but the muscles in my back are a little tight, so I thought I should rest here awhile."

"When my mamm was expecting Karen, she used to complain of her back hurting a lot, and lying down to rest always seemed to help." Doretta seated herself in the rocking chair. "So relax there as long as you want, and don't worry about helping with lunch. I will take care of feeding Rosetta, and I'll make our lunch too. All you have to do is tell me what appeals to you."

"Rosetta is fine for the moment." Eleanor motioned to her daughter, playing happily across the room with her toys. "And I'm not hungry yet, so why don't we stay here and visit awhile?"

Doretta leaned comfortably against the back of her chair. "Okay. Just let me know when you're ready to eat and I'll head straight for the kitchen to get lunch made."

"Sounds good." Eleanor sat up and positioned a cushion behind her back.

"There's something I've been wanting to ask you." Doretta swirled her tongue around the inside of her mouth. "But if you'd rather not answer, I'll understand."

"Go ahead. What do you want to know?"

"I was wondering how you held things together during the time Vic was drinking and refused to get help. Did your faith in God become weak when Vic got progressively worse?"

Eleanor folded her hands in a prayer-like gesture. "I did question God a few times, but I never stopped praying or believing that He would give me the strength to deal with the situation. No matter how bad things looked, I continued to seek God's will, all the time asking Him what I should do." Eleanor smiled. "I also found help through the letters you sent. You were such an encouragement to me. It was a comfort to know that I could trust you not to tell anyone the things I shared with you. Another thing I did that was really the most important was to read the Bible along with my devotional book every day."

Doretta sat quietly, letting her friend's words sink in. It was a comfort to know that the letters and words of advice she'd offered had been helpful to Eleanor when she'd gone through such a troubling time in her marriage. During the time Doretta had written those letters, she'd felt God's presence and was certain that He had given her the right words to share. *Why then,* she asked herself now, *have I not felt His presence and a sense of direction in my own life during this past unsettling year?* She glanced at the devotional book lying on Eleanor's coffee table. *I think I should start reading that, along with some passages from the Bible. I will also pray and ask the Lord to speak to me through His Holy Word.*

Grabill

"Anything from Doretta in that pile of letters?" Elmer asked when he entered the kitchen where Amanda sat going through the mail.

She shook her head. "I guess she's been real busy helping Eleanor and hasn't found the time to write."

He frowned. "At least she could leave us a message more often. I mean, how long does it take to make a phone call?"

Amanda shrugged.

"You're not condoning our daughter's inconsiderate behavior, I hope."

Amanda placed the envelope she held on the table and looked directly at her husband. "I am not condoning anything Doretta has done. I just don't see the point in getting worked up because she hasn't kept in touch as often as we'd like."

Elmer took the seat across from her. "She's been gone a whole month now, and how often has she called or written?"

"I don't know. I haven't kept track." Normally, Amanda would have been just as upset about not hearing from their daughter as Elmer was right now, but she had decided that no news was good news, so what was the point in getting worked up over something she couldn't control? Amanda had been doing what she and Betty both decided — praying regularly for Doretta and Warren, and she told Elmer that.

"I've been praying for her too," Elmer said. "In fact, I pray every day for all five of our kinner."

"As do I." She looked at her husband calmly. "We need to trust the Lord to reveal His will to Doretta. If she is supposed to return to Grabill, He will make that clear.

And if it's meant for our daughter to remain in Pennsylvania, we'll need to accept it and not try to make her feel guilty."

"Do you think she might eventually find someone there and end up getting married?"

"It's doubtful since Doretta believes she must keep the promise she made to William. Unless she comes to a place where she feels released from that commitment, our eldest daughter will probably never allow herself to fall in love again and get married."

Elmer shook his head slowly. "Now that would be a real shame."

Warren sat at the desk in his office going over a list of things he needed to order for the store. This was cold and flu season, and he needed to keep his shelves stocked with plenty of cough syrup, natural decongestants, chest rubs, herbal teas, and several other products his customers liked to use for their fall and winter illnesses. One of the items he was almost out of was an herbal tea for sore throats that was particularly soothing when a teaspoon of honey was added to each cup. Many people had told Warren that it was one of the most helpful remedies he sold.

Another product that sold well these days was vitamin C with citrus bioflavonoids. The supplement was used to strengthen a person's immune system, and taken as suggested on the label, it delivered twenty-four-hour support. Warren took anywhere from three thousand to five thousand milligrams of vitamin C per day during cold and flu season. He felt that he needed it in order to stay well so he could keep his store open to the public. Since becoming an adult, Warren had believed in trying to maintain his health through good eating habits and by taking nutritional supplements.

Warren finished the list and leaned back in his chair with his eyes closed. As often occurred, a vision of Doretta came to mind. Her pretty auburn hair, gentle spirit, and the kindness in her brown eyes had captivated him for as long as he could remember. *If only she could love me as I love her. If Doretta knew about William's journal entry, would it make any difference?* Feeling a tightness in his stomach, Warren opened his eyes. *Should I leave a message on Eleanor's phone and tell Doretta what I'd wanted to say before she ran out of my store? How would she respond if I hired a driver and went to Paradise to tell her in person? I could take William's journal along and let Doretta read my brother's written words for herself.*

He shook his head. *No, for now at least, I'll need to give this more thought and pray about it before I decide what to do. Besides, I can't close the store right now and leave my customers no local place to shop for nutritional items. And Mom sure can't run the place by herself.*

Warren remembered the day he had spoken to Amanda at her home and asked to speak with Doretta. After telling him that Doretta had gone to see her friend in Pennsylvania, Amanda had said, "My daughter has never fully recovered from your brother's death, and she needs this time away, which is probably something she should have done sooner. Hopefully, this will give her a chance to think things through and come to grips with whatever feelings she is still dealing with. Doretta has come a long way from the depressed state she was in for so many months after William died, but her recovery has not been complete."

I shouldn't go behind Amanda's wishes and do what I think is right, Warren told himself, *but oh, it sure is tempting.*

Betty fiddled with her apron's waistband as she glanced at Warren's office door. He'd been in there a long time. Could he really be that busy filling out orders, or was Warren doing something else right now? *He's been awfully tired lately. Maybe he's taking a nap.* She shook her head. *That's not likely. Warren's dedicated to making his business succeed. I doubt very much that he would sleep on the job, no matter how tired he may be.*

Betty thought about the question Amanda had asked her when she'd popped in for supplements awhile back, wondering if Betty enjoyed working here. Even now, the question seemed odd to Betty since she'd only started helping Warren in the store that day. *I still can't believe that Amanda called us out of the blue to let Warren know that her daughter was quitting. It left my son scrambling to fill her position at the last minute. I suppose Amanda felt obligated to do it because she didn't want to upset Doretta any further. I probably would have done the same thing if Warren had asked me for a similar favor.*

Betty rubbed a spot on her lower back where a muscle had tightened. It had been several weeks since she'd had a chiropractic adjustment, and she could certainly use one right now. There was no time for that, though. They'd been busy all morning, and this afternoon hadn't been any better so far, which meant there was no way Betty could take time away from the nutrition center today.

She thought back to the first week Warren had opened the new business and how she'd offered to work here. She had been a little put out at first because he'd turned her down and hired Margaret. But now, with Doretta gone, Betty felt that she had no choice but to help her son. Warren had put the word out that he was looking to hire someone full-time, but so far not one person had applied for the job.

It's too bad Margaret's working at the harness shop and seems to like her job, or I'd go to her myself and see if she'd want to come back here and work for Warren. Betty grabbed a broom and started sweeping up some dried mud one of their customers had tracked into the store, thanks to their muddy, wet boots. *Even if Margaret was free to come back, I guess Warren would never consider rehiring her because she wasn't reliable the first time around. At least the young woman had more energy than I do, and she probably didn't end up with a backache by the end of the day. Whatever made me believe I was up to the task? Guess I just need to keep taking one day at a time and hope my strength holds out.*

Betty had finished sweeping and was on her way to the storage room to put the broom and dustpan away when Warren stepped out of his office. "Paperwork all done?" she asked.

He gave a nod.

"You were in there quite awhile. There must have been a lot to order."

"I had several things on my list," he said, "but after I'd written up the orders, I stayed in my office longer, doing some thinking and praying."

"About your business?"

"No, about Doretta."

"I'm not surprised." Betty moved closer to him and placed her free hand on his shoulder. "You miss her, don't you, Son?" It was difficult not to tell him that she knew Doretta loved him. But if she repeated to Warren what Amanda had said, she would be going back on her word.

"Jah, I miss her a lot. I wish I hadn't messed things up with Doretta. If I'd kept my mouth shut and hadn't blurted out that I love her, she would still be working for me, and you'd be at home doing all of the things I'm sure you'd rather be doing."

Betty couldn't deny that there were plenty of things at the house that needed her attention and that many of them were chores she enjoyed doing. But she didn't tell Warren because there was no sense in making him feel guilty.

"I've thought about going to Pennsylvania to talk with Doretta. I could apologize for what I said and see if she would agree to come back."

"Why would you want to apologize for telling her what was on your heart?"

Warren pulled his fingers down the side of his face and gave a little grunt. "I'm not sorry for loving her, Mom, but I should have known she wasn't ready to hear me say those words. It's been a full year now since William died, and Doretta hasn't let go of her feelings for him. I believe that she sees me only as a friend and maybe not even that anymore."

She's in love with you, Warren. Betty's inner voice screamed to say those words, but she held her tongue. If she didn't keep her word to Amanda and told Warren the truth, it wouldn't solve a thing — unless Doretta could release herself from the promise she had made to William. Betty reached around and massaged the kink that had remained in her back. *Which is why she needs to know what he wrote in his journal.*

"I just need to accept the fact that Doretta

might never come back to Grabill and move on with my life." Warren shook his head. "Only thing is I'm not sure what direction my life should take. I have no desire to have a future with anyone but her."

"I have an idea," Betty said.

"Oh? What's that?"

"Why don't you take your brother's journal over to the library and make a copy of the page where his last entry was posted?"

"What for?"

"You could mail the copy to Doretta. I'm sure if she read it, she'd have a different perspective on things — especially regarding the promise she made to William."

Warren shook his head vigorously. "That's not a good idea, Mom. No, I can't do that at all."

"Why not?"

"Because even if Doretta felt released from her promise after reading William's journal entry, it might seem as though I was pleading with her to love me the way I love her. As much as I want Doretta to know what William wrote, I've decided not to say anything."

The bell on the front door jingled, announcing a customer had entered the store. "I'll go see who came in while you put those things away." Warren pointed to the broom and dustpan.

"All right. We can talk more later." Betty turned to the storage room then looked back over shoulder. She couldn't help noticing the slump of her son's shoulders as he made his way up the aisle toward the front of the store. Betty bit the inside of her cheek. *If there was only something I could do to make things better for Warren and Doretta.*

CHAPTER 34

The weeks spent in Paradise rolled by, and before Doretta knew it, Christmas was only a few weeks away. As she sat on the end of her bed in the guest room reading the devotional book that had been on the coffee table, her gaze came to rest on a particular Bible verse, Proverbs 27:9 NLT. Silently, she quoted it: *"The heartfelt counsel of a friend is as sweet as perfume and incense."*

I gave Eleanor counsel when she went through so many trials early in her marriage, she thought. *And since I've been staying here in the Lapps' home, my dearest friend has counseled me.*

Doretta reflected on the conversation she'd had with Eleanor yesterday, when Rosetta was down for her afternoon nap. Doretta had brought up the topic of the promise she'd made to William before he died and how she wished she'd never made such a promise. Eleanor had listened quietly, and after Doretta began crying, Eleanor had shared her opinion on the matter. Doretta closed her eyes and remembered what had happened:

"You've been dwelling on that promise far too long, my friend." *Eleanor moved closer to Doretta.* "You can't go through the rest of your life bound by a promise that was made to a man who is no longer living. It's time for you to move on with your life and let it go."

"Is that what you truly believe?" Doretta asked tearfully.

"It's not what I believe; it's what I know. You need to do what is right for you now. William would not want you to continue grieving for him and hanging on to a promise that was fulfilled the day he died. Just as in a marriage, a husband and wife agree to remain faithful and stay true to their mate until the day comes that one of them dies. After that, they are free to marry again if they choose. The promise they made to each other on their wedding day is no longer valid."

Doretta sniffed deeply and swiped at the moisture on her cheeks. "I — I see what you mean, but even if I went back home feeling released from that promise, I think it might be too late for me and Warren to have a relationship."

Eleanor patted Doretta's hand. "If two people love each other, it's never too late."

Doretta's thoughts returned to the present, and she turned to a new page in the devotional. This one began with a verse found in John 14:16, where Jesus spoke to His disciples: "And I will pray the Father, and he shall give you another Comforter, that he may abide with you for ever." After getting into God's Word these last few weeks, Doretta had become fully aware that the Holy Spirit was her comforter and counselor and that she needed to seek God's will and guidance every day for the rest of her life. It was the only way to find true inner peace.

A knock sounded on Doretta's bedroom door, and she called, "Come in!"

The door swung open. Eleanor stood with a pained expression while holding her stomach. "My labor has started. In fact, things are moving rather quickly, Doretta. Could you please go out and call my midwife? Oh, and the number for Vic's boss is on a piece of paper taped to the wall in the phone shed. He'll need to be notified too so Vic can leave whatever job he's on and be here for the birth of our baby."

A surge of adrenaline shot through Doretta, and she leaped off the bed. "I'll go do that right now!"

She grabbed her jacket, raced down the hall, and hurried out the front door. "Dear Lord," Doretta prayed out loud, "please help the midwife and Vic get here on time, because I don't think I'm up to the challenge of delivering my friend's baby."

Doretta felt relieved when Sharon, the midwife, arrived. Vic came in a short time later. They were both in Eleanor's room with her now, and Doretta had been trying to keep Rosetta entertained in the living room. She wished she could take the fussy little girl outside, but the weather was too cold.

Rosetta's toys no longer held her interest, so Doretta needed to find something else that would keep the child occupied. She had tried feeding Rosetta a snack of cheese and crackers, but most of them had ended up on the floor.

What can I do to make her stop fussing? Doretta asked herself. Suddenly, an idea popped into her head — something she hadn't done in a long while. Doretta took the little girl by the hand and led her to the upstairs guest room so, in case they got too noisy, they wouldn't disturb Eleanor's concentration as she delivered her baby.

Doretta sat on the floor in front of the little girl and began to sing and yodel. "Oh, there was a silly horse who went down the road — *clip-clop, clip-clop,* singing, 'Yodel-lay-hee-hee — yodel-lay-hee-hee.' As the horse went *clippity-clopping* on his way, he sang louder: 'Yodel-lay-hoo-hoo; yodel-lay-hoo-hoo. Oh-lay!' "

With an upturned face, Rosetta looked at Doretta and giggled.

"You like that song, huh?" Doretta repeated the lyrics she'd made up on the spur of the moment. "Oh, there was a silly horse who went down the road — *clip-clop, clip-clop,* singing, 'Yodel-lay-hee-hee — yodel-lay-hee-hee.' As the horse went *clippity-clopping* on his way, he sang, 'Yodel-lay-hoo-hoo; yodel-lay-hoo-hoo. Oh-lay!' "

Rosetta's little lips moved rapidly as though she was trying to copy Doretta, but all that came out was a babbling sound and more giggling.

Doretta smiled. She had the child's attention now, so she switched to another yodeling song she'd made up when she had first learned to yodel at the age of ten.

"A silly sheep rolled over in the grass; Oh-lo-lo-dee! Oh-lo-lo-dee-dee-oh! The sheep got up and ran to the barn: Oh-lo-lo-dee! Oh-lo-lo-dee-dee-oh!"

Doretta continued yodeling and singing one silly song after another until Vic joined them in the bedroom and announced, "The baby's here, and it's a boy!" He bent down and swept Rosetta into his arms. "You have a baby brother, my sweet little girl." He looked at Doretta and grinned. "His name is Stephen Edward, and he and his mudder are doin' real well."

Doretta shed joyful tears as she stood up and gave him and Rosetta a joint hug. "Thank the Lord!"

Vic handed his daughter back to Doretta. "I'm going out to the phone shed to make a few calls. My parents and Eleanor's folks will want to hear the exciting news that they have another grandchild now."

"Jah, I'm sure they will." Doretta was eager to see Eleanor and Vic's son, but that could wait awhile. Right now, Eleanor needed to rest, and soon it would be time for Doretta to start supper.

After Vic went out the door, Doretta pressed a gentle kiss on Rosetta's forehead. "Your life is about to change, little one. It won't be long and your brother, Stephen, will be old enough for the two of you to play all sorts of games together."

Doretta thought about her own siblings and some of the fun things they'd done

468

together while growing up. She missed them and her parents very much, but there was someone else she missed even more.

Grabill

"Are you sure you don't mind if I make a quick trip to the library? I have some books that are due today, and I don't want to pay a fine for returning them late," Betty said to Warren when they were between customers.

"It's fine, Mom. Things have slowed down some this afternoon, and I'm sure I can handle things on my own while you're gone."

"Okay. I'll just go get my jacket and tote bag and be on my way."

"You may need your scarf and gloves too," Warren said. "It's pretty cold out there today. I wouldn't be surprised if we end up with some snow soon — maybe even by Christmas Day."

"I'll bundle up." Betty hurried to the back room and put on her warm outer garments. Then she peeked into her tote bag to make sure the books she'd checked out, along with William's journal, were still there. *Of course, why wouldn't they be?* She clucked her tongue. *I put them there this morning.*

Even though Warren had told Betty that he'd decided not to say anything to Doretta about William's journal entry, Betty felt strongly that Doretta should know. She had been tempted many times to let Warren know that Doretta was in love with him, but something always held her back. *It should be Doretta's place to tell him rather than for him to hear it secondhand from me. Besides, if I told and Amanda found out, she'd be upset with me for not staying true to my word.*

Betty picked up the tote bag and left the room. *If Warren knew I had taken his brother's journal from the house this morning, he would have questioned me about it, and then I'd have had some explaining to do. I don't want Warren to know that I plan to use the library's copy machine to make a duplicate of William's last journal entry page.*

A few minutes later, Betty said goodbye to Warren and went out the front door.

Struggling against the chilly wind seeping around the neckline of her jacket, she hurried on down the sidewalk and crossed over into the next block where the library was located. It wasn't a big building, like the one in Fort Wayne, but for the size of Grabill, the smaller library seemed adequate — at least for most people's needs.

Betty checked books out here frequently and enjoyed reading historical novels during what little free time she had these days. She read mostly after retiring to her and Raymond's bedroom each evening. After a busy day at Warren's health food store, sometimes Betty would only make it through a few pages before falling asleep with the book on her chest. Sometimes she would wake up with the book still in that position, while other times whatever she'd been reading would be lying on her nightstand. She knew that Raymond had placed the book there when he'd come to bed and found her sleeping. *He's such a thoughtful husband. I did the right thing when I said yes to his marriage proposal almost thirty years ago.*

Fighting the force of the blustery wind, Betty pulled the door open and stepped into the library, appreciative of the warmth it offered. She removed her gloves and scarf and put them in her tote, then headed for the area where books should be returned. After getting the books out of her tote and putting them in the RETURN slot, Betty found the copy machine and took out William's journal. She opened it to the page where William had written his last entry, placed it facedown, closed the lid, and put her finger on the button to make a copy. Her first try produced nothing, and Betty wondered what she had done wrong. She gave it a second try, but still nothing printed.

Betty pursed her lips. *I wonder if it's out of paper.* She went to speak with the librarian sitting behind the long front desk and told her about the situation with the copy machine. The woman nodded and agreed that a lack of paper was most likely the problem. She also said that she would send someone over to help.

Betty waited impatiently near the copy machine, hoping no one she knew would come into the library and ask what she was doing. She wanted this plan she'd come up with to remain a secret — at least until she'd had the chance to send off the copy, which would be as soon as possible.

She glanced around several times, struggling with impatience while she took in some of the things within her sight — sturdy bookshelves lining the walls, computers for the library patrons to use, tables for students to work at, filing cabinets, and a children's section with picture books on the shelves along with several chairs for people to sit in while they read. Betty also heard sounds in this building that she'd never noticed before, like the ticking of a clock, fingers tapping on a keyboard of one of the computers, and toddlers laughing and singing during story time. Betty smelled some unique odors — a musty carpet smell, no doubt from the rain they'd had lately, spicy cologne from an older man who walked by, and the odd aroma of pencil shavings from the sharpener nearby.

Before leaving, she needed to put the copy of William's journal entry in an envelope she'd already addressed. On her way back to the store, she'd stop at the post office. Hopefully, the lines of people mailing letters or packages wouldn't be too long. Betty wished she had thought to open Warren's desk and put a stamp on the envelope before coming here. If she didn't get back to the nutrition center within a reasonable time, Warren would no doubt question her about what had taken so long when she finally returned to the store. Explaining the primary reason she'd come to the library was definitely not what Betty wanted to do. Warren wouldn't approve of her interfering in his personal life, and she would regret having followed through with her plans.

While Betty continued to wait, she recalled the last comment she had made to Warren on the topic of William's journal, after he'd explained why he didn't want to send a copy of the last entry to Doretta. *"All right. We can talk more later." Those were my exact words, so I'm sure he thought I was in agreement with him. And now I've gone behind his back, and I must ask myself: what if my little plan fails?*

Several more minutes went by, but when Betty's patience had worn about as thin as a blade of grass, a young woman finally came over and filled the copy machine with fresh paper. "It should work fine for you now," she said, offering Betty a timid-looking smile.

"Thank you." Betty hit the button again, and this time a piece of paper came out with Warren's last entry clearly visible. *What a relief!* Now all she had to do was stuff the envelope and head for the post office. Barring anything unexpected, Warren would be none the wiser. If this plan worked, Doretta would return home, Warren would be happy, and Betty could give up working at the nutrition center. *Yes, indeed,* she told herself, *this could work out well for everyone involved.*

CHAPTER 35

Paradise

"Are you sure that you can't stay with us any longer?" Eleanor asked when she entered the guest room, where Doretta was busy packing her suitcases.

Doretta shook her head. "Christmas is tomorrow, and your parents will arrive sometime today to spend the holidays with you and get acquainted with their new grandson. Besides, my driver will be here to pick me up soon." Doretta made a sweeping gesture of the room she had cleaned thoroughly, including putting fresh sheets on the bed. "Another thing — you'll need this guest room for your mamm and daed, and I've probably overstayed my welcome anyhow."

"No way!" Eleanor moved across the room and took a seat on the end of the bed. "It's been so wonderful having you here, and Vic and I appreciate all that you've done to help out." Eleanor teared up. "I shall miss you, my dearest friend. I hope you'll come back to visit us again."

"I will. I'll miss you and your little family, but I'd like to spend Christmas with my family, and it'll be fun to surprise them when I show up."

"Yes, I understand, and it will be a nice Christmas for them and you. I hope things work out for you to get your old job back, too."

Doretta's brows furrowed. "That may not happen since Warren's mother has been working at the nutrition center since I've been gone." She gave a brief smile. "As you know, my mamm has kept me informed through her phone messages and letters."

"Speaking of letters . . . one came in the mail for you yesterday. Vic brought a stack of mail in when he got home from work yesterday, and I didn't have the chance to look through it till I went to the kitchen this morning." Eleanor got off the bed. "I'll go get it right now."

Doretta sat in the rocking chair, holding baby Stephen while waiting for her driver to arrive. He was a chubby little fellow, weighing almost nine and a half pounds the day of his birth. But oh, what a sweet baby he was, only crying when he needed to be fed or have his diaper changed.

Rosetta sat on the couch still wearing her pajamas as she cuddled up close to her mother. Doretta would miss both of these precious children, but she knew without reservation that her place was at home now.

"Did you read the letter I gave you earlier?" Eleanor asked, looking at Doretta.

"No, not yet. I put it in my tote bag, and I'll read it as we're traveling down the road. It'll be a distraction from watching all the drivers going too fast, and it will keep me from falling asleep. At least for a little while," she added with a chuckle.

"Maybe you should try to sleep as much as you can so you're wide awake and refreshed when you get to Grabill."

"Jah, maybe so." Doretta stroked the baby's soft cheek and sighed. "Eleanor, you're so blessed to have these two children. I can't help feeling a bit envious."

"Your turn will come. You'll see. By this time next year, you might be a married woman."

"I'd like to believe that, but I'm afraid Warren might be upset with me for running out of his store and quitting my job. Warren said he loved me, but he may have changed his mind." Doretta heaved another sigh, this one a little deeper than the last. "And when I tell him what's on my heart, he may not believe me or he might not even care anymore."

"I can't imagine that he would not believe you or wouldn't care about what you have to say." Eleanor looked at Rosetta, who had now fallen asleep with her head in Eleanor's lap. "She doesn't normally wake up this early, but I think hearing our voices woke her."

"Sorry about that," Doretta apologized. "It's hard to whisper and still be heard."

"Not a problem. She's sleeping pretty soundly. I doubt that our voices will wake her now."

The toot of a horn sounded from outside, and despite the harsh noise, Rosetta continued to sleep. Eleanor stood and laid her daughter on the couch. "That must be your driver, so as much as I dislike the idea, I guess it's time for us to say our goodbyes."

Doretta stood and placed Stephen in his cradle near the couch.

After they'd hugged and promised to stay in touch, Doretta put on her outer garments, slipped the straps of the tote bag over her shoulder, and picked up her two small suitcases.

"I wish Vic hadn't left so early for work

this morning, or he would be here to help you with those," Eleanor said after she'd opened the front door.

"It's okay. I can manage. And I certainly wouldn't want you to pick up even one of the suitcases. They may be small, but they're both heavy with the Christmas gifts I bought for my family."

"I know, and I'm being careful about not doing too much too soon." Eleanor followed Doretta out the door and said goodbye again as Doretta stepped off the porch. She was partway across the grass when Mary Beth left the van and came to help with her luggage.

"Thank you." Doretta could barely get the words out because of the constriction she felt in her throat. She had learned so much since she'd come here, and Doretta felt closer to God now than she ever had. If things worked out at home the way she hoped, any minor trace of depression that might still linger in the shadows of her mind would be completely erased.

Grabill
As they approached the nutrition center, Doretta's heartbeat picked up speed. On the way there, she had opened the envelope Warren's mother had sent her with a copy

of the last entry in William's journal. Reading what he'd said had been the confirmation Doretta needed regarding the decision she'd made before leaving Pennsylvania. She wondered if Warren knew about the journal, but she figured if he had, he would have surely said something to her about it.

How will Warren respond when I show him this? Doretta asked herself, reaching into the tote bag to take out the envelope. *I hope he will be as pleased to read it as I was.*

"I shouldn't be too long," Doretta told her driver when they'd pulled into the store's parking lot. She smiled. "And from here, we can go straight to my parents' house."

Mary Beth nodded. "Not a problem. Take your time. I don't have to be anywhere until this evening, when my family will be getting together for our Christmas Eve supper."

"Okay, thanks." Doretta got out of the van and stepped onto the porch. When she opened the door and went inside, the sight before her caused a knot to form in her stomach. Warren stood behind the counter holding Margaret in his arms.

Heartsick, Doretta turned and was about to leave, when Warren called out to her, "Don't go!"

Her ears were ringing, and it was difficult

to breathe or to think rationally. *I'm too late. Warren and Margaret are together as a couple again.*

"Doretta, please, come here and talk to me."

She felt his hand on her shoulder, and it took all her strength to turn and face Warren. "Looks like I've come here for nothing, but I may as well give you this before I go." Her hand trembled as she handed him the envelope.

"What's this?" He stared at her.

Doretta swallowed hard. She would not give in to the tears pushing on the back of her eyes. At least not until she got into Mary Beth's van. "Guess it's not important now since you're back with Margaret. You can open it after I leave if you want." Doretta whirled around and rushed out the door.

Warren's gaze clouded as he stared at the closed door. *What just happened here? Did I give her the impression that I'm back with Margaret? What's in this envelope she gave me?*

With no thought of Margaret, whom he'd left behind the counter, or even the customers milling around the backside of the store, Warren raced out the front door after Doretta. She was almost to her driver's vehicle and had reached for the door handle when he shouted, "Doretta, please wait! Margaret and I are not together again!"

She turned, and as he approached the vehicle, she looked at him with tears swimming in her dark eyes. "Really? Then why were you hugging her?"

"She came into the store to say she was sorry for all the unkind things she had said and done while we were dating. Margaret will be moving to another part of the state next week, and she wanted to make things right with me before she goes."

Doretta rubbed a spot on her forehead just above her right eyebrow. "Why is she moving?"

"She's taking a job at a farm where they train horses with all kinds of problems, and they need another trainer. They'd heard about Margaret's ability with horses and reached out to her to see if she would be interested in working for them."

"Oh, I see." Doretta looked at the envelope she had given Warren. "Are you going to read it?"

"What does it say?"

"You might want to open it and read it yourself when you have the time."

"I'll do it now but not here. Can we go back inside and sit in my office? I'd like you to be with me when I read it."

Doretta hesitated and finally nodded. He led the way, and when they entered the store, Warren was glad to see that his mother had resumed her place at the check-out counter and was talking to Margaret. *"Kumme,"* he said to Doretta. "Please come with me."

When they entered Warren's office, he took a seat behind his desk and Doretta sat in the folding chair nearby. Her heart pounded as he opened the envelope and read the words on the piece of paper his mother had copied from William's journal and sent to her. When Warren finished reading, he looked at Doretta strangely. "Where'd you get this?"

"Your mother sent it to me while I was at Eleanor and Vic's."

"Oh, boy . . . My mamm is sure a sneaky one, isn't she? So she made this copy without my knowledge and sent it to you?"

"Jah."

He leaned slightly forward. "I guess she wanted you to know the truth."

"Are you surprised by what your brother wrote?" Doretta asked.

He shook his head. "Not at all. I'm the one who discovered William's journal, and I was planning to tell you what his last entry said, but after I declared my love for you, you ran out of my store before I could say anything about the journal."

"I'm sorry about that, Warren. I should have waited to hear what you'd wanted to say, but —"

"It's okay. I took you by surprise."

She nodded. "I want you to know that I was planning to come back here even before your mother's letter came."

"Really?"

"Jah. Like Margaret, I owed you an apology."

He tipped his head. "You've never said anything unkind to me or tried to get me to do things your way, like Margaret often did."

"I'm sorry that I didn't stay and listen to what you had to say," Doretta apologized again. Her cheeks warmed, and she lowered her gaze. "I'm also sorry for not admitting that I am in love with you, and I hope I haven't ruined things between us by quitting my job and running off to Pennsylvania."

"Did I hear that right? Did you just say that you love me, Doretta?"

"Yes, I did."

Warren jumped up and came over to where she sat. He lifted her chin so she looked directly at him. "You really, truly love me?"

"Jah. Very much."

"And you no longer feel bound by the promise you made to William?"

"No, I was released from that promise the day he died. I just hadn't realized it because I still loved him so much."

"We both loved my bruder, and we always will, but we know now that he would have been okay with it if you'd chosen me instead of him." He bent his face close to Doretta and brushed his lips gently across hers. "So if you're willing, I'd like permission to court you."

Heat radiated throughout Doretta's chest as she gave him an affirmative nod.

Warren looked up and briefly closed his eyes. "Thank You, Lord." Then he pulled Doretta gently to her feet and kissed her soundly. She knew, without a doubt, that this would be her best Christmas ever.

EPILOGUE

Eleven months later

Doretta sat beside Warren at the bride and groom's table, toward the end of the meal that had followed their wedding service. This was one of the happiest days of her life, and she almost felt the need to pinch herself just to be sure she wasn't dreaming. So much had happened since she and Warren had begun dating. In addition to drawing closer through time spent together, Doretta had continued to grow spiritually and emotionally. Besides working at the nutrition center with Warren, she spent some of her free time writing letters to her friends, Eleanor and Irma. She was thankful that both young women had been able to come to Grabill and join them for the wedding along with their husbands and children. In fact, Irma and Eleanor had been Doretta's witnesses at the wedding service this morning. Doretta thought it was nice that Warren had asked her brothers, Glen and Isaac, to be his witnesses.

Margaret hadn't come to Doretta and Warren's wedding, but her parents had. Margaret's mother had dropped by the nutrition center last week, and she'd mentioned that her daughter had been dating an English fellow who worked with Margaret. Margaret had told her folks in a recent letter that she would not be joining the Amish church and wanted to live in the English world, where she would have more opportunity to do the things she liked. Doretta wasn't totally surprised by this, because Margaret had never seemed committed to the Amish way of life. Hopefully, she had found a good church to attend and would put her faith and trust in God.

Doretta felt a sense of joy when Warren gave her hand a gentle squeeze under the table. "I love you, fraa," he whispered in her ear.

"I love you too," she whispered back. "And I'm ever so thankful for second chances."

"Same here." Warren leaned even closer. "I would kiss you right now if there weren't so many people looking at us. I can just imagine the reaction we would get if I did kiss my bride in front of them."

"That's okay." She smiled. "Your kisses can wait till we are alone."

"If my brother was here, I think I know what he would say to us right now."

"Oh? What's that?"

"William would say that we should be happy and always keep God at the center of our lives."

She nodded. "I believe you are right." Doretta thought about John 14:18, a verse of scripture she had read recently: *"I will not leave you comfortless: I will come to you."*

Thank You, Lord, she silently prayed, *for giving me words of comfort during the last two years, through family, friends, and especially from faithfully reading Your Holy Word. You have never left me — it was I who walked away from You for a time. In the days and years ahead, please use me to offer trust, comfort, and wisdom to others in need.*

DORETTA'S APPLE MUFFINS

Ingredients:
2 1/4 cups flour
1 tablespoon baking powder
1/2 teaspoon salt
1 1/2 teaspoons cinnamon
1/2 cup sugar
1 egg, beaten
2/3 cup milk
1/2 cup vegetable or coconut oil
1 1/2 cups apple chunks
Cinnamon-sugar mixture, using equal parts
    cinnamon and sugar

In large bowl, combine flour, baking powder, salt, cinnamon, and sugar. In another bowl, combine egg, milk, and oil. Stir into first mixture until everything is moistened. Stir in apples. Spoon into muffin tins that have either been greased or lined with paper baking cups. Fill each cup three-quarters full. Sprinkle cinnamon-sugar mixture on top. Bake at 400 degrees for 20 to 25 minutes. Cool and serve.

Dear Reader:

Depression is a topic that some people prefer not to talk about. Perhaps it's because they are embarrassed or feel that they might be judged or looked down upon by other people because they don't understand the problems or possible consequences of depression. A lot of humans have been programmed to believe that they must project strength to those around them. While it might be difficult for a person to admit they have feelings of depression, talking about it and the emotions that go with being depressed is essential because the feelings a depressed person has are very real.

I chose to write about the issue of depression because many people struggle with it and are misunderstood. Sometimes, even the depressed person doesn't understand the reason they feel so unhappy.

They just know that they are. There are many reasons a person might be facing depression, such as periods of prolonged stress, hormonal changes, a chemical imbalance, genetics, a major life change, an illness that doesn't get better, financial difficulties, or the loss of a loved one, such as the character in this novel had to face.

Symptoms of depression can include things like difficulty concentrating, problems making decisions, persistent feelings of sadness, crying spells, trouble remembering details, fatigue, feelings of worthlessness, insomnia, excessive sleeping, irritability, not wanting to socialize, feelings of guilt, an increase or decrease in appetite, persistent headaches, feelings of helplessness, loss of interest in activities once enjoyed, or suicidal thoughts.

When I was in my early teens, my mother was diagnosed with bipolar disorder, caused by a chemical imbalance. I had witnessed her mood swings numerous times, including deep depression. During this time, she spoke negative or harsh words, stayed inside the house with the curtains closed, neglected her physical appearance, and showed no interest in doing the things she used to do for fun. Eventually, her mood would switch to an emotional high. When her emotions ran high, I did not understand what she seemed so excited about or why she did some really strange things, like inviting people she barely knew to our house. She would often give things away to these people, and sometimes she expected me and my sister to give some of our toys to children we didn't know. With no understanding of her condition early on, I had believed that, during her bouts of depression, my mother did not care about me or my sister. Once I understood my mother's condition, I often had to remind her to take the medication the doctor had prescribed for her. If she took it regularly, things got better, but if she forgot or refused the medication, her mood swings came back, often worse than before.

There are many ways to manage depression, such as reducing stress, socializing with others, engaging in activities previously enjoyed, exercising regularly, eating a balanced diet, joining a support group, asking a close family member or friend for support, praying, reading Bible verses, and in some cases, taking certain natural supplements or prescribed medication. Of course, people with severe symptoms of depression should always consider seeking help from a health care professional.

It is my hope that if you or someone you know is dealing with depression, you'll choose to reach out for help. Please, don't let fear of the unknown or worrying about what others might think keep you from opening up to the people you trust and who you know care about you and want to help. The key to recovery is not trying to deal with your unhappiness alone. Sharing details about your depression with people who understand and are not judgmental can be healing, and it will benefit you in many ways. You should never go through this experience alone.

Love & Blessings,
Wanda Brunstetter

DISCUSSION QUESTIONS

1. In this book, Doretta suffered from depression after her boyfriend, William, died, and she also had to learn to cope with her own injuries. In the beginning, she wouldn't accept help from anyone. Have you or someone you've known ever been deeply depressed? Did you seek help from someone or try to deal with it on your own?

2. When Doretta's injuries from the accident got better, she tried to stay busy all the time so she wouldn't have to deal with her grief and depression. Is keeping busy an answer for extreme sadness, or are there better ways to deal with despair?

3. Doretta's friend Eleanor wanted to help Doretta feel better emotionally, so she wrote her letters that she hoped would offer comfort. At first, Doretta did not do

any of the things Eleanor suggested, and she even refused to answer her friend's letters and phone calls. Why do you think a person suffering with depression might pull away from friends and family and be unwilling to accept help for their depression?

4. Doretta's boyfriend was an identical twin to his brother, Warren. Although identical twins look and even sound alike, they may have different personalities and be skilled at different things. Sometimes there might be jealousy and rivalry between twins, but the closeness twins share creates an unbreakable bond. How did Warren deal with his brother's death? Why was it difficult at first for Warren to talk about the feelings he had for William?

5. Warren's girlfriend, Margaret, had a special way with horses and often helped owners deal with their horse's behavioral problems. But Margaret's ability and determination to help horses got in the way of her job at the nutrition center on several occasions, causing her to arrive at work late or leave early. Warren got frustrated with Margaret's unreliability, but he put up with it for quite a while before

telling her that she no longer had a job working for him. Why do you think Warren took so long to ask her to leave?

6. After her accident, Doretta's faith in God wavered and she became filled with doubts. Have you ever felt your faith in God waver while going through a trying time? What did you do to strengthen or regain your faith?

7. When Warren's twin brother died, their mother worried about Warren and became overly protective. She also tried to do too much for him. How did this affect Warren, and what did he do in order to deal with it? If you had been in his mother's place, how would you have handled losing a son?

8. When Doretta was injured in the accident, her mother worried about her and sometimes said or did too much. How should a parent show support to adult children going through troublesome times without treating them as if they are still children?

9. After Warren broke up with Margaret and she realized she wouldn't be getting a marriage proposal, she saw no reason to join

the Amish church. What did that say about her spiritual life and desire to be part of the Amish community she had grown up in?

10. After Warren read the final entry in his brother's journal, should he have told Doretta about it right away? Why do you think he held off talking with Doretta about his brother's journal even though it involved her?

11. Do you think Warren's mother was right in letting Doretta know about William's last journal entry and what it had said? Or should she have respected Warren's wishes and said nothing? Would things have turned out differently in this story if Doretta had never learned about William's journal?

12. Doretta made a promise to William that she would never love another man except him. Do you think she should have felt bound by that promise after William died?

13. Is there ever a time when it's okay for a promise to be broken? Have you ever made a promise to someone and wished you hadn't?

14. Who was your favorite character in this story and why? What was the thing you liked most about them?

15. Were any of the Bible verses mentioned in this novel meaningful to you? What scripture passages mentioned could help someone suffering from depression?

ABOUT THE AUTHOR

New York Times bestselling and award-winning author **Wanda E. Brunstetter** is one of the founders of the Amish fiction genre. She has written more than one hundred books translated in four languages. With over twelve million copies sold, Wanda's stories consistently earn spots on the nation's most prestigious bestseller lists and have received numerous awards.

Wanda's ancestors were part of the Anabaptist faith, and her novels are based on personal research intended to accurately portray the Amish way of life. Her books are read and trusted by many Amish people, who credit her for giving readers a deeper understanding of the people and their customs.

When Wanda visits her Amish friends, she finds herself drawn to their peaceful lifestyle, sincerity, and close family ties. Wanda enjoys photography, ventriloquism, gardening, bird-watching, beachcombing, and spending time with her family. She and her husband, Richard, have been blessed with two grown children, six grandchildren, and two great-grandchildren.

To learn more about Wanda,
visit her website at
www.wandabrunstetter.com.

The employees of Thorndike Press hope you have enjoyed this Large Print book. All our Thorndike Large Print titles are designed for easy reading, and all our books are made to last. Other Thorndike Press Large Print books are available at your library, through selected bookstores, or directly from us.

For information about titles, please call:
(800) 223-1244

or visit our website at:
gale.com/thorndike